LIKE A LOVE STORY

A STORY

ABDI NAZEMIAN

BALZER + BRAY
An Imprint of HarperCollins*Publishers*

Balzer + Bray is an imprint of HarperCollins Publishers.

Like a Love Story
Copyright © 2019 by Abdi Nazemian
All rights reserved. Printed in the United States of America.
No part of this book may be used or reproduced in any manner whatsoever
without written permission except in the case of brief quotations embodied
in critical articles and reviews. For information address HarperCollins
Children's Books, a division of HarperCollins Publishers, 195 Broadway,
New York, NY 10007.
www.epicreads.com

ISBN 978-0-06-283936-7

Typography by Michelle Taormina
19 20 21 22 23 PC/LSCH 10 9 8 7 6 5 4 3 2 1
❖
First Edition

*This book is dedicated to Jonathon Aubry
for giving me my own true blue love story,
and to all the activists and artists who have
made so many love stories possible*

SEPTEMBER 1989

"It comes as a great shock around the age of 5, 6, or 7 to discover that the flag to which you have pledged allegiance, along with everybody else, has not pledged allegiance to you. It comes as a great shock to see Gary Cooper killing off the Indians, and although you are rooting for Gary Cooper, that the Indians are you."

—James Baldwin

REZA

There should be a limit on how long any human being has to wear braces. Also, there should be another name for braces. Mouth invaders, maybe, or teeth terrorists. Although I suppose an Iranian boy these days shouldn't even *think* the word *terrorist*, so I take that back. Maybe I should just call them friends. They've accompanied me as we moved from one country to another. But it's been three years now, and I'm done. Tomorrow, I start my senior year of high school, in a new school, in a new city. This is it. My last chance to not be invisible.

I'm watching two television shows at once on the largest TV screen I have ever seen. Everything in this home, and in this country, is jumbo sized. It isn't even a normal television. It's a projection screen. Abbas says the quality of the image is a lot better. And the image can split, so you can watch multiple things at the same time. As if the split screen television weren't stimulating enough,

3

he also has an endless VHS collection and closet full of board games. The only games my dad ever played were called "How fast can I empty this bottle?" and "How many times can I leave my family and come back, only to leave again?" My mom wants me to call Abbas "Baba" or "Daddy," but that's never going to happen. No man with this many versions of Monopoly could ever be my father.

I'm watching *The Golden Girls* on the television, and in a smaller box at the bottom of the television, I'm watching *The Neverending Story*. I grab ahold of the edge of my braces, the part that digs into my gums, and pull. Hard. I yank on those braces like I am playing tug-of-war with them, and soon they start tearing off. I feel a sharp pain, and with it, sudden freedom. It feels right. Maybe freedom always comes with pain. That's what my dad used to say about the revolution. There's blood too, lots of it. I see it on my nails, now ruby red like my mother's.

My mom, who is at her desk reading *Architectural Digest*, sees me and screams.

"Reza, what have you done?" she asks. "Are you out of your mind?"

I look at her as the taste of blood clogs the back of my throat. She removes a tissue from a gold box and approaches to help clean me. But as she's about to touch my face, I push her away and grab the tissue.

"I can clean it myself," I say. I hear the edge in my voice and immediately feel guilty. I wish she knew the truth—that I'm trying to save her. Just in case my blood is toxic. Just in case you can get it from having too many thoughts of boys in locker rooms.

"You really are out of your mind," she says, with enough tenderness to make me feel guilty again.

I want to tell her that of course I am. What else could I be after what our family has been through? But instead I just say, "I think I need an orthodontist."

We moved so recently that I don't even have doctors here yet. My mom sighs, unsure of what to do. I can feel the wheels in her head turn as she whispers to herself. Then she finds the yellow pages and starts flipping through them until the ruby-red fingernail of her index finger rests on the image of a smiling man.

"He looks capable," my mom announces.

"Hard to tell," I say. "All these guys have crooked teeth."

My mom smiles finally. Almost even laughs. Her own teeth are, of course, perfectly straight and gleaming white. There's something unspoken here; that she doesn't want to call Abbas and disturb him at work. She doesn't want him to know that his new stepson is the kind of deranged kid who rips out his own braces. She likes to deal with problems privately and quietly. That's her way.

"I can't handle this right now," my mom says. But she rushes me to the orthodontist, proving that she can, in fact, handle this right now. That's the thing about her. She always can handle it right now.

As I lie on the orthodontist's chair, listening to the

doctor and my mother chat, my mind zones out. I do this sometimes. I'm afraid of speaking, of saying the wrong thing, of revealing something about myself I shouldn't. So I listen. And if I listen too long, the voices become hazy, like I'm hearing them through an ocean. When I was a kid, I would sink into the bathtub every time my parents would fight. Or more specifically, when my dad would yell, and my mom would appease. I could still hear them from below the water, but they sounded far away. And I felt safe. Well, almost.

There was so much blood, Doctor. Should I call you Doctor?

I have so many Persian patients. I love your people.

Can we be done by the time my husband gets back from work?

And so beautiful. Do all Persians have such long eyelashes?

The orthodontist puts on his blue gloves, which makes me feel a little better. I wish the whole world could wear a giant latex glove around itself, like a shield of armor. It would not be so different than Iran was, with women in their chadors. They thought those chadors were protecting men from their impure thoughts. Maybe latex around everyone would protect me from mine.

"You have such a quiet child," the dentist says. "My own kids won't stop talking."

"I'm not a child," I say, coming out of my haze. "I'm seventeen. I should be allowed to make my own decisions."

"Reza," my mom says. "When you are my age, you

will thank me. I promise you." My mother has made many promises to me. That the revolution would never succeed. That my father would change. That I would grow into a good-looking man.

I don't tell her that I will never be her age. I have known this from the moment we left Iran and landed in Toronto. I was eleven years old, and there was so little I knew about the world. But I knew that my dad would never change, and that my mom had finally found the strength to leave him. But there was something else I knew, something I knew from the moment I first went swimming with some other boys, and one of those boys' swim trunks fell. I knew that I longed for other boys, to touch them, and hold them, and be with them. I hid that knowledge away, buried it. It was safe inside me. Then we landed in Toronto, and my mom and my sister made a beeline to the airport newsstand, giddy over the selection of fashion magazines, choosing which to buy, discussing Isabella Rossellini's beauty.

Does she not look vaguely Iranian?

Well, Iranians and Italians do not look so different.

No chadors. I can't believe it.

She looks identical to her mother. You both look like your father.

I think I want to be the first Iranian supermodel.

My eyes were glued to another section of magazines, and to the cover of *Time*. "The AIDS Hysteria." My mom and my sister were so immersed in analyzing Isabella's skin tone that I managed to covertly flip through the magazine, and inside I saw sickness, disease, lesions, young men dying. I knew that I liked it when boys' swim trunks fell. But the fact that this would kill me, this was something I did not know until that moment. Until *Time* magazine informed me that I would die soon.

I've been living in fear ever since.

"I just want to be able to smile this year," I plead, to both my mom and the orthodontist. Before getting the braces, my incisors were so high on my gum line that even when I smiled, they were invisible to the outside world. This horror was among the many reasons I never smiled, but let me be honest, I had many other reasons for not smiling.

"Is that too much to ask, to be able to smile without scaring people? To be able to start at a new school without being the four-eyed, metal-mouthed kid everyone makes fun of? To actually have someone . . . like me?" I can feel my face burning.

My mother suddenly smiles. "Oh," she says. And then adding a few syllables to the word the way she loves to do, "Ohhhhhh." I have no idea what is going on in her overactive mind, but then she declares, "I understand. You want to have a girlfriend!"

She does *not* understand. She never does.

My mother turns to the orthodontist. "Is there anything we can do?" she asks. "We need your approval, of course."

I don't understand why she treats this orthodontist as her accomplice, and not as a man that we just randomly chose from the yellow pages. Or as a creep who likes talking about her beautiful eyelashes.

The orthodontist makes a deal with me. He will remove the braces if I wear a retainer every night without fail. I shrug in acceptance, and a small smirk of victory forms on my face.

When we get back home, I rush into my room, which is too big for me, and stand in front of the mirror. I run my tongue around my mouth, reveling in the feeling of smooth teeth. Maybe I'm a little fixated on my teeth, maybe I have spent too much time analyzing them, measuring with my ruler the microscopic movements they made day by day. But now that the braces are gone, I can already tell that this obsession only saved me from thinking about the sad state of the rest of my appearance: my thin, nondescript body (not tall enough to be lanky, not stocky enough to be athletic), my cheeks with their remnants of baby fat (which have been mercilessly pinched by my sister), and my thick mop of unkempt hair.

The pathetic state of my appearance is only reinforced when Saadi walks into my room without knocking. My sister may be in college now (or at least pretending to be in college, since no one trusts her to show up to class or read a book), but I have inherited a new stepbrother. He's six feet tall. He plays lacrosse, whatever that is. He's the same age as me, but he's twice my size. He walks around the house in white boxer shorts and a white baseball hat, and he calls me "the little prince," since I'm named after the former shah of Iran, even though my dad hated him. I suppose that reveals a lot about how present my dad was in my life, even back when I was born. I think I hate the shah too. Maybe if he had been strong enough to stop the revolution, we would all still be living together in a place where people look like me.

He starts opening my drawers. "Where's my Fine Young Cannibals CD?" he asks.

"I, um, did not touch it." I keep my gaze fixed on the mirror, but in the reflection, I see him bending down to open a bottom drawer. For a moment, I compare his thick legs to my scrawny ones, but after that moment passes, I don't think of my legs at all. All that exists are his legs, his back, his shoulders. I hate myself. I wish I had braces in my mouth again so I could rip them out a second time. I wish I would die, and if there is an afterlife, I could find my dad there and tell him that I'm just as messed up as he was.

"Can you stop staring at me," he says. It's not a question, it is a command.

I quickly look out my window at the city streets outside. At the base of a tree, trash bags are piled up, and I feel so nauseous that I can almost smell them.

"I was not looking at you," I scoff.

"Why do you talk like that?" he says.

"Like what?" I ask.

"So formal. Like you're fresh off the boat. Loosen up. Weren't you in Canada the last few years? Don't they talk like normal people there? It's 1989. You talk like it's 1889."

"I don't know what normal people talk like," I say. And this, I think, is exactly why I do not usually talk.

"Your family should've left Iran during the revolution like the rest of us," he says. "I don't know why you stayed."

We stayed because my dad believed in the ideals of the revolution, even though my mother knew they were immediately corrupted. Also, because my mother was not ready to leave him yet.

"I said stop staring. You better not be a fag," he says. "One per school is more than enough."

My heart races. Is it because this hairy beast has figured out in a few moments what my mother has not figured out in seventeen years? Or is it because I now know something about my new school that I would never have imagined in my wildest dreams . . . . that there will be someone like me there?

"I'm not a . . ." But the word won't escape my lips. I want to say it. I know that if I say it, he won't think I am one.

He opens a drawer and pushes some of my underwear aside—starched white briefs, which, next to his boxers, seem like what a little boy would wear. My room used to be his, before he got upgraded to what used to be the guest room. "I'm just shitting you," he says. "I know you're not. My mom says homosexuality is luckily a problem that Iranians don't have. I guess we don't have that gene or something. But Art Grant definitely has that gene." He moves on to another drawer and finally finds what he's looking for. "Here it is," he says. Once he has the CD in his hand, he looks at me. "Hey, little prince, my dad asked me to take care of you at school."

"Oh," I say. "Um, I don't know if that is necessary. I can take care of myself." That's untrue, but I am good at disappearing into the background.

"I figured," he says. "You look like a strong, self-sufficient person." There's a hint of a smile on his lips. "I'll be watching you from afar though, just to make sure you're okay." He smiles bigger now, and then adds, "I'll always have my eye on you." He says it like a threat, and I know it is.

When he leaves, I close the door and put a chair in front of it. I need privacy. I find the yearbook the school sent me. It's on my bookshelf, where it sits next to the summer reading I had to do (Maya Angelou, Bram Stoker, George Orwell) and the Homer books I will be reading this fall. I quickly flip through the yearbook, scanning the small square black-and-white photos of my new classmates. Most of them look shockingly similar, the boys with their collared shirts and side-parted hair, and the girls with their ponytails and pouts. I notice a girl named Judy who looks so different from the rest, with heavy eye makeup and a piercing gaze, and I think that it's nice someone else at the school doesn't belong.

But I'm looking for Art Grant. I go to the Gs, but at first I don't find him, until I realize Art must be a nickname. He's listed as Bartholomew Emerson Grant VI, and he's very hard to miss. His hair is shaved at the sides, and a soft Mohawk at the top sways toward the right side of his face, which is turned slightly, probably to reveal the earring in his left ear. He has a smirk on his face, like he knows exactly what people are thinking of him, daring anyone looking at this picture to call him a fag again, telling the Saadis of the world to go to hell. Even in black and white, his eyes look like a cat's, defiant, challenging you. My mom once told me that no matter where you stand, you'll think the Mona Lisa is looking right at you. That's how I feel about this picture. Like Art is looking right at me. Like he sees me.

I quickly close the book, overwhelmed by his image, but his face haunts me. I cannot stop thinking about him, and his shaved scalp, and his studded ear, and his devilish lips. I need to stop thinking about him, and I know there's only one way to do that. I lie back on my bed, close my eyes, and unzip my pants. I see Bartholomew Emerson Grant VI come to life, enter my room, climb into bed with me. He kisses me, undresses me, tells me not to be scared. But then he's gone, and all I can see are images of dying men with lesions.

I hate myself. I hate these thoughts. I hate Bartholomew Emerson Grant VI.

I close my eyes tighter, and my breath quickens. When it's over, I breathe out all the air inside me, hoping that with the last bit of oxygen leaving my body, this sickness will leave me too. I know this is a phase. It must be. I grew out of needing my stuffed rabbit with me all the time. I grew out of hating eggplant, and of putting McDonald's french fries on every Persian stew my mom made. I will grow out of this. I must, because I cannot ruin my mom's new marriage. And because even though my mom can handle anything, I don't know if she can handle me dying.

I need to live, and to live, I can't ever be what I know that I am.

ART

It's the irony that hits me first. That I have never felt more alive, while I'm surrounded by people who are dying. In a city that feels completely segregated, this community center is overflowing with people of all races, ages, genders, and income levels. Bankers and dancers, all in one place, with one purpose. To fight the power, to screw the system, and to show the presidents and CEOs of the world what we're made of. There's nowhere else in the city with this much energy in it, nowhere with this much color, this much diversity. Maybe death is the great equalizer. Except it's not. Because gay people seem to be doing most of the dying. My people. The final irony, that here in this place, it's okay for me to be gay. I try to be gay at home, but with my parents' judgment and denial, and all those photos of Ronald and Nancy Reagan staring at me from within their silver picture frames, it doesn't work out so well. At school, the starched gray-and-navy-blue uniforms they make us wear basically tell us to conform to heterosexual norms, OR ELSE. Here in this room, I don't need to be gray and navy, I can be a proud-ass rainbow.

"There's a new report out," a woman says. She's super tall, her hair is buzz-cut, and she wears overalls and a black bra, which makes me love her already. She looks like the kind of woman who could play Molly Ringwald's best friend in a prom movie. I pull my camera up from around my neck, where it's pretty much always dangling, and I snap a photo of her. She speaks with an edge to her voice, a tremble of anger and fear. "It's hidden in the back of the newspapers, of course. They don't like putting our stories on the front page. It says teenagers are the plague's newest victims. *Teenagers.*"

The eyes of the room turn to me and Judy. Almost three hundred people are massed in this dingy space, but we're the only teenagers. And fabulous ones, too. Judy's wearing a frayed azure-blue top over striped leggings with combat boots. She designed the outfit herself. Like with a sewing machine. She's brilliant that way. She jokes that the reason she'll make it as a fashion designer someday is 'cause AIDS is wiping out her competition, but that's not why. It's 'cause she's beyond talented. We keep our eyes on each other. "Oh God," Judy whispers to me. "Please tell me they're not going to make us speak."

"Our whole culture is in severe denial," the overalls lady continues. "*TEEN. AGERS.* They are out there having sex. And nobody is talking to them about the

16

risks. We need to protect them!" When she says the word *teenagers*, she says it with a level of passion that scares me, like there's something about being a teenager that's so intense that the word needs to be spoken like a warning.

"I guess this is one advantage to the fact that no one wants to sleep with us," Judy whispers. "We won't get AIDS."

Judy and I haven't made a celibacy pact or anything, though that's what our parents and our sex-ed teacher have recommended. It's just the reality of our situation that there are ZERO romantic prospects in the world for us, which has the benefit of making us each other's everything. I'm the only out gay kid in our whole school, and Judy isn't exactly the kind of girl most guys go for, though she has certainly pined for a few. I think she's gorgeous, of course. She looks like a cross between Cyndi Lauper and a Botero painting. But as she often says, gay guys finding her gorgeous doesn't do much for her. Also, she's allowed to make AIDS jokes 'cause her uncle Stephen has AIDS and makes AIDS jokes all the time. He says he's too close to death NOT to make fun of it.

"Speak for yourself," I say. "The whole basketball team wants to sleep with me." I pause for dramatic effect, and then add, "They just don't know it yet."

Judy smiles and swats my shoulder, which is bare thanks to the tank top I'm wearing, purchased at the merch table at a previous meeting. Judy and I have been coming to these meetings for a few months now. At first, Stephen wouldn't let us come. But we begged, and we got our way. He still hasn't let us go to an actual protest, but we're working on it.

"Shut up," Judy says. "We are at a serious gathering of serious people discussing a serious issue about *TEEN. AGERS.*"

Judy's uncle Stephen stands up, adjusts his shawl, and clears his throat. He's high drama, and we love him for it. Once upon a time, he was also the most handsome, charismatic man I had ever met. Now he looks like a ghost. But at least he's still alive. His lover, José, is gone, as in not with us anymore, as in deceased. The hospital threw his body in a GARBAGE BAG when he passed. He's one of the ninety-four friends Stephen has lost to the disease. He keeps a list. He also keeps a pot of jelly beans and adds a jelly bean to the pot every time someone dies. He says that just before he dies, he will eat every one so that his friends will be with him. As he begins to speak, I snap a photo of him. "What about an action at the department of education?" Stephen asks. "We could demand a change in their sex education policies. We could demand condom distribution. We could dress up like librarians. I have the perfect blouse!"

Another man—thin as a rail with hollow cheeks—stands up. "We don't have the time or the resources to be distracted," he says. "We know who the real enemy is. The price of AZT is obscene. We have our plan, and it's going to need all our attention."

"Well, that's what affinity groups are for," Stephen says. "And I'm on board with our plan. Like all of you,

I'm ready to risk getting arrested . . . again."

There's some laughter in the room, solidarity in the number of times they've all been booked and released. That's the way it usually works. ACT UP members are given civil disobedience training, and they're usually released without being put through the system. But there have been exceptions, and no one wants to be that exception. I see a man in a leather jacket in the corner of a room eyeing a handsome young dancer type. They cruise each other with heat. For meetings about a deadly sexually transmitted virus, these gatherings are surprising breeding grounds for hookups. I snap a photo of the two men.

"But we also need to find a way to stop new cases," Stephen continues. "And what better place to start than by educating young people?" He looks at Judy and me, and he adds affectedly, "Our innocent, pure young people."

"If my face isn't enough to scare young people into having safe sex," the thin man says, "then I don't know how protesting outside the department of education will help."

He's right. I look at his face and realize it's the face I've been seeing in all my nightmares since I first understood what sex was, and since I first understood that Judy and I would never get married and have kids like we said we would, because I really do want to sleep with the basketball team. And the football team. And every member of Depeche Mode and the Smiths. I basically want to sleep with everyone with a Y chromosome. But this man's face—gaunt and covered in caked-on concealer doing a poor job of hiding purple lesions—is the face that stops me from acting on any of my abundant desires. It's the face my dad and I were looking at five years ago when we were sitting outside one of those awful French bistros where all the men wear identical suits and all the women wear dead animals on their backs. One of those faces walked by us, leading a poodle on a leash, and my dad looked at it—the face, not the poodle—with a grimace of disgust and said, "They deserve it, you know. Maybe when this is all over, we won't have any more of them in the city. Maybe even in the world. Wouldn't that be something?" And then the face walked away, leaving me and my father alone, steak frites in front of us and a new barrier in between us.

How was he supposed to know that only a few months before, I'd had my first wet dream, about Morrissey? How was he supposed to know that I had discovered—after a childhood spent assuming I was just like others—that I was not only different but despised? That he had just suggested the world would be a better place if his own son dropped dead after a few years of lesions, diarrhea, and blindness? I wanted to reach over and strangle him. To exterminate him and anyone with that kind of hate in their hearts. I could see the headlines—*Old Money! New Scandal! Greedy Banker Killed by Effeminate Son. Revenge of the Gay: Son Brutally Strangles Father.* But I didn't kill him. I just ate my steak in silence and listened as he told me about his latest trades.

"We do have two teenagers here with us," Stephen says, pointing to me and Judy. "My beautiful niece Judy, and her best friend, Art. Not to put them on the spot or anything, but maybe they could tell us something about their experience."

"We have no experience!" Judy says, way too boisterously. "Not in that department, I mean. None. Nada. We're basically Doris Day and Sandra Dee."

A man in the corner with fuchsia hair says, "And even if they had experience, do you think they'd want to tell a roomful of grown-ups including their uncle? Have you forgotten what being a teenager is like?"

"Bite your tongue," Stephen says. "I only just turned nineteen." When he says this, he sounds like he's in one of his melodramas. Stephen loves old black-and-white movies. It's funny, 'cause he's the most colorful person I know. He's brighter than color. He's Technicolor.

"I have something to say." That's me talking. My palms are sweaty, and my voice shakes. "I, um, it's about something that I think is, um, super important. It's just, well, I think that there's something that would be missing even if the department of education spoke to teenagers." I pause for a long time, and Stephen gives me a nod of support. "It's the parents," I finally say. This is it, the gist of what I want to say, and once I start, I can't stop. "It's the parents who have to change first. Because so long as parents are telling their kids that being gay is a sin, or that this disease is God's way of killing gay people, or that celibacy is the only way not to die, or that they can get it from sitting on the wrong toilet seat, then nothing else matters. Because teenagers, well, I mean, we don't tell grown-ups what we do because we already know how they're going to react. We already know that they'll either pretend we never said what we said or they'll ground us or blame us. And you know, most people don't really have parents like you."

"Thank God—I'd be Daddy Dearest," one man in the back cracks, but Stephen quiets him with a flick of his wrist.

"I don't know what I'm saying," I say. Stephen gives me another nod. Here's what I think I'm saying: that Stephen is the dad I wish I had, the dad I was supposed to have, the man I consider my spiritual father. And that life for gay people is inherently unfair, because most gay people are born into families that just don't get them at all. And that's the *best-case* scenario. The worst cases . . . being abused, kicked out of the house, thrown into the streets. I guess I'm lucky my own case is somewhere in between. I mean, I know my parents think I'm a pervert, but they also haven't disowned me or anything. But that's probably because if they did that, then their whole social circle would inevitably find out why. And they're saving face as long as they can. They just care how things look to their bridge club. When I told them what they should have already known from the Boy George posters on my wall, my dad just walked out of the room, like this was a business meeting he was cutting short. And my mom . . .

she looked at me with disappointment, like I'd gotten a B-minus in math or something. Then she told me that it would all be okay, so long as I didn't tell anyone or do anything.

They never mention that conversation, not even when I wear eyeliner or tank tops or dye my hair or blast Madonna so loud that our place sounds like a pride parade. They've basically chosen to ignore *me*, and I've chosen to make that hard for them. "I guess I'm just saying that I think someone should protest parents. Or maybe not, like, all parents. But someone should protest *my parents*."

I finally shut up. And then the man with the fuchsia hair turns to me and says, "Gimme their address, and we'll handle them."

I sit down, my face hot and my hands shaky. I've been to a few of these meetings with Judy, but this is the first time I've spoken. Thankfully, the conversation is steered back to their next action. Six men are going to dress as traders, use fake badges, and infiltrate the floor of the New York Stock Exchange to protest the pharmaceutical company that is making AZT prohibitively expensive. As I listen, it suddenly hits me how hard being eloquent is, how angry I am, and how I have no idea how to be an activist. That's when I raise my hand and stand up again. All I say is "I want to help."

Stephen glares at me, but I stare him down. This is when it comes in handy that he's not really my dad. I don't need his permission. And nothing's more important to me than ending AIDS. Yeah, it's because I want to help people, and I don't want to die before my time, and I'm filled with love for Stephen, and I'm inspired and swept up in the electric energy of this room. But it's more. I don't know how I'll ever begin to live while this disease is raging. Who will love me when all they'll see when they look at me is the possibility that I may kill them? Judy will meet someone eventually. She'll probably have kids, be a famous designer, live in a fancy Upper West Side condo overlooking the park with her hot architect husband. And me . . . I'll either die or be eternally single because guys are too scared of me. So what choice do I have but to do something about this?

"Art," Judy whispers to me. "These things are dangerous. There are always cops . . ."

I ignore her. "Yeah, I want to help," I say, more firmly this time. "Just tell me where to be."

I don't know how, but I know that this decision will change my life. I'm a little psychic sometimes. I see colors. I can't describe it, but I know that in this moment, it's like a bright-pink light shines around me, and it just feels right. I hand my camera to Judy. "Hey, take a picture of me," I whisper.

"Why?" she asks.

"Just because," I say. "I want to remember this moment."

JUDY

At first, I see only his eyes. They're staring at me from above his long blue locker door. Brown doesn't do justice to the color of these eyes. My eyes are brown. His are something else entirely. Other eye colors conjure up so many beautiful images. Blue eyes bring to mind deep oceans and endless skies. Green eyes bring to mind rolling fields of grass or ancient emerald stones. But brown doesn't conjure much, does it? Mud. Dirt. Excrement. Pretty much describes my eyes. But his, they are more like the richest caramel ever created. They look like a vast desert, endless, beautiful, romantic, like some gorgeous Saharan desert, not that I've ever seen those places outside of some old Marlene Dietrich movie my uncle chose as one of our Sunday-night films.

Once my dull brown eyes manage to glance away from his caramel ones, I look down and see his bare feet, also caramel colored, with a few stray black hairs on each toe. So basically, I see the top of his eyes, one long locker, and bare feet, and I can't help but think that maybe this mystery man is naked, and that behind that locker, he's mooning our whole high school. His index toe is bigger than his big toe. I notice that right away because Art once told me that guys with an index toe longer than the big toe are supposed to be phenomenal in bed, or are going to be really rich. I don't remember anymore. Art has a lot of theories and superstitions, like people with gaps between their front teeth are supposed to be geniuses, which he obviously thinks is true because he and Madonna have huge gaps between their front teeth. If I were Art, I would start spreading a theory that fat girls with avant-garde fashion sense and severe black bangs are the chosen people.

"You're Judy, right?" the mystery man asks in a shaky voice, his mouth still hidden by the locker.

Wait, he knows your name, Judy. Maybe he traveled from a distant land to find you. But what will you wear for your wedding? Not some boring wedding dress. Maybe like a slip with an absurdly long veil.

I look up to his eyes (still perfect) and down to his feet (still perfect). Eyes. Feet. Eyes. Feet. Oh, and I haven't even mentioned his hair: black, thick, wavy. I let my mind wander, imagining he really is naked behind that locker, and that soon he will reveal himself to me: body, heart, and soul. Art always says I'll be the first to meet my soul mate, and I always say he's totally wrong. But maybe he's not. Art says he sees auras around people and things. I think he makes that up to seem interesting, but maybe not.

"Um, yeah, I'm Judy," I say. "And who are you, naked man?"

Shut up, Judy. That wasn't an internal monologue. He can hear you.

"I'm sorry?" he asks with a laugh, and now I notice his sexy accent.

"Oh God, I'm the one who's sorry," I say. "It's just that you're not wearing any shoes, so from where I'm standing, it kind of looks like you might be naked behind there."

I sound like an idiot, but what else is new? This is why I limit my conversation partners mostly to Art and Uncle Stephen. I know they're not going to judge me no matter what lunacy comes out of my mouth. And yeah, I have parents. And yeah, they judge me, usually silently or through annoyingly supportive suggestions about how I could slim down. For the record, my parents have female baldness and cancer all over their family trees, so a little extra weight is the least of my problems.

He closes the locker door and reveals he's very much *not* naked. Oh well, that fantasy is over. But he's also definitely not wearing our school uniform. His khaki shorts and white polo shirt are appropriate for the September heat wave, but most definitely inappropriate for this prisonlike school my parents choose to send me to, even though it's killing them financially.

"My stepbrother told me this was the uniform," he says. "Luckily, I brought tennis shoes for gym class, so I was just putting my sandals away."

That's when I notice that in addition to the aforementioned, and very hot, Middle Eastern accent, he also has a weird choice of words. "We call sandals flip-flops here," I say. "And we call tennis shoes sneakers."

He nods as he ties the laces of his white sneakers. "Thank you, Judy."

I let myself imagine bending over and tying his shoe-laces for him, massaging his legs in the process. God, I'm a perv. Art always says that straight people are ultimately much pervier than gay people, and if we were the only variables in the sample set, he'd probably be right. Art has a dirtier mouth, but I have dirtier thoughts. I have to—there's no way other people's brains are this gross. I mean, I'm seriously picturing myself rubbing this guy's thighs right now.

"Hey, so how do you know my name, mystery man?" I ask, attempting flirtation, but the minute the words escape my lips, I realize I probably sound pathetic bordering on creepy.

"Oh," he says. "They sent me this." He pulls out a yearbook from his locker.

"And you actually studied it?" I ask. I haven't looked at our yearbook since sophomore year, when me and Art went through and rated all the guys together, hating ourselves for giving tens to all the biggest assholes, like there was an actual correlation between a guy's dickishness and hotness.

He nods. I don't mean to make him feel bad. I hope I didn't.

"I don't remember everyone, but you stood out."

Of course you did. You're the only fat girl in there.

"So, um . . . ," I stammer, trying to make scintillating conversation and failing. "What's your name? I haven't studied the book like you."

"I'm Reza," he says. "I'm not in the book yet. There wasn't time to include me. I just moved here from Toronto, by way of Tehran."

"You didn't wanna move to Tokyo next?" I ask, but he doesn't seem to get the joke. "You know, cities that start with *T*."

"Oh," he says. "I understand."

If this were Art, we'd be riffing by now, listing off every *T* city we knew. I search for something else to say. "Well, I wish my picture was cuter. I look like a girl who cut her own bangs in a sad attempt to look like Louise Brooks but achieved Cousin Itt instead."

"Judy?" Reza says quietly, and when I look up, he asks, "What are bangs? And who is Louise Brooks? And Cousin Itt?"

I laugh. "Bangs," I say, pointing to my forehead, "are this ugly shape my hair makes on my forehead, which was both an attempt to cover up my forehead acne and

29

an effort to look like Louise Brooks, a silent-film star of the 1920s who never made it in talkies. And Cousin Itt is a hairy creature from the television show *The Addams Family*."

I can tell he wants to ask me what talkies are. That's definitely a question I asked my uncle a while ago, but he just says, "You look good."

I don't say anything, because I'm freaking out inside. A beautiful boy just told me I look good. I need to seal this deal before some skinny girl scoops him up from under me.

Other kids are zipping past us, going to class, gossiping about their summers, and yet it's like Reza and I are all alone. He has a weird quality about him. A calmness. He speaks softly, chooses his words carefully. It's disconcerting and exciting, maybe because I'm so used to being around Art, who spews words from his mouth like an active volcano.

"Perhaps you can cut my hair someday," he says.

"First of all, I won't touch your hair 'cause it's perfect," I respond. "If Rob Lowe's hair follicles and a perfect ocean wave had a baby, they would birth your hair."

What the hell is wrong with you, Judy? Why are you talking like this?

"And second of all, my attempt at cutting my hair was disastrous, so my uncle fixed it. If I look halfway normal, it's because of him. Okay, what's your first class?" I ask Reza. He takes his schedule out of his pocket and hands it to me. "We both have English with Tompkins first," I say. "Follow me."

But before we can start down the hallway, Art rushes toward me frantically, his face obscured by a winter hat, which is an odd choice for a sweltering September heat wave. When he's uncomfortably close to me, he takes the hat off, revealing hair dyed a strange shade of lavender that wouldn't look out of place on the mane of a My Little Pony. "How bad is it?" he demands.

"It looks fine," I lie, because Art is my best friend, and as his best friend I know that if I tell him he looks like a My Little Pony, he'll go apeshit. Art says he's a little histrionic because both of his parents are so rigid and rarely show emotion, so he overcompensates.

"Okay, you're clearly lying," Art says. With his hat back on, he shifts to the right and eyes Reza. "Who are you?" he asks. "And what do you think? Honestly?"

Reza stares at Art with what I can only read as either fear or disgust, and my heart sinks a little. It suddenly hits me that if and when I finally fall in love, the chance that my heterosexual lover is a homophobe is high. And I can't love a homophobe. Definite deal breaker, right alongside dirty fingernails and guys who don't wash their hands after they pee, which Art tells me is another important epidemic that women are unaware of due to bathroom segregation.

"Hello!" Art says to Reza. "Do you speak?"

Reza clearly doesn't know what to do with Art's

super-intense energy.

"What do I think about . . ." Reza trails off. He's still staring at Art like he's studying him, and it's starting to piss me off a little. My best friend isn't a circus freak. But then I tell myself that maybe Reza is staring because he's curious. I try not to jump to a negative conclusion. I know I can be defensive, protective, judgmental. Take your pick.

"About my sherbet hair!" Art whisper-yells. "Is it the worst tress trauma since Pepsi burned Michael Jackson's scalp to a crisp?"

I turn to Reza and explain, "Michael Jackson is a pop star. He started out as part of the Jackson Five before releasing what I still consider to be his masterpiece, *Off the Wall*, then . . ."

"I know who Michael Jackson is," Reza says.

"*Thriller* is his masterpiece, and don't change the subject please. I need an honest opinion." Oh, that's another thing about Art. When he's in the room, it's all about him. Don't even try to divert attention away from him.

Reza doesn't give an honest opinion. He doesn't say anything. And this makes Art crazy. "Okay, whatever, you can't even be bothered to answer a simple question. I'm done here," Art says. But Art doesn't leave. He hovers around us.

Reza has a far-off look. He shrugs. "I should, um, get to class."

He awkwardly gives me a kiss on each cheek, and as he does, he rests his hands on my love handles for a moment, like they're a hand pillow. I wish I hadn't eaten that bagel for breakfast.

Finally, Reza lets go of me and walks down the hallway. Once he's safely out of hearing distance, I turn to Art. "What is wrong with you?" I ask, irritated.

"Um, hello," he says, lifting his hat once more to reveal his hair.

"Art," I say, "I was having a moment with that guy."

"Oh," he says. "You mean, like a sexual-healing, super-freak, touched-for-the-very-first-time moment."

I blush and nod. "I don't know. I think so. He's new, and cute, and seems, I don't know, different. Maybe they like girls like me in Tehran and Toronto."

"Or Taipei," Art jokes, and I smile, because I love that our brains sometimes work the exact same way.

"Or Türkmenabat," I say.

"How long have you been waiting to throw Türkmenabat into casual conversation?" Art asks.

"I mean, since I was born." I'm smiling now. This is me and Art. This is what we're like when we're at our best. Like two puzzle pieces that decided to escape the rest of the puzzle because we fit so good.

"Look, I'm an asswipe and I'm sorry," Art says. "I promise you that my number one goal from now on, other than pissing my parents off by dyeing my hair the gayest color that's not rainbow, will be to aid your mission of romancing that stone-cold hottie. You got that, Frances?"

Oh yeah, Art sometimes calls me Frances, usually when he's said or done something stupid and needs my forgiveness. My uncle named me Judy for his "favorite *Homo sapiens* of all time," and Judy Garland's real name was Frances Gumm. Art likes to think he's the only person who knows the real me. His real name's Bartholomew, by the way. Bartholomew Emerson Grant VI. He comes from a long line of men who would probably be horrified to share a name with him.

"I got it." I sigh. "Do you think this is the year I'll finally get a boyfriend?"

"I hope so," Art says. "And if it's him, more power to you. His ass is *Beyond the Valley of the Dolls*." That's a movie my uncle made us watch. "So does this mean your crush on Ben Stark is over?"

"Yeah, that ended when he misspelled *fabrication* in his editor's letter for the school paper," I say. I shake my head, wondering how I could ever have had a crush on anyone but Reza, and say, "Come on, My Little Pony, let's get to class before the bell rings."

"You wench, you lied. I do look awful." He groans. "I'm going to burn you at the stake."

"We *love* My Little Pony," I counter.

"Iron-i-cal-ly," he says, stretching out every syllable. "The way we love Stacey Q, scrunchies, and *Mommie Dearest*."

I hold Art's hand before he can bolt out of school, and we walk toward English class together. On our way in, we run into Darryl Lorde, who takes his white baseball hat off and greets Art with "Hey, faggot, you know hats aren't allowed." Then, when Art takes his hat off, Darryl leaps back. "Whoa, I didn't think you could get any gayer."

Art just smiles. He's used to Darryl by now, the ringleader of our school's homophobes, who is so good at sports that he can pretty much get away with anything. "I did it just for you, Darryl," Art says, then winks.

Darryl shakes his head in disgust, then heads into class. I can hear him fake sneeze when he passes Reza, but instead of saying "Aaaa-choo," he says, "*Aaaa-yatollah!*" And his dumb cronies laugh. I shoot him a dirty look and glance over at Reza, who seems to be trying very hard to ignore what is happening.

Art and I are the last ones to arrive. As we walk in, Art fake sneezes himself, blurting out, "*Aaaa-ssholes.*" But no one laughs this time. A few people stare at us like we're aliens, including Annabel de la Roche and her gaggle of girlfriends, who all look like they subsist on multivitamins and iceberg lettuce.

There are only two empty seats left. One is next to Reza. "Take that seat," Art whispers to me. I hesitate, and when I do, Art practically pushes me into it.

Reza whispers to me, "Why is your friend so aggressive?"

Before I can respond, Art leans in close to Reza. "Because life is short and I'm not going to let it be boring too." He catches himself, then backs off. "Sorry, I'll go sit up front and leave you two lovebirds alone."

Oh God, Art, *lovebirds*? Seriously?

"I'm sorry about Darryl," I say to Reza.

"Who?" he asks.

"The idiot who was making fun of you," I say.

Reza shrugs. "I'm good at tuning things out," he says. "Denial is even more Iranian than ayatollahs."

I giggle nervously, not sure where to take the conversation next. "Sorry about Art, too. He comes on a little strong."

He nods. Then in a hushed voice, he says, "There was nobody like him in Iran or Toronto."

"I'm sure Toronto has gay people," I say, way too defensive. "As for Iran, I don't know, maybe they've killed them all."

Okay, this is over. You've definitely scared him off.

"Oh," he says. "I'm sorry to offend."

That's all he says. And it's enough to make me feel like total shit about myself.

"No, I'm the one who's sorry," I say. "I'm just sick of people making fun of him."

"Was I making fun?" he asks.

"No," I say. "No, not at all. You were just making an observation, which was probably totally true. In fact, I'm the offensive one. I'm the one who assumed that he's basically like all other gay people. When in fact you were right. Absolutely no one in Toronto, or Iran, or any place where humans live, is anything like Art. Maybe that's why I get defensive of him. 'Cause he's special."

Reza just nods, almost like he's agreeing with me.

We both look up at Art, so hard to miss with that hair. He's flipping through some notecards. Not just any notecards. The Queer 101 notecards Uncle Stephen made for him to explain important gay concepts like conversion therapy, the Cockettes, and Quentin Crisp. And those are just a few of the *C*s. I can see that Art is reading #67 John, Elton.

"I talk too much," I say. "I'm sorry."

"Do not apologize for talking. Most of my life, I've talked too little."

He smiles hesitantly, stopping himself midsmile. It's like he's just learning how.

"I'm not, by the way," I say.

Stop. Stop now.

"Not what?" he asks.

"I mean, we're best friends, and he's on the upper echelon of the Kinsey Scale, but . . ." I can tell he has no idea what the Kinsey Scale is, and I explain. "Oh, that's this scale, this thing that says some people are into men, some are into women, and some are in between."

"Oh," he says.

He seems extremely uncomfortable with this conversation, and I want to change the subject immediately, but instead, I say, "I'm on the side of the scale that's totally hetero. That's it. I just wanted you to know. I have no idea why I'm telling you this."

Yes you do. Because he's cute, and unlike the rest of the boys at school, he doesn't seem like a total tool.

"Oh," he says. He closes his eyes for a moment. After a beat, he says, "Me too." Then he smiles awkwardly. And I smile back.

#75 Love

Love might just *happen* to them, but for us, it's not as easy. For us, it's a fight. Maybe someday it won't be. Maybe someday love will just be . . . love. But for now, love is the four-letter word they forgot we care about ever since they discovered that other four-letter word, AIDS, the disease formerly known as GRID. Gay-Related *Immune Deficiency*. That's what they called it at first. They changed the name eventually, once it became clear we were not the only ones who would die. But the stink never wore off. It never does when they want to control you. Marilyn was *always* Norma Jeane, and they never let her forget it. When her ideas got too big, they reminded her she was nothing but an orphan. And AIDS will always be GRID. It is *our* disease, born of our *deficiencies*. But I'll tell you what we will never be deficient of. LOVE. We love art and beauty. We love new ideas and pushing boundaries. We love fighting against corruption. We love redefining archaic rules. We love men, and women, and men who dress like women, and women who dress like men. We love tops and bottoms, and top hats, especially when worn by Marlene Dietrich. But most of all, we love each other. Know that. We love each other. We care for each other. We are brothers and sisters, mentors and students, and together we are limitless and whole. The most important four-letter word in our history will always be LOVE. That's what we are fighting for. That's who we are. Love is our legacy.

REZA

Our dining room is extravagant and ridiculous. Just sitting in it makes me feel uncomfortable. It looks like it was designed for an ancient royal shah. Anything that can be gold is gold, and anything not made of gold is crystal, glass, or emerald green. The paintings on the walls are mostly old Persian portraits from the Qajar dynasty, but then there's a portrait of Abbas, done in the same style, as if to imply that he is one of those royals. I'm surprised there's no painting of Saadi done in the old Qajar style, except instead of wearing an ornate robe and headdress, he would be wearing boxer shorts and holding a lacrosse stick.

"There is no doubt we are headed toward a recession. And if others have doubt, they are wrong. I know we are. Just look at real estate prices. They're starting to dip and it's only going to get worse. We were living in a bubble, and it's popping as I speak. Nobody is spending on luxuries like real estate and expensive furniture any-more."

That's Abbas talking. My stepfather. He's bald and very tall, one of the lankiest Iranians I have ever seen. And he speaks with so much authority. If there's one thing I have learned since my mom married this man, it is that when he talks, you listen. If I could interject, here is what I might say: *First of all, you are still living in a bubble. Just look around this home. And second of all, stop subtly suggesting my mother shouldn't start working again.* Because that is what is really happening right now. My mom was an interior designer in Toronto. She did okay. Well enough to support me and my sister, although we certainly did not live in a gold-leafed wonderland, and we certainly did not go to a fancy private school with starched uniforms, children of famous people, and lacrosse teams. I don't even know how Abbas and my mom met. Probably ages ago, since Persians all know each other anyway. All I know is one day, my mom sat me and my sister down and told us she was getting married again. She said she and I would be moving to New York, while my sister stayed in Canada for college. And that was that.

"It is not surprising that prices are starting to dip in the city," Abbas continues. "People are afraid of getting mugged, beaten, raped. What happened in Central Park is just the beginning. I love it here, but if I were to do it all over again, I would think twice before buying in the city."

My mom just smiles, an eye toward the pot of *ghormeh*

sabzi, and says, "Honestly, Abbas, I have no idea how you trained your cook to make Persian food this well."

"Oh, my mom trained her," Saadi says. "These are her recipes." There's no obvious venom in the way he says this, but his intent is hard to miss.

That's when I deduce that it wasn't Abbas who picked out the decor of this mausoleum we are living in. The gold, crystal, glass, and emeralds of the dining room, the old paintings, the cacophony of rugs, the lacquered picture frames and heavy curtains, they were probably all selected by this woman I have never met. For a moment, a feeling of warmth toward Abbas washes over me. Because if he was married to a woman this tacky and over-the-top, and then traded her in for a woman as classy as my mother, then perhaps he isn't as bad as I want him to be.

"Her recipes are delicious then," my mom says diplomatically.

"So, Reza *jan*, how was your first week of school?" Abbas reaches over to me and tries to playfully punch my shoulder.

"School is okay," I say.

This is a lie. School is terrible. I'm the new, dark kid who has no idea how to make friends. They make Iranian hostage crisis and ayatollah jokes about me. And I'm scared of the other kids, none more so than Art, who attracts and repels me, sometimes in the same moment. There's one good thing about school, and that's Judy. She is kind, and funny, and she seems to like me, seems to see something in me that I wish I could see in myself.

"Tell us a little more," my mom says. "What is your favorite class?"

"Um, I don't know," I say. "English, I guess. We're reading *The Odyssey* and I think it's good."

Saadi nods his head. "Awesome book," he says. I saw him yesterday in his room, reading the CliffsNotes.

"I wish you would read the *Shahnameh* as well," Abbas says. "We have our own history and literature."

"We could all read it together," my mom says. "Like a family book club."

I can see the wheels in Saadi's head turning, trying to figure out the chances that someone has written CliffsNotes for the *Shahnameh*. When he figures out that the chances are zero, he says, "Right, like we have time to read two epics in one semester."

Abbas doesn't admonish his son. Instead, we sit in silence, nothing filling the space but the sound of four mouths chewing. There's a point during all our family dinners so far when everybody's attempts at conversation fail. We sit and say nothing, chewing as quietly as we can. In Iran and in Toronto, we never had a quiet family dinner. My dad and my sister didn't know how to be quiet.

And then the doorbell rings.

"I'll get it," my mom says.

"It's for me," Saadi says, getting up. "It's my project partner for biology. Don't be shocked by how he looks. He's a queen."

Saadi moves toward the front door and opens it. I

don't see Art, but I can hear him. "Hey, what's up?" he asks Saadi.

"Nothing," Saadi says. "Let's get this over with."

Saadi and Art enter the dining room. It's the first time I have seen Art out of the school uniform, and now the rest of him matches his lavender hair. His jeans are ripped at both knees and splattered with paint. He wears a sleeveless black T-shirt, with zippers at both sides and a decal of a woman with big hair on it. And his combat boots have thick heels on them, so when he walks in, it sounds like my mom sounds when she enters a room. He has a camera around his neck, a fancy one with a big lens.

"Family, this is Art," Saadi says. "We have to work on a science project."

"Hey, family," Art says, waving his right hand, revealing a single fingernail painted black.

"Hello," Abbas says. He stands up and shakes Art's hand politely. "I'm Abbas, Saadi's father. You are a class mate of his?"

"Oh yeah, we're real close," Art says, his voice thick with sarcasm.

"This is my wife, Mina," Abbas says, and my mom dutifully stands and shakes Art's hand. "And you must know my other son, Reza."

I freeze for a moment. I do every time Abbas refers to me as his son, which I am clearly not. Nothing about me says that I belong in his world of high finance and high-rises.

But I know it's my turn to stand dutifully, and I do.

"Hello, Art," I say, and I approach him to shake his hand.

"Hey, Reza," Art says. When he shakes my hand, he holds it a little too tightly, and I catch a hint of the smell of his armpits. His sleeveless shirt has sweat stains on it, inevitable if you are outside for more than a few seconds. Smelling him makes me uncomfortable, and I pull my hand aggressively away from his. He looks at me funny when I do, but I have no idea what he's thinking.

"Are you hungry, Art?" my mom asks. "We have stew and rice. Have you ever had Persian food?"

"We're going to study," Saadi says.

"It's okay," Art says. "I don't eat meat anyway. I don't believe in killing living things. Except Jesse Helms."

My mom and Abbas flinch at that, more than a little offended, as if his clothes and hair were not enough.

"And yeah, I've had Persian food. My parents have lots of Persian friends. Kind of inevitable when you live on the Upper East Side post-1979."

"Who are your parents?" Abbas asks. "Do I know them?"

"Dad, I want to be done studying before *Quantum Leap* is on," Saadi says. "Can you let us go, please? And he's Bartholomew Emerson Grant VI, so he passes whatever test you're giving him."

I stare at Art, wondering what the significance of his name is, what special lineage he comes from. I zone out as the conversation speeds up—Abbas is excited by this newfound piece of information. The sounds become hazy. All I see is Art, like I can hear his heartbeat through the fabric of his tank top, underscoring the conversation.

Oh of course I know your father. We've never done a deal together, but we've tried.

Probably for the best.

Tell him I say hello. And your beautiful mother.

What a lovely coincidence. We'd love to have your family over for dinner.

And I'm so sorry about the loss of your grandfather. What a man!

The expression on Art's face seems to question whether the death of his grandfather was a loss at all. I know that ambivalence. I felt it when my mom told us about my dad. By that point, I hadn't seen him in four years, not since we left Tehran. And I felt a hollow sadness, a sharp pain, but also relief. We could start over.

"He was a great man," Abbas continues, perhaps hoping for some response from Art.

Art does respond now, but not about his grandfather's greatness. "This is the raddest dining room I've ever seen," he says. "Could I take a picture of it?"

My mother stands up. "Oh, of course," she says, exceedingly polite. "We will just get out of the way."

"No, no, you're a crucial part of it. All of you."

My mom sits back down. Art raises his camera to his face, closes one eye, and focuses. The four of us sit, smiles frozen on our faces, and wait for him to click. "Brilliant," he says, with a fake British accent.

Then Saadi pulls Art out toward his bedroom, leaving me alone with Abbas and my mom.

"I wonder why Bartholomew Grant allows his son to dress like that," Abbas says.

"American parents are so different," my mom says. "They let their children get away with murder."

"Murder is one thing," Abbas says. "Purple hair is another thing altogether."

My mom laughs, and I get a glimpse of what she sees in him. Maybe it really is more than money. I also find myself wanting to defend Art, and I don't know why, because I too hate his purple hair, and his dirty high-heeled boots, and his sweaty armpits.

"Well, thank God, none of us have children like that," my mom says. "We have wonderful children." She tousles my hair and smiles as she says this, and I realize she probably has not told Abbas a shred of truth about my older sister and all her issues.

"We do," Abbas says. "We are very lucky."

I force a smile, and I remind myself to be grateful. "I feel very lucky too," I say, and my mom beams. "I also feel full. May I be excused?"

"Of course," my mom says.

Before leaving the room, I give my mom and Abbas a kiss on each cheek and thank them for dinner.

I'm in my room reading *The Odyssey*, and I can hear the faint voices of Saadi and Art in the room next door. I can't tell what they're talking about, and although the subject matter of their conversation is probably restricted to the mundane details of their homework, I still want to hear everything. I try to refocus on the book, but I'm on page one of over two hundred, and I'm not exactly feeling focused. I think about my own odyssey, from Iran to Canada to New York. I find myself turning the page without even remembering a thing I have just read. I used to be a reliably good student, always capable of getting the straight As that my mother desired from me. But now, finding myself unable to read a single page, I wonder if maybe I was only good because I was compensating for my sister's perpetual problems. If she hadn't been around to scare me into behaving, would I have studied as hard, or tried as desperately to please my mom? I turn another page. I'm still not paying attention, even though I highlight a sentence or two in an effort to convince myself I'm still diligent.

Then the door opens. No knock. I assume it's Saadi, but Art walks in, and I jump back in surprise.

"Whoa," he says. "I'm not Freddy Krueger. You weren't jerking off, were you?"

"Um . . . no," I say. I hold up *The Odyssey* and push it toward him, just in case he has bad eyesight or something. "I was reading. For school."

"I can see the book," he says, laughing. "You can put it down now."

I put the book down on my lap, using it to hide my growing erection. A few seconds pass, but they feel eternal. Finally, I ask, "Is there, um, something you need? From me?"

He sits on the edge of my bed and begins to unpack his

book bag, removing the mess of items inside and laying them down on my floor. First, a bright-yellow Discman. Then his own copy of *The Odyssey*. Then a purple folder, and a white binder with a pink triangle sticker on it. Then some jelly bracelets. As he keeps riffling through his things, he peeks up at me.

"I was just wondering, what's the deal with you and Judy?"

He pulls a few pins out and lays them on the carpet. I cannot take my eyes off one that reads ACT UP, FIGHT AIDS in block letters. "Sorry, what?"

"You," he says, pointing his finger at me and pressing it into my chest. "And Judy."

"Oh," I say, a little terrified of him.

He doesn't take his finger off my chest, and I try to push it away. But when I do, he grabs ahold of my hand and squeezes it tight. "Don't evade," he says. "Because Judy's my best girl, and I'm not interested in seeing her heart broken. So, if you're not into her, move on now, okay? And if you are into her, then she loves going to the movies, especially revival houses. She can't get enough ice cream—her favorite is mint chocolate chip. She lives for avant-garde fashion. And her favorite flowers are yellow roses, the brighter the better."

He still has a grip on my hand, and I find myself getting harder. Very, very hard. I try to reposition myself to hide the damning evidence, but he still won't let go of me. "Can you release me please?" I ask. But he doesn't, and we end up struggling, our bodies circling each other until finally he lets go. I pull the covers over me, my breath heavy.

"Why are you so weird?" he asks. "You're not like your brother, are you?"

"Brother?" I ask.

Art points his finger toward Saadi's room. "Your brother. I call him and his friends 'white hats' 'cause they're always wearing those dumb white baseball hats. It's like code for 'I'm a dick who's afraid to sit too close to a fag.'"

"I do not, um, I don't think you are supposed to use that word," I say.

"What, fag? I'm allowed to use it," he says defiantly. "Because I am one. Major fag. So major I've written a fan letter to Boy George and received a handwritten response. So major I'm joining the ACT UP protest of the New York Stock Exchange this month." He rattles on and on before catching his breath and turning his attention back to his book bag. He pulls out a crumpled T-shirt. "There she is," he exclaims. And in an instant, he takes his sweaty tank top off and he isn't wearing a shirt. I try to look away, but I don't. I'm too interested in his lean body, in the wisps of hair on his lower back, in the freckles on his shoulders. Then he throws the crumpled T-shirt on. "My advice for New York heat waves. Always carry a change of T-shirt and underwear in your bag."

I imagine the extra pair of underwear in his bag and try my hardest to think of anything else. I think of my dad's drunk rages. I think of my sister sneaking in late at night, of my mom crying. I think of my mom getting the phone call that my dad died, and of her sitting me and my sister down and telling us the news with glassy detachment. But in between all these thoughts is the same nagging question: what kind of underwear does he wear?

"I guess I'm gonna take off," Art says. He puts his headphones on and stands up. "Hey, what do you think of the new Madonna album? It's the shit, right?" Before I can answer, he says, "And don't say you hate Madonna, because I don't trust people who hate Madonna."

"Oh, I, uh, I don't know her music very well," I say, suddenly wishing I did. "My mom mostly listens to Persian music. I like that holiday song. What is it called?"

"'Holiday,'" he says curtly.

"Oh, right," I say. "My sister always played that."

"And what do you listen to?" he asks, in a way that makes me feel he will hate whatever the answer is.

"Whatever is on, I suppose."

He puts his headphones on my ears. "This is what's on," he whispers to me, his breath hitting my face just above my eyes. Then he presses play, and I hear an aggressive guitar followed by Madonna's voice telling me that life is a mystery, and that everyone must stand alone, like I didn't know that already. But soon, the music transports me to some other magical land. Art lets the whole song play. When it ends, he pulls the headphones off me and says, "The second song's even better."

"It is, um, really great," I say, unable to find the right

words to describe the transcendent experience of hearing that song.

"Yeah, I know, she's the queen of the world." He sits next to me again, speaking faster, his hands moving quickly. His passion for the subject spills out of him. "You know about the Pepsi commercial, right?"

"Um . . ." My stammering must make it obvious that I don't.

"Sorry, but were you living in Tehran and Toronto, or were you living under a giant rock? Madonna did a Pepsi commercial to that song, and a few days later she released the video to the song, where she dances in front of burning crosses and kisses a black saint. Pepsi told her to pull the video. She said fuck you. So . . . they pulled the commercial, and she kept the five million. That's what you call a badass bitch move. Do what you want and keep the money."

I stare at him as he talks, mesmerized by his confidence. "You might be allowed to use the *f* word," I say, "but I don't think you're allowed to use the *b* word."

"What, bitch?" he asks.

I nod and smile. "You are not a woman."

"Honorary," he says. "Just like Judy's an honorary queer. Speaking of, you never answered my question. Do you like Judy?"

I feel trapped. I don't know what the right thing to say is. If I say no, then she may never spend time with me again, and she is the only friend I have made. And also, I'm scared of Art, of how he makes me feel, of his directness and self-assurance. I wonder how he got to be that way. Maybe his parents support him unconditionally, cheer him on no matter what. I bet they do. That's what American parents are like.

"She's, um, very cool," I say, hoping that will make him stop. "Probably the coolest girl I have ever met." That's not a lie. I can't tell the whole truth, but I also hate telling lies.

"Okay," he says. "That'll do for now. She's a great kisser, you know. We practiced with each other."

I don't say anything to that. I'm too busy daydreaming about what it would be like to practice kissing with Art.

He stands up again and clicks open his Discman. He pulls out the CD, then finds the case for it in his bag. He throws it on my bed. "A present," he says.

"Oh, I can't accept that," I say.

"Whatever. I can easily steal another twenty bucks from my parents to replace it. My dad's so easy to steal from. He just leaves his money in a money clip on the mantel when he showers." Art throws on a few of the jelly bracelets and dumps all the other items that were in his bag back in, in no apparent order. "See you at school?" he asks.

"Um, okay," I say. He's about to leave when I stand up and call his name. When he turns around, I stumble over my words, but finally I ask, "When did you know that you were, um, you know, homosexual?"

He puts his bag down and smiles. "I had a wet dream

about Morrissey. He's a singer. A hot one with an accent. I love accents."

"Is that a serious answer?" I ask, self-conscious about my accent.

"Seriously," he says. "But I should've known sooner. All my friends were girls. And there was Judy's uncle Stephen. He was always around. You know me and Judy have been friends forever, right?" I nod, but I say nothing because I don't want him to stop. "I always felt more connected to him than to my own dad. I guess I should've known that whatever Uncle Stephen was . . . is what I was too. It was just so obvious that we belonged to the same tribe or something. But before that wet dream, I didn't understand, you know? I had no frame of reference. Why?"

"No special reason," I say.

"So you're cool with me being gay?" he asks. "Because Judy was afraid you'd be a homophobe."

"Oh, no, of course not," I say, as if it's a matter of politeness.

"Cool," he says. "Case closed." Then he waves his hand and leaves. Just like that.

I notice his backpack on the floor. I could run out and return it to him, but I stay put. I lock the door, and I pull out the sweaty tank top he threw in there and a pair of black briefs. I put on the Madonna CD he gave me, and as I listen to the sound of her voice calling me home, I push his scent against my face. It makes me feel wobbly, and I sit on the floor as I catch my breath. Then I keep searching through his bag, feeling the smoothness of his jelly bracelets and leafing through his notebook, like I'm searching for his secrets. But I immediately feel awful about snooping, and I slam his notebook shut. He doesn't even have any secrets, I remind myself. He is the open book. I'm the one with secrets. I close my eyes. The second Madonna song comes on. She tells me to express myself. I wish I knew how to do that.

Then I pull out a stack of worn, oversize index cards, held together with a rainbow scrunchie. My eyes catch the top of the first card, which reads #1 Adonis. Then #2 Advocate, The. Then #3 AIDS. I stop cold. Just that word on a piece of paper scares me, makes me feel like it could be transmitted to me, and I quickly flip past it. The cards are alphabetical, each with a number on top and a subject, followed by a handwritten scrawl, almost illegible. You can tell they were written quickly and with passion. Some entries are longer than one card, sometimes two or three, stapled together. I scan through the cards. I wonder what secrets they hold. There are one hundred and thirty-one of them in total, and a few leap out at me. #9 Baldwin, James. #18 Brunch. #26 Condoms. #28 Crawford, Joan. #53 Fucking Reagans, The. #54 Garland, Judy. #75 Love. #96 Radical Faeries. #127 White Night Riots. #131 Woolf, Virginia. But one card calls to me above all others. #76 Madonna. I pull it out and start to read.

ART

I catch a glimpse of myself in one of Wall Street's intim-
idatingly tall glass buildings, and at first I can barely
recognize the image as me. My hair isn't lavender anymore—it's dyed back to its natural chestnut brown and
cut into a conservatively short haircut. My earring is
gone, and the hole that once housed it already seems to
have closed up. I'm not wearing a tank top, or a Silence
= Death slogan on my clothes, or a concert T-shirt of
Cyndi, Boy George, or Madonna. I'm wearing a bor-
ing-as-dirt gray suit, a white shirt, and one of my dad's
many crisp red ties, which feels like it chokes me. At least
I have my camera around my neck, so I don't feel like a
completely lost soul. Then I see Stephen in the reflection
behind me. "Ready?" he asks. He's wearing a dark-navy
suit, light-blue button-down shirt, and striped tie. The
concealer he wears is so subtle you wouldn't even know

there's any makeup on his face.

I turn around to face him. Behind him are seven more men in suits. None of the people frantically rushing in and out of these colossal buildings see anything but a group of traders chatting before their workday begins. Only we know the rage that hides behind these suits and ties and conservative haircuts.

"My heart's beating really fast," I say.

"That's normal," Stephen says. "The first time I protested, I felt like Judy Garland playing Carnegie Hall. Just breathe and enjoy your first drag show."

"Drag show?" I ask.

"Look at us," he says. "We're serving Wall Street *realness*." He winks at me, because calling something *realness* is a throwback to a ball he took us to last summer. It was the most fun ever. "All we have to do now is act."

When Stephen first told me and Judy about ACT UP, he said it wasn't so strange that he had found his calling as an activist, because it was close to his first love, acting. Acting, activism, action, they're all based on creating authenticity in an artificial world. Stephen never was an actor, though. He was a lawyer, and not the kind who got rich defending corporations and screwing people over. He helped refugees resettle into the country. But he had to stop working when his health got bad, or maybe the agency he worked at thought he'd scare the refugees. There was something ironic about a man with AIDS helping resettle immigrants, since people with AIDS are banned from entering the country. But his lawyering is all over anyway. Activism and being a rad uncle are his only jobs now.

"You loaded up your camera with fresh film?" he asks.

"It's ready to go."

"Remember, take some photos and then run. We made a deal, okay?" The deal is that I'm allowed to photograph the action but not be a part of it. Because he won't have me getting booked by the cops, even if chances are I'd immediately be released.

"I don't care about getting arrested," I tell him.

"And I don't care that you don't care. Leave the risks to those of us who are going to die soon," he says.

I hate when Stephen does this. He makes these throwaway jokes about his imminent death, which I choose to believe isn't coming anytime soon. I choose to believe that a medical breakthrough is on the horizon and will arrive just in time to save his life. But I don't say this. I've tried before, and it upsets him. He says he wants to have hope, but not *too much* hope. "Too much hope will just kill me faster," he said to me once. I don't know exactly what he meant by that. But another time he said to me, "It's the anger that's kept me alive, you know. Without the anger, I'd have joined José by now. I just have too much to scream about to leave just yet."

Behind us, one of the seven men, the most handsome one, calls out, "It's almost nine. We should go in. Here are your badges." The man hands us fake trader ID badges, with false names but our real photos on them. I stare at mine for a moment, thinking this is exactly who my parents pray I will turn into one day. Something else hits me hard—that when I strip away the punk hairdos and the alternative style, I look so much like my dad. I think about how easy it would be if this were who I was, a person who liked his red ties, and his boring haircuts, and his trades and deals and golf games. A person who didn't like boys, who didn't hate convention, who wasn't so angry. For a moment, I even wish for this, for an easy life. But this wish just makes me angrier, fuels me more. It reminds me that what I want, what I truly want, is to be loved and accepted for being me.

"We're going in through the west staircase. As soon as we make it to the trading floor, we need to move fast. We need to do this before security realizes and stops us. Does anyone have to use the bathroom? Best to use it now." Everybody shakes their heads. "Okay, let's do it. And remember why we're doing this. Burroughs Wellcome's stock has risen forty percent since they started selling AZT, and the drug is still unaffordable for even a person with above-average income. We will shame them into lowering that price even if they throw us in jail for it again."

We enter the building without a hitch, flashing our fake ID badges to a bored security guard. I feel like I did when Judy and I snuck into Danceteria once, except this time what waits for us on the other side isn't a live performance from Grace Jones. It's the New York Stock

Exchange. As we walk up twenty flights of stairs, the men all joke with each other. "Nice ass," one of them says to the one in front of him, as he gently spanks it. The one in front shimmies a little. "Now remember," another says, "do not cruise the traders, no matter how much they may resemble Christopher Reeve." I love this about these guys, their ability to laugh through their anger, to find light even in injustice. When we reach the top, Stephen turns to the group, and in his most dramatic Joan Crawford, he says, "Don't fuck with us fellas. This ain't our first time at the stock exchange." The men all nod to each other in solidarity, and then we open the door.

I momentarily freeze when the door opens to reveal the trading floor. There's something majestic about it. All those people in their muted colors, all those computers, all those lights. People moving so fast that they barely notice each other. You can almost hear the numbers crunching. You can almost feel bank accounts getting fatter, and land being destroyed, and people being taken advantage of, and the stink of greed and death being spritzed into the air like those perfume samples in the Bloomingdale's lobby. Everything about the energy of this place says that what happens here changes life, for the better if you're one of the chosen few, but mostly for the worse.

"Art!" I hear my name being screamed and I snap to attention. Stephen and five of his friends have already chained themselves to the balcony of the stock exchange. "Art!" Stephen screams again. I realize I haven't taken a single photograph. My camera is dangling limply from my neck. I raise it up to my eyes, closing one of them, my eyelid twitching nervously, my hands shaky. I snap one photo, then another. Behind me I hear voices: "Hose those faggots down. They like that," one says. "Throw 'em in jail. They like that more," responds another. It's just high school, I think to myself. It's all high school. This is just another locker room, another safe space for straight assholes to spew their hate. I point my camera at the homophobes and snap. I imagine the click and the flash are bullets, plunged DEEP into their hateful asshole hearts.

"It's almost nine," another voice says. In the chaos, I can't tell if it's an activist or a trader. I move my camera toward the activists now. It's almost nine. It's showtime.

The bell rings. The opening bell, marking another start to another day of financial corruption. Except this day, nobody hears it. What they hear, what we all hear, is the sound of foghorns. Loud and invasive, they take over the space. I snap away as the activists blow those foghorns, and I see the hint of a smile on Stephen's face. I wonder if he's also thinking about that time he told me that Cher's voice is like a foghorn, calling all the queens to her shores and warning them of the many navigational hazards ahead. Probably not. He's probably thinking of how he's changing the world, righting its wrongs. And it's more than a smile on his face now. It's a look of sheer exhilaration. He's LIVING right now. It's like he's the most alive person in the world. And then I realize I am LIVING too, and it feels amazing.

The activists unfurl a banner that reads "SELL WELLCOME," a message to the traders about the pharmaceutical company that has jacked up the price of AZT. They've shut down trading. They're my heroes.

"Art, run. Now!" It's Stephen again. Police have entered, and immediately my pulse races and I start to run. Maybe the idea of getting detained sounded fun in theory. But now I know that when cops are after you, none of it is fun. I look around as I flee and realize how much of the chaos I missed. The hissing traders. The threatening police. And the media. The cameras, the video cameras, the reporters, all filming us. All filming *me* as I took pictures of them. I make eye contact with one of the video cameras as I bolt the hell out of there, back to the stairwell we came in through.

I speed down the stairwell to the bottom, my camera hitting my chest as it bounces up and down. On the bottom floor, I collapse and catch my breath. I wonder if Stephen has been handcuffed yet, if this action will work. Will the drug price come down? And when will the next action be? Because I'm not done. I need to feel this again.

When I exit the building, the morning sun hits me hard, as does the September heat. I take my suffocating tie off and consider throwing it in the garbage. It seems to symbolize everything I hate about the world. But then I think better of wasting a perfectly fine piece of fabric, and I wrap the tie around my head like a headband. Judy would approve of that. She loves repurposing things when she designs. As I sneak around the side of the building, I see a few media trucks parked outside, and I see spectators, a lot of them, frozen across the street, staring at the building. Maybe we've helped them see something.

And then I *see something* . . . Reza. At least I think it's him. He's in that crowd, staring at the building with fascination. I crane my neck forward trying to get a better look. I take a step closer to the crowd. But I still can't be sure. I put my camera to my eye and I zoom in on the crowd. And through the lens I can now see him clearly. He looks forward, until he doesn't. Until he looks right at me. I click. And then he rushes away.

I can't tell which direction he went, but I run. I want to know what he was doing there, and why. But I don't see him anymore. I walk past countless buildings, countless people, but I can't find him. Finally, I give up. I need some water, and I turn onto Fulton Street, where I see a deli. Next to the deli is a record store, and inside is Reza, browsing nonchalantly.

"Hey," I call as I walk into the store, but he doesn't look up. "Reza!"

Now he looks up. "Oh, Art. Wow, hi, wh-what are you doing in . . . this place?" He's nervous and stammering, and so full of shit it reeks.

"Um, what are *you* doing here?" I ask.

"Oh, I heard this was a great record store," he says. "And I just received my allowance, so . . ."

"So you decided to go record shopping at nine in the morning . . . on a school day . . . blocks away from where you knew I was protesting."

He looks down at the records, flips through a few, maybe deciding what to say next. "If we go to school now, we will only miss one class."

"I'm not going to school today," I say. "I can't. Not after what just happened."

"What just happened?" he asks.

He looks at me blankly, and I search his eyes for what is going on behind them.

"I was at a protest," I say. "You were there too. I saw you."

"No," he says, now suddenly cool as can be. "But white people think all Persian people look alike. It's okay, though. I'm not offended."

I smile in disbelief. He has mastered the art of deflection, and also, he's been hiding a dry sense of humor.

And then he changes the subject, pulling a record up. "Look," he says. It's Madonna's *Like a Virgin* record. There she is on the cover, in a wedding dress. "Is this a good one?"

"They're all good ones," I say. "She doesn't do mediocre."

"Maybe I will purchase it," he says. "Since I already have the *Like a Prayer* CD thanks to you. But I think I prefer records. Do you think they sound better?"

I don't know what I'm supposed to say. I don't feel like bantering about the vinyl versus compact disc debate right now. I want to know why he was there, and what his deal is.

"Why does she call her records *Like a* something?" he asks. "Do you know?"

"I don't know for sure," I say. "But I think it's because she's all about the difference between what something looks like and what it really is. She's *like a* virgin, but not really. Something is *like a* prayer, but not really. I guess she's pointing to the illusion of sex and religion."

"Oh" is all he says.

But I can't stop. Now we're not bantering anymore. Now we're talking about something deadly serious . . . Madonna! "Stephen thinks that's why she's so popular with gays. Why divas in general are so popular with gays. Because we can see what's hiding beneath the artifice. We know what it's like to be one thing on the outside and another on the inside. All of us."

I realize I've started speaking of *we* and *us*, as if I'm including Reza. And he doesn't correct me. And I have no idea at what moment I thought—no, I knew—that he was one of us. Does *he* know it? Am I wrong?

"That's why Stephen thinks we'll always be more into female divas, even when the world is enlightened enough for gay men to be pop stars and movie stars. Because worshipping a gay male star would be too literal for us. We need layers and symbolism. We communicate in code. As does Madonna. That's what I think the *Like a* thing is all about."

Am I communicating in code? And if I am, what the hell am I even saying?

"I see," he says now, and he sounds so proper, so stiff,

so scared. We lock eyes, and I find in his a sadness so deep and bottomless that I want to reach inside him and heal it. And in his sadness, I recognize my own, which I usually cover up with anger. I have a crazy thought . . . if he's from Iran, he probably knows a bunch of people who died in the revolution, just like I know a bunch of people who died of AIDS. Most of the other kids in school don't know anyone who died, except for their grandparents maybe.

I reach into the Madonna section to pull out another record, and as I do, our hands graze each other. I feel something. Is it electricity? I don't know. It feels like a cousin of what I felt up there at the protest. It feels like being reminded that the point of BEING alive is to FEEL alive.

"In between *Like a Virgin* and *Like a Prayer*, she released *True Blue*," I say as I pull the record out. "It's interesting, right? Sex and religion aren't clear-cut to her, but love is. She didn't call it *Like a True Blue*."

"*Like a Romance*," he says.

"*Like a Love Story*," I add.

We each hold records in our hands, our fingers touch each other, and our eyes are locked in some secret shared space we never knew existed until just now.

And then he says, "I'll purchase them both. I think I love Madonna." And he pays for the records.

We walk for a bit, toward the subway. He says he's afraid of taking the subway, and I tell him that's absurd. "The subway is the one place in the city where you can be guaranteed *not* to run into the exact kind of *assholes* who are afraid to ride the subway," I say.

He asks if I just called him an asshole, and I say maybe. We might be flirting. Or we might not be. I have no idea how to read him.

Then I remember something. "Hey, you have my backpack?"

"Your book bag," he says. "I am so sorry. It's been sitting in my room for days. I promise I haven't touched it."

I think about what's inside, a bunch of junk, and then I remember my most prized possession is in there . . . those notecards Stephen made me when I asked him what OUR history was. I can't believe I left those. That shrink my parents sent me to would probably say I left the bag there hoping Reza would open it, hoping he would read those cards and feel what I felt when I read them . . . some connection to the past, to a community, some sense of belonging. "It's okay," I say. "Just give it to me next time we see each other."

"Okay," he says.

He's about to go when I call him back. "Hey," I say. "I'm just wondering . . . were you in Iran during the revolution?"

"I was," he says. "My mother wanted to leave, but my father didn't. We went to Toronto six years ago, when my mother left him."

"Oh," I say. "So your dad's still there?"

"No," he says. "Well, not exactly. He, um, died."

There's something so final about those words. He

doesn't embellish them. He doesn't say he passed away, or something like that. "I'm so sorry," I say.

Reza shrugs, like there's nothing else to say about the subject.

"I've lost a lot of people too," I say. "People I knew through Stephen. They've died. All around me." I stop myself from saying more. What I'm thinking is that if Stephen is my spiritual father, the dad I was meant to have, then we're both being raised by widows. But I don't say that. Because Stephen's not my father, and because Reza doesn't look like he wants to continue this conversation.

"I'm sorry," he says. "Death is never easy."

"Yeah, death sucks," I say. And then, desperate to end on a positive note, I add, "But life can be awesome, right?"

He smiles sadly, like he's not ready to answer that question yet.

He braves the subway alone and heads back to school. But I don't. I can't. I go back home, where my parents are waiting for me.

My dad's in one of his perfectly tailored business suits. My mom's in a Jane Fonda aerobics outfit, but not even the sunshine yellow of her leotard and leggings can mask her distress.

"We saw you on the news," my dad says, his voice laced with barely concealed rage.

My mom says nothing, because she's really good at letting my dad speak for her.

I say nothing, because I know that I won't be able to control my anger once I open my mouth.

"Look, we love you, Art," my dad says, like he's exasperated. "I wouldn't have come home from work if I didn't love you," he continues. "But this is getting serious. You could have been arrested. You could have jeopardized your future."

I roll my eyes at him.

"Art," my mom says, her voice trembling. "You have such a bright future ahead of you. I just want you to have . . . a future."

There it is. It's not my criminal record we're worried about anymore. It's my death.

Then dad does what he does best. He offers me a deal. "I'll tell you what, Art. If it's what it takes, then I'll write a check to any AIDS charity of your choice. Ten thousand dollars." My mom looks at him in shock. "If you promise to stay away from these protests," my dad says. "And from that man."

"That man" is Stephen, of course. I wonder what he would do in this situation. Would he take the deal? I can almost hear him telling me that the money will make more impact than one passionate teenager ever could.

"Okay, you're on," I say. We shake on it. My dad's handshake is so firm that it almost crushes me.

"This is the right thing, Art," my mom says, visibly relieved. She takes my hand in hers awkwardly. "Thank you," she says, with a deep breath and a smile.

The relief that washes over my mom's face makes

me feel sick for a moment, because I have no intention of keeping my end of the bargain. I'll just wait for the check to ACT UP to clear before doing anything risky again. Then it'll be too late for them to cancel the payment. I avoid looking at my mother. I tell myself that I'm Madonna, and my parents are Pepsi. I'm the badass bitch here. Did Madonna also feel guilty when she took their money?

But deceiving them was the only choice. I couldn't say no to that donation, and I'm not done either. I'm only getting started. For the first time in my life, I know what being gay is all about. It's not about the wet dreams, or the jerking off, or the ability to impersonate your diva of choice. It's about the feeling you get when you look into another person's eyes and have an out-of-body experience. It's about whatever the hell I was feeling when I really *saw* Reza for the first time. It's about love. How can I not keep fighting for that?

As I walk away from my parents, another thought, and a feeling of terror, washes over me. Judy. Judy. Judy. I won't hurt her. I won't. And yet . . . I resent her right now. Her heterosexuality gives her the ability to declare crushes openly and without fear. She assumed he was straight, because why wouldn't he be? Because the whole world is pretty much straight. I resent that she has a privilege I'll never have. And I hate my resentment. I love her more than anything. I have other privileges. She's my everything. *What do I tell Judy?*

JUDY

I'm in my bedroom, staring at fabrics, desperately trying to drown out the sound of my mother's book club. I pick up a sunflower-yellow fabric I've always wanted to use for something but never have because it was just too bright and beautiful and optimistic to be wasted on my life. Don't get me wrong, my life has had its moments, but this fabric deserves better.

Maybe tonight is worthy of it, Judy. A first date. Is it a date? It's so not a date. You invited Reza to Sunday movie night with your uncle and Art. What kind of a pathetic move is it to invite a guy you like to the gayest movie night ever, with your uncle who will most likely be wearing makeup and a kimono, and your inappropriate best friend?

I'm a chicken, and I need a buffer, and the thought of being out alone with Reza, even in the world's lushest yellow fabric, scares me half to death. I hold the fabric up against my body and second-guess it immediately. Art says I'm a summer, which means I look good in this kind of hot color, but maybe he's wrong. Maybe I'm a winter. Maybe I'm frigid. I think about what I could do with the fabric. It could be a dress. It could be flowy. It could be asymmetrical. It could be simple and classic, even though I don't do simple and classic.

But I can't get inspired when the sound of my mother and her friends invades my room, and our apartment is so small that you hear everything from everywhere. That's the thing about having parents who insist you go to the best private school in the city. They end up living in the only nearby place they can find, which is tiny and has no heat. They say they moved here just before I started kindergarten so I could be closer to the amazing school I still go to, because education means everything, but I secretly think another bonus for them was the fact that we have to walk up six flights of stairs, which they think would be good for my waistline, and theirs. And yes, I was big back then too.

We rarely have guests, but my mom's book club rotates hosts each time, so every fourth meeting, the ladies colonize my space. I love books. I love clubs. I just have a problem with this particular book club because they only read self-help books. Not a joke. Their current choice is *The 7 Habits of Highly Effective People: Powerful Lessons in Personal Change*. Pretty much every book they've ever read involves a colon or a semicolon in the title. My mom asks me to join the book club every time they make a new choice, as if whatever crappy book they're reading next will tempt me into having Sunday brunch with a group of ladies who wear pastel and love to discuss ways of making their lives better, even though their lives have not changed since I was born. And yet . . . and yet . . . every one of those women is married. Every single one somehow attracted a man while wearing pastel and filling her bookshelves with books about how to be the best you. Which makes me wonder if I'm not the best me. I wonder if Reza would prefer a pastel Judy with highly effective habits. I crack my door open to spy on them.

"Okay, let's discuss habit number four," my mom says. "I really loved this one, and I can already feel it changing me. Think win-win!"

"I had trouble with this one," my mom's friend in pink pastel says. "It says not to make any deal unless both parties feel that they win."

"But isn't that such great advice?" my mom's friend in blue pastel says. "The other night Jim and I argued and argued over what movie to see. He wanted to see *The Abyss* and I've been dying to see *Parenthood*."

"Oh, it's so good," my mom's friend in red pastel says. (Yes, there is such a thing as red pastel.) "There's a scene with Dianne Wiest and a vibrator that . . ."

"Shh!" my mom says. "The walls are thin. Judy can hear everything."

"Well, at least she doesn't have headphones on her ears all the time like Jonah," pink pastel says. "He's always listening to music, like he's not present at all. And therein lies my problem with habit number four. I'm all for win–win in adult relationships, but with kids . . ."

"Well, children are the exception to everything," blue pastel says. "Carl and I had this joke after Reagan made that speech about how we don't negotiate with terrorists. We decided that in our home, we do not negotiate with teenagers."

They all laugh, like this is funny, like comparing us to terrorists is somehow apropos. I hate that I use, or even think, words like *apropos*. That's my mother's influence. She says education is the only reason they break their backs to send me to a school they can barely afford, but the other reason is that she worships rich people, wants to talk like them, and dress like them, and always be happy like she imagines they are. I look at her, smiling. She's always smiling, even though I know that inside, there's pain and sadness and yearning. She works as a teller at a bank and pretends it's the most exciting job in the world. She pretends to be happy with my dad, with his dull accounting job, with the world in general, with everything except me. She wants me to be thinner, to smile more and be more pleasant, and to have girlfriends. In the friends-who-are-girls sense, not in the lesbian sense. Sometimes I want to shake her and be like, *Look around, this world isn't pleasant. Why do you have to act so pleasant?* But obviously I don't, 'cause that would just confirm what she already thinks about me. That I'm weird and aggressive and do things just to be different. That's what she said to me once. "Judy," she said, "life is so much easier when you fit in. All you have to do is *choose* to be interested in things others are interested in." She also told me once that even though she loves her brother, he chose a difficult path. Those were her exact words. "He chose a difficult path, sweetie, but that doesn't mean we don't love him to death." Then she said, "Sorry, bad choice of words at the end there." But seriously, she thinks he chose to be gay. That he chose to get sick. That he chose to bury all his friends.

I turn back to the fabric. I've pretty much decided the yellow is it. I've been saving it too long. My parents were given this crazy expensive bottle of wine once by Art's parents—it was an anniversary gift or something. They told me they were going to save it for a truly special day. That was six years ago. I can't be like that. I wonder if all children want to be the opposite of their parents. Art does. I do. I guess if you had a really cool parent, maybe you'd want to be just like them. But the thing is, most parents are uncool.

I think of Reza. What does he like? Who does he want me to be? And as soon as I think that, I hate myself for it. If Uncle Stephen has taught me anything, it's that you shouldn't be who anyone else wants you to be. "People can smell inauthenticity," he said. "Better to just be yourself, and easier. I was a queen when I met José, and he didn't seem to mind." I wish I could feel like that, like a queen. And Reza could be my king. Maybe we could go back to Iran and bring monarchy back to his country. Imagine all the amazing fabrics I'd have at my disposal there. I could probably make gowns out of peacock feathers and diamonds.

I have drifted so far away from figuring out what to do with this fabric, and there's only one thing that helps me when I'm blocked. I head out toward the freezer, toward ice cream. On my way, I pass the ladies. They've moved on to habit number five now.

"Personally, number five is my favorite," red pastel says. "I always try to understand first, and then be understood."

"I started to get a little bored by this point," pink pastel says. "Isn't he just saying something we've known a long time? To listen. To have empathy."

"There was a point at which I started to think that this is just a version of the Bible," my mom says. Oh God, no. My mom brings the Bible into every book club conversation, like it makes her smart or something. She's not even religious. She just read it in college. "Oh, hi, Judy!"

They all turn to me with way too much excitement, like Central Park pigeons that just spotted an almond croissant. Judy! Judy! Judy! They're *really* friendly.

"Hi, everyone. Hi, Mrs. Wood. Hi, Mrs. Fontaine. Hi, Mrs. Foley." I smile.

"You know, I've asked Judy to join our book club. I think the kind of literature . . ."

Literature. Mom refers to self-help as literature.

". . . we read would be so useful for teenagers . . . ," she continues.

Don't you mean terrorists? I want to say. I have so many issues with her, but I try to be diplomatic. "I'd love to,"

I say. "It's just that Uncle Stephen and I always do our movie nights on Sundays, and you guys always meet for Sunday brunch, so . . ."

"How is Stephen?" pink pastel asks, her face suddenly contorted into something resembling an attempt at concern.

"He's hanging in there," my mom says, with a sad glance my way.

"Cancer is just so sad," blue pastel says. I feel a surge of anger. I want to correct her, but I stop myself.

My mom just shrugs and says nothing. She doesn't say the word AIDS, and neither do her friends. And she's not alone. For almost a decade now, families have been lying about why their sons and brothers have been dying. Just go through the obituary section. Lots of pneumonia. Lots of cancer. I guess they're not totally lies, but the reason these men *could* die of pneumonia or rare cancers is because of AIDS. I told Uncle Stephen how much I hated that my mom won't say the word. But he told me to let it go. "Those are your mother's friends. That's her community. Let her have her process."

"Well, Judy, if you're watching a movie tonight, I highly recommend *The Naked Gun*. To finish my story about Jim and me fighting over what to see. We made the night a win-win by not going out to the movies, and renting *The Naked Gun*. We stayed in, ordered Chinese, and laughed and laughed."

"Oh, thanks for the recommendation," I say. "The thing is that Uncle Stephen doesn't really screen movies made after the death of Judy Garland, unless they are somehow relevant to movies made before her death. Like we watched *Beyond the Valley of the Dolls* 'cause it was a sequel to the original, and *Mommie Dearest* is a frequent choice 'cause it's about Joan Crawford."

My mom grimaces a little. I think I'm being too weird for her. I probably shouldn't speak around her friends.

"*Mommie Dearest!*" pink pastel says. "That movie was so scary. I still have nightmares about it."

"Oh, we think it's a comedy," I say.

Shut up, Judy.

"A comedy?" pink pastel says. "It was about child abuse. What's funny about child abuse?"

"Um . . ." I don't have the answer. I know Uncle Stephen would be able to explain this. If he did, he would end up telling this woman that everything can be laughed at. Including child abuse. Including AIDS. Including them. And they wouldn't like that. "I don't know," I finally say. "I guess it's just so over-the-top."

"Well, I had an alcoholic father," pink pastel says. "And that kind of rage *is* over-the-top." Her tone is sharp. She's miffed. Not quite angry though. These ladies, like my mom, just get miffed. Anger is too hot for them.

I choose to end this unfortunate exchange by heading to the freezer. Before I can even open the door, my mom calls out to me in her most benign tone, "I made a delicious beet salad and some poached salmon. It's in the Tupperware in the fridge."

This, in case anyone in the room missed it, is my

mother telling me *not* to open the freezer because that's where my comfort resides. I open the fridge. I unlatch the Tupperware. I stare at the beet salad. The beets do look beautiful. That color would make a nice fabric. Then I remember I need to get into a creative zone. And only one thing helps with that. I take the pint of ice cream, pull a spoon out of a drawer, and head back to the room. "Have a great book club, everyone." My mom gives me a *miffed* look. Maybe it's about the ice cream. But just in case, I say, "I'm sorry about what I said, Mrs. Wood. I would never laugh about what you went through. And thank you for sharing that experience with me."

My mom smiles, impressed.

"Apology very much accepted, sweetie," pink pastel says. "I'm happy this was a learning experience for you."

I force a smile and squeeze the ice cream container hard as I head into my room. It's frozen, but I manage to dent it a little with the force of my grip. They go back to discussing habit number five. Except they made no effort to understand me at all. They just shamed me into apologizing and *learning.*

The ice cream works. It does every time. I don't know what I'll do if ice cream ever stops working. I guess I'll have to experiment with other desserts to fuel creativity. Eclairs, maybe. Or plain whipped cream. Joey Baker brought an empty can of whipped cream to school once to suck the air out of the can. Sadly, that is indicative of the male population at our school. And believe it or not, I once had a crush on Joey because he was weird and different and really good at science, and because next to homophobes like Darryl Lorde and Saadi Hashemi, he was a prize. But Reza seems so different. It's almost like this country has just lost it when it comes to raising decent guys. They're either homophobic or self-involved or they suck on cans.

I spend the afternoon at the sewing machine. I'm inspired, and in some kind of zone. I put the latest Madonna in the CD player. Art's obsessed with her. I love her too, though sometimes I wish she'd remained kinda pudgy like she was in the beginning. Overall, I think I prefer Debbie Harry, 'cause she's stayed true to her downtown roots, whereas Madonna seems all about conquering the mainstream. I won't care about the mainstream when I design. I'll be happy just designing for the freaks. But no concerns about Madonna's thinness or mainstream cred is gonna stop me from listening to *Like a Prayer* ad nauseam, because it's undeniably brilliant. That song she sings with Prince comes on. It's called "Love Song." As I sew, I think that this would be my dream. To someday have a guy like Reza who loves me, and supports me, and dances to love songs with me. And to be a wildly successful fashion designer who makes clothes that people like Prince and Madonna wear.

My mother enters right after I put the outfit on. It's turned into a bright-yellow dress, which I pair with black-and-white striped leggings and a chunky black necklace Art got me for my birthday last year. "You were hard at work," she says.

"Yeah," I say. "It was a good day." I would ask her opinion, except I know that if she's in an honest mood, she'll say I look like a circus clown, and if she's in a conflict-averse mood, she'll tell me I look great! in a fake voice indicating that she's lying.

"Maybe you'll design something for me someday," she says brightly.

"Maybe . . . ," I say. "It's just . . . I don't think you'd wear anything I design."

"It would be like a commission," she says, annoyed I'm not playing along. "You would have to design something that fits the client. In this case, me."

"Yeah, but the thing is, I have a style. A look."

My mom sighs. I exhaust her. "You know, even some of the biggest designers do custom orders. What if Jackie O. called you tomorrow? Would you tell her she has to dress just like you, or would you make her something classic and beautiful?"

"I don't know, Mom," I say. "Can I answer that question when Jackie O. actually calls?"

My mom shrugs and smiles. "Sweetie," she says, as she sits on my bed. Uh-oh—when she begins a sentence with *Sweetie*, something is up. "You do understand why I don't tell people what Stephen has."

"It's so stupid," I say. "I'm sure they all know. He's been on the news protesting. Twice."

"They've never met him," she says. "They don't know what he looks like."

"There are pictures of him all over the living room!" I argue.

Then we both just look at each other with the kind of sadness that makes me want to bury myself somewhere, because we both know that the Stephen in the picture frames and the Stephen on the news look nothing like each other.

"It's just . . . it's just easier this way," she says. "And he does have cancer. Kaposi's sarcoma is cancer."

"I know that," I say. "It's just . . . if no one dies of AIDS, then how will the shame ever go away?"

"But so many people die of AIDS," she says. "Rock Hudson died of AIDS!"

"And he was outed because of it," I say. "Not exactly a poster child for gay pride."

"Stephen is sick," she says. "I don't understand why we have to politicize it."

"I don't know," I say. "I guess maybe because *he* politicizes it. Can't we just, like, follow his lead?"

She nods. She knows what I'm trying to say. She knows how wrong it is that one disease could be more socially acceptable than another.

"I know what you're thinking," I say.

"It's not what I'm thinking," she says, conflict etched all over her face. "It's what others think."

"Why do we care what others think?" I'm pacing the room now.

"Sweetie, come sit next to me." She pats the bed, like

that'll convince me to calm down.

"I know what other people think. That they deserve it. That he deserves it."

"No," she says. "Not at all. Nobody deserves this, and nobody I would call a friend would say that."

"What then?" I ask, staring her down. "I just don't get it, Mom."

"It's not a disease that you get at random. It's a disease you get because of a behavior . . ."

"Oh my God, Mom, stop! He's your brother!"

"And I love him. I worshipped him when we were kids. Don't you think I know how magnetic he is? Don't you think I emulated him when I was young just like you do now? Don't you think I understand why *Mommie Dearest* is funny? I'm his sister. I've let him be like a parent to you. I haven't seen my own mother for over a year in solidarity with him, because I hate the way she treats him. It's just not always so simple, Judy. I'm *not saying* he did this to himself, or that he deserves it, or that anyone does. I am saying that the reason people might prefer to say someone died of cancer or pneumonia is because certain things are private. I'm saying there are discussions I would rather have with him, with you, but not with women who wouldn't understand. That doesn't lessen my love for him, and he knows it." She catches her breath. I think she may not have breathed for that whole monologue.

"Well, I'd like to *make* people understand."

"Fine," she says. "That's your choice, and I'm not stopping you."

"You know, not everything is a choice, right? Like maybe he didn't *choose* to be gay, and maybe I can't just *choose* to be thin."

"I'll give you the first one," she says.

How generous of her.

"And think of the things he did choose to do," I continue fervently. "He could've been some fancy lawyer, right? He *chose* to help refugees and asylum seekers. You always say yourself how noble that was."

"It was," she says.

"And now he *chooses* to be an activist. He's always choosing to change the world. What have you chosen?" This last question was cruel, and I know it. *Stop when you have the moral high ground, Judy.*

"I chose to work hard, marry a good man, and raise you right," she says, defensive. Then she takes a breath. "I'd say my brother and I both did some pretty good things."

I hate when she does this. It's always when I say something totally bitchy that she's at her nicest, like she wants to shine a light on my awfulness.

"Sweetie," she begins again. Uh-oh. "I know we are very different women, and I'm generally okay with that, especially since I was once not completely unlike you, so there's hope we'll grow closer. . . ."

Oh God, please don't let me turn out like her.

"Mom, where is this going?"

"I just want us to be close, especially because . . ." She trails off. "Your uncle, he may not be around much longer." I feel the tears coming, but I've just done my makeup, and it looks good. I try to squeeze them back. "And I want to be here for you. And I want you to be here for me."

She's done it. She's succeeded in making me cry, and in making me sit next to her on the bed. She grips my hand in hers. She seems to glance with disgust at my nail polish. Half the nails are black, and the other half are yellow. "I just don't get it," she says.

"It's a look," I say. "And I wanted to bring together the black and yellow of the outfit."

"No," she says. "Not your nails, which are strange, I must admit. I just don't get how somebody so vibrant could . . ."

"Mom . . ." I'm too sad to say anything else. She's crying too.

She wipes the tears from her eyes and looks at me again, assessing me. "You put a lot of effort into an outfit for Sunday movie night," she comments.

"Not really," I say.

"Last week, you went in sweatpants and that leather vest I hate."

"Last week, I felt run down," I say.

She glances at me with interest. "I know you better than the back of my hand, you know. Of course, I won't look at the back of my hand 'cause it looks so old. Hands are the first to go." She places her hand on my cheek. "Whoever he is, just don't come on too strong. You can be a little intense. And if you invited him to your uncle's, don't let Art scare him off either."

I want to say that maybe this guy likes intense, that maybe this guy likes girls that come on strong, but I say nothing. Because I will not confirm that there is a guy. That will lead to follow-up questions, and I'm not going there. "It's just another movie night," I say.

Mercifully, my dad peeks his head into the room just then. "Well, this is sweet," he says. "My girls are having a moment." He's still in his racquetball outfit. We all have our Sunday routines. "What are we talking about?"

"Oh, girl talk," my mom says, with a wink my way, as if we're suddenly coconspirators or something. But the thing is, she's kind of made me feel like we are. And I wonder, who would Reza feel more comfortable with? My parents and their safe world of pastel, racquetball, and self-help, or Uncle Stephen and Art's world where we laugh about child abuse and do Mae West impersonations?

I want my parents to leave the room so I can call Reza and cancel my invitation. The whole thing was a terrible idea. They do leave eventually. But by that point, the woman who answers the phone at Reza's house tells me he's already gone. "He just left with his friend," she says.

"Oh," I say. "Weird—he's meeting me."

"Oooooh," she says, with way too much interest. "That's nice. Are you a friend of his?"

"Um, yeah," I say, "I'm Judy."

"Oh, of course, he's mentioned you," she says. "This is his mother, Mina. I'd love to meet you soon."

I smile a little. *He's mentioned you to his mother, Judy. That's a good sign. A really good sign.*

"Is he, um, bringing a friend with him?" I ask.

"They said they were both meeting you," she says. "He left with the hedge fund man's son. He had left his bag here last time. What is his name again? It's very long."

"Oh, Art," I say. "Bartholomew. Okay. Well, I'll see them soon and, um, nice to chat with you."

I hang up the phone. It's a little weird that Art picked Reza up, and a little weird that he had left a bag there to begin with. But I don't let myself get too in my head. I'm sure there's a reasonable explanation, or given Art, some unreasonable but hilarious explanation. I fix my makeup again, getting ready for showtime.

#54 Garland, Judy

The gay movement as we know it might not exist without Judy Garland. Some say that the queens who started the Stonewall riots, fighting back against decades of police brutality, homophobia, and oppression, did so in part because they were mourning Judy's death. Perhaps we identified with her for generations because, like us, she was brutalized and victimized by the system and because, like us, she somehow created so much beauty out of it all. And perhaps once she was gone, we were ready to stop being victims ourselves.

By age sixteen, Judy was one of MGM's most valuable stars. She was Dorothy, after all. The studio gave her pills to wake up, to lose weight, to go onstage. But the thing about Judy is that no matter how much artifice they imposed on her, and no matter how many pills they gave her, her raw authenticity still shone through. That's why she was able to give the greatest performance ever put on film in *A Star Is Born*. She lost the Oscar for that movie, and not just to anyone . . . to Grace Kelly! To a woman who was born so perfect and privileged that she was allowed to keep her name in an era when the studio system pretty much gave everyone a new identity.

The day our Judy was born, my sister and her husband couldn't agree on what to name her. My sister favored the name Ernestine, after our mother, and her husband wanted to name her Carol, after his mother. I held newborn Judy in my arms as they argued. For a moment, it seemed one of those names would be the first name and the other would be the middle name, but they couldn't agree on which would go first. And then . . . I whispered the name Judy, because when I gazed into my baby niece's eyes, I could tell that she had an authenticity that would shine through any expectation the world imposed on her. I saw in her a force of nature that would never accept limitations. And I hoped, no, I knew, that someday, she would be a great friend to this friend of Dorothy.

REZA

I don't know why I do it. Abbas already gives me an allowance, something my mother could never do when she was raising us alone and paying for everything from the sporadic money she made from interior-design clients. Back then, I never desired much that money could buy anyway. My mother bought my clothes. My mother bought my notebooks for school. My sister bought records when we could afford them, and we would listen to those along with a few old cassettes my mother brought with her from Iran. Consumption was not yet in my vocabulary. But now I want things. I think about things. Well, I think about one thing. Madonna. I think of Madonna constantly. I cannot explain it. I love her music, but there's something deeper, like she is saying all the things that I want to be saying. It is out of desire for her that I sneak into Abbas's bedroom when he showers on Saturday.

We are alone in the apartment. Saadi is practicing

lacrosse. My mother is at the hairdresser, living a life of leisure she is quickly growing accustomed to. And me, I'm about to become a thief. In Iran, they would likely cut my hand off for this, but then again, they would also have cut my hand off for masturbating more than I brush my teeth, and for what I think about when I masturbate, and for the time I used the toothbrush as a tool to help me masturbate, thinking about Art.

Abbas sings Billy Joel in the shower. My father only sang when he was drunk, and his voice always had a threatening edge to it, even when he was singing a love song. I remember Art saying how easy it is to steal from his father. I enter the room. I wonder where Abbas keeps his money. It's not on any tabletop that I can see, or in a drawer. Then I find his pants, hanging from a chair. A wallet in the right pocket weighs them down. I creep closer. The shower is still on. He is still singing. I think about what I want to buy, and I reach my hand in. The first thing I see inside the wallet is his driver's license, with a much younger photo of him, back when he had hair. Then, in the pouch, I find bills. Three hundred sixty dollars in different denominations. I wonder how much would make him notice. I decide fifty dollars is a good number, take it, and run out. Art was right. It's easy. So is spending it.

I'm staring at my new purchases as I get ready for Judy's movie night. Two posters of Madonna now hang on my wall. In one, she's in a wedding dress, the words "Boy Toy" on her belt. In the other, she has her arm raised suggestively, a cross dangles from her neck, and her cutoff shirt reads "HEALTHY" in block letters. I decided on this one because that's what I want to be. Healthy. Forever. There's one more purchase, and I am wearing it. It's a T-shirt with a decal of Madonna's face on it. I love it.

A knock on the door startles me as I assess my new look and the posters I just hung on the wall. My mother enters. "Wow," she says. "Did you go shopping?"

"It is, uh, just . . . I'm not used to having an allowance, so I used it." I feel myself trying to sound relaxed and failing.

My mother gets very close to the HEALTHY poster. "Why does she have to show her armpit?" she asks. "A bit vulgar, no?"

"I like it," I say.

She looks at me with a smile, then runs a hand through my hair. "My first crush was Alain Delon. He was a French actor. Gorgeous. I would rip his photos from magazines my aunt brought back from France and put them on my wall." She smiles again, lost in memory. "I just hope the woman you marry will not be show-ing her armpits and her belly button all the time. You will discover all this soon enough, but there are women you have fun with and women you marry. Madonna is a woman you have fun with."

What I want to say is . . . *and there are women you want to be.*

The doorbell rings. "Who is that?"

"Oh, right, that's why I came in," she says. "The door-man called and said your photographer friend is here."

"Is he studying with Saadi?" I ask.

"I don't think so. The doorman said he was here to see you."

My heart. It seems to be bouncing inside my body, hitting the edges of me in different locations, until it sinks into my stomach and stays there. I don't move.

"I can answer it," my mom says. And she's gone. To open the door. For Art. Who is here to see . . . me?

I can hear them from within my room, saying their obligatory hellos, and my mother giving Art a kiss on each cheek. Last time, it was a handshake. "Reza is in his room," she says.

I hear the stomping of his platform shoes getting closer and closer. I close my eyes and tell myself not to act as scared as I feel.

"Hey" is all he says when he comes in. His camera is, as always, dangling from his thin neck.

I say, "Hey."

And then he sees the posters, and my shirt, and he says, "Whoa."

"What?" I ask, wondering if we will only speak in one-word sentences.

He lifts his camera to his eye, adjusts the focus, and snaps a photo of my posters.

"Have you joined the fan club yet?" he asks.

I shake my head.

"You should," he says. "You get a magazine in the

mail. And you get dibs on concert tickets and stuff like that."

"Cool," I say, still trying desperately to sound normal.

"Since we're both headed to movie night, I figured I'd swing by and get my backpack. Then we can go together."

"Oh, of course," I say, and I pull the book bag from my closet and hand it to him.

He unzips it and peeks inside. He pulls out the note-cards and breathes a sigh of relief, then puts them back in. "Thanks for taking care of it," he says. "There was actually something really important in here."

"Oh," I say, maintaining what I hope is a very inno-cent expression. "What?"

"Just, um, study cards," he says. "But you know, they're the only ones, so if I lose them, I fail."

"At what subject?" I ask.

"Life," he replies with a crooked smile.

I look down. I realize the number of sins I have committed since moving to New York is mounting. I snooped in his bag. I stole from my stepfather. And now I lied to Art. Though of course, I have lied to him before. I pretended it was a coincidence I was outside the protest, which was a ridiculous charade. I was drawn to it because I had heard him discuss it. I had to be there. I try to convince myself that the city made me steal and lie and snoop, but I know that's not true. And I don't feel bad either. What I feel right now is not guilt; it's disappointment that I read only a few of those notecards. I should have read them all before he surprised me like this. Well, all except the ones about AIDS. I want to know more, but I'm still too scared.

"So should we head?" he asks. "Stephen might pick some three-hour movie, so we don't wanna be late."

We say goodbye to my mom, who is watching the giant television with Abbas, wrapped in a cashmere blanket. She looks so relaxed, like she has aged backward. I wonder what she would be like if she had married a man like Abbas to begin with.

The air outside is still hot as we begin our walk. New York is very good at controlling the temperature inside, but once you are outside, you are battling the elements. The mugginess makes me sweat a little bit, which only makes my nerves worse, which then makes me sweat more. "See," he tells me, "I told you to pack an extra shirt. How many Madonna shirts did you buy?"

"Just one," I say.

He looks at me with interest. "You made a good choice," he says. "And it fits you well."

I don't know what to say to this. I just smile.

"Come on, let's get on the subway here," he says. "He lives too far downtown for us to walk."

He runs down the steps, so I do too, though I don't skip the way he does, like he's running on a trampoline. His jeans fit so well from behind that I find myself staring at him, wishing they would fall down. Maybe I can add sorcery to my list of sins and make that happen.

On the train, he asks, "So what has Judy told you about her uncle?"

"She said he has movie nights," I say. "And that they are always old movies."

"Did she say that he was gay?" he asks.

"She did mention that," I say.

In front of us, a young couple kisses each other aggressively, sucking each other's bottom lips like sliced oranges they want every last drop of juice from.

"And did she tell you that he has AIDS?" he asks.

"I, uh, she did not say that," I say, my heart beating. I had gathered from some of what I read that Judy's uncle wrote those notecards, and I had guessed from what he wrote that he has AIDS. But now I realize that I am about to be in a room with a person who has AIDS. I want to turn around and escape to a safe place. I want to go back to Canada, before I knew about this disease. I close my eyes and imagine that poster of Madonna. HEALTHY.

"I'm not trying to scare you or anything," he says. "I just think it's good to be prepared. 'Cause he looks sick, you know. Have you ever met someone with AIDS?"

I shake my head.

"You probably have and don't know it," he says. "That's the thing. Nobody goes to get a test. And people can have HIV for years without knowing it, and then suddenly, they die. But the thing is, it's not sudden. They've had the virus for years. Anyone could have it."

He isn't making me feel better. I wish this subway were air-conditioned. Sweat is sticking to me, to my clothes. I feel suffocated.

"You okay?" he asks.

"I'm just hot," I say, too quick.

"Hey, you know you can only get AIDS from sex and needles, right? You need semen or blood involved. You won't even get it from kissing. You're not gonna get it at a movie night, if that's what you're worried about."

"I said I'm just hot," I snap back.

"Got it," he says, an edge to his voice.

We don't talk after that. We watch the couple across from us kiss so aggressively, I'm sure they are drawing blood from each other and getting AIDS. And what about the hangnail on my finger, which is red from all the times I've picked it and is now touching the dirty seat? What if someone else was sitting here before me, and they had a bleeding hangnail in the same exact spot? What about toilet seats—people could bleed on them, or worse, masturbate on them? What about cuts on fingers when we shake people's hands? What about . . .

I pull my shaking hand up quickly, off the possibly bloody seat, and place it on my lap.

"You sure you're okay?" he asks.

I nod. I wish he would stop looking at me like this, like he can see inside me. I wish he were not sitting next to me. I wish the train weren't bouncing up and down, forcing my body to shift closer to him with its movement.

Then he takes his own hand and puts it on my lap. "Hey," he says, with tenderness that only serves to underline my discomfort. "Whatever it is, it's okay."

I don't say anything. His hand feels so good on my lap, his temperature cooler, his grip stabilizing. Our hands are just inches away from each other, but with each bounce of the train, they shift closer, like magnets drawn to each other, until finally they touch. One of his fingers now rests atop my hand. Just one finger, and yet it ignites my whole body with excitement. His skin is rougher than mine. I don't dare move. I let our skin touch for the few seconds it takes for the subway doors to open, and for him to declare we have arrived at our stop.

He looks at me as he pulls his hand away, and I can't take my eyes away from his. Then he smiles, nods, and leaps up. He throws his arm between the doors as they're about to close. They reopen and I rush out, already wishing I could remain here underground with him forever.

He leads the way to the apartment. I have not been to the East Village yet. It's like stepping into a music video. It's colorful, and loud, and smells like hundreds of spices being cooked into one hot stew. He stops me in front of a Korean deli. "Hey," he says. "Hold up a sec. I need to get something here."

I realize I was going to bring one of Abbas's bottles of wine with me as a gift for Judy's uncle. My mother insisted I bring something. And of course, I forgot it. "Good idea. I forgot a gift. We should get some wine here."

"Reza, delis don't sell wine." He laughs. "And anyway, you look like a kid."

"You're right," I say, immediately wishing I hadn't

said something so dumb in front of Art. "We can bring something else. Let's look."

We go inside, and I hear two men say his name.

"Art!" one says.

"Art?" the other asks.

I turn to face the men. One is a tall black man in a fake fur coat that reaches his feet. The other is a freckled redhead who wears a red knit Christmas sweater, except the Santa Claus on the sweater has lipstick and earrings on. Their faces are gaunt, like skeletons. Skin clings tightly to their bones. Eyeballs seem to pop out of their faces.

It's movie night, isn't it?

Has Stephen shown you The Women *yet? It's my absolute favorite.*

It's a wonder we're still together, him being a Joan fan and me being a Bette fan.

It's so good to see you guys outside of a meeting.

Did you hear? AZT is 20 percent cheaper now.

It's still 70 percent too expensive, but it's a step.

Fur and Christmas sweaters are an interesting choice in this heat.

We're both always freezing these days.

Who's your cute friend?

Oh, this is Reza. He's fresh off the boat from Tehran and Toronto.

Did he not want to stop off in Torino?

Art taps my shoulder and I blink my eyes. I say a meek, "Hello, nice to meet you."

"I'm obsessed with that queen," the man in the fur

says. "Those outfits. The gowns, the hair. Honestly, that homely Queen Elizabeth should take some tips from her."

"I'm sorry?" I say.

"Farah Diba!" he says. "Your queen. The glamour. The opulence. The extravaganza."

"Farah *Diva*," Christmas sweater says.

"Farrah Fawcett has nothing on her," fur coat says.

"Thank you," I say, as if he has complimented me. And then, stupidly, I say, "I don't know her, though."

The man in the Christmas sweater smiles. "Well, there's still time. She's not dead yet. Come on, baby, let's let the boys be."

"Wait!" Art says. And when he has their attention, he adds, "Could I take your picture? You just look so fabulous tonight."

Fabulous? They look like they are going to die.

The men stand in front of the refrigerated section of the deli, which seems ironic since everything inside is fresh. Fur coat is taller than Christmas sweater, and so he rests his head atop Christmas sweater's head. They smile. Art snaps.

"Glorious," Art says.

"Make me look like Mahogany," fur coat says.

The men hug Art before they leave, and I cannot help but watch as their skin touches his. One of them has a lesion just above his wrist, and it grazes Art's neck as they hug. I want to push it away, to create a barrier between us and these men.

Art and I head to separate aisles. I find a bottle of non-alcoholic cider and purchase it with the money my mother gave me to take a taxi tonight. Art tells me he will be right out. As I wait outside, a group of people across the street are dancing, a portable stereo at their feet. And then I see a flower under my face. A single pink rose.

"A present," Art says from behind me.

I turn around and see him smiling. "That's a nice idea," I say. "Does her uncle like flowers?"

Art blinks just once, then looks right at me like I'm an idiot.

"What?" I say.

"Nothing," he says, his face reddening. "I just thought . . . It's nothing."

And that is when I realize that the rose was meant for me. My heart beats with equal parts excitement and fear. I can't believe that this beautiful, fearless boy actually has feelings for me. "I understand."

"Maybe I read the signs wrong," he says.

Of course he didn't. I feel frozen.

"But if I didn't," he continues haltingly, "then we can only do this on one condition, which is we tell Judy. Because I can't live lying to her."

Hearing him say the word "live" reminds me of what he represents. What all men like him represent. Death. I can't do this. I have to stop him before it goes any further.

"I am sorry," I say, my heart breaking a little more with each word I utter. "I think you are mistaken."

"Oh," he says, clearly hurt. "Okay."

We stand in silence for a moment. I wish I could disappear.

"I wasn't gonna say anything," he says, shaking his head. "I guess I thought . . . I mean, the other day in the record store . . . and then I held your hand on the subway."

He wasn't holding my hand. His finger touched mine, that's all. Now I worry, and I search his finger for any sign of a hangnail. If his hangnail touched my hangnail, and he has AIDS, which he probably does, then I have AIDS, and I have destroyed my mother's life.

"I think we should go," I say. "Can we please go?"

"I'm so confused," he says. "What's up with the Madonna thing?"

"I have a crush on her," I say. "It's normal. My mother's first crush was on a French actor."

He nods. Then he looks at me with anger in his eyes. "Just wipe the word *normal* out of your vocabulary, okay?" he says. "I hate that word."

"And I hate being here," I say, becoming angry myself. "I was supposed to take a taxi with air-conditioning. I was supposed to not arrive sweaty, and not arrive with you."

"I didn't make you come with me, you know," he says. "All you had to say was thanks, but no thanks."

"I thought you were my friend," I say.

"I am your friend," he says unconvincingly. "I guess I was just stupid, or selfish. . . . I just thought we could be more."

I want to touch him and tell him how I feel. I long to take his rose, put it in water, and tuck it into my copy of *The Odyssey* when it dies, so it will be forever preserved. But I can't, not without the fear.

"I wish you hadn't said anything," I say.

He looks at me for a long time, as if challenging me. Then he says, "Me too." After a short silence, he adds, "I'm sorry. I guess I . . . I don't know what got into me."

"No, I'm sorry," I say.

And then he says, "Don't tell Judy about this, okay?"

"I thought you could not lie to her."

"That was when I thought we might be a thing. But if we're not a thing, then why would we tell her?" His voice shakes. "To humiliate me more?"

He walks in front of me. I don't know what else to do but to follow behind him.

ART

What the fuck? No, honestly . . . WHAT THE FUCK? I know I read the signs right. MADONNA! The posters, the T-shirts. Then I second-guess myself. Maybe straight men can like Madonna. I do some quick math in my head. *Like a Virgin* was the first album by a woman to sell five million copies in the United States alone, and is close to ten million now. How many people live in this country anyway? Could all ten million people be queens and women? Maybe, or maybe not. And I know he was flirting with me. It couldn't have been a coincidence he was outside the stock exchange. And he let me put my hand on his. Well, okay, it was just a finger, but I know he felt the electricity. He didn't pull away like a straight dude would. But maybe men from other countries are different. Stephen told me once that in Cuba, men hold hands all the time. The irony of José's life in Cuba was that all the straight men would hold hands with each other, and the gay men were too afraid to. Maybe it's a cultural thing.

He's walking behind me. I thought he'd run away. But he's still walking behind me. He's so proper and polite. I've figured it out. He wasn't flirting with me. He was just being POLITE!

I turn around just before we get to the apartment. "Why don't we go in separately?" I say. "It'll be less weird."

"Oh, okay," he says.

"Okay," I say.

"Okay," he says.

"So I'll go in first, and you wait a few minutes."

"But it is rude to be late," he says.

"Judy and her uncle aren't like that," I say. "I'll see you in there."

I want to go in first. I don't know why, but I just need to be in Stephen's apartment. It's my favorite place in the city. I love everything about it. I love all the pictures of him and José. They give me hope that someday I'll find someone to fall in love with. And yeah, maybe that person will die, or maybe I'll die, but isn't that better than never loving? I love the black-and-white living room, his colorful collection of jelly beans that represent all the friends he's lost, the framed pictures of old movie stars, and the record collection.

It's Judy who opens the door, and the minute I see her face, I want to punish myself somehow. I don't deserve her. She looks fabulous. She's in a sunflower-yellow outfit I've never seen before, and then I remember her buying that fabric. We were together. She said something about how it was too special for her life, and I said something about how she could make a cute dress for our daughter out of it. I hate that joke now. I hate that we acted like our getting married and having children was a thing. Why did we think being each other's consolation prizes was okay? I deserve more. She deserves more. She certainly deserves a much better best friend than me. And maybe she deserves Reza.

"Hey," she says. "Where's Reza?"

"What do you mean?" I ask evasively. "I'm sure he's on his way."

I go inside. I can smell something Stephen is cooking in the kitchen. He calls out, "Hello, my beloved Art. Just you wait till you see what I'm making."

"I thought you two were coming over together," Judy says.

I sit on the couch. "Um, no, Frances," I say. "Why would we come together?"

Shit. I shouldn't have called her Frances. She knows I only do that when I've royally messed something up.

"Um, because I called his place," she says. "And his mom said you stopped by to pick him up."

Double shit.

"Oh, yeah," I say. "I actually just went to pick something up, not pick *him* up." But I did try to pick him up, as in hit on him. I'm an asswipe. I'm a traitor to my best friend. I've inherited my father's complete disregard for others.

"Right," she says. "A backpack."

We make eye contact. She seems to know too much. What else does she know?

"I left it there when I was studying with his stepbrother," I say. "You know Saadi won't even sit next to me when we're studying, even when we're both looking at the same notebook. It's like he thinks I'm a leper or something."

"So did you see Reza?" she asks pointedly.

"Oh," I say. I try to think fast. What do I say? "Yeah, he was getting ready."

"Did he seem excited?" she asks.

"I think so," I say. But what do I know? I thought that I could see colors and auras around people and that Reza was emitting a beautiful pink glow. That's why I got him a pink rose. I was dead wrong.

Stephen enters the living room. He's wearing a red apron and his face is flushed. "Tonight, we celebrate. The price of that goddamn drug has come down."

Yes, there are things to celebrate. Things much more important than one dumb rejection. "It's such good news," I say, trying hard to sound excited about it.

"I can't believe it happened so fast," Judy adds.

"The world can change," Stephen says. "If you fight hard enough for that change. Don't forget that."

The world *has* changed. It all feels so different now. Something between me and Judy feels broken, and I want to repair it. But how? And does she even feel it?

"The price is still ridiculously high," Stephen says. "But it's a step. And we have some plans to keep the pressure on."

"He's making arroz con pollo," Judy says. That was José's favorite dish. Stephen only makes it when he wants to summon José's spirit, when he wants him in the room with us.

"He deserves to be here tonight," Stephen says. "He would have loved this moment. And don't worry, Art, my dear. For you, I have also made arroz con tofu." Stephen takes the apron off and wipes his face with it. That's when I notice he's drenched. He's always sweating, but tonight it's more extreme. I tell myself it's because he's been cooking. Everyone sweats when they're in the kitchen. Stoves and ovens are hot. It's normal. Reza was sweating too, and that didn't mean he was dying. I tell myself to stop worrying about Stephen. He hates concern. "Before the guest of honor arrives . . . ," Stephen says, and he sits next to me and leans in close to me conspiratorially, "tell me everything I need to know."

"He's just a guy," Judy says.

Stephen holds his hand up to silence her. "She's too embarrassed to tell me what I need to know. Art, speak."

"Um, he's from Iran," I say.

"I know that," Stephen says.

"He's nice," I say.

Stephen looks at me, disappointed. Judy also looks at me, like she knows something is up. Because she knows that I would normally have a lot more to say than this.

"Okay, well neither of you is divulging anything of interest," Stephen says.

"He's cool," I say. "And I think . . . I think he's not like American guys, you know. Like, he's into Madonna. When I was picking up my bag at his place, he had posters of her on his wall."

"Interesting," Stephen says. "It's the rare icon who can reel in both straight and gay men. Of course, straight men want to screw her, and gay men want to be her."

"Great," Judy says. "He likes 'em in killer shape. That'll work in my favor."

"He also likes them daring and stylish," Stephen says. "And like a virgin."

"Ew, Uncle Stephen. Can we talk about something else?" Judy asks. "I'm already nervous enough."

Stephen smiles and says, "Nope, can't talk about anything else." He stands up next to Judy now and holds her hands. "My baby girl's first date. This is your first date, right?"

"Yes," she says with pride. "Of course. I would've told you. We have no secrets."

"Speak for yourself," Stephen says. "I have a secret or two, but nothing you kids need to know about now."

I think about Stephen's secrets. I think about the one thing he has never told me: who made him sick. Was it José? Or was it someone else? Did Stephen have it first, or did José have it first? And does Stephen even care? Does it even matter who gave it to who?

"Well, I don't have any secrets," Judy says.

I have secrets. I have guilt. I have shame. Stephen said once that getting AIDS helped free him from the last remnants of shame inside him. "I shame my shame," he said. I wish I could do that now, but I can't. My shame is too fresh.

Then Judy says, "Where is he?"

Where is he? A very good question. He should've come up by now. I told him to wait a few minutes, but it's been more. Did he go home? Is he done with us all? Have I ruined my best friend's chance with him?

"I'm sure he'll be here soon," Stephen says. "So tonight, I was thinking we could watch *Ziegfeld Girl*. We haven't seen that one in ages, and it's a safe choice for your new friend."

Ziegfeld Girl, a movie we've seen before. Stephen loves it because it stars not one but three of his favorite actresses, Judy Garland, Lana Turner, and Hedy Lamarr. Judy loves it because the fashion is insane. Gowns and capes and diamonds and crowns made from stars. I love it because it's about sisterhood, about three women who couldn't be more different but who stand with each other in solidarity. And the first time we saw it, that's what I thought we were. Me and Judy and Stephen, sisters in solidarity. A tribe.

"Sure," Judy says. She seems more concerned now.

Where is he?

I think about Lana Turner, and about how Stephen once told us that even though she and Ava Gardner dated and married all the same men, they were also great friends. Maybe Judy and I can be like Lana and Ava. Maybe we can both have Reza and still remain great friends. If it worked for them, why couldn't it work for us? But then I remember Reza doesn't even want me. And that Lana and Ava were both gorgeous women, so of course they were both desired, and of course they remained friends because if their man strayed, they could attract another with a snap of their fingers.

Then, finally, the ring of the buzzer. He's arrived.

The minute it takes for him to take the elevator up is interminable.

When the doorbell rings, Stephen tells Judy to open it. "He's your guest," Stephen says as he wipes more sweat from his face. He hasn't been in the kitchen for a long time now, and the apartment is air-conditioned to a crisp, but the sweat still pours. I'm starting to get worried now, and so is Judy.

"Are you okay, Uncle Stephen?" she asks.

"Of course I'm okay, silly," he says. "Don't waste your youth worrying about my hot flashes, please. Every girl goes through menopause at my age."

Judy opens the door, and Reza stands on the other side. He's holding the bottle of cider in one hand and a bouquet of yellow roses in the other. He must have gone back to the deli to buy them. "These are for you," he says to Judy, handing her the flowers.

I can't see Judy's face from behind, but I can feel her beaming. I feel my body shake, but I can't even figure out what emotion is causing it. Anger, maybe. Jealousy. Hurt. Some combination.

"Wow," Judy says. "That's so sweet. Thank you. Wow. How did you . . . did you know yellow roses were my favorite?"

"I did," Reza says. "Art told me."

Judy looks back to me now and smiles. "Wow," she says. "Wow."

I don't move. I don't react.

Stephen approaches the door. "Hi, Reza. I'm Judy's Auntie Mame, but you can call me Uncle Stephen." Judy looks a little mortified. But Reza doesn't get the joke. He shakes Stephen's hand, and then Stephen wipes more sweat from his face. Reza smiles politely, but I can tell he's afraid. He doesn't cross into the apartment.

"This is for you," Reza says, handing Stephen the cider.

"My favorite too," Stephen says, an obvious lie. Then, playing up the joke, he says. "Did Art tell you that non-alcoholic cider is my favorite?"

"No," Reza says. He's totally missed the joke. He doesn't get Stephen's humor.

"He's just teasing you," Judy says. "That's what he does."

"I don't mean to be rude, but there's something I must say," Reza says, and that stops me cold. What is he about to say? I feel a bead of sweat on my own brow and wipe it off. Why is everyone sweating tonight? What is he about to say? "I just thought it would be nice to spend some time alone with Judy. I have an allowance, and we could go out, if that's okay with your uncle." I breathe a sigh of relief. At least he didn't reveal my secret. At least he didn't out me.

Judy turns around. She looks different, like a woman.

"It's fine with her uncle," Stephen says, a proud smile on his face.

It's not fine. It'll be the first Sunday movie night we've skipped since we started. We didn't skip Sunday movie night the week after José died, or when Judy had the flu. Sunday movie night is sacred. It's church. And it doesn't work without the three of us. Without each one of the Ziegfeld Girls.

"Um, well, I guess I'll see you guys later then," Judy says.

"Well, let me put those beautiful flowers in water," Stephen says. "We wouldn't want them to die."

That last word seems to linger in the air. Before handing the flowers to Stephen, Judy breaks one in half and places it in her hair. "Just 'cause it matches my outfit," she says.

Stephen tells them to have fun, then disappears into the kitchen with the bouquet. Reza then waves to me and says, "Goodbye, Art." Goodbye. Just like that. With finality. Like a send-off. I stand up to say goodbye. I watch them go to the elevator. As they do, Reza places a hand on Judy's back, protectively, like a boyfriend would.

I stand alone as the door closes, feeling sick to my stomach. When Stephen returns, I turn toward him and see he has placed the flowers in a pink ceramic vase. They look perfect, and I wish they had been mine. I'm filled with envy, and I hate myself for it. "Nice guy," Stephen says. "I wish my first boyfriend had been that nice."

I want to say that he's not her boyfriend, but I don't. "I'm happy for her," I say. Can he tell I'm lying?

Stephen goes to the kitchen and brings back a bag of jelly beans. "Two more to add tonight," he says. "It was a bad day." He pulls out a red jelly bean. "Pete," he says. "Such a beautiful dancer." He drops the jelly bean into his pot. Then he takes out a turquoise jelly bean. "Miss Mia Madre," he whispers.

I gulp down hard. I remember Miss Mia Madre, a drag queen he loved. She'd always be at the ACT UP meetings, though usually out of drag there. "But she still looked healthy," I say. "She hadn't even lost any weight."

"She was healthy . . . and then she wasn't," Stephen says. "AIDS is a little like meteorology. They can predict tomorrow's weather with some degree of accuracy, but anything further out is pretty much a guess."

That fills me with panic. I need Stephen here for more than another tomorrow. But I don't go there. "I think . . . I think I took some pictures of her."

"I'd love to see them," Stephen says. "She was born Pedro Martinez, you know. In New Jersey, of all places. Such an ordinary name for an extraordinary soul." He throws the jelly bean into the pot. "It's over a hundred now." He sighs. Then he collapses on the couch. "Maybe it's for the best those two went out," he says. "I'm feeling worse than usual tonight. I can't beat these fevers any-more. My glands feel like golf balls. I wouldn't have been much of a host."

I sit next to him. I say nothing. He sits up and holds my hand. His is so clammy that it slips a little in mine.

"Hey," he says. "Let me tell you a story."

I nod. I love his stories.

"My sister and I used to be best friends. We did every-thing together. We were partners in crime. We spoke at least once a day, we reported every detail of our lives to each other. Remind you of anyone?"

I can feel him trying to make eye contact, but I evade his gaze.

"She met Ryan before I met José. And when she did, things changed. She didn't call me every day anymore. Some days she forgot. And then two days would pass, or three. Eventually, we spoke once a week. And when we did, she wouldn't report every detail of their lives to me. I pressed, but she didn't feel right. She didn't want to tell me everything about their intimate life because their intimate life trumped ours."

"It's a really sad story," I say. He thinks I'm melan-choly because I'm losing Judy, and I guess it's true, but only partly. The other part I'll never tell a soul about, even Stephen.

"You haven't heard the ending yet. I, of course, being the demanding bitch that I am, was very upset with her. I wouldn't take her once-a-week calls. I withheld infor-mation from her about my life, just for revenge. We still spoke, but it wasn't the same."

"Is that the happy ending?"

"Eventually, I met José. I fell in love. And then I understood what had happened. Because what happened between us, the intimate moments, the love and the sex and the fights and the negotiations, they were our secret world. And to tell anyone all of it, even my sister, would have been betraying him."

"Is that the end?" I ask.

"I suppose," he says. "The moral is, the dynamic of friendship changes when one friend finds romance. But change doesn't mean it's over."

I could ask Stephen if he thought Reza seemed gay. I could tell him about all the little fleeting moments that passed between us. I could tell him that I think I love him too. But ours will never be a love story. And what's love, anyway? I don't have time for love—I'm too angry to have time for love.

"So when's the next action?" I ask, desperate for something to take my mind off things. "I want to be involved."

"Art," he says, "you can't be a part of every single one."

I give him a gaze of steel.

"We're in the early stages of planning something against the church. In December. We figure the closer to Christmas, the better. Show them exactly how lacking in Christmas spirit they really are."

"I'm in," I say decisively. "What can I burn down?"

Stephen laughs. Then he picks up his apron again and wipes himself. He's really soaked. "Don't say the word burn to me right now. I feel like my head's in an oven."

"Can I do something to help?"

"Pay attention in science class," he says. "Then cure AIDS."

I want to cry. "I suck at science," I say. I think about studying biology with Saadi, about Reza next door to us. "I can sit here and watch a movie with you. Keep you company." I'm the one who needs company.

"That sounds nice," he says.

We watch *Ziegfeld Girl* as planned. I eat arroz con tofu. It's not very good, but his cooking never is. I don't care. It reminds me of the days when Stephen was strong, José was alive, and Judy was my uncomplicated best friend. Stephen doesn't touch his plate, just slowly sips bright-orange Gatorade from a wineglass. He has no appetite, and the more he eats, the more diarrhea he has. And since Judy Garland is framed above his toilet, he tries to minimize his diarrhea out of respect.

I don't like the movie as much this time. I realize that Judy, Lana, and Hedy all go their separate ways in the end. Their sisterhood has an expiration date, like a carton of eggs.

JUDY

The air is warm and muggy. I love these summer nights, when you can almost feel a hint of autumn coming but summer just won't say goodbye. The yellow rose tugs at my hair. No one has ever given me flowers before, let alone yellow roses. When I declared them my favorite, I never thought anyone would. As we step out into the evening, Reza says, "I don't know this neighborhood very well."

"I can lead the way," I say.

"To be honest, I don't know this city at all," he says.

I smile. "I don't mind being your tour guide."

"Okay," he says. "I would like that."

Wow, Judy. Have you seriously found a guy who likes you being bossy?

I lead him to Saint Mark's Place. It's my happy place. It's where punk shops and comic book stores and wig shops coexist. It's where hippies, drag queens, and musicians unite. It's where I get pretty much all my ideas. As we walk, I feel a pang of worry. Uncle Stephen seemed so ill tonight. The sweating, it wouldn't stop. He's had fevers and flus before, but this one looked awful. Maybe I shouldn't have left him. I have this constant fear that each time I see him will be the last, and that I won't tell him all the things I need to tell him. That I won't get to say goodbye.

"The neighborhoods are so different in this city," Reza says. "This is nothing like the Upper East Side."

"Uh, definitely not," I say. We get to the beginning of Saint Mark's. "This is where I want to live when I grow up. Right at the edge of Saint Mark's Place. I want a small apartment overlooking the street, and in the window, I want to put a few mannequins wearing my designs. I'll swap the designs out every month, and I'll do seasonal displays. It won't be, like, a store or anything. It'll be my home, but it'll entertain people who walk by."

"You and Art are lucky," he says, wistfully.

Art. Something was up with him. All that business with the backpack was weird. And he called me Frances, which he does when he feels guilty. But maybe I'm overthinking it. Or maybe he was just concerned about Stephen like I was.

Stop thinking about Art and Stephen, Judy. Enjoy this moment. That's what Uncle Stephen would tell you to do.

"You both know who you are, what you want to be," he says.

"What do you want to be?" I ask.

He shrugs. "I have no idea. I guess I just . . . want to

go to college, so I have more time to figure it out. I like school. Well, I like class at least."

Something strikes me. That maybe the reason Art and I know what we want to be is because we've been partially raised by Stephen, and we feel how fleeting time is, how quickly it can be taken away.

"So, my favorite place here, if you're hungry, is Yaffa. It's got really yummy tahini dressing, and the waitresses are so badass."

He's craning his neck, taking in this street for the first time. The leather. The piercings. The tattoo shop down the street. There's a dog wearing pink vinyl. There's a man in a corset. There's a hippie smoking grass. There's Manic Panic, my favorite place on the whole street. It's closing soon, supposedly, which totally depresses me. I wish I could freeze time on Saint Mark's, just so it never changes.

"That's my favorite store," I say. "They sell crazy hair dyes and punk things. The women who started it are so amazing. They even sang backup for Blondie." He looks at me, confused. "Blondie. One of the best bands of all time, led by goddess Debbie Harry, who could literally wear anything and look good."

I'm talking too much. What guy wants to hear about hair dye, and about Tish and Snooky's backup career? What does he care?

"That restaurant sounds nice," he says. "Should we eat?"

We go inside and sit. The waitress wears black vinyl

platform shoes, a short black skirt, and a crop top. I've seen her before. Art and I love her look. "Isn't that cute?" she says as she hands us menus. "The flower in your hair matches your dress. I love that."

I love that she noticed. I'm so yellow that I feel like sunshine.

Say something charming, Judy. What do people talk about on dates? About how much they like each other?

For a long time, we say nothing. We stare at menus. We can't even see each other.

Then he says, "Judy, can I ask you a question?"

"Of course," I say.

I think he's going to ask me something deep, but he says, "What should I order?"

I laugh. "I'm obsessed with the tahini dressing, but you can pretty much get it on the side of anything you order. Like if you get a burger and fries, dip them in the dressing. If you get salad, get extra dressing. Honestly, if you get pancakes, douse them in tahini and they'll taste amazing."

"Okay," he says. "Maybe we should ask them for tahini dressing soup."

I laugh too loud. It's not even that funny, but I love the idea of both of us slurping salad dressing like soup.

"You have a nice smile," he says.

"Thank you," I say. He's so sweet and so vulnerable, and so different from every other guy I've met, and without thinking, I say the first thing on my mind. "And by the way, thank you for not being a typical asshole guy."

Idiot, Judy. Who wants to hear the word asshole *on a date?*

The waitress returns, and we order salads.

"Do you know that before school started, I ripped my braces out? Before that, I would never smile."

I suddenly laugh. "Oh my God," I say. "Did you bleed?"

"Oh, yes," he says. He's laughing too, now. We have found some kind of groove. "There was so much blood. And my mother was too scared to tell her new husband that her son is crazy, so she found an orthodontist in the yellow pages."

"No!" I say.

"I'm very serious," he says, laughing his beautiful laugh. "But I convinced them to take the braces off. Now I wear a retainer at night."

"Aw, that's cute," I say.

"I haven't told anyone about that," he says. "Not even my stepfather or stepbrother knows."

"Your dental secrets are all safe with me," I say. I lean in covertly. "And by the way, I would've liked you even with braces."

He smiles again. Our salads arrive. "You are too kind," he says.

"No, seriously," I say. "I'm a lot of things, but I'm not kind. I can be an awful, unforgiving person. I judge everyone, except Art and Stephen. I hate people."

"You do not hate people," he says. "You love Art and your uncle. You just said you love those ladies who sing backup."

"Those aren't people," I say. "Those are downtown legends. I love downtown legends. I hate everyone we go to school with, except for you and Art."

"I don't know if I blame you," he says. "They are mostly not very nice."

"I know," I say sympathetically, thinking of the terrible things I've heard said to him in the halls. "And usually Darryl Lorde is the ringleader."

He nods in agreement. There's a short silence, and then he says. "Judy, I'm sorry about your uncle."

I tense up a little bit. I haven't touched my salad, but now I start to nervously devour it. "Thanks," I say, my mouth full.

"I don't know if Art told you, but my father died." His salad is still sitting there, wilting as he speaks. "It was strange because I hadn't seen him in years. When he died, at first, I felt nothing. I just went about my day like nothing happened. My sister raged and screamed and threw things. I thought something was wrong with me. But it hit me much later. Like, a year later. And in some ways, I don't know, maybe I still haven't accepted it." He waits a beat. I say nothing. Then he says, "That's the most I have ever told someone about him. I . . . You make me feel like I can say anything to you."

Uncle Stephen once told me that nobody can *make you feel* anything. If you feel it, it originates from you. "God, I'm sorry," I say. "How did he . . . "

"He just drank too much," he says. "His liver . . ."

I'm filled with a sudden appreciation for my boring

father, his accounting job, and his once-a-week glass of whiskey.

"I just wanted you to know," he says. "I understand what it feels like to lose somebody important to you."

I nod. Why is he so sensitive and cute? Who is this perfect? "Stephen's lost so many friends. And then we lost his partner, José. That was hard. But I don't think I'll cope at all if Stephen goes. I just . . . I pretend it won't happen, you know, I pretend he's invincible." I feel a knot in the pit of my stomach. I think of the sweat pouring down his face earlier today. I gotta change the subject before I cry. "So what else did Art tell you about me?" I ask.

"Oh, he told me about the yellow roses," he says. "And that you like ice cream."

"And you remembered!" I say. "I mean, that's just so . . . thoughtful."

"I'm always thinking," he says, and the way he says it makes me feel a little like he's talking about something else, something that has nothing to do with me, or salad, or ice cream.

"What do *you* like?" I ask.

"I don't even know," he says. "I just . . . This is what scares me so much about you and Art. You remind me that I have no idea who I am."

"You like Madonna," I say.

He nods.

"Favorite song?" I ask.

He doesn't even think. He immediately says, "'Oh, Father.'"

"Mine is 'Borderline,'" I say. "I know it's an old one, but it just gets me. Like it's about so many things. Borderlines are everywhere, between lovers, between straight and gay people, between countries.

"And by the way," I continue, "I'm not one of those stereotype peddlers who think liking Madonna makes you gay. She's an equalizer. Not to mention that men from other countries are so different. Art went to Italy and France with his parents, and he said that *every* man there seems gay. I've never left the country, but when I'm a designer, I'll go *everywhere*. Maybe I'll even move to Paris when Saint Mark's Place is so gentrified that it sucks. I'd like to be in a place where all the men seem gay. A world of men who act gay, but who like women, and with delicious croissants everywhere!"

Shut up, Judy. You sound like a freak. Avoid culinary and homosexual topics immediately.

"Not that you seem gay at all, by the way," I say quickly. "It's just the Madonna thing."

"I suppose I like what she has to say," he says haltingly.

"Your dad died, so you were raised by a strong woman, and it sounds like your sister is intense, so two strong women in your home. It's obvious why you'd like a strong woman like . . . Madonna." I was about to say *a strong woman like me*, but what kind of conceited thing to say is that?

Change the subject, Judy.

"It was so nice of Art to tell you what I like," I say. "He's a really great friend."

"Yes, he is," he says. "A great friend, to you."

The way he says *to you* has a sting to it. Maybe something did happen between the two of them. Maybe they just don't like each other. But that can't be a deal breaker. I can't give this guy up because he and Art don't like each other.

We talk for an hour, about his sister, who sounds badass and hilarious. She would often come home from clubs when Reza was waking up. About his mother, who must be tough as steel. It's so obvious how much he loves her and wants to make her happy. I tell him about my parents, about how typical they are, and how they've sacrificed their lives to give me a life that I don't even want. How fashion means so much to me. And Uncle Stephen—how without him, I wouldn't even be me. I'd be someone named Ernestine Carol, or Carol Ernestine.

He's the one who asks for the check. And when the waitress brings it, he insists on paying. "A real gentleman," she says, not to him, but to me, like she's telling me how rare a real gentleman is.

Oh, I know, fabulous waitress.

After Reza pays, he excuses himself to the bathroom, and the waitress lingers. "You're glowing," she tells me. "You don't glow like this when you come in with your other friend."

"Am I?" I ask. "I guess it's because my other friend is gay."

"You're also looking gorgeous tonight," she says. "I love your dress."

I love downtown. I belong here. "Do you think he likes me?" I ask conspiratorially.

"Definitely," she says. "Body language, baby. He was leaning in. His hands were on your side of the table most of the time. His feet were too."

"Really? I didn't even notice."

Of course you noticed, Judy. Why are you lying?

She takes Reza's money and heads to the back. When Reza returns, we step outside. The waitress's words run through my mind. As we walk, I try to observe his "body language." He walks next to me, but not so close we're touching. His hands are in his pockets, nowhere near mine. But then, at one point, his foot grazes mine. "Oh, sorry," he says.

Maybe he did that on purpose. Maybe he was communicating his desire to touch you with this accidental kick.

"I think we should get ice cream," he says. "Since you love it. And I love it, too."

I smile, really excited, like we have something highly unusual in common, as if 99 percent of the world doesn't love ice cream.

He gets chocolate and coconut. I get mint chocolate chip and French vanilla. As we eat, we pass a street vendor selling jewelry, sunglasses, and hats. We stop and browse. I throw a beret on him, and he laughs. "I look like a fool," he says.

"No, you look adorable," I say. "Like an existentialist."

He puts the beret back in its pile, unconvinced.

"Hey, could I make you over?" I ask.

"Make me over into what?" he asks.

"You know, like, make clothes for you. If I made clothes for you, would you wear them? I promise they will be very cool, and cut to perfection."

He looks at me with surprise. "I would really like that," he says.

My eyes fall on some pins the vendor is selling. Tiny laminated fish, one beady eye staring out through the plastic. "Are those, um, real fish?" I ask.

"Of course," the vendor says. "These pins are special. Fish represent life."

"Do they?" I ask.

"Read the Bible!" the man says.

"We'll take two," Reza says. He pays for the pins and puts one on himself, then one on me. As he pins me, his hand grazes against my boob. *Body language.* I feel like one of those pretty girls in fifties movies, getting pinned by the guy in the varsity jacket. Except our pins have dead fish in them, and his varsity jacket is a Madonna shirt, and my cheerleader uniform is a fabulous sunflower yellow outfit. I take my last lick of ice cream.

And that's when I look across the street at Manic Panic, and I see . . . her.

Debbie Harry.

She's dressed in head-to-toe red. Red leggings. A body-hugging red dress, the back low-cut. Red boots, with stilettos. Her hair is ice blond, a red streak through it, like a punk Jean Harlow. She wears a chunky cross around her neck, and another necklace with big silver Xs running up and down it. Her lips are ruby red, too. I say, "Holy shit Reza, that's DEBBIE HARRY." No, I don't say it. I scream it. And in doing so, I alert everyone on the block. Debbie must hear me too, because she waves to me, then steps into a black car.

It's a sign. It must be sign. When does this just happen? When does a guy bring you your favorite flowers the same night you see Debbie Harry on Saint Mark's Place?

"Is that the backup singer you were telling me about?" Reza asks.

"No!" I say. "That's the LEAD SINGER. That's one of the most fabulous stars in the whole world. And we . . . saw . . . her."

Art will hate that he missed this moment. He'll act happy for me, but he'll be green with envy as I describe her red perfection.

Don't think about Art, Judy. This is your moment.

"I like to see you so happy," Reza says.

My whole body feels alive, like a new life is beginning, like Debbie has transferred some of her energy to me. And that's when I lean in and kiss Reza.

Rapture. That's what it feels like.

I pull away. "I think I was supposed to let you do that," I say. "If you even wanted to."

He blushes, his eyes nervously darting around.

"Unless you didn't want to . . . ? If so, I'm really sorry." Suddenly I feel like the biggest fool on earth.

"Do not apologize," he finally says. "I'm so happy you did that. You have no idea how good that makes me feel."

Now *he* pulls *me* in, his hands on my love handles. I understand why they're called love handles now. It's rapture.

DECEMBER 1989

"Always be a first-rate version of yourself, instead of a second-rate version of somebody else."

—Judy Garland

REZA

Judy's home is everything my new home is not, by which I mean it feels like a home. There are no chandeliers. No gold, no crystal, no ancient paintings. I don't feel like I'm in a museum in this place—nothing about it says look but do not touch. The pink and yellow flowers on the sofa fabric have long faded to gray. The wallpaper on the living room walls has started to peel at the edges, revealing the plaster and dried glue beneath it. The teacups don't match, and they were clearly collected over many years as a family, from universities, tourist destinations, corporations, and concerts. The one I am currently handed by Mrs. Bowman reads "Dad of the Year" and it's chipped. I will need to watch my lip every time I take a sip to make sure the cup doesn't cut me. But I like that they have kept this chipped cup in their cupboards. I like that the dad in this house was dad of the year.

"Is it okay?" Mrs. Bowman asks me.

"I'm sure it is," I say, as I blow on my tea, still steaming.

"I know you Persians are masters of the tea," she says, with a playful smile that erases any possible offense I may feel at hearing her say *you Persians.*

"Mom, can you try being a little more sensitive with your words? How would you feel if he said, 'I know that you Americans are masters of the . . .'" Judy pauses and sighs. "God, we're not even masters of anything. It's so depressing."

"We invented musicals," Mrs. Bowman says, holding her smile.

"Yeah, but they're just a bastardized version of opera," Judy says. "All we do is take other cultures, steal their treasures, and take the credit. We have no culture of our own."

Judy's mother sighs, in much the same way Judy just did. Their mannerisms are remarkably similar beneath their divergent facades. Mrs. Bowman turns to me. "I'm sorry if my words offended you, Reza. I promise you that I only meant well."

"Oh, I was not offended," I say.

"Well, I was offended on your behalf," Judy says, placing her hand around my waist. She likes to do this, put a hand on my body. Sometimes around my waist or my shoulder, sometimes on my leg, through my fingers or my hair. It usually makes me feel safe for a moment, and then it reminds me of everything I cannot give her, everything I am pretending to be, and everything I felt when Art's hand touched mine. But that already feels like a lifetime ago.

I take a sip of the tea. Though it did not come from a teabag, it tastes like it did. It has none of the richness of flavor my mother's tea does. "It's delicious," I say. And then, wanting to lighten the mood, I add, "This master of the tea approves." I'm such a liar. Everything I say is a lie.

"You see," Mrs. Bowman says, with a look toward her daughter. "He likes my tea. Perhaps you could take some lessons in graciousness from your new . . . boyfriend."

A wave of tension passes through the room. Boyfriend. Girlfriend. We have not used those words yet, at least not in front of each other. I can feel Judy scanning my face for a reaction, but I stare at the linoleum floor. This word has just underlined my deceit with its specificity.

"Yeah," Judy says, squeezing my waist. "*You Persians* have such good manners."

I don't laugh, but Mrs. Bowman does. She pulls Judy in close to her. "Listen, I'll be at book club for most of the afternoon, so if I don't see you, I hope it goes well."

"Thanks, Mom."

"And Reza," Mrs. Bowman says, "once my daughter has approved, I'd love to meet your parents and your brother as well."

I smile and nod. We Persians have such good manners. But what I want to say is that they are not my parents. I have a stepfather and a stepbrother now. They don't belong to me, and I don't belong to them. Like

Cinderella, I'm an impostor in my home, and like her, all I want is a prince.

"Okay, may we be excused now?" Judy asks.

"You were never *not* excused," Mrs. Bowman says, and she turns away from us toward a dog-eared book above the microwave. "It's a free country."

The title of Mrs. Bowman's book leaps out at me. *When BAD Things Happen to GOOD People.* The words *bad* and *good* are capitalized, like warnings. Bad things have happened to me, but I am not a good person. I'm a liar and a thief. Have bad things happened to Mrs. Bowman? I remember that her brother is sick. Maybe that's why she's reading this book.

As Judy takes my hand and leads me to her bedroom, I think about how easy it was to meet her parents. I met them weeks ago, and there was no pomp or circumstance about it. Judy brought me by her house for a casual dinner. Her mother made pasta and salad and insisted I call her Bonnie. Her father asked me questions about the revolution with genuine interest and insisted I call him Ryan. Since then, I have been welcome in their home. Easy. Nothing about tonight will be easy. Unlike this family, mine doesn't come from a free country. We have rules and expectations. I had offered to bring Judy by the house to meet my mom and Abbas, but my mom rejected that suggestion, worried about what kind of impression it would make on Judy that they wouldn't take her out to dinner first. I wanted to say it would send the impression that they were relaxed, normal people, but I let her have her way. My mother made and canceled three restaurant reservations before we finally settled on a place. She decided her first choice was too stiff, her second choice was too far downtown for Abbas, who generally won't go below Fifty-Ninth Street, and her third choice too loud. At dinner in our ornate dining room, she asked me where I thought Judy would like to go. Perhaps, my mother said, we should choose the restaurant Judy would like. That's when Saadi made his first of what I knew would be many cracks. He said Judy would like any restaurant that serves food, the more of it, the better. A moment of silence, and then the revelation that Judy is overweight. I could see my mother taking this in, accepting that her son's first girlfriend may not be the perfect Persian princess she once imagined. I glared at Saadi and revealed some more important details about Judy to my mom and Abbas. I told them that she designs clothes, and that she loves Saint Mark's Place, Debbie Harry, and avant-garde art. That's when Abbas decided we should go to Mr. Chow, which is where the rich and the avant-garde meet, where Warhol liked to eat when he was alive and wanted overpriced dumplings. My mom wondered if we could get a table, and Abbas said that of course he could. This is the thing about the Abbases of the world. They may prefer to stay above Fifty-Ninth Street, but if they want to go elsewhere, they have access. That's what money buys you, access to any corner of the world you want to explore and the safety to return home.

"I hope you like it," Judy says. "And obviously, if you

don't, then you don't have to wear it." We are in her room now, and she sits at her sewing machine, a pint of cookies-and-cream ice cream by her side.

"I'm sure I'll like it," I say.

"Don't do your polite Persian thing with me, okay? I want you to feel free to be rude with me. To be yourself."

"But I am not rude," I say.

"Right, of course," she says, shaking her head. "It's like sometimes I think that deep down, everyone is an asshole, and nice people are just hiding their true selves. Does that make me horrible?"

I shrug and spoon a bite of ice cream into my mouth.

"Maybe it just makes me a New Yorker," she says. "Honestly, whoever decided children should be raised in this city is the horrible one."

If only she knew what being raised in Tehran was like.

"Obviously I'm happy about it, though. Nobody raised in Peoria would design this fabulous shirt for you."

Now I take a spoon of ice cream and feed it to her. She accepts it as she continues to sew. "This is the life," she says. "When I'm a famous designer, I'm going to make sure I have a gorgeous man feeding me ice cream while I work. He'll have one of those ice cream trucks, but instead of some dumb jingle, it'll play 'I Love Rocky Road' by Weird Al on a loop."

I look around her room, at the posters on her wall. David Bowie in pants that look inflated. Debbie Harry in a gold leotard. Pages ripped from fashion magazines and taped to the walls with abandon. Models I don't recognize, wearing dresses with zippers down the sides, men's shirts way too big for them with belts cinched around them, gowns with sequins on them, clothes so shiny that some of them look like they were made for another planet.

She looks over at me and smiles. "You okay?"

I look away. She asks me this question a lot, and I never like it. We don't ask this question in my family. We know that the answer will always be yes, but that the truth will always be no, so what's the point in asking the question? "Of course," I say. Does she ask me this all the time because she senses that something is not okay, or does she ask this question because this is what Americans do?

"I'm sorry about my mom," she says. "I hope she didn't upset you."

"Not at all," I say. I mean it, too. I have much more monumental things to be upset about than the assumption that I know a lot about tea, which is true anyway.

"Okay," she says. "She's just not that culturally sensitive, I know, but she means well, which I guess is worth something."

"I like her," I say. "And I like your father too."

"Cool," she says, her head down, assessing her work. After a few more seconds, she pulls the fabric out of the machine and reveals it to me. "Ta-da," she says.

I could see pieces of the shirt as she was working on it,

but I was not prepared for the explosion of colors, deep orange and royal blue and gold. The sleeves are blue, and there is the illusion of an orange vest laid atop the shirt. On the back are two thick stripes, outlined in gold, and inside the gold stripes are tiny figures of plants and goats and flowers. The level of detail is so intricate that I find myself studying the shirt like a piece of art. "Wow," I say.

"Does wow mean you like it?" she asks. "Or does wow mean it's too much and you would never wear it and you think I'm a freak for making it for you?"

"No, it's just . . ." I search for the right words. "It belongs on David Bowie, not on me. I am not worthy of it."

"At least try it on before saying that."

She hands me the shirt. The fabric is softer than I imagined. It feels luxurious. It's not until I'm holding it in my hand that I realize the colors are reminiscent of ancient Persian clothing, and that the tiny figures running down those stripes look like miniatures. It hits me how much time and care Judy has put into this one shirt, for me. I am not unworthy of the shirt. I'm unworthy of her.

"Is it . . . Persian?" I ask her.

She smiles. "I didn't want it to be too obvious," she says. "I went down a total rabbit hole of research at the library about Persian style. Oh my God, Reza, honestly, it's beyond. The robes. The shawls. The vibrant colors and the vests and the level of detail. I mean, you guys come from the epicenter of everything gorgeous."

"Wow," I say.

"I wanted it to be a surprise." She claps her hands together. "Come on, try it on. I want to see how it fits."

I unbutton the black cardigan I'm wearing. The fish pin Judy and I bought together is on it. We have worn those pins every day since we bought them on Saint Mark's Place. When I place the cardigan down on Judy's bed, the eyeball of the fish seems to be staring at me, judging me. Then I put my hands at the base of my favorite T-shirt and pull it off. When I lay it down on the bed, Madonna's eyes seem to be judging me as well. I love Madonna so much, but I know she would hate me. All she tells me to do is express myself, and here I am hiding. I don't like having my shirt off. I hate how thin I am, and I hate the thick hairs growing on my chest, and I hate the birthmark on the bottom of my back. It's the first time I have taken my shirt off in front of Judy. Even when she took my measurements, I kept a T-shirt on. I can feel her looking at me, then looking away, then looking back at me. Is she thinking I look better with clothes on? I think about Art taking his shirt off in front of me, of how beautiful he was.

I put my arm through the left sleeve first, and then the right. As I reach for the buttons, I realize they are gold. I was so focused on the colors and pattern that I did not even notice this detail. When I'm done, I look at myself in her mirror. I look like a new person, like a person who has a strong sense of self, like a person confident enough to stand out. The person in the mirror is who I want to be.

"You look like a rock star," she says. "Do you like it?"

"I do," I say. "Very much."

She claps her hands together again, her excitement bursting out of her. She stands in front of me and takes my hands in hers. Her hands are so soft, and her nails are smooth and lacquered with her purple nail polish. She whispers, "I think you inspire me."

"Oh," I say.

"Maybe you'll be the Marlene Dietrich to my Josef von Sternberg. I'll surround you in beauty. I'll design, and you'll be my muse."

"Maybe . . . ," I say. She gets closer to me and I suddenly feel panicked. I know I'm supposed to kiss her. I've seen this in movies. She's everything I *want* to want, and I hate that I don't want her. I want magic powers that will turn her into Art. I want to kiss Art's lips, smell his scent, see his bare chest again. I close my eyes and press my lips gently against hers.

She pulls her lips away from mine after a few seconds. "I'm excited to meet your family."

"Me too," I say. "Of course, you've already met Saadi."

"Is he nicer at home than he is at school?" she asks skeptically.

"No," I say.

She laughs, and the sound of it lifts me up. I love the

life in her, the passion and the vision. I imagine this is what Madonna was like, back when she was our age. Bold and confident. Madonna would hate me, but she would love Judy.

Judy looks down at the pint of ice cream, melting into a soup. She picks it up and feeds me a spoon. "Finish it, please," she says. "I don't need it now that I'm done."

"Maybe we can add some tahini dressing to it," I suggest. "Tahini ice cream soup."

"Stop," she says playfully. "You're driving my taste buds crazy."

I slurp the ice cream like soup, which makes her smile. But there's something melancholy in her gaze now, and taking her lead once again, I whisper, "Hey, you okay?"

"Yeah," she says. "I guess I'm a little nervous. Like what if they don't like me? What if they think I'm some unsophisticated American girl?"

"What?" I say. "Who would think that?"

"I would think that," she says, revealing an insecurity I hadn't known was there. "I do think that."

"Judy," I say softly. "You don't think that. I know you don't. You are . . . beautiful, and so cool, and so good."

The capitalized words from Mrs. Bowman's book cover seem to float above me and Judy like clouds, the word GOOD above Judy's head, and the word BAD above mine. Maybe I do know who I am. Maybe I have found myself, as Americans like to say. I am BAD. I lie with every kiss. I lie with every touch and every gaze.

"Thanks for saying that," Judy says.

"I'm not just saying it. I mean it." I wish she under-stood how much I mean it, that despite all my lies to her, the most important truth is that I think she's incredible, like sunshine in a dark world. And I wish she knew that her ability to even utter all these doubts out loud means she thinks highly enough of herself to respect the emo-tions inside her. I would never let my doubts leave the prison of my brain.

She takes my hand. "Hey," she says. "Thanks for checking in."

I have checked into her life, like a hotel room. I only wish that I could truly inhabit this room, untouched by my desires.

ART

We're standing outside Saint Patrick's Cathedral, one of Andy Warhol's favorite places in the city, and it's as opulent, ornate, and glamorous as Warhol himself. It's also a place of judgment and repression, and because of that, it makes no sense to me that Warhol loved it. It mystifies me that only two years ago, a memorial mass was held for him here, that its pews were filled not with gay haters and pro-lifers, but with Yoko Ono, Grace Jones, and Halston, with the freaks and goddesses from his Factory. Maybe this was Warhol's personal fuck-you to the church, his way of telling them that he was so big and so powerful that his circus could invade their halls at will. Stephen was there for Warhol's mass, not inside, but outside. He saw them all walk in, the fabulous people in their downtown twist on Sunday church couture. He thinks that despite his queerness and his celebration of those cast aside, what Andy wanted more than anything was acceptance by the God he still worshipped.

"Shall we go become one with God?" Stephen asks. Next to him are five activists, including many I recognize from the meetings and two I recognize from the New York Stock Exchange protest.

"Remember not to make a scene today," a woman in a gray coat and jeans says. She has curly red hair and glasses. She's not a member of ACT UP; she's a part of another organization called WHAM!, Women's Health Action and Mobilization, which is joining forces with ACT UP for this. "Today is just a chance to scope out the place, come up with ideas."

"Sorry I'm late," a voice I recognize calls out from behind me. I turn around to see Jimmy, wearing the same black fur coat he wore the last time I saw him, inside the Korean deli, that awful night I thought Reza and I were going to fall in love and live happily ever after. I hate that night and want to forget everything about it except for Jimmy and his fabulous coat. I love that he's wearing it to church.

Jimmy kisses everyone on the cheek, saving me for last. By the time he gets to me, everyone else has begun to enter the church. Jimmy locks his arm in mine. "Art, *mon amour*," he says with a conspiratorial wink. "You just get more handsome, while the rest of us degenerate into one giant lesion."

"You look like Mahogany," I say.

"I look like Mahogany with an eating disorder and jaundice," he says. "Darling, do you remember that photo you took of me and Walt in the deli?"

"Of course," I say.

"Could you . . ." His voice quivers. He takes a breath of crisp winter air. I can feel the shallowness of his breath, his lungs working overtime to do their job. "I think it was the last photo of the two of us together while he was still . . ." He takes another big breath in, but this time, he doesn't finish the sentence.

I know the end, of course. Walt is dead. Died almost two months ago, just weeks after I saw them. And I should've given him a copy of that photo as soon as I found out. I'm sure he would've appreciated it. But the thing is that I never developed that roll of film. I knew it would remind me of Reza, and I didn't want to see any of those photos.

"I'm on it," I say, putting my hand on his shoulder.

We are almost at the entrance of the church when Jimmy whispers to me, "Do you believe in God?"

I pause for a moment. I don't know what the right answer is. If I say yes, I'm lying. If I say no, I'm telling a dying man who just lost the love of his life that there is nothing left for him but dust. "I don't know," I finally say.

"I didn't think I did," Jimmy says. "But since getting sick, I've started to wonder, or to hope . . ." Another breath, and then he says, "Hey, do you know that Walt died the day after Bette Davis? Honestly, that queen was such a fan that he had to follow Jezebel to the afterlife. You didn't see me croaking when Joan died, did you?"

I laugh, grateful that he lightened the mood. But I feel his pain. His body is wasting away. His lover is gone. And he doesn't even have a copy of the final photo taken of them because the kid who took it is too self-involved to develop the roll.

"Welcome," a woman says when we reach the entrance. She holds her hand out to us, first to me, and then to Jimmy. She fixes her gaze on him as she shakes his hand, inspecting him. "I hope you enjoy today's mass," she says.

As we move away from her, I tell Jimmy, "I hate that she stared at you like that."

"Honey," he says, "white ladies were staring scornfully at my queer black ass long before I had AIDS. I'm used to it."

"Is it awful that I think this place is absolutely gorgeous?" Stephen asks, approaching me.

"Good Lord," Jimmy says. "Next you'll be telling us that you find Reagan gorgeous too."

"Not in the least," Stephen says. "But I could have my way with Cardinal O'Connor." Seeing the shock on our faces, he quickly says. "It was a joke. Jesus Christ, I'm not that desperate."

I realize that both Stephen and Jimmy just took the Lord's name in vain without thinking much of it, and it makes me think about how adeptly religion has seeped into every part of our language. Even those of us who want to shake the shackles of religion off us are tied to it somehow. I look up and take the vastness in. The cathedral is majestic and so imposing, like the church wants to remind you of its power through its architecture. Near the entrance is a gift shop. Candles are for sale, and Bibles, and postcards, and pens, all there to raise funds for the church, the money going toward reaching more people with their message of intolerance. It feels completely absurd to me. I know that ACT UP meetings have a merchandise table too, but that's because we have no money and no funding. The church has countless cathedrals just like this one, real estate everywhere, and they still want people to give them more.

We make our way to pews in the back of the church. I sit in between Stephen and Jimmy, but pretty soon, we are standing as Cardinal O'Connor enters in his ornate robe, looking like an extra from a Cecil B. DeMille movie. I look over at Stephen, Jimmy, and the rest of the activists as O'Connor enters, and daggers shoot from their eyes, all pointed straight at this man. This awful man, who was brought to New York to bring conservatism back to the Catholic Church by a Vatican that wants to push back against some of the reforms the church has taken on recently. Cardinal O'Connor made it his business to take our condoms away, so we can all die.

As the choir sings a song, Stephen whispers to the group, "So the idea being batted around is that we all lie down in the aisle when he does the homily."

A woman in front of us shushes him. I close my eyes for most of the ceremony. It's not my first time in church, and most of the memories it brings to mind are bad ones.

But this time, something about the choir moves me. The sound of all those voices harmonizing together is undeniably beautiful, and the acoustics of the space make it sound like the voices are surrounding me. If angels do exist, I suppose this is what they'd sound like. And the voices remind me of the choir in "Like a Prayer," and I think that if it weren't for all the bullshit rules of Catholicism, then there would be no Madonna, because what is she if not a rebellion against all of this? I guess I need to be grateful for that. I hear her song playing in my head, and I imagine Reza's face when he listened to it for the first time. I could feel it washing over him. I could feel him come alive, forming into something new in front of my eyes, and then he pulled away from me. I keep my eyes closed until the choir stops, and I imagine myself kissing Reza's lips, his eyelids, his nose, his chest, his thighs. I imagine everything that would disgust the church and the Cardinal, all set to their holy music. I guess that's the thing. I don't want to burn this place to the ground. What I want is to make them see that I AM HOLY. These thoughts of me and Reza, they are holy. Well, except for that part about him being my best friend's boyfriend now. That's a sinful detail.

"The Lord be with you," O'Connor says.

"And with your spirit," the room responds. All except our row. We're not playing this game. We're not going to do his call-and-response and eat his tasteless wafer. We're here on a mission, to get ideas about how to invade this space and open people's eyes to the church's complicity in our deaths. The mass is long and boring. In his homily, O'Connor makes multiple references to protecting "the unborn," and I can feel the WHAM! woman's blood boiling. It's amazing how gung ho he is about saving the lives of fetuses, but then he turns a blind eye to all the actual humans DYING right in front of him.

When it comes time to take communion, we decide to head out.

But I'm not ready to leave. Not when I turn and see the prayer candles waiting to be lit. There's a suggested donation to light a candle, but I know that God isn't about money exchanging hands to make wishes come true. And I know that I don't believe in a God who can grant wishes, but if there's even a chance that such a God exists, then I have some wishes that I'd like granted. I figure making a wish is like an insurance policy, and so I close my eyes and light a candle.

I want to wish for Reza to come back to me, but that will be next. That can't be my first wish, not when I'm surrounded by death. Not when Stephen looks so weak. So I wish for Stephen to get better, for a miracle drug to become available before his time is up, for the color to return to his skin and for the weight to return to his body. I light the candle and watch the wick come alive.

And then the next wish. Another candle lit. This wish, for AIDS to be cured entirely. Not just for Stephen to survive, but for every person with AIDS to be cured. And for all the queer kids like me to get to fall in love without fear looming over us like the spires of this cathedral.

And now, another candle. This one is for Reza. I close my eyes as I light the candle, and I imagine him across from me. *I'm wishing for you*, I tell him in my fantasy. *I'm asking a God I don't even believe in to make you mine. And I think the only reason I'm having these doubts about God's existence is you. That feeling of connection I had with you, it made me feel, I don't know . . . that there must be something bigger than us. It made me feel that maybe there is a God. So I'm asking God, and all those angels and saints that I don't believe in either, to make you love me, and to watch over you, and to make you happy, but most of all to make you mine.*

I open my eyes. I feel a presence around me.

Is it Reza? Is it Andy Warhol? Is it God?

Nope, it's that unbearably chipper woman who greeted us at the door.

"You made a lot of prayers," she says, as she places five bucks in the donation box and lights a candle herself. As she reaches her arm toward a back candle, the gust from her arm extinguishes one of my candles. Which one was it, the one for Stephen, the one for AIDS, or the one for Reza? I don't even know. My heart speeds up. Is this God sending me a sign?

The woman's wick stays lit. "It was a beautiful homily, wasn't it?" she asks me.

"Sure," I say, and quickly scurry away.

Outside, Stephen, Jimmy, and the rest wait for me at the corner, already engaged in heated debate about what to do next. Some want this protest to be more peaceful, less in-your-face, because if they offend too many people, their message could get lost. Others want it to be even more aggressive and bold, because their target is so aggressive and bold. "Let's not argue now," Stephen says. "These are just ideas. They need to be discussed at the meeting."

"A word of advice," the WHAM! woman says. "Whatever you do, don't become divided. If there's one lesson I've learned from the women's health movement, it's that you need to build a true coalition. If you show them that you're divided, creating change will be close to impossible. They'll just play you against each other."

Those words echo in my mind as Stephen, Jimmy, and I separate from the group and head toward downtown. It's a beautiful day, the winter sun shines on us, the air crisp and fresh. I love early winter in the city, before the snow turns to slush, before the cold has been with us so long that we're collectively frozen into a stupor. Come to think of it, I love the beginning of every season. Everything feels more vital, more exciting, when it's new.

"Shall we walk downtown?" Stephen asks. "While we still can."

"Speak for yourself," Jimmy says. "I'll probably make it a few blocks before I run out of breath."

. Stephen locks his arm into Jimmy's. "Come on,

strength in numbers. We're not dead yet."

Stephen and Jimmy lead the way downtown. I walk behind them, just like Reza walked behind me that night after I gave him the flower. I pull my camera up to my eye and snap a photo of them from behind as they walk.

"Two widows," Jimmy says. "Who would've thought?"

"Maybe José and Walt are watching us right now," Stephen says.

"I doubt it," Jimmy says. "If there is an afterlife, Walt is too busy drinking martinis with Bette Davis to be watching over me. He was done with me."

"Don't say that—he was not done with you," Stephen says. Then he adds, "Maybe he's huddled up with Walt Whitman, commiserating over how they hated the name Walter."

"Celebrating and *singing* themselves," Jimmy says.

"Every atom belonging to him belongs to you," Stephen says, continuing the Whitman quotes. "He's still here, a part of you. Just like José is still here in me."

"Do you wish you had gone first?" Jimmy asks.

Stephen pulls Jimmy closer as they continue to walk slowly. Walking behind them, both with them and apart from them, I catch every single person who stares at them, some with fear, some with pity, some with compassion, some with hatred. I pull my camera up and snap more photos, but this time, I let Stephen and Jimmy be nothing but a blur. I focus on the background, on the pedestrians, on their gazes. I don't want to run through my film too fast, so I wait until someone stares, and then I snap.

"Sometimes," Stephen says, "I think it would've been easier to go first, but then I think of José here without me. I'd rather be the one in pain."

"Me too," Jimmy says. "I don't know who the lucky one is. Walt, for being spared more of this. Or me, for getting a little more time."

"Maybe we're all the lucky ones," Stephen says. "We had love."

Jimmy lets out a hearty laugh. "Better to have loved and lost your love to Kaposi's sarcoma than never to have loved at all."

If they're the lucky ones for having had love, then what does that make me? Will I ever have love? Probably not, because I'm a self-pitying narcissist. Look at me. I'm listening to two beautiful, noble, HOLY men who are not only facing death themselves, but also lost the loves of their lives, and what am I thinking about? Myself.

Two men in business suits walk past us. They look at Stephen and Jimmy with sneers that remind me of my father. I press my camera, hear it click, feel it capture the violence of their scrutiny. Stephen and Jimmy should be revered and worshipped, not feared and derided. They are the saints who belong in God's cathedrals, they are the icons that belong on the posters on our walls. And that's when I have an idea. A new project. I'll photograph them and show the world how beautiful they are. I'll pose them as saints, re-create old religious iconography. No, they're too good for that. I'll turn them into Dietrich and Garbo. I'll light the photographs like the Old Hollywood photos of George Hurrell and Clarence Sinclair Bull, all haze and gauze and smoke and shadow. I'll make the world see what I see, that these men and women are mythic, larger than life. Maybe I won't have love, but I'll have something else. A purpose. Love would just distract me anyway. Rage will be way more productive.

I make a choice. I choose rage.

JUDY

I can't believe I'm in Mr. Chow. I can barely focus as Reza's stepdad orders food for everyone, imagining all the people who could have sat in this chair before me. Maybe Debbie Harry sat here, or Madonna, or Candy Darling. I don't see anyone famous right now, except for a model I think I recognize from the pages of *Vogue* who is literally tearing a dumpling apart with her chopsticks and placing the wisps of lettuce within into her mouth. She's very tall and very skinny, and I pity her. I want to ask her if it's worth it, to eat shredded lettuce and champagne for dinner just so you can look like that. I don't think so. "Judy *joon*, last chance. Anything special you would like to order? Anything you do not eat?"

I realize Reza's stepdad is talking to me and focus back on our table. "Oh, I'll eat anything," I say.

I think I catch a smirk on Saadi's face, but I'm not sure. He's probably thinking some variation of: *She looks*

like she'll eat anything. Or, *She's already eaten everything.*
He doesn't even have to say a word—I can feel the con-
descension emanating from his lacrosse body, from his
beefy arms busting out of his polo shirt, and from his
white baseball hat dangling from the back of his chair.
Seriously. He wore a white baseball hat to Mr. Chow.
He's taken it off, thank God, at the urging of his dad, but
still. I see vintage Halston here, and this season's Gaultier
too. I see bodysuits, palazzo pants, suede blazers, vinyl
jackets, and deconstructed clothes that redefine geome-
try and the shape of the body. And Saadi wore a white
baseball hat. But the best outfit in the whole place is the
one next to me. Reza looks incredible in his shirt, like a
star. Maybe it's a good thing Madonna isn't here tonight,
'cause she'd swipe him away from me and put him in her
next video. And he's mine. I have to keep reminding
myself of this because it still feels so unreal to me. He's
mine, he's mine, he's mine.

"Judy *joon*," Reza's mother says. "it is so nice to finally
meet you."

"Oh, you too," I say, a little too brightly. "All of you."

"We've already met," Saadi says. "We go to school
together, remember?"

I nod and force a smile. "Of course I do." How could
I forget all the times his buddies called Art a faggot in
front of me, all the times Saadi just stood there as Darryl
Lorde spewed hate. Saadi never said a word to stop Darryl, which makes him an accessory to the crime.

Accessories. So many insanely fabulous accessories

in this room, none more gorgeous than the brooch on Reza's mom's shirt. It's a gold bird, with bright jewels filling in its features. It glimmers in the light and complements her silk shirt perfectly. The woman is stunning.

"Mrs. Hashemi," I say, "I'm a little obsessed with your look."

"Please, call us Mina and Abbas. We are not formal people." They both smile. She's wearing silk, and he's wearing a suit that looks like it was custom-made in Rome, but they're not formal people.

"Okay, Mina . . . that brooch is, like, so magnificent."

"Oh," she says. "I'm so glad you noticed. This is one of the few things I took with me from Tehran."

"I can see why it was a top priority," I say.

"Well, after my children," she says. "They came first, and this brooch was a close second."

I laugh a little too loud, grateful for her humor. Women this beautiful usually aren't very funny. My theory is that they never develop a sense of humor because their beauty gets them through life too easily. I think the best-case scenario is to be born really ugly and remain ugly for most of your childhood, so that you're forced to develop humor, intellect, and thick skin, and then blossom into a supermodel when you're a grown-up. I wonder if handsome men have this issue too. Probably, but I haven't given it as much thought. Anyway, I bet Reza's mom didn't look this good when she was my age. She seems too cool for that.

"So tell us, Judy, how did you become interested in fashion?" Mina asks. "And before you answer, can I say that I very much like what you've done with my son." She places a hand on Reza's cheek, and he blushes. "He looks like a new person, like a handsome man. My baby boy is gone."

"Okay, Mommy," Reza says, embarrassed. I love that he still calls her Mommy, pronounced in an accent that makes it sound more exotic than infantile.

"There is a lot of money in fashion these days," Abbas says. "Do you know the current valuation of LVMH?"

"Um, I don't," I say. "I'm sorry."

"You can make billions these days. The important thing is building a strong brand name. Because then you are not just selling clothes. You are selling a lifestyle. And when you are selling a lifestyle, you can sell anything. Perfume. Linens. Candles."

"Oh wow," I say, laughing. "You think really big."

"So do you," Saadi says, with a smile. "Obviously."

I flinch a little. Asshole. I know it's a crack about my weight.

Don't take the bait, Judy.

"I'm glad you noticed," I say, shooting him daggers with my eyes.

"Calvin Klein is a perfect example," Abbas says. "He makes most of his money from underwear and perfume now, and how much work does it take to design underwear?"

"I don't know," I say. "I've, um, never designed underwear."

"Maybe you should," Saadi says. "Reza could be your model."

Reza blushes. This dinner is getting weird fast.

"Of course you should," Abbas says. "If you want to be a billionaire."

"My dad's all about the money," Saadi says. "If you can't tell."

"It is just exciting to see a young person who knows what she wants to do," Abbas says, with a stern look toward his son that speaks volumes. "Perhaps it's time you started thinking about what interests you professionally."

"I have a little time," Saadi replies, his mouth full.

"The operative word there is *little*," Abbas says. "We all have a little time, and we should do our best with it."

"I think the decor of this restaurant is so exciting," Mina says, her attempt at changing the subject both obvious and awkward.

Mercifully, some food arrives, and it smells so delicious and fragrant. I watch as plates of noodles, dumplings, chicken skewers, and Chinese broccoli are placed in front of us. I think of all those times I've been out to restaurants with Art, and how annoying it is that he won't eat meat or anything that touches it, and how, as always, I need to modulate what I want for him. Mina insists I serve myself first, and I do, filling my plate up with food. Soon, we're all eating, and the conversation turns to a variety of subjects, from the Central Park Five to what my favorite classes at school are to how I feel about wearing a uniform when I'm so into fashion to Iranian politics. Reza barely speaks. I mean, he says a few words here and there. A *yes* or a *no* or a *that's delicious*, but he doesn't contribute many complete sentences. I wonder if he's always this quiet around his family or if it's just tonight.

In the middle of the meal, two men enter and sit at the table next to us. One of them is skin and bones. There's a dark lesion on his upper neck. He nods toward our table as he sits, almost in apology, like he's sorry for subjecting us to his illness in the middle of an otherwise pleasant dinner. Abbas and Mina smile politely, but in a glacial and forced way. Saadi almost sneers. Reza just looks scared. Which reminds me of how, in the two months since we started dating, he hasn't come over to Uncle Stephen's once. I've invited him to Sunday movie night multiple times, and each time he has some excuse about why he can't come. He has some plan with his family, or he's behind on homework, or he's got a stomachache. I'm pretty sure the real reason is that he doesn't want to hang out with someone who has AIDS, but I haven't pressed him on that point yet. I guess I don't want the answer. Because if he tells me that's the reason, it might make me fall a little out of love with him.

When the two men sit down, I smile extra big at

them, trying to compensate for anyone making them feel unwelcome or shut out. But even my smile probably bugs them. I'm still giving them special attention, treating them like they're somehow different, singling them out, and I immediately feel bad about that. That's when I feel something on my knee. Reza's hand. I hook my fingers into his, and he clasps onto me under the table, giving my hand a squeeze. I don't know what the squeeze means, but I think he knows what I was thinking when this man walked in. I turn toward Reza and smile, and that's when he whispers, "You have some food in your teeth."

"Oh God, gross." I run my tongue around my teeth, then smile at him.

"Still there," he says.

I put my napkin on the table. "I'll be right back," I say, trying hard to keep my mouth closed as I speak.

On my way to the bathroom, I smile at the man with AIDS again. *Stop it, Judy.* But then I realize it's not just him I'm smiling at. I'm smiling at everybody. I smile at the woman speaking rapid French to her girlfriends. I smile at the man with the Tom Selleck mustache, who may actually be Tom Selleck, come to think of it. When I get to the bathroom, one of them is out of order. I turn the doorknob of the functional bathroom and it's locked. A female voice from inside calls out, "Yeah, I'm in here."

"Sorry," I call out. And then, I add, "Um, take your time."

As if that isn't awkward enough, when I turn back,

I run right into Saadi. "Personally, I think pooping in public bathrooms is rude," he says, smirking.

"Um, you're gross," I say.

"What do you think people do in bathrooms?" he asks. "Design underwear?"

I don't even respond to that. We stand against the hallway wall for a few seconds, and then he says, "Wow, that person is really taking their time. I hope they light a match when they're done."

"You know we don't need to talk," I say.

"So what's the deal with you and the little prince?" he asks.

"Who's the little prince?"

Why are you not ignoring him, Judy? Ignore him.

"My stepbrother," he says. And then, with a smirk, he adds, "Your boy toy."

"He's the same age as you," I say.

Saadi smiles, like I've set him up for a perfect response. "I know," he says. "But he's so small and cute."

I just shake my head. I don't want to talk to him. I just want to pick the food out of my teeth and go back to the table.

"So what's with him and Madonna?" he asks.

"I don't know," I say. "What's with you and your white hat?"

Stop engaging, Judy.

"I look cute in it," he says, his overconfidence anything but cute. "Have you seen his room? There's a new picture of Madonna every day. Two posters was weird enough. Now it's like a shrine or something."

"If you have a point, make it," I say.

"I think you know my point," he says with an arched brow.

Why is the person in the bathroom taking so long? Hurry up, lady. I'm about to go ballistic on this dude.

But she doesn't hurry. And I can't hold back any longer. "You know something, you're an asshole," I say. "And so unoriginal too. Guys like you are everywhere. In fact, you don't even need to speak anymore, because I know everything you're going to say next."

"Fine," he says, holding his hands up. "I'll shut up now. I was just trying to save you."

"Oh, please," I say. "Save me from what?"

He doesn't say it. He's a jerk, but there's only so far he'll take it. I know what he's thinking though, some version of "I'm trying to save you from getting AIDS from your gay boyfriend who loves Madonna so much."

"Did you follow me to the bathroom to harass me?" I ask.

"You asked me not to speak," he says. "Now you're the one asking me questions."

"Shut up," I say.

"I did not follow you to the bathroom to harass you," he says. "I came to the bathroom because I ate too much roughage."

"You're certifiably disgusting," I say. "And by the way,

I can tell you from experience that Reza isn't gay, not that you said the word. You're probably too afraid to say it. You probably think that speaking it means you'll get the disease."

"Oh yeah, are you sure?" he asks. "Does he get hard when you kiss him?"

"Get away from me," I say. "That's none of your business."

"Which means he hasn't gotten hard." Saadi smirks.

"Of course he has," I say, hoping the lie isn't too obvious.

"Uh-huh." It's obvious Saadi doesn't believe me. "In that case, I would bet his eyes are closed, and he's thinking about Tom Cruise when he kisses you."

The bathroom door opens. The skinny model emerges from inside, smiles sheepishly at us, and then returns to her table. I rush into the bathroom and close the door behind me.

I approach the mirror and smile big. There it is, a bright-orange piece of chicken stuck between my teeth. Disgusting. How long was it there? Will Reza's mother forever think of me as the girl with food in her teeth? I pick at it with my nails, but it's stubborn.

Saadi's wrong about Reza. He's so wrong. Reza holds my hand all the time. He loves kissing me. He loves spending time together and he lets me dress him, and . . . Okay, it's not like we've gone further than kissing, but that's as much my fault as his. It's not like I'm sexually experienced myself. He's probably just scared, or shy. Lots of straight men like Madonna. Saadi is such a stereotype himself that he can only think in stereotypes. He doesn't even know Reza. Even though they're stepbrothers, they just met. Screw Saadi.

I run the sink, crouch down, and take some cold water into my mouth. I swish it around to loosen that piece of chicken, then spit. I smile. It's still there. Am I supposed to feel around for a hard on when he kisses me? Is that what girls do? I don't even know. I remember that my skirt has safety pins running down the side of it. So obvious. I undo one of the safety pins and point the tip at the chicken. Finally, I get it out of my mouth. I put the pin back, wash my hands, and take a deep breath before exiting the bathroom. When I leave, Saadi isn't even there anymore. He probably didn't need to use the bathroom. He did just come to harass me.

Reza doesn't go home with his family. He walks me to my subway station, holding my hand.

"I think my mom really likes you," he says.

"Really?" I ask, a big smile on my face. "I mean, I'm not fishing for more compliments, but you know, I don't mind compliments."

"Fishing," he says as he touches the fish pin on his shirt. "That's funny."

"Fish represent life!" I yell, and we both laugh.

"She really did like you, though," he says. "I know when she doesn't like someone. And anyway, she'd be crazy not to like you."

"What about your stepdad?" I ask.

He shrugs. "I don't know him well enough to read him yet," he says, with a hint of sadness.

"I'm sure it's hard to suddenly be a part of a new family," I say, thinking about what a jerk Saadi is.

He nods.

"But I'm glad your mom married him," I say, smiling. "Because if she didn't, we wouldn't know each other. And that would suck."

We reach the station. He faces me awkwardly. "I guess this is goodbye for tonight," he says.

"You want to come to Uncle Stephen's with me?" I offer. "Art's probably there. It'll be fun."

"Oh . . . thank you . . . ," he stammers. "I'm so tired, though."

"Are you scared to hang out with my uncle?" I ask, bracing for the response.

"What? No," he says. But he's clearly lying.

I take a breath. "You know it's not like a cold. You can't get it from being in the same room with someone."

"I know," he says, looking away.

"Okay, I just . . ." I don't finish. I want to say that it's important to me that my boyfriend gets to know my uncle, that no one can really know me without getting close to Stephen. But I don't want to push too hard, afraid I'll push him away.

"I understand," he says. "I'll spend time with him soon. I think it's been nice, for now, to get to know you without so many people around."

"Yeah?" I ask.

I move closer to him, so close that he looks softly out of focus, like Montgomery Clift in *A Place in the Sun*. I imagine that I'm Elizabeth Taylor in that same movie. Of course, the real Montgomery Clift was gay, and Uncle Stephen told me that he and Liz were best friends, just like me and Art, but that Liz was a little in love with him. And I wonder . . . I feel the heat of Reza's breath on my face. I want him to press his lips against mine, and he does. I pull him close as he kisses me, placing my hands on his lower back, forcing his body to become one with mine. I could inhale the entirety of him, I could seriously just make him a part of me. That's how much I want him. I run my hands up and down his back, and then I pull away from him a little, just far enough to give my hand space to touch his chest, and then move down to his torso. As nonchalant as I can, I move my hand down, feeling his crotch. I feel something hard. Is it him, or is it his zipper? I can't even tell. I've never felt a hard-on before. Aren't they all different sizes?

He pulls away from me. "I should go."

"Wait," I say. "One more."

I pull him in again.

Kiss him.

Feel him.

Press my body against his. I feel like a total perv. I wish Elizabeth Taylor was here right now, so I could ask her if she had to feel Montgomery's hard-on to know if he was into her or not.

With my body crushed against his, there is no

question. He's not hard. It was just his zipper. But maybe he's just nervous. Or maybe it's because we're in public. Or maybe he's exhausted.

This doesn't mean anything, Judy. Don't make it mean something.

We say goodbye, and then he walks away.

As I descend onto the subway platform, and then onto the train, I can't stop questioning everything. So what if he wasn't hard? It's not evidence that could be admitted into a court of law, or a court of love. If Art were sitting next to me, he'd say it's not *hard evidence* and we'd laugh. Art told me once that the subway was the hottest place in the city, as in sexual heat, not physical temperature. He said that all those bodies rubbing against each other basically made it a clothed, coed bathhouse, not that he's ever been in a bathhouse. I think he says things like that just to get a rise out of me, but as a crowd of people enters the subway, I can't help but look at every man's crotch, trying to assess how easy it is for a man to get hard.

When I enter Uncle Stephen's apartment, he's lying on the couch with Art next to him, a box of half-eaten pizza in front of them. *Mommie Dearest* is playing on the television. It's almost over. They're watching the scene where Joan replaces her daughter Christina in a soap opera, literally playing a part meant for a woman half her age. They're reciting each line at the screen, so loud that you can't hear the actors, and it sounds like the movie is dubbed.

"How was the date?" Uncle Stephen asks.

"Great," I say, a little too quickly.

"More detail please," Uncle Stephen says.

I sit in between them on the couch. "Let's just watch the movie."

Art pulls me in so that my head is on his chest. This is so simple, so easy. To rest my head on the chest of a boy I love as a friend, without having to worry about whether and how he loves me back, knowing we'll be each other's everything forever because friendship is so much easier than romance. Art's heart is beating rapidly. On the end table next to the couch is a new picture frame. Inside is a photo of Uncle Stephen, Art, and me from this past Halloween, when we joined the ACT UP protest of Trump Tower, which Uncle Stephen explained to us is a symbol of all the real estate subsidies given to luxury buildings while ten thousand people with AIDS in the city are homeless. The protest was incredible. There was a man dressed as Dorothy holding a sign that read "Surrender, Donald." There was a man dressed as Freddy Krueger holding a sign that read, "Nightmare on Trump Street." And us. Uncle Stephen was dressed as Joan Crawford, and Art and I were Christina and Christopher. Art was Christina and I was Christopher. We were a nuclear family. We made sense. We still make sense. I start reciting the lines along with them. And I think how much less complicated things felt before we met Reza, back when we knew the roles we were playing and the script we were reciting.

#115 Taylor, Elizabeth

First she was a doe-eyed child star. Then the most beautiful woman in the world. By twenty-six she was a grieving widow, by twenty-seven a brazen homewrecker, by twenty-eight a near-death survivor, and soon an Oscar winner, and the world's highest paid actress. She was married seven times (but not to seven men—you do the math), and she became the best friend to none other than Michael Jackson (who seemed unable to befriend anyone who wasn't a child or a chimp). But her most important role is as a *fighter*. She fights for us. She throws fundraisers, starts foundations, testifies before the Senate. She even stands up to America's highest-ranking bully and mean girl. The. Fucking. Reagans. Ronald Reagan . . . hadn't he already inflicted enough pain upon the world through his abominable acting work? He was even out-acted by a chimpanzee in his most famous role. Now that takes effort. But he one-upped himself by watching as we died, silently enjoying the genocide like it was dinner theater for him and his equally talentless wife (try sitting through one of *her* movies). It was Elizabeth Taylor who lobbied her old Hollywood pals until he said the word publicly for the first time in 1987. Take that in for a moment. We had been dying in droves for six years, and our president had yet to say the word AIDS. I hope people remember that. And I hope people remember that without her, there would be less glamour in the world, but also less goodness, and less courage.

REZA

Being in JFK airport feels like you're in every city in the world at the same time. Every language is spoken here, and every kind of person is represented. Families, couples, students, all coming and going. I stare up at the list of arriving flights and imagine myself flying to all these cities, disappearing into Paris for a week, or Rome, or Hong Kong. What would my life be like in Buenos Aires? Who would I be there? My mom sometimes watches that television show that takes place in a bar, and sings along to the theme song, which is about how nice it would be to go to a place where everybody knows your name. But what I'm thinking as I look at these cities is how I would love to go to a place where nobody knows my name, where nobody expects anything of me. Who would I be in Lisbon? Or San Francisco? I would have no mother there, no stepfather, no one to disappoint. I could even die without hurting anybody but myself.

"Where is she?" my mother says, exasperated. Her exasperation belongs to my sister, and her expectations belong to me.

"I don't know," I say, searching the crowd of arriving passengers for her. An old woman in a wheelchair being pushed by a flight attendant emerges to the arms of a family holding a banner that reads "Welcome to America, Grandma!" A beautiful woman coolly approaches an older man and gives him a peck on the cheek before throwing her carry-on bag into his arms. A men's soccer team wearing matching maroon jerseys and shorts comes through the arrival door, talking over each other loudly in Spanish. I don't know what they are saying, but I don't care when they have legs like these. If I go to a place where nobody knows my name, I want it to be the place these men are from.

"Zabber!" She screams her nickname for me. "There you are."

I turn my attention away from those soccer players' bodies and see my sister. She doesn't come through the arrivals door. She stands by the entrance near the street. She wears ripped acid-wash jeans with a pink heart sewn into them, a body-hugging black sweater, and a bomber jacket. Her lipstick is ruby red, her nails are hot pink, and her hair is crimped and piled atop her head in a messy bun. She holds a small suitcase.

"Tara!" I scream back, and without looking over at my mother, I rush into my sister's arms. When she holds me, I melt into her body a little. She feels familiar. She reminds me of a time when I knew what to expect. But her scent is new. She smells like cigarettes, maybe, and a new perfume.

"Did you not arrive with the other passengers?" my mother asks.

"My flight was overbooked, so I ended up on an earlier flight," Tara says. "I tried to call and tell you, but no one answered."

"Oh," my mother says, suspicious.

"The good news is they gave me credit for the inconvenience, so next time you don't have to buy me a ticket." Tara looks at my mom with annoyance. I know what Tara is thinking: that my mother is always suspicious of something. "Or maybe you don't care about airline credits anymore now that you're so rich."

"Tara, please," my mother says. "Let's not begin like this. It's so nice to see you." My mom takes Tara's hand and pulls her into a limp hug. They kiss each other on both cheeks, each marking the other with a small smudge of red.

"God, you even smell expensive now, Mom," Tara says.

Tara has not yet learned the first rule of our new life, which is that we don't talk about the money we now have. Tara has never been good at rules, whether spoken or unspoken, and it's like all she wants to talk about as we head home is money. Seeing our life through Tara's eyes, I understand. When we left Toronto, we were a family that had been living in a cramped apartment and did laundry once a week because we didn't have a lot of nice clothes. Now my mother is wearing a Versace blouse, holding a Chanel handbag, and picking her daughter up at the airport in a Mercedes Benz.

Tara notices everything. She notices that our car is spotless and points out that parking a car in Manhattan must cost more than her college tuition. I'm in the back seat as we head into the city, and I can see Tara in the front passenger seat, taking in the city as we enter, the grime and the height and the energy of it. She has the fire this place requires, not me.

"Tara, may we speak frankly before you meet Abbas?" my mother asks as she takes a wrong turn onto Madison Avenue. I realize my mother is purposely extending the car trip to have this conversation.

"You know me, Mother," Tara says. She calls her *Mother* when she wants to annoy her. "I'm nothing if not honest."

That's not true at all. Tara lies all the time. She lies about where she goes, and who she goes with, and what she does when she's there. But the thing about Tara that's so fascinating is that she makes you feel like she's always being honest, because of her confidence and delivery.

"I have not told Abbas about some of your past mistakes because I don't want him to judge you on your past . . . ," my mom begins, and I know that this conversation will go very, very badly.

"They weren't mistakes, they were choices," Tara says, her voice already rising.

"Just as I would not want to be judged based on my past mistakes," my mother continues, staring ahead at the road, going in the complete wrong direction now. "Perhaps moving forward, we can keep our emotions a little more private."

"Oh, okay," Tara says snidely. "So basically, you want me to hide who I am to make you and your new husband more comfortable."

I stare at the store windows, all those fancy boutiques with their perfectly proportioned mannequins in the windows, draped in luxurious fabrics. I imagine Judy at her sewing machine, creating the different looks. I see her surrounded by colors and fabrics and ideas. We pass a store that's working on a new display. In the window is a man disrobing a male mannequin. I look at the mannequin's body and find myself getting a little hard. I cover my crotch with my hands. I imagine that Art is the mannequin, standing in the store window naked. How sick do you have to be to be turned on by a piece of plastic? In the background, their argument continues.

I just want him to see the sweet you, the real you. . . .

As opposed to the fake person I used to be?

You were young. Everybody is a fake version of themselves when they are young.

No, it's old people who are fake. They forget who they really are.

You won't feel that way when you're my age.

You just look young 'cause you have money now.

Please do not talk about money in front of Abbas. People

with money do not talk about money.

I know, I know. And people with dead dads don't talk about dead dads 'cause it makes people uncomfortable. God forbid we cause anyone discomfort.

You are causing me discomfort right now, not that you care.

"Hey, Zabber, thanks for all the support. Much appreciated." Hearing my nickname snaps me back to attention. We are pulling into the garage now, my mom having accepted that she must eventually turn the car in the right direction and go home.

"Reza, my love," my mom says, agitated, "what have I done to deserve your sister's awful treatment of me? Tell me."

"I'm still in the car!" my sister yells. "Don't talk about me like I'm not here. Can you tell her how annoying that is, Zabber?"

This is what they do. They make me a referee of their eternal competition.

My life could change again very soon. Tara is about to meet Abbas and Saadi for the first time, and given her propensity for destruction, we could all be on our way back to Toronto by tomorrow. But to my surprise, Tara is on her best behavior when Abbas greets her at the door. When she turns on the charm, she is irresistible, and she turns it on now, all smiles, compliments, and questions. She says things like "Wow, what a beautiful painting," and "Has anyone ever told you that you look like a younger Marlon Brando?" and "Seriously, it is so nice to finally meet you after hearing so many amazing

181

things from my mom and brother." The closest she comes to mentioning money is when she says, "I feel like Annie when she sings 'I Think I'm Gonna Like It Here,'" which is a charmingly appropriate way to acknowledge that these new surroundings are opulent and that our new stepfather is Daddy Warbucks.

I can tell that after just ten minutes, Abbas already loves her. He smiles at her in a way he has never smiled at me, like he can't wait to hear what she will say next.

"Saadi!" Abbas yells out. "Come meet your new sister."

"Did you name him after the poet?" Tara asks.

Abbas beams. "Yes," he says. "Are you a fan of our ancient poets?"

"Well, they were like the first rock stars," Tara says. "Rumi. Hafez. Khayyam. Saadi. They said everything we need to know about love and wine way before John Lennon and Mick Jagger did."

"And they said it better," Abbas says, impressed.

My mom smiles in relief, and perhaps in pride, seeing her daughter through Abbas's eyes now.

"And what about Forough Farrokhzad?" Tara asks. "People think Iranian women are all cloaked under chadors with no rights or ideas of their own, but we had our own bold feminist poet decades ago."

"She was incredible," Abbas agrees.

And then I hear Saadi's door open, but it's not just Saadi who emerges from the room.

Art.

I have successfully been avoiding him. Sitting far from

him in class. Making excuses when Judy is spending time with him. Not showing up to those Sunday movie nights. Keeping my Discman and headphones handy, so that I can put them on when I see him in the distance, creating a buffer of sound between us.

Art, in black jeans that hug his legs, and a leather jacket, his camera swinging across his chest, hitting the zippers of the jacket. Like a pendulum, each swing one more heartbeat, each clink of the camera one more second further from that moment when I could have kissed him. Further and further from that possibility.

"Sorry, we were studying," Saadi says, holding his hand out to Tara. "Nice to finally meet you."

"Yeah, you too," Tara says.

Art seems to be staring right through me. I look anywhere but at him, and in my search for a point of focus, I find Tara gazing at me curiously. She knows me too well.

"Hey, I'm Tara," she says to Art, holding her hand out.

"Oh cool, you're Reza's sister?" Art asks. "I've heard about you."

"And I can confirm that everything you have heard is true," she says.

Everyone laughs. She can take a potentially tense situation and bring humor to it. I don't have this skill. I don't even know if I have a sense of humor. What I know how to do in tense situations is shut down and disappear.

"Come, let's get you settled in, Tara," Abbas says warmly. "I hope you don't mind sharing a room with your brother."

"We're used to it," she says, turning to me with a smile of solidarity.

Tara follows my mom and Abbas toward my room. I stand with Art and Saadi in the foyer, wishing I could break the tension with humor. Then Saadi punches me in the shoulder.

"Ow," I say. "What was that for?"

"For not warning me that your sister is smoking hot," he says.

"You realize she's your sister too now," Art points out.

"Yeah, thanks," Saadi says. "Maybe don't lecture me about appropriate sexual behavior when you like butt sex."

Art responds with a middle finger in Saadi's face.

"Later," Saadi says. Then Saadi leaves, and I stand with Art. His camera has stopped swinging now. Nothing but stillness, and the heat of his body. I have a new fantasy. To go somewhere where no one knows my name, but to go with Art. To go somewhere where he can be the only person who knows me. He can rename me whatever he wants. He can call me *Baby* or *Sweetie* or *Honey* or just *Reza* if he wants. I can belong to nobody but him, exist only for him.

"Are you avoiding me?" he asks.

"Of course not," I say. I almost say *Why would I do that*, but I stop myself, because he might just answer that question, and I don't want him to.

"Okay, because I know Judy's life would be easier if we were friends."

"Oh," I say. "But we *are* friends."

For a moment, I had forgotten about Judy. I had imagined going to a place with Art, and leaving her behind. I hate myself for thinking that, and worse, for wanting it.

"Got it," he says. "Just wanted to clear the air."

"Okay," I say. The air is anything but clear.

We stand across from each other for a few deep breaths. "Hey, did you see *People* named Madonna one of the best-dressed people of the year?"

"Yeah," I say. I already have that issue in my room. I have every magazine Madonna is on the cover of, and every record, and more posters. I have amassed a collection, funded by my allowance and supplemented by the money I have made a habit of stealing from Abbas's pocket when he showers.

"I kind of wish they said she was the worst-dressed, you know. Like, I kind of wish the mainstream world didn't get her. That she could just be ours. Is that selfish?"

I don't know who he means when he says "ours."

"Are you doing anything fun for the holidays?" I ask. This is the question everybody at school seems to ask each other, and I pull it into the conversation now, hoping for an innocuous answer.

"In the ultimate statement of Christmas spirit, I'm joining this ACT UP protest of Saint Patrick's Cathedral. Has Judy told you about it? It's gonna be epic. EPIC."

"Oh," I say. Judy hasn't mentioned it. She doesn't talk about Art a lot when she's with me. And then, repeating the response everybody at school says to any question, I say, "Cool."

"Then my parents are taking me skiing in Aspen, which'll suck, but whatever. My real holiday is going to be that protest. What about you?"

"We are going to Miami," I say, wishing Miami was closer to Aspen.

"Miami!" Art repeats with excitement. "There's a nightclub there that Madonna goes to all the time. I'll get the name of it. You have to go look for her."

Art thinks I'm the kind of person who goes to nightclubs, the kind of person who looks for Madonna at places other than newsstands and record stores and MTV.

"Um, yeah, we're totally going to that nightclub," Tara says. She's standing a few feet away from us now. She approaches me and puts an arm around me. "I love our room. Who knew my little brother was a Madonna fanatic?"

"I like her," I say, trying to sound casual.

"Like her?" Tara parrots. "You have her plastered all over your room. You have every record she's ever released in there, including some European and Japanese editions of singles."

A moment passes between Tara and Art, a glance, a wordless conversation.

"I should go," Art says. "But it was nice to meet you, Tara. And in case you don't already sense it, your new stepbrother wants to bone you, so be careful."

"No shit," Tara says. "But thanks for the warning."

"I'm brutally honest," Art says.

"Oh my God, me too," Tara says.

They hug each other goodbye, and I can hear Tara whisper something in Art's ear before he leaves, but I don't know what. I wish I knew, but I'm too afraid to ask.

When Art is gone, I can feel his absence. I am at once deflated and relieved. Tara pulls me in close and leads me toward our room. We collapse on the bed together, lie next to each other just like we used to when we were little. She would talk, I would listen. "Hey, I want to tell you something," she says.

"Okay." I look away from her, at my wall, at that poster of Madonna and the HEALTHY shirt.

"I wasn't on that flight today. I've actually been in New York for a few days already. I drove here with my new boyfriend. He's a DJ. He spins house music at this club in Toronto, and he wants to make it in New York. There's no music scene there."

"Tara, what are you talking about?" I ask. "Aren't you going back for college in January?"

"Hell, no!" she says. "Are you kidding? When you meet Starburst, you'll understand."

"His name is Starburst?" I ask. I'm trying not to sound like my mom would.

"It's a DJ name. His real name is Massimo, which is the hottest name ever. He's Sicilian and unbelievably sexy.

And he got himself a one-bedroom in Hell's Kitchen that I plan on moving into as soon as I tell Mom about him. So you won't have me as a roommate for long." She takes a breath. "I really want you to meet him."

"Tara, are you sure . . ." I don't finish the question.

She turns me so we are facing each other. "Listen to me, baby brother. When you're in love, you'll do anything for it. You'll see. That's why people write songs about how mountains aren't high enough and rivers aren't deep enough to keep them from the person they love. It's so powerful."

"I know. I have a girlfriend," I say.

"Mom told me," she says. "Are you in love with her?"

The way she asks the question, I know that she knows the answer. Tara sees me, and maybe she always did. I let the question linger in the air. I lie next to my sister, thinking that I don't love Art either. If I did, I would do anything to be with him. I would climb mountains, swim rivers, risk disappointing my mother, jeopardize her new marriage, accept the possibility of catching a deadly disease. Maybe I'm not brave enough for love.

When I open my eyes, my sister sits cross-legged next to me, staring down at me. "So," she says, "the art in this house was cute."

"Yeah," I say.

"There's one piece of art in particular that I thought was adorable," she says. She looks at me with bulging eyes, her neck craning toward me like a chicken.

"Oh, I get it," I say. "We're speaking in code."

"Are we?" she asks. "Did you think the Art was cute? I think maybe you did."

I don't say yes. I don't say no. I just nod and stare at the ceiling, thinking there's room for more Madonna posters up there, then imagining that Art will crash through the ceiling like an angel, a messenger from a place where only he knows my name.

ART

I put flyers all over the school but not a single person shows up. They have the pink triangle on them, advertising the first lunchtime meeting of a new school club, our very own ACT UP affinity group. I don't know what I expected. I didn't expect crowds of lacrosse players to swarm through the doors, but a stray theater geek would've been nice, or a fashionista or two, or maybe even a supportive teacher. At least a few freshmen, sophomores, and juniors looking for something on their college applications that would make them appear more compassionate than they are. For our class, college applications are already in, so there's no reason for anyone to take on a new extracurricular activity unless they actually care about it, and I guess no one in the senior class other than me and Judy, who should be here by now, cares about the countless people dying in our very own city. But they're all just strolling down the hallway, acting all carefree and happy like there isn't a war raging outside these halls.

Jimmy once told me that AIDS is like war. Governments and powerful people don't give a shit because it's not their kids being sent to the war. It's not their kids dying. But I'm their kid, and I'm in this war. My classmates, however, are definitely not. They've all applied to colleges, and now they can relax, throw parties, experiment with drugs and alcohol, make out with random classmates they likely won't see again for the rest of their lives. They've probably all applied to a handful of top schools, a handful of mid-tier schools, and one or two safety schools. I didn't. I applied to two schools, Yale and Berkeley. One because I wanted to get my dad off my back. The other because it's in the city I dream of living in: San Francisco.

"I'm so sorry I'm late. I got caught in a conversation with Mr. Horney about my Jane Austen paper," Judy says, rushing in. She's wearing a metallic silver trench coat she designed herself over her uniform, with that stupid dead fish pin on it. Judy and Reza have worn those ridiculous pins ever since their first date, like some weird symbol of their union. As if they want to remind me that I'm not a part of their private little heterosexual world, in which they're blessed with Debbie Harry sightings and hand-holding and good-night kisses. "Is it over?" she asks.

"It never began," I say bitterly. "No one showed up."

"Seriously? I told Reza to show up." She looks

disappointed, but I can't tell if it's because nobody gives a shit about AIDS activism or because her boyfriend doesn't give a shit. Her BOYFRIEND. She's started calling him that.

"Well, he didn't," I say. "You don't need to turn him into one of us, you know. He can, like, not care about the things we care about."

Judy sits next to me. She places a hand on my knee and squeezes. "Do you think the school thought twice before hiring a teacher named Mr. Horney?"

I laugh. We've made fun of his name before, but it never stops being funny.

"Speaking of horniness," I say, "are you getting some?"

Judy blushes a little but doesn't take the bait. She tells me close to nothing about her and Reza. I don't know if he's a good kisser. Or if he's felt her up. Has she seen him naked? Because if she has, I want a description. "Okay, we're changing the subject," she says. "Tell me what you're taking pictures of lately."

I tell Judy about my photo project, how I want to photograph activists but make them look like old movie stars.

"I love it," Judy says, clapping her hands together in excitement. "Can I design clothes for them?"

"Obviously. Maybe it can be the first project of our school's ACT UP affinity group, which, as you can see, is a group of two."

"I'm in," Judy says, and we start planning the shoots. For a moment it's just me and Judy against the world again, and it feels great.

Then Darryl Lorde peeks his head into our room as he's walking by with some friends, including Saadi. Every single one of them wears a white baseball hat and a sneer, but Darryl's sneer seems extra cruel today. He's a sadistic asshole and he'll run the world someday, unless the rules of the world change. "Is this the fag meeting?" he asks.

"Yeah," I say. "But don't worry, closeted fags are welcome too."

"Oh, cool," he says. "I'll let your dad know if he hasn't moved to San Francisco yet."

"Wow," Judy says. "So much wit."

"You guys should be quarantined," Darryl says.

"Move along, Darryl," Judy says. "We're having an official meeting."

"You know you can't start an official school group without a faculty sponsor and at least five students," he says. "So stop plastering your propaganda all over the hallways, or the Young Republicans Club will have something to say about it. We have twelve members, you know."

"Ooh," I say. "You're bigger than a football team and just as dumb."

"We're not the ones who'll be dead next year."

He says this so coolly, so matter-of-fact, that it feels

like I've been punched in the gut. The fact that I could be dead next year doesn't even register as shocking to him in any way. It's just another insult to throw my way. If I were dying on the street, he'd make some popcorn, kick his feet up, and enjoy the show.

His friends all chuckle their deep-throated straight-dude chuckles. Like my death is a sitcom and they're its laugh track. Like the death of my mentors and fathers is funny. Saadi's laughter makes me feel sick, knowing that Reza has to share a home with him.

"Hey, here's an idea," Darryl says. "Maybe you should just kill yourself now, save your parents the hell of watching you grow lesions all over your face."

My blood boils. My fingers tense into a fist. Before I know it, I leap out of my seat and tackle Darryl to the ground, taking him down like I'm one of the gorgeous ladies of wrestling. "Go to hell, you fucking ASSHOLE!" I scream as he writhes below me, his scared, beefy body stronger than mine but unable to overpower the force of my rage.

"Get off me, fag!" he yells.

"Not until I give you AIDS," I say, and I spit on his face. I don't know why I say or do that. I know I don't have AIDS. I know that if I did, I couldn't give it to him by spitting on him. But right now, I want nothing more than to be able to give this prick and every homophobe out there this disease. They deserve it. THEY should be quarantined. Judy screams for me to stop, but I ignore her. I scream that I'll give him AIDS at least five more times.

"You're sick," he says as he finally finds the strength to push me off him.

My body rolls toward the wall, but I'm not done.

I swing a punch at his face—and miss.

Then I grab ahold of his leg and try to yank him toward me. "You're right. I'm sick with AIDS, and I'm gonna bite you and give it to you. Like a vampire." I flare my teeth and go for his bare ankle.

"Art, stop, please stop, you're scaring me!" Judy pleads.

I pull Darryl's foot toward my face. He pushes his leg up, kicking my chin hard in the process. My teeth hit my lips. My head doubles back, hits the wall with a thud. The camera swings to the left and smacks against the wall. My eyes flicker with the shock of pain.

When I open them, I see blood on my hand and on my shirt. We are surrounded by people now. Students. Teachers. Most of them look horrified. Annabel de la Roche and her friends look at me with pity in their eyes, which is even worse than horror. Nobody but Judy will stand anywhere near me. She holds me close, some of my blood on her fingernails, like polish. She keeps whispering *Oh my God, oh my God, oh my God*, and then manages an *Are you okay?* I pull my camera close. Remove the lens cap. The lens is cracked. I let out an audible gasp of sorrow. I would rather lose teeth than my camera. Judy whispers that a camera can be replaced. I know that, but

THIS camera can't be replaced.

"This is insane," Darryl says. "You don't . . . do you really have it? Do you have AIDS?"

"Fuck you," I say.

"That's not an answer," Saadi says. "Just tell him if you have it, dude."

"Go to hell, *dude*," I say, turning to Saadi. "We study together, you know me, and you just stand there while your sociopath of a friend . . ."

"Yeah, right, I'm the sociopath," Darryl says, cutting me off. "You're messed up."

Our principal, Mrs. Starr, approaches with a look of fear on her face. "What in the world happened here?" she asks. "Are you all right, Art?"

"He attacked me," Darryl says. "He jumped me and said he was going to give me AIDS."

"Is that true?" Mrs. Starr asks.

"It's true," Saadi says. "I saw the whole thing." Yeah, and he did nothing.

"Yup," I say to Mrs. Starr. "Every word is true."

"We'll discuss that after we take you to the nurse."

"I'm fine," I say. "It'll heal."

Mrs. Starr crouches close to me, but not too close. She won't come near my blood. I think about what a big deal it was when Princess Diana shook the hand of an AIDS patient without gloves. Seriously, this is the world we're living in. A world where people are afraid to shake hands with gay people.

"Art," she says, "you need to see the nurse."

"I was in the middle of the first meeting of my affinity group," I say. "And I plan to finish it."

"I saw the flyers," Mrs. Starr says. "That group isn't school sanctioned and therefore can't meet on school property. But if you want to start a sexual minorities alliance, I would sponsor it."

"Oh, would that make you feel more comfortable?" I ask.

"It would certainly have more members," she says.

"I'm a member of Art's affinity group," Judy says proudly, and I love her for it.

"I don't need numbers," I add. "I need passion. I need people to CARE that we're dying." I look at all the shocked students staring down at me, like I'm some zoo animal. They'd throw peanuts at me if they could. I scream out at them. "I'm starting an ACT UP affinity group at this school. We need to fight back and end AIDS, and show the world that young people in this country give a shit. Who's with me?"

Silence.

"Art, let's get out of here," Judy whispers. "They're not worth it."

It's when the crowds start to part, that I see him standing in the back, behind a group of kids. Reza. He looks shell-shocked, but he doesn't take his eyes off me. Or maybe he's looking at Judy. I don't know. But he doesn't move, and I want to shake him, make the person I know is underneath all that fear break free. I want to kiss him and kill him at the same time.

"Okay, clear out, everyone," Mrs. Starr says. "The show is over, and so is lunch. Get to your afternoon classes." As the crowd starts to disperse, she looks at me once more. "There is no ACT UP group at this school, Art. And you're looking at a lot of detention."

"Whatever," I say, having run out of eloquent things to say.

I watch as Darryl, Saadi, and their complicit buddies walk past Reza. "What are you staring at, ayatollah?" Darryl asks Reza as they pass him, and Reza says nothing, and Saadi says nothing.

Eventually, there's no one left but me and Judy, and Reza, who approaches us. He doesn't come too close, though, and this distance feels like a dagger being plunged into me.

"Are you guys okay?" Reza asks.

"Do I look okay?" I snap back.

"Jesus, Art, he's not the enemy," Judy says.

"Anyone who isn't a friend is an enemy," I say.

"I thought we were friends," Reza says.

"No, we were just saying that to make Judy feel better. But it's obvious we're not. You didn't show up to my meeting. You're too scared to come close to me right now. You stood there while your brother's buddy tried to kill me."

"He's not my brother," Reza says. "And I didn't come

to the meeting because I was . . ."

"Studying?" I ask.

He nods.

"You're always studying when Judy hangs out with me. You're always studying when we have movie nights. Not that I want you there. It's our thing. It's our tradition, like those fish pins are yours. You should never have been invited in the first place."

"Art, come on," Judy says.

"No, he's scared of me. Of us. Look at him. He's scared of getting too close." I grab Judy's hand and thrust it toward Reza. "Hey, your girlfriend has my blood on her fingers. You scared she has IT?"

"Art, stop!" Judy demands.

"Fine, I'll stop," I say. "I'm leaving."

"Leaving where?" she asks. "It's the middle of the day. We have class."

"What are they gonna do, expel me?" I know I sound like an ass, but I don't care. My wrath knows no boundaries right now. I want to lash out at everyone and everything that doesn't understand me, at everyone and everything that isn't queer, and yeah, maybe that even includes Judy. I want to erupt, to explode, and then to be reborn in a new world where I don't have to feel different every day, a world where our blood is immune to infection.

I exit the school into the cold air, and it hits my face like a slap. The pain is still there, and as I walk the streets,

I can feel people's eyes on me. I walk. And I walk. And I walk. To the only place where I might possibly feel at home right now.

When he opens the door, he's wearing one of his kimonos and he looks like he's been sleeping and sweating. The concern in his eyes softens my anger. His hand on my face makes me cry. "What happened?" he asks.

"I . . ." But I can't seem to get a word out. I just cry. He pulls me into his arms and closes the door behind us, and I sob onto his silk kimono, probably destroying it.

"Shh," he says. "It's okay." He strokes my hair. I can feel the clamminess of his hands on my skin—he has a fever. He smells metallic from all the medication he takes. "It'll all be okay," he says.

"How can you say that?" I ask. "José is dead. Everyone who's good in this world is dead or dying. The world is ending. Our world."

He doesn't say anything. He leads me to the couch and sits me down. He leaves for a moment, then returns with a warm, wet cloth and an ice pack. He holds the cloth to my face, carefully wiping the dried blood from my lips and my cheeks. Then he holds the ice to my lips. "You'll be okay," he says.

"Why am I so angry?" I ask. "What do I do with all this anger?"

"Not whatever you just did," he says. "What *did* you do?"

"I jumped a kid who called me a faggot at school," I say.

Stephen nods. He moves the ice to the other side of my face. It chills me and makes me feel better. "We need to be better than them," he says.

"Why?" I ask.

He shrugs. "Because we have no choice. We're held to different standards."

"He cracked my camera lens," I say.

"I can buy you a new lens," he says.

"No," I say. "No." I lift my camera. I point it at Stephen and manipulate it until his face is in focus. The crack in the lens shows up in the viewfinder, like a thunderbolt from above that cuts his face in half. It makes the image look like it was attacked. I snap a photo. "I'll keep it for now. I want to photograph you and your friends if you'll let me. I'll make you beautiful. But there will be a crack in each image, so everyone knows. So everyone remembers that we're under assault."

He smiles. Nods. He gets me.

"On one condition," he says.

"What?" I ask.

"No more beating people up, not even the worst homophobes."

"Deal," I say.

We shake on it. Then we put on *Cover Girl*, an old Rita Hayworth and Gene Kelly musical. Stephen says he needs something candy colored and optimistic, but he falls asleep almost as soon as the movie starts. His breathing is labored when he sleeps, like he's gasping for air. I watch the movie to the end. Rita plays a singer who performs in her boyfriend's nightclub. She gets discovered and almost chooses fame and money over love, but in the end she chooses love. I decide there's nothing optimistic about it. What's optimistic about other people falling in love?

JUDY

I know that dressing like Madonna won't make me look like her, or allow me to magically turn men on the way she does, but I decide that the time has come for me to inspire Reza to do something more than kiss me. Art's parents invited my parents to go see *City of Angels* tonight, which means Reza and I will have my place to ourselves. No mom offering him tea and talking to him about her fascination with Persian rug patterns. No dad asking him to play racquetball with him sometime, and telling him how proud he must be of his fellow Iranian Andre Agassi. No book club. Just a boyfriend and a girl-friend in an apartment free of parents. So that's why I'm making myself lingerie, inspired by the slip and garter Madonna wears in the "Express Yourself" video. If Reza likes her, then I'll turn into as close an approximation as I can manage. I can be sexy. I can writhe around the room wearing next to nothing, lick milk out a bowl like a kitty, do whatever it takes to turn him on. It's been two months now, and I'm ready. I'm ready to feel his skin against mine. I'm ready to put all those lessons about how to use a condom to use. I mean, what's the point of education if the knowledge is never implemented? I don't even eat ice cream as I design. I don't need it this time, since I'm basically copying an existing outfit in my size. All I need is skill, which I have, and a body, which I have. When I'm done, I try it on and stare at myself in the full-length mirror. I don't look like Madonna, but I look hot. And if I love myself, then others will love me too. That's what Uncle Stephen told me once.

I see my doorknob turn, my mom trying to shove her way in like she always does. "Sweetie, will you zip me up? Your father can't seem to make a zipper work. Why is this door locked?"

I quickly throw a sweater and jeans on over the lingerie and open the door. I force a smile. My mother is wearing her little black dress, the same one she wears anytime she goes somewhere nice. She says the beauty of the little black dress is that it can be worn anywhere and never goes out of style. I want to explain to her that when the little black dress first became popular, when Audrey Hepburn wore one, it was like a revolution. Back then, women were supposed to be all busty and curvy and frilly, and here came this skinny, boyish woman wearing sleek, simple clothing. She was a middle finger to the establishment. But then her style became the establishment, and now it's like all the moms of the world want to look and dress like her. I hope that when I become a designer, my creations never become the establishment. And if they ever do, I'll change. I'll reinvent.

"What were you doing in there?" she asks, peeking into my room for a clue, like I'd be stupid enough to leave one for her.

"Turn around. I'll zip you up."

She hesitates for a moment. She doesn't want to turn around yet. She wants to know why I would lock the door. But she turns, and I carefully zip her up. "Honestly," she says. "What is it about men and zippers and clasps? Your father still can't help me put on a necklace either."

"Hand me the necklace," I say.

She does. The necklace is gold, with a tiny little diamond dangling from it. Simple. Elegant. Classic. The clasp is small and tricky. You'd need a microscope to see it. My hands are behind her neck, and she pulls her hair up for me. There's something so painfully intimate about this, these rituals of ours. "This necklace belonged to my mother," she says softly. "She gave it to me for my thirtieth birthday."

"So she was capable of kindness back then," I say coldly.

"She's capable of kindness now," my mom says. "Just not toward Stephen."

"Are you defending her?" I ask.

"I am not," she says. "But I think it's important for

you to remember that we are complicated people. Who we are at our worst doesn't define us, just as who we are at our best . . ."

"She won't speak to her own son," I say.

"And she deserves our silence," she says. "But she also read to me every night when I was a little girl, and made us the most delicious birthday cakes every year, and took us on trips, and gave me this necklace."

"Yeah, well, I'm sure Ronald Reagan read to his kids too, but that doesn't mean I forgive him for killing all of Uncle Stephen's friends."

I finally clasp the necklace.

She turns to face me. "You know Reagan didn't literally kill them, right?"

"He could have stopped it."

"Maybe," she says.

"Definitely," I say.

"That's the thing about the past, sweetie," she says. "You can never go back and say a different outcome is definite." She lets out a sigh and shakes her body, like she's ridding herself of my bad energy. "So, how do I look?"

"Fine," I say. And then, because I know I need to be kinder but don't want to be fake, I say, "You look just like Audrey Hepburn."

She smiles. She loves hearing that. "We'll tell Art's parents you say hi."

My dad emerges now. He's wearing the same blue blazer, white shirt, and khakis he wears every time he goes out. Not exactly style icons, my parents. Yet I can't help but feel a twinge of affection for their consistency. "Nice of them to invite us," my dad says. "Such nice people."

"Kind of," I say. "Except they basically don't want Art to be gay."

"Sweetie," my mother says, "no parent *wants* their child to be gay. They should accept it, but don't ask them to *want* it."

"When I have kids, I *want* them to be gay," I say. "But I'll accept them if they're straight."

"You'll change your mind," she says. "You'll want grandkids."

"Major assumption there, Mom," I say. "Anyway, I'm sure Art's parents would never mention any of this to you at the theater. I'm sure they don't even tell people their son is gay, or that he just beat up a homophobe at school."

"Did he . . . Is he . . . You know, it's none of our business, and we're going to be late." My mother goes to the living room to grab her purse, then returns and gives me a peck on the cheek. "Are you seeing Reza tonight?" she asks.

"Yeah, he's on his way," I say.

"Have fun, and lights out by ten," my dad says, with a smile that indicates he knows how absurd he sounds.

My mom lingers after my dad leaves. There is something unfinished about our conversation. There's always something unfinished about us, like we're a sentence that ends in a comma.

"I don't want grandchildren too soon," she finally says.

"Gross and goodbye," I say.

"I'm assuming no girl who has helped her uncle distribute condoms would . . ."

"Mom!" I squeal. "Goodbye."

Seriously, how does she know tonight is the night? It's like she has some maternal sixth sense about me.

"Bye, sweetie." She gives me a hug this time, and I hug her back.

The twenty minutes it takes until Reza arrives feel like multiple lifetimes. Time has slowed down in our tiny apartment. And when he knocks on the door, time speeds up, going too fast.

"Hi," he says before giving me a quick kiss on the lips.

"Hi," I say, smiling nervously. "Come in."

I lead him into the kitchen, where we stand awkwardly. "Do you want something to drink?" I say.

"I'm okay," he says.

"Food?" I ask.

He shakes his head. "I have to tell you all about my sister," he says. "Her new boyfriend has named himself after a candy."

"Wait, let me guess," I say, excited to have found a little game to ease my own tension. "He goes by Pop Rocks." Reza shakes his head. "Fun Dip." He shakes his head again, laughing now. "Big League Chew! Bazooka! Ring Pop! Push Pop!"

Reza is cracking up now. "No, but these are so good. DJ Bazooka."

"Wait, he's a DJ?" I ask. "You left that detail out."

"Yes, and his name is DJ . . ."

I cut him off and practically scream, "DJ Gobstopper."

"DJ Starburst," he says.

"It's definitely catchy," I say. Then, with a flirtatious smile, I add, "Speaking of DJs, I just got the new Pat Benatar greatest hits record. Wanna go to my room and listen to it?"

"Sure," he says.

We head to my room, and I put the record on. We lie down, side by side on my small bed, our bodies crushed into each other, listening to Pat tell us that love is a battlefield, like we needed to be reminded.

We make it through side A of the record without doing anything but tongue-less kissing. I get up and turn the record around. Side B begins. We are shadows of the night now. The lights are dim. The city is dark, and I think of all the couples all around this city who must be making love right now. I feel empowered. I tell Reza that I have a surprise for him, then I remove my sweater. And my jeans. I stand before him, in my slip and garter, offering myself up to him.

"Oh wow," he says.

"You like it?" I ask, desperate for validation.

"You look just like Madonna in the 'Express Yourself' video," he says.

I smile. "That's the idea. I figured since you like her so much . . ."

"Wow," he says again, which I try hard to convince

myself is a good response. It's better than *gross* or *ew*. But my heart is sinking a little. I'm all too aware of everything he's not doing. Like pushing me down on the bed, passionately making out with me, ripping the slip off me.

I sit down on the edge of the bed. He lies next to me, looking sideways at me. Neither of us moves. "It's okay to . . . touch me," I say, my voice shaking now.

"Okay," he says, but he does nothing.

"Have you ever, you know . . ." I don't say more. Instead, I say, "It's my first time, too. I've never done anything with a boy except practice kissing with Art."

Shut up, Judy. No guy wants an image of you making out with your gay best friend.

"I mean, he doesn't count, though, since he's gay. You'll be my first."

"Okay," he says again, his voice dry and distant.

I feel like he's miles away from me, and I want desperately to pull him back into this moment. I take his hand and I place it on my waist. "Is that okay?"

"Yes," he says, but still his voice and his gaze are somewhere else. Somewhere far away. I wish I knew where so I could go there with him. All I want is to feel close to him, and instead I feel like we're floating away from each other, like we have no gravitational pull.

I move his hand up to my breasts. Art told me that men would go nuts for them someday, and this is that day. I'm ready for him to go nuts for them. He doesn't. His hand just sits on my left boob, limp. No heat in his touch, no electricity. I feel a void inside me growing bigger and deeper. I've never felt so desperate for anything. I would give up so much just to have him want me right now.

"I love your feet," I say. "I remember seeing them the first day we met, and thinking, those are perfect feet."

You sound like a lunatic, or like some kind of foot fetishist.

"And I also love your back," I say, stammering, trying to save this clearly botched attempt at sexiness. "Your skin is so . . . soft." I pause, and then, my voice shaky, I ask, "Which parts of my body do you like?"

He doesn't answer the question. He opens his mouth once to try, but no sound comes out. Maybe it's for the best. I don't think I want to hear what he has to say. And then he pulls his hand away. Covers his face with it in shame.

"Judy . . . ," he whispers from beneath his fingers, barely audible. "I can't do this."

"I'm sorry," I say quickly. "I'm so sorry. I pushed you too far. I'm sorry." I know how pathetic I sound. I know he's rejecting me, and I think I know why. But I want to keep him. I need to hold on to him as long as I can.

"Judy . . . ," he whispers again, and now he takes his hands off his face and holds mine with them. His eyes are welling, no tears yet, but the formation of them, like a looming threat of what's to come. "I am the one who is sorry."

"No, don't be sorry," I say. "Don't even say anything else. It's okay. I can wait!"

"I can't do this to you anymore," he says. His eyes are fuller now. A wave is coming to the surface of his face, about to explode.

"Let's just go watch a movie," I say, trying to escape this conversation.

"Judy," he whispers.

"What do you want to watch?" I interrupt him. I don't want him to utter another word. "My parents don't have a lot of options, but I think they have *Police Academy*. Have you seen it?"

"Judy, you know what I'm about to say," he says, with kindness that enrages me. If there's one thing I don't want from him right now, it's kindness. I want passionate, animalistic lust, or the promise of future passionate, animalistic lust. Instead, I get kindness, and worse, pity.

"I don't know, and I don't want to know," I say harshly.

"That night," he says. "That night I brought you the flowers . . ."

Now I'm thrown. "That night?" I ask.

"Art and me, we . . ." He trails off.

"Art?" I ask, my face tense, my hands shaking. "What does Art have to do with this?"

I catch a glimpse of myself in the mirror. I feel humiliated and alone. Art. And Reza. Did something happen between them? I was ready for something else, maybe, but not that.

"He gave me a flower," he says, choosing his words carefully. "And we . . . I can't explain it, but I think . . . I think I like men."

"Okay, back up," I say, annoyed now. "You like men . . . or you like . . . Art? Because one of those options is a lot worse than the other."

"I am so sorry," he says, with even more pity. "I love you, Judy."

Somehow hearing him say he loves me just makes it all so much worse. This hurts so much that I *want* to be angry, because at least anger will mask the pain I'm feeling. "You didn't answer the question," I snap. "If you're going to say something, then just say it."

"I like men, *and* I like Art," he says, like he's amazed he just said it out loud. "And I love you."

"Stop saying that!" I yell, pushing him away from me. I stand up, turn away from him. "You can't love me and do this to me. You don't get that privilege!"

I grab for my sweater, for the comfort of hiding behind fabric again. I was an idiot to think a guy who wasn't gay could like me. How could I have been so blind to all the signs right in front of me?

"You can go now," I say as I put my pants on, my fingers trembling.

"I feel horrible," he says earnestly. I know he means it, but I don't care.

"You should," I say coldly. "You should go rot in hell for what you did to me."

"I will," he says, anguished.

"Good, now that we agree, can you leave?" I say bitterly.

Pat Benatar is still singing, but I pick up the needle and turn the record player off. It's quiet now. Nothing in this room but his duplicity and my humiliation. He stands up and faces me. He doesn't say anything. He just looks me in the eyes, and tears flow down his cheeks. I turn my face into steel.

"Go," I whisper. I want him out before I start crying myself. He doesn't deserve my tears. What was I thinking dressing myself for him, when I've known all along that the only person anyone should dress for is themselves? How did I let myself lose so much of myself in him?

"I don't want to leave you," he says. "I want to be here with you. I want to be your friend."

"You're not my friend," I say icily. I want to hurt him like he hurt me.

"Okay," he says. "I will go." He doesn't move.

"Go, then," I say. "Why are you still here? Go!"

He opens his mouth to say something else but stops himself. He moves toward me, probably to give me a pity kiss, but I flinch.

"Reza, I don't want you here. Get out."

Finally, he leaves.

I want to throw on every outfit I have in my closet. I want to wear so many layers that the broken heart underneath the lingerie is deep below the weight of fabric, deep enough to lose all sensation.

I used to love being alone in this apartment. I would look forward to the rare night when both my parents were out, when I could blast any record I wanted and design anything my imagination dreamed up without interruption. But I'm not just alone anymore. I'm lonely too. I get the difference now.

I replay the last few months in my head, and it all makes sense now. All those awkward moments between them, between us. Art lied to me. His best friend. His parents are at the theater. He might be alone at home too.

Like a zombie, I head to the phone. I dial Art's number. Three rings. Ring, ring, ring.

"Hello?" he says.

I just breathe.

"Hello, who is this?" he says.

His voice. I knew that voice before it cracked, before it knew how to tell a lie.

Say something, Judy.

"Um, okay, bye," he says, and hangs up, leaving me with nothing but silence.

#63 High School

There may be no harder place to be queer than high school, a place of bullies and slurs, a place steeped in rituals of heterosexuality. Who's dating who? Who kissed who? Who will be homecoming king and queen? Who will be your prom date? And you have to play along, because if you don't, your difference has a spotlight on it.

I tried to play along. I took a girl to the prom. I kept my eyes on the locker room floors when other boys were changing. I talked about my crushes on the girls with the biggest breasts. Still they called me a fairy. Still they beat me up. Still they left notes in my locker that read "die, faggot." And still my dad asked me why I didn't just fight back.

But high school ends. Remember that, even when it feels eternal. And when it ends, there are places to go. The Village, Provincetown, San Francisco. Pockets of cities and towns where boys take boys to dances and dance their nights away, writhing their bodies against each other in a primal effort to shed all the trauma of their past. Places where girls settle down with girls, places where boys can dress like girls on the street and get high-fives instead of fists against their gorgeous faces. Maybe someday high school will change. Maybe someday there can be two homecoming queens, maybe someday girls can ask other girls to the prom, gay boys can enter locker rooms without fear. But if it doesn't, then just remember that high school ends. And that there is another life waiting for you, over the rainbow.

REZA

It's Sunday morning. *The* Sunday morning I have heard Art talk about with so much anticipation and excitement. The day of the church protest. It's freezing outside, so bitterly cold I think my eyelashes will freeze as Tara and I walk to meet DJ Starburst for an early breakfast.

Once we sit down, I can't stop staring at DJ Starburst. He's undeniably good-looking, and clearly enamored of my sister. But he doesn't look like he should be named after bright, gooey candy, with his long black hair, brooding eyes, and all-black clothing. At some point in the conversation, I have an idea that he should change his name—perhaps he could be a dark chocolate instead. Something like DJ Skor. But I don't suggest it. Instead, I listen as the two of them relive their courtship for me.

"I was on the dance floor when we met," Tara says, talking way too fast, like she's still drunk from the night before. She snuck out last night. She does that a lot, and no one but me notices. "The music was so good. I think it was a remix of Duran Duran singing "All She Wants Is" with some house beat behind it, and I was freaking out. I looked up at the DJ booth to see who the genius was."

"And the genius was me," Starburst says in his Italian accent. He speaks deliberately, each syllable oozing charm. I can see what she sees in him, but I wonder if what my mom says about women you have fun with and women you want to marry applies to men. I wonder if Starburst is a man you have fun with.

"I think I blew him a kiss," Tara says. "Did I blow you a kiss?" She looks at him coyly.

"You did. And it was like the strobe lights created a spotlight on you," Starburst says, oozing lust for her. Then, turning to me, he says, "Your sister's eyes were like lasers to my heart."

"Oh," I say. "That's so sweet." Also, a little weird, but I'm trying to keep an open mind.

"I knew right then I could love her," he continues.

"And I knew I could love him," Tara says.

He kisses her, she kisses back. Their tongues are sloppy and passionate, and they are probably tasting each other's breakfasts: eggs Benedict for him, blueberry pancakes for her with loads of syrup to sate her sweet tooth. I never kissed Judy like this. She probably wanted me to. I wonder what I would do if Starburst did to my sister what I did to Judy. Would I be able to forgive him?

"Obviously, I made my way up to the DJ booth to

make a request," Tara continues.

"She requested New Order," he says. "Which made me realize not only was she beautiful, but she also has taste."

"Then we basically made out for the rest of his set," Tara says, with no hint of shame.

I force a smile. "Great," I say, trying hard to act like I want to hear about my sister making out with a DJ all night.

And they don't stop there. He reminisces about their first dates, their shared dreams, her promise that she would move to New York to be with him. She shows me a ring he gave her on their second date, metal with a small skull on it. He shows me a tattoo on his lower back, her name written in Farsi script. She says she was going to get a tattoo of his name but chickened out, too afraid of the needles. I feel grateful for that. I can only imagine how our mother would react if she discovered a tattoo on Tara's skin. They make out again. I can taste their passion. It all seems so unbelievably fast. How can two people just look at each other through the glare of strobe lights and know they are in love? How can they be so sure? And if this is possible, is it possible for me?

"So?" Tara says, picking a blueberry out of her pancake and flinging it at my face.

"Ow," I say, but I pick the blueberry off the table and eat it. I have barely touched my own omelet, my appetite a distant memory since I broke Judy's heart.

"We need your advice, little brother," she says. "You're

the only person who knows all the players, and who isn't predisposed to hate me. It's time for me to tell the fam that I'm staying in New York and moving in with my man. How do we handle this delicately?"

Tara handles nothing delicately. Even if you gave her a feather, she would find a way to turn it into a weapon and stab you with it. "I don't know," I say. "Maybe go back to school first and . . ."

"No, that's not an option," Tara says curtly. "I'm staying in New York. I'm living with Massimo." Hearing her use his real name somehow makes their relationship, and their plans, a lot more serious.

"Do you . . . do you have enough money to live . . . in case they . . . ," I stammer, but I know they understand what I am saying. In college, Tara's life is taken care of. If she chooses to quit school, there is no guarantee.

"I make okay money as a DJ," Massimo says.

"But then you have to spend most of what you make on new records," she says to him.

"I'm not quite at the level where labels give me free records," he explains.

"But he will be," Tara says, beaming with pride. "And I can wait tables, or bartend. We'll be fine."

I nod, taking this in, imagining the look on my mother's face when she finds out my sister is going to quit school to become a bartender and live with a DJ.

"I'm trying to change, Zabber," she says to me. "I'm trying to handle this differently than the old Tara. The old me would've just blurted this out, probably after a few drinks, had a huge fight with Mom, put you in the middle of it. I don't want to be that person anymore. I just want to love who I want to love and be who I want to be."

It's all I want too. To love who I want to love. To be who I want to be.

"I know you understand," she says.

I know she does, too. She asked me that first night if I thought Art was cute, and I nodded. I did not say anything else, just a nod. But it was enough. And she only said one thing to me after I nodded. She said, "I always knew and I think it's great." That was enough too.

"I think you should tell Mommy first," I say, "and alone. Just you and her."

Tara looks over at Massimo apologetically, and after kissing her twice on the hand, he says, "It's okay. I don't need to be there."

"And then," I continue, "I think you should ask Mommy how she would choose to tell Abbas. You should make her part of the plan and the decision."

"Okay, that's good," Tara says pensively, like she's taking mental notes. "Thanks."

"Also, I think you should find a college in New York to transfer to before you—"

Tara bites her lip hard, then stops me. "I can't transfer to college here."

"Why?" I ask.

She bites her lip again. "I never showed up to class in Toronto," she says casually. "I just . . . it's not my thing."

"But Mom was paying!" I say, a little too strongly,

annoyed on behalf of my mother, who worked so hard to raise us before Abbas was in her life, who sacrificed the prime of her life for us.

"I didn't waste the money," she says. "I managed to get a refund . . ."

"Did you give it to Mom?" I ask.

"No, of course not—that's my money. If she was gonna spend it on college for me, then I can spend it however I want." She flares her nostrils at me, defiant. This is the old Tara. This is the kind of terrible decision she makes. "And it'll tide us over until I get a job here. It's not easy to get a job in the States without work papers."

"That's like stealing from her," I say.

Then I have a flash of me rummaging through Abbas's pants, taking money from his pockets, spending it on Madonna posters, records, magazines. I'm no better than her. I just know how to hide my wrongs better. At least she is open about who she truly is.

"We don't have to bring that up," Tara says dismissively. "I like your advice. I'll have a calm one-on-one with her, I'll make her part of the decision . . ."

"Whatever," I say, suddenly angry with her. Maybe she thought I'd appreciate being a part of her process or something, but it only makes me feel complicit. "And you know what, please stop making me a part of all your lies."

"Don't judge me for my secrets because you have your own," she says, flinging each word at me. "You're not exactly the poster boy for truth."

"*Amore, calmati*," Massimo whispers to her as he pulls her close to him.

She doesn't even speak Italian, but she smiles and whispers, "*Si, amore.*"

We sit in silence. Her words were daggers inside me, and the cuts are only now starting to truly hurt. I know she's right. My own life is one big lie I've shielded people from because I've been too afraid to hurt them. Maybe that's why Tara lies too. Maybe she's just afraid of hurting us. But then I remember all the screaming matches with our mom, that time she bleached her hair and destroyed the bathroom paint in the process, that time she had to have her stomach pumped, and when our mom caught her in her bedroom with a boy, or when Tara borrowed her favorite dress and burned the bottom of it. And now, love. *Love.* How can she love him? She's known him two weeks! I've known Art for two months now. I'm overtaken by a desire to kiss him the way my sister kisses Massimo. I want to scream at my sister and tell her that it's my turn now, my turn to make waves. If she tells our mom all this now, then I'll need to spend the rest of the year fixing her mess, smoothing the cracks she creates in our family, playing the role of a good boy I know I am not and that I'm sick of being. Maybe this is really why I'm angry. Because I want what she has.

"I'm sorry," I say, standing up. "I have to go."

"Zabber, I'm sorry," Tara says with genuine regret. "I'm so on edge. I didn't mean it the way it sounded. You know I support you no matter what."

"I know you do," I say, hating myself for lashing out at her.

"I just wish you supported me too," she says pointedly.

I'm reminded again that I want love, passion, life.

"I do support you, but I also have to go," I say. "I . . . I have somewhere to be."

What is Art doing right now? Is he already in the cathedral? Or is he getting ready for the big day, dressing himself up in fancy clothes?

"With Judy?" Tara asks.

I nod. I could tell Tara where I'm going, but I don't have the energy for that right now. I just want to be near Art.

"I thought you said you broke up," Tara says, suspicious.

"I'm sorry," I say. "I'll see you later." I begin to walk away, but some melodramatic impulse makes me turn around and add, "I have my own life to live, you know."

I don't know what has gotten into me. I don't know who the boy is who just said that to his sister. But I like him. He sounded a little bit like Madonna in *Desperately Seeking Susan*, defiant and edgy, a person no one messes with. This is the person I feel myself becoming as I walk the frigid streets of the city toward the cathedral. I don't even walk, I strut. I treat the city like my runway. I will myself to turn all my nerves into confidence, to release all the butterflies in my stomach into the cold city air, so that there will be only one butterfly left. Me.

As I get close to the cathedral, I can hear them. It

sounds like thousands of people, and when I turn a corner, I realize that it is. Maybe five thousand. All kinds of people. Young and old, men and women, from every background. They swarm like bees, screaming and chanting and singing and holding signs like *ACT UP Fights AIDS, Stop the Church, Keep Your Religion Out of My Body*, and *Thou Shalt Not Kill* over a photo of the cardinal.

Well-dressed newscasters are everywhere, with their hard hair and their hard smiles, trailed by cameramen, holding equipment, wires connecting back to trucks parked around the perimeter of the church. A man dressed like Jesus screams that he too wants to go to heaven. A group of women sing a song about their bodies belonging to them. A black drag queen in an evening gown and a large white hat raps on top of a box, rhyming *homosexual* with *indefensible*, and *Catholic* with *Sapphic*, and *AIDS* with *renegades*. This is nothing like the New York Stock Exchange. There were some spectators there, some media, but nowhere near this. I enter the crowd of people, and as soon as I do, I feel myself turning from butterfly into caterpillar again, longing for a cocoon. How will I find Art among all these people?

I push my way past crowds, making eye contact with person after person, their energy and passion transmitting into me, giving me strength. I was too young to remember much of the Iranian Revolution, too young to have gone out into the streets with my dad, who was a part of it. But I remember him describing the energy to me, and I remember driving by a protest. It felt like this. Crowds, chants, anger, passion. I close my eyes and take it in. For a moment, I'm seven years old again. My country is in the throes of chaos. My father is the chaos. My mother fears the chaos. My sister is becoming the chaos. I am in between, hoping for order, not realizing it will never come, at least not to this country. And soon enough my mother will choose to escape to a new life, while my father will be eaten alive by his own demons. I open my eyes again. I pray that the revolution for these people turns out better than my father's did. That unlike him, they live, and that unlike him, they create a better world.

"Hey," a man says to me. "I know you."

I blink my eyes. Do I know him? And then I remember. It's the man from the deli, the one in the fur coat, the one Art took a picture of. He's wearing the same coat now, and holding a sign that reads *Keep Calm and Rage On*.

"You're Art's friend, right?" he asks.

I didn't think he could get any thinner, but he has, in just two months. There is a lesion on his neck now, big and dark and purple.

"Hi," I finally say. "Yes, my name is Reza."

"Right," he says. "Reza. Isn't this magnificent? Listen to all these people. It's the sound of centuries of repression being beaten into the ground. It's the sound of change."

"Do you know where Art is?" I ask urgently.

"I think he wanted to be in the church," he says. "You know Art. He's got to be at the center of the action. Come on."

He gifts his sign to another protester, then takes my hand to lead me inside. I freeze when I notice another lesion on his palm. I feel its texture on me. I remind myself this isn't how you get infected, and I grip his hand so tight that the lesion disappears in our united palms. There's no purple anymore. Just my brown hand gripped into his black one.

"You know I've wanted to scream at churches since long before this disease," he says. "This is like a lifelong dream come true."

"What did you want to scream?" I ask as we get closer and closer to the church.

"Just a great big fuck-you for messing with my brain as a kid, for making me feel shame, for making my momma think she shouldn't love me for who I am." He takes a breath. "Of course, I wasn't Catholic, but it's all the same to me. I don't care if you're Baptist, Catholic, Protestant, Muslim, Jewish, or one of those adorable little Scientologists. If you *use God* to tell people *created by God* that they're sinners for who they love, then I give you a great big middle finger and I invite you to sit on it." He raises his free hand up into the sky and points his middle finger at the cathedral and screams a loud guttural scream, years of emotion coming out of his tired lungs. I notice a gold ring on his ring finger when he does this, and I remember the man who was with him at the deli, the man who isn't with him now. I hope he's just lost in the crowd.

We reach the entrance to the cathedral and step inside. Worshippers have gathered, seated quietly in pews, ignoring the sounds of protest outside. The cardinal enters, the mass begins. It all feels mundane and normal until a group of men and women walk to the center aisle and lie down in it, quietly. They just lie there, their arms over their hearts, like corpses, the visual symbolism of what they are doing obvious and powerful. It's a die-in.

Then I finally see him. Sitting in a pew. Taking photos of the men and women lying down in the nave.

Art. A winter hat on his head.

Art. His fingernails painted black, his camera covering his face.

Art. Taking a photograph of Judy's uncle, who is one of the men lying down like a corpse, pretending to be dead.

I imagine Art dead, and the thought fills me with dread, but instead of making me want to run away in fear, it just makes me want to make the most out of every second he and I have on this earth together.

The gaze of Art's camera restlessly darts from one end of the room to another until his lens points right at me.

"Reza?" he seems to whisper like a question, though maybe I imagine this.

I freeze. Art cocks his head, indicating I should join him, and I do. I quietly sit next to him.

"Hi," I whisper.

"Hey," he whispers back. "What are you doing here?"

"I don't know." I clasp my hands tight on my lap, look up to the ceiling, to the nave, and then to Art, and then to the faces of worshippers and back to him. His lip is still swollen from the fight at school, a hint of a bruise on his cheek. I want to kiss it, to heal it.

"Is Judy with you?" he asks.

I shake my head. "I came by myself. I was at breakfast with my sister, and I was walking home, and I . . . walked here instead."

Art nods. His eyes search mine.

"Does Judy know you're here?" he asks deliberately, like each word is its own question.

I don't answer. I feel too guilty about what I did to Judy. And what if Art's love for Judy overrides any feelings he ever felt for me? What if he hates me when he finds out I hurt her?

The mass continues, the cardinal speaks of God and duty and morality. The people in the pews nod and listen, listen and nod. They will not let their Sunday homily be disturbed by this protest. They go on with their rituals as if nothing unusual is happening, as if right now I did not just make one of the most important decisions of my life.

Art takes pictures. One click after another. And then he tries to change the film in his camera, but his hands are too frozen, and he struggles. He cups his hands in front of his mouth and blows into them.

"Here, let me try," I say, taking the film and the camera from his lap before realizing I have no idea how to work his fancy camera. "What do I do?"

"Just help warm up my hands," he says with a sly smile. "It'll be easier."

He moves his cupped hands toward me, and we both

blow into them. Our cold cheeks press against each other, creating immediate heat. Our breath seems to merge into one gust of steam. I don't feel cold at all anymore. I feel my temperature rising with each breath. After a few breaths, he pulls his hands away, grabs his camera, and changes the film. But his gaze is on me as he does it. It's amazing how he doesn't even have to look at the camera as he changes the film. It's second nature to him. I want him to love me like that. Like it's our nature.

I suddenly wish that I was religious. That, like my grandparents, I prayed five times a day. Because I have something to pray for now, something to believe in. I have faith in myself, in love. I would kneel more than five times a day to pledge my faith to whatever this is I'm feeling.

"YOU'RE KILLING US!" a man in the pews screams, standing up.

The church stirs. The activists lying down do not move.

The worshippers do not move.

Art stands up to photograph the screaming man. He pulls his hat off, revealing his hair has been dyed in streaks of pink.

"YOU'RE KILLING US. YOU'RE KILLING US," the man repeats. "STOP KILLING US."

Others join him. They scream about the church's policies on condoms, abortion, and needle exchange. They say the church is causing teenagers to get sick, women to get sick, men to die in shame. The chaos that existed outside the cathedral invades it now, swarming in, the floodgates open. People run, people push, and I hear Art's camera clicking and clicking, capturing it all from the pew, while at the front the cardinal hangs his head. They are like opposing forces, the cardinal and Art, standing at opposite ends of this space, at war.

"Art, get out of here," Judy's uncle says. He's standing up now. "Get out, go home before they make arrests."

"I'm not going anywhere," Art screams back.

Judy's uncle sees me. "Reza?" He speaks my name as a question too, just like Art did, but I don't feel like a question anymore. I feel like an answer now.

Art keeps taking pictures as the protest gets more heated. When the police swarm in, he looks up at me, takes my hand, and says, "Come on, let's go." His hand in mine, I can feel both of our heartbeats in our fingertips.

"Isn't this incredible?" he asks. "Don't you feel alive?"

"Art, go home now," Judy's uncle yells. "The police are everywhere."

Art leads me out the main entrance. When we taste the fresh air, he turns around and yells out at the church, "GO TO HELL!"

We try to get out of the chaos, but a video camera is pointed in our faces. A newscaster stands by the camera with a microphone. Art, unprovoked, grabs the microphone and speaks into the camera with ferocity. With his free hand, he tries to pull me close to him, but I squirm away.

"My name is Bartholomew Emerson Grant the Sixth,"

he says, pronouncing each syllable carefully. This is the first time I have ever heard him use his full name, and I know exactly why he does it. He wants to be sure that all the powerful people who recognize this name listen. He will use anything he has at his disposal to make change. "And I am here protesting the Catholic Church's policies, which are a direct attack on the lives of gay men and women, and all women. Cardinal O'Connor wants us dead. He wants us exterminated, and we won't go quietly. Fags and dykes are here to stay. We are holy and we deserve the same rights as everyone else." Art catches his breath, looks at the crowds around him. "We are on the right side of history," he says. "And we are going to survive to write that history. Wait and see."

The newscaster takes the microphone back and sticks it in my face. "And who are you and why are you here?" she asks.

The camera and the microphone feel like they are attacking me, shining a spotlight on my fears and cowardice. I had the courage to come here, but I am not Art. I am not ready to be seen on television, and more important, to be seen on television *by my mother*. I hide my face in my hands and turn away from the newscaster.

I am somewhere else now. I exist only inside my own anxiety, imagining what my mother will say if she finds out who I am. But the violence around me pulls me back to this moment. Protesters lie down in the road. Police arrest people. The chaos becomes louder, uglier, with screams of *Get down*, and *Pigs*, and *Where's your badge?*

The arrested do not resist. When the police get them, they go limp, like corpses.

Luckily, the newscaster has moved on, but I am still frozen in fear. I want Art to protect me, but he has his camera in front of his face. He documents the arrests until he sees Judy's uncle is one of the men being arrested.

"Stephen!" he yells, and runs toward him, and I run after Art.

Art yells at the police to let Stephen go. "He's sick. Just let him go."

I watch as Art puts a hand on one of the officers, attempting to pull him off Stephen. "Art, don't," I beg. "Stop."

I rush toward Art. And that's when I feel it. Something pulls us apart. Policemen. Two of them. One of them yanks Art away and handcuffs him. The other pushes me to the ground. My cheek hits the cold pavement hard. My heart beats so fast that I might have stopped breathing. All I see are our bodies, so many bodies on the ground like corpses. And the voices feel so distant. Stephen's voice. Art's. The police.

These are children, officers.

Get down and stay down.

They're just kids! They were trying to help me.

I'm seventeen. You make a habit of harassing seventeen-year-olds?

Shut up.

Reza. Reza, come back. Where are you taking him? Reza? Let him go!

Art, don't resist. Don't fight.

REZA!

I am standing again. The police have yanked me back up as fast as they took me down. I have no control over my body anymore. No control over my emotions. I feel fear but also excitement. Maybe even relief. Is my life over, or is it finally beginning?

"Reza!" Art yells as he is pulled away by one of the cops.

"Art!" I scream. "I came here for you."

"It'll be okay, Reza," he says. "They always release protesters. Don't resist. That's the most important thing, okay?"

I hold Art's gaze as long as I can, my eyes fixed on his. I wish I could read his expression.

When he's out of view, I close my eyes. I go limp, letting the police lead me. But the irony is, I have never felt more in control. This is not the Iranian Revolution. I'm not a kid who is afraid of his father, desperate to please his mother, living in the shadow of his sister. That is not me anymore.

I'm seventeen, and yes, I still have fear in me, but I have strength too.

I am the chaos now.

ART

I replay his words in my mind. I hear them ringing in my head as the police take me to the station. "Art, I came here for you." They echo inside me as I am released. "Art, I came here for you." Those words inhabit me. They fill a void in me I never knew existed until I heard them. What did he mean? Did he come to the protest because he was inspired by me? Or did he come because . . . I don't even let myself think it. I can't set myself up for disappointment.

The words still reverberate in my head when I leave the police station and go back into the winter freeze, where Stephen waits for me, leaning against a newspaper stand. "Hey," he says.

"Well, that was an adventure," I say with a smile, still giddy from Reza sitting next to me in that church, from the feeling of his hot breath in my hands.

"You okay?" He places his palm tenderly on my

cheek. The gesture immediately makes me think of how my own dad never touches me, never hugs me.

"Has Reza been released yet?" I ask.

He shakes his head. Stephen must catch the worry in my eyes, because he says, "He'll be okay. They always release us."

"He's not like us, though," I say. "He hasn't been through civil disobedience training. And he's not thick-skinned. I just . . ." What I want to say is that I want to protect Reza from all this. I want to go out and fight so that he won't need to.

Stephen looks at me and asks, "Art, where's Judy in all this?"

Judy. What about Judy? I hate myself right now. It's like all the shame I've worked to push below the surface has risen and multiplied and created a tsunami of self-loathing. I can feel her next to me, her hatred, her disappointment.

"I don't know," I say. "I don't know why Reza showed up. I don't know what happened between them."

"You haven't spoken to her?" Stephen asks, with just enough judgment to make me feel even guiltier.

"I haven't called her this weekend, but she hasn't called me either," I say, realizing how defensive I sound.

Then I hear Reza's voice. "You should go be with Judy," he says. I don't know if he's talking to me or to Stephen.

"Reza, are you okay?" I ask. I want to approach him, to hold him, but Stephen's presence stops me. All my feelings for Reza are a betrayal of Judy, and Stephen is a harsh reminder of that.

"I'm okay," he says, his voice shaky, his eyes welling. "I think I'm okay."

"Reza, what happened with Judy?" Stephen asks.

Now Reza's tears start to roll down his beautiful cheeks. "I told her I couldn't be with her. I told her everything. That I think I'm . . ." He stops for a long beat before he says the word, "gay." Then he takes a breath and adds, "And that there was something between me and Art." My heart swells hearing him say that out loud. Then my mind instantly goes to Judy.

I think back to last night, to that hang-up phone call I got. It was Judy, it must have been. She was calling to tell me off, and I deserved it. Fuck. I should have called her back. I should have checked in on her. We talk at least once a day. And I knew she had a date with Reza last night. Fuck.

"Oh my God," Stephen says. I search his eyes for what he's thinking. I can see him pulled between an impulse to be there for Reza, who had the courage to come out, and to lash out at Reza, for betraying his beloved Judy. "I'm sorry," Stephen says. "I have to go."

"Stephen, please!" I call after him as he walks away from us.

He doesn't look back at me, but he does stop. "It'll be okay, Art," he says. "But I have to go. Someone needs to be there for her." And he's off. Gone to support his niece, who I just royally screwed over. He's not my father, he's not even my uncle. He's hers. He doesn't belong to me in any way, and he's probably done with me now.

I'm alone with Reza. It's so cold out that barely anyone is walking on the street. It feels like it's just us in the world, or us against the world, because everyone seems to have turned on us. I wished for him, and now he's here with me. So why does it feel so bittersweet? "Art, I came here for you," I hear him say again, and I wish he would say it again right now. Wish he would remind me that I matter to him.

But instead he says, "I'm so scared, Art." He's shivering. Maybe from cold. Maybe from fear. Probably from both.

"I know," I say, taking his hands in mine. "But this won't even be on your record. As long as you don't get arrested again in the next six months, it'll be forgotten about." I try to sound as soothing and supportive as Stephen sounds when he reassures me, but I can hear the worry in my own voice.

"It's not that," Reza says. "It's . . . I was on the news. I thought . . ."

I'm such an idiot. He's not worried about the arrest, or about Judy. He's worried about his family. I can only imagine how upset they'll be, how much they'll hate me too. They'll blame me for corrupting their son, just like my parents blame Stephen. Ugh, why am I thinking about my role in this? Why am I making it about me?

I don't know what to say. If I tell him it'll be okay, it would be a lie. I know firsthand how cold and

239

unsupportive parents can be, how deeply their homophobia can cut. "I'm here for you," I say. I wish I could think of something better than that generic platitude, but it's all that comes to me.

"I wanted to see you. To be with you. I didn't think I would be on the news," he says quietly. "I didn't . . . I'm not ready to tell my mom."

"I know," I say. "I know. I get it."

He sobs, warm tears falling down his cold cheeks. "What if she won't look at me anymore? What if my stepfather doesn't want to stay married to her because of me?"

I take his hands in mine. I cup them and blow into them, warming him up. Do I see a small smile through his tears?

"I hate this," I say, shaking my head. "I hate that a moment that should be joyful is filled with so much anguish."

"I also feel joy," he says through tears.

Now we both laugh, because it's just so absurd, and because there's nothing else to do. I kiss his sweet hands, his slender fingers, and I hold his hand to my cheek. "I can be with you if you want, when you tell them."

He shakes his head. "No, that wouldn't feel right," he says. "I need to do this alone."

"Okay," I say. "I can walk you home."

"That would be nice," he says.

We walk home, side by side. "What was it like when you first told your parents?" he asks.

I want to lie, but I can't. He deserves my honesty. "It was horrible, Reza. But I got through it. And you will too. I can promise you that."

He nods somberly.

"And if they kick you out, we'll go somewhere together."

He laughs. "Like where?"

"Like San Francisco," I say, excited. "I've always wanted to move there anyway."

"Why?" he asks. "You're already in the greatest city in the world."

"Yeah, but San Francisco is the *gayest* city in the world," I counter. "It's a place where queers are the defining part of the city's identity. There are queers in New York, but no one thinks of New York as a place for queers. They think of it as a place for everyone. When someone wants to call you a fag, they don't tell you to go to New York, they tell you to go to San Francisco. That's what Darryl Lorde always used to say to me."

I hear Darryl's voice in my head.

Go to SAN FRANCISCO, fairy.

You belong in SAN FRANCISCO with flowers in your hair, faggot.

Why don't you just admit you're from SAN FRAN-CISCO?

"San Francisco," Reza repeats. "Maybe the two of us will go there someday."

"What do we have here anyway?" I ask. "My parents hate me. Judy and Stephen are pissed at us. If your family doesn't want you, we'll go. The two of us. Because I want you. Okay?"

He looks over to me with a sad smile. "I want you too," he says.

When we reach his apartment building, he holds me tight, like he's grasping on for life. "Can I call you after?" he asks.

"You can call me anytime," I say.

"Do you have any last words of advice?" he asks.

I want to think of something brilliant, something that will solve all his problems. Instead, I utter another generic platitude. "Just be yourself," I say.

He nods. Then, with sincerity that almost breaks me, he says, "I think this is the first day I've even come close to being myself."

Then he lets go of me and heads inside. The absence of his physical presence next to me makes me feel an unbearable emptiness. I miss him. I want him by my side always. As I walk home, I realize I have my own parents to face. It won't be easy. They'll have certainly heard I was on the news as well.

I steel myself for a fight as I enter our apartment. As expected, they're waiting for me. My father looks enraged. My mother looks like she's been crying.

"We made a deal," my father says as soon as I walk in, as if I've done something blasphemous. Deals are his religion, and breaking one must mean I'm even more of a sinner than he already thought I was.

"I know," I say. "I'm sorry. I just had to be there, Dad.

The cardinal is trying to . . ."

"This isn't about the cardinal, Art." My dad stands up now, probably to appear more threatening. "This is about you. You lied to me."

"To us," my mom says, her voice shaky. I wonder if they were fighting before I got here. I rarely hear them fight. It wouldn't be proper.

"No more money," my dad says. "Not a cent. You will never see that man again. You will go to Yale in the fall. You will major in business and intern at the firm in the summers. You are done humiliating me and this family."

Now I'm really pissed off. I tear my scarf and hat off and throw them on the couch dramatically. I take all the mixed-up emotions I'm feeling about Reza, Stephen, and Judy and unleash them on my dad. "Oh, because I can't go make money without you," I scream. "Because I have no talent. That's what you think of me. You don't even ask to see my photographs. Ever."

"Art, I've looked at your photos," my mom says, trying hard to keep the peace.

"Mom, the last time you asked to see my pictures was a year ago," I say. "And all you said is that they were nice."

"But they *were* nice," she says helplessly. "I liked them."

"They're not nice. I'm not nice, and I don't want to be nice. I'm angry, Mom. My photos are full of my anger."

"You wouldn't even have a camera if it weren't for my money," my dad says curtly.

"Why does it always come back to money for you?" I

ask, enraged. "I don't want your money. I want—I don't know, maybe your love and respect."

"Then earn them," my dad says.

"I shouldn't have to earn your love and respect," I say, incredulous. "I'm your son. That part should be unconditional."

I can feel my mom trembling. "Art, sweetie, we do love you. We do," she says.

"And by the way, Dad, the camera was a gift from Stephen," I say. "You don't even know that. You don't even know what he's given me."

"Given you?" my dad snaps.

"Yeah, he's given me a community," I say.

My dad shakes his head. "You're too young to have a community. At your age, all you have is a family."

"QUEERS!" I yell at him. "We're queers, Dad, and we have a community. We're there for each other."

"Is this because I didn't love you enough?" my mom asks, approaching me. She clutches onto my arm and whispers urgently. "Because I could love you more. I did my best, but I could do better. I could help you."

"Don't you get it, Mom? Loving me more won't make this go away. Loving me more would mean accepting me." My voice cracks. I hate that I still want their approval, will probably always want it. "That's the only way for you to love me more, Mom."

"We are doing this *because* we love you," my dad says. "I understand you don't see that now. But someday you will. And you'll thank us. And it's okay for you to think of us as the enemy right now. That's the job of parents sometimes."

"I have to get out of here," I say. "I feel so suffocated."

"You're grounded," my dad says sternly.

I laugh in his face. "I can't be grounded, Dad, because you don't control me. Life is short, and I'm going to live mine."

"Life is not short," my dad says. "It's longer than you think, and the things you do at your age have consequences. Getting arrested, not going to a great college, you'll see, all these decisions and moments add up."

I know they do. That's what I'm counting on.

And I also know about consequences of my actions. I don't regret the protests, or the arrest, and I don't regret being with Reza now. But I regret having lied to Judy. Today was, in a way, as close to perfection as I've ever had, but one thing was missing: Judy. I don't even know who I am without her friendship, and I need to go see her, to make her understand, to earn her forgiveness.

"I'll see you later," I say to my parents.

"Art," my mom yells out to me as I'm halfway out the door.

I turn around, exasperated, giving her my best *what is it?* look.

"Don't forget your scarf and hat," she says. "It'll be freezing out there at night."

"Let him freeze," my dad says. "Let him see there are

consequences to his choices."

My dad walks into their bedroom and slams the door. My mom grabs my scarf and hat from the couch. She gently places the hat on my head, then folds the scarf in half and loops it in the front the way she likes to. I suddenly feel like her little boy again, the one she would dress in cashmere scarfs. I remember the wonder she had back then, how often she would tell me how lucky we were. She was raised with so little, and now she had everything. She had me.

"Mom," I say, my voice barely audible.

"It's okay," she whispers haltingly. "You don't need to say anything. You and your father are both stubborn men."

"Mom, I think . . . I . . . I think I like a boy." I let out a sigh. I don't know why I open up to her, but I'm caught up in the moment. "And I think he likes me, too."

"Oh, Art," she says, backing away from me like I just slapped her in the face. I want her to hold me, ask me about him, *something*. Instead, she says, "I can't hear about this. Please. I can't."

I turn from her and leave. Why do I try? Why do I leave myself vulnerable to feeling this deep hurt? And is that exactly what I'm setting myself up for by walking to Judy's house now?

I could close my eyes and walk the path to Judy's house. I know every store on the way, every trash can, every flaw in the concrete of the sidewalks, every doorman.

I've walked this path countless times, each time knowing that at the end of the yellow brick road, Judy would be waiting for me with open arms. This time, each step is tentative, filled with unease, my feet taking a few extra seconds with each ascent and descent.

I knock on the door. She must recognize my knock by now. I recognize hers. She knocks in twos, a firm tap-tap each time. I always know when it's her. I can smell her when she's near me in the hallway. I swear I always know when it's her on the phone, like even the ring sounds different.

The door opens. Stephen answers it. "Art," he says. He looks me in the eye, and just that small gesture makes me feel a little better. Maybe he doesn't despise me. "It's good you came."

Judy stands behind him, in the arms of her parents.

"Hey," I say.

She shakes her head at me in disbelief, with the same look of disappointment that Cardinal O'Connor had when the protesters started screaming today, the same look my mom gave me when I told her I liked a boy. Except this time, I deserve the contempt. I deserve every single dagger her eyes throw at me. I didn't feel like a criminal when I was arrested, but I do now.

JUDY

I hate the way my body is shaking. I wish I could stop it. My mom and dad each have an arm around me, and I can feel their hands squeezing me, steadying me. I try to pinpoint what exactly I'm feeling. Is it anger, fear, sadness, or as is often the case on an SAT question, "all of the above"?

"Hey" is all he can think of to say.

"Hi" is all I can think of to say back.

All of the above. The answer is definitely "all of the above." I'm so pissed off at him, and so afraid of confronting him, and so sad that our friendship is over. My mind spins with possibilities of going to college somewhere he would never go, picking one of those liberal arts colleges in remote towns, surrounded by trees and sky and miles of open road, no city near us, no Art.

"Maybe the two of you should go for a walk," Stephen says.

"Sure," Art says. "Judy, I . . ." He doesn't finish the sentence. He can't. What can he possibly say to defend himself?

"You what?" I spit out. "You're sorry?"

"Well, yeah," he says, caught off guard.

"That's not enough," I say. "That'll never be enough." I've never heard my voice like this. It's harsh, rough, laced with bitterness that I didn't know I had in me.

"She's very upset," my mom says, stating the obvious. "Maybe you two should speak when things have cooled off."

"Things will never cool off," I say viciously.

"Of course they will," my mom says. "It's like that Joni Mitchell song . . ."

My mom is about to sing. She is seriously about to sing some old folk song. I bet it's the one about the seasons going 'round and 'round, or maybe it's the one about seeing clouds from different sides. I have no idea. All I know is that if she starts singing to me right now, I'll lose my mind, so I quickly blurt out, "A walk sounds good." I grab one of my father's winter coats from the coat rack and throw it on. It's brown and worn and ugly, and it's exactly what I want to wear right now. I want to disappear, crawl into someone else's skin.

Before we leave, my parents each hug me, and Stephen gives me a hug and a kiss on the cheek and whispers something to me. "Friendship is far more tragic than love. It lasts longer," he says. "Oscar Wilde said that." I don't respond. What is he trying to tell me? That I should be more upset about losing Art than I was about losing Reza? If that's his point, then it's so obvious. Reza may have been my first "boyfriend," a word I'll always put in quotation marks when using it to describe our fake relationship, but Art has been my best friend since forever ago. Obviously, losing my best friend is more tragic. But if Stephen's point by saying "it lasts longer" is that Art and I will somehow kiss and make up, then he's wrong. This friendship is over.

Nobody hugs Art before we leave, and he doesn't try. But before we go, my father stops Art by calling his name. "Judy has always been a great friend to you," my dad says sternly. "What you did to her was beneath you." I can feel the way those words sting Art. They're so simple, so direct, so true. My dad, a man of few words, but a man of words that actually matter. I don't know if I've ever loved him more than in this moment.

As we walk down the interminable stairs to get outside, we say nothing. Art walks in front of me, his legs moving both quickly and hesitantly, like he wants to get out of here and wants to turn back at the same time. I used to love following behind Art. I felt like he knew where he was going. He seemed to have all the confidence and charisma I lacked, the aura of a natural leader. Now I want to push him down the stairs and lead the way myself.

When we get outside, it starts to snow. The snow was timed for this exact moment. Gods and goddesses are crying frozen tears as they watch us. "Which direction should we go in?" Art says.

"Who cares?" I snap back.

He starts to walk north, and I stay alongside him. We walk in silence for a few steps, and then he says. "There's nothing like first snow, right?"

"Seriously, you wanna talk about the snow right now?" I ask, irritated.

"I guess it's like, I don't know if this'll make sense, but it's like us in a way. Like at first the snow falls and it's perfect, but inevitably it turns into slush, but then, maybe, the springtime comes and flowers bloom and things get better again and . . ."

"Oh, just stop it," I say.

"I'm only trying to . . ."

"Stop it!" I scream. I take a breath of cold air in and out, the steam escaping my mouth forming a little shield around me. "The seasons just happen, Art. This did not just *happen*. You didn't just lie to me and hit on my boyfriend by accident. You did it on purpose. Don't turn this into some natural thing between friends that will get better with time. It isn't, and it won't, and I guess we can just go home now, because there's no point in talking. What's the point? What's the point? What's the point?" I yell. I don't know why I keep repeating that. Maybe I wish he could answer it.

"You're right," he says, defeated.

"Great," I say. I throw up my hands and realize I forgot gloves, and that my fingers are a little frozen. "What's the cliché, I'd rather be happy than right?"

"Something like that," he says. "But I'm not happy, Judy. I can't be happy without you. You're my best friend, and I messed up."

"Royally," I say.

"I feel so awful, Judy," he says, and I can feel the guilt and remorse in his voice. "I've been feeling bad about it since the moment I realized I had feelings for Reza. I'm wrong, and I'm an asshole, and I'm so, so sorry."

I don't want his guilt or his remorse. I don't want apologies. I want to understand how he could do this to me. "I just don't get it," I say, softening a little. "How could you like a guy and not tell me?"

"Because you liked him too," he says sadly. Then he stops walking. "No," he says. "That's not true. It's so much more than that. You've had crushes before, Judy. But I never have. There's never been a guy at our school that I *could* have a crush on without fearing he'd beat me up. I don't know how to have a crush. I don't know how to talk about it. Everything I was feeling was wrapped in fear and shame, and then this added layer of you, my best friend, liking him, and then dating him. I didn't know what to do."

I start to walk again, and now it's him who follows me. "You could've told me," I say. "You could've been honest."

"You don't understand," he says, and now it's *his* voice that's laced with bitterness.

"Then make me understand," I say, challenging him.

He looks over at me. He no longer looks apologetic. Now he looks angry. "We aren't two girlfriends fighting over the guy they both like, Judy. I'm gay. I'm not like you. I can't just have crushes. I can't take a guy I like to school dances. I can't even contemplate dating without thinking of death and being disowned by my parents. None of that applies to you. I know we're best friends, and I know we've always done everything together, and been there for each other, and maybe when we were younger, it felt like there was no difference between us. But there's a huge difference. All that time that we were growing up together, I was dealing with these feelings of being different, ashamed, thinking I was wrong and gross and . . ."

"I know all that," I say. "But you always seemed so confident."

"Whatever confidence I had was my attempt to mask everything underneath it. God, Judy, how do you think it feels to have your dad tell you that gay men deserve to die, that AIDS killing us off is a good thing? Your parents love you, they encourage you, you get annoyed with them because they're too nice to you sometimes. My parents want me dead."

"That's not true," I argue. But I know in a way it is. They don't want Art dead, but they want him to be a different person than the one he is, and maybe that's the same thing.

"I never thought I'd have this, Judy," he says sincerely. "I never thought I'd get to have a boyfriend. Maybe I didn't tell you because I wasn't prepared for it, because nowhere in my imagination did I practice the scene of talking about my crush, or of having a relationship, or of having sex even . . ."

"Wait," I say, realizing he just mentioned having sex. "Have you and Reza had . . ."

"NO!" he screams. "God, nothing has even happened. Nothing physical. But I just, I guess, I don't know, I'm so sorry, Judy, I really am, but I just want you to see it from my side, to try to understand how hard it's been for me, and not just this situation, but everything that has to do with love and sex. Maybe I messed it all up, and maybe it's too much to ask right now, but I want . . . I guess I just want you to be happy for me, because it all feels empty without that."

I always wanted this moment. For Art to find a guy. But why did it have to be the one guy I wanted? "Yeah, that's definitely too much to ask," I say, hating myself for rejecting him. But I have to. It just feels like the distance between us is too wide now.

"I know," he says, despondent. "I know."

"It's not like I've had a boyfriend before. He was the first. Why him?" I look away from Art, avoiding his gaze.

"I don't know," he says. "I didn't plan any of this, Judy."

We walk in silence again for a bit. For a moment, he almost had me sympathizing with him. But then I realize what he's done. He apologized, but the apology was trumped by how sorry I am meant to feel for him because he's gay. And that pisses me off even more, because no one in the world has given him more support and sympathy than me. Well, maybe Uncle Stephen, but Art wouldn't even know Uncle Stephen if it weren't for me. I am the victim here. I'm the one who's been wronged.

I must shake my head or something, because he says, "What? Just tell me what you feel, Judy."

"It's *always* about you," I say, exasperated.

"I didn't mean to make it about me," he says. "I swear."

"No, but it's what you did, and it's what you always do," I realize how much time I've spent catering to Art's needs. "And I don't care what else you have to say. Your actions have spoken for you. You're self-centered, and you've always had the world served to you on a platter and you're upset when that's not the case. You want to talk about how we're different?" I start to walk faster— the cold air doesn't even feel cold anymore because my body feels like there's a fire inside me that is raging. "How about we talk about how you're filthy rich and my parents barely make ends meet? How about we talk about the fact that the nicest things we have are all presents from your parents? How about we talk about how I need a scholarship to get into college, but you can waltz into Yale? Yale! You can literally get arrested and still get into an Ivy League with your money. And you're a man, so gay or not, you've got that."

"What does this have to do with me and Reza?" he asks desperately.

"This is not about you and Reza," I say. "And it's not about me and Reza." That's when it hits me how little I've thought about Reza today, and how much I've thought about Art. This is my real heartbreak. "Are you an idiot?" I ask. "This is about me and you."

He stops again. I don't want to stop walking. I'm on a roll. I'm saying things I never even knew I felt.

His lips tremble a little, and then, in a defensive whisper, he says, "I don't know what to say. I don't know how to apologize for my parents' wealth or my gender."

"And I don't know how to apologize for my heterosexuality," I snap back.

We're at an impasse now. We've both said what we never dared admit aloud before.

I start walking again, but toward home this time.

"Judy, please," he begs as we walk. "I know we can make this right. I know we can figure it out."

"No." I hold my hand up.

"This will suck without you," he says. "All of it. Our last few months of high school, me and Reza . . . what about Sunday movie nights?"

"What about them?" I say, being intentionally cruel.

"Stephen loves them as much as we do." He's desperate now, grasping at straws.

"Don't use my dying uncle to get forgiveness that you don't deserve," I say. "Stephen has lost over a hundred friends. I think he can handle the grief of not having us both at Sunday movie nights."

"You're still going to go?" he asks, incredulous.

"He's *my* uncle," I spit out. "I'll do whatever he wants me to do, and he'll do what I ask him to."

Stop now, Judy.

"Please don't . . . please don't make him stop seeing me," he says. I can see tears forming in his eyes. They fall down his cheeks. It's like the thought of losing Uncle Stephen is more devastating to him than the thought of losing me, and this reminds me of all those times I wondered whether Art would've liked me as much as he did if I didn't have a gay uncle he looked up to. These tears give me my answer. I guess I always knew it, though. I just looked the other way, like I did with so many things when it came to Art.

We reach my apartment building. We face each other. His tears stop. His cheeks are moist, and his eyes are gauzy.

"Goodbye, Art," I say. It sounds final.

"You'll still see me, you know," he says. "In the hallways. In class. Let's be civil, at least."

"Goodbye, Art," I say again.

He fixes his stare on me and tries one final plea. "I know there's a version of this where I say I'll give him up, but I can't do that. I care about him too much. If you were a real friend, you would understand."

"Guess we're not real friends then," I say. Just saying those words brings tears to my eyes. I don't want him to see me cry, so I turn away from him.

"Guess not," he says, his voice full of sorrow.

"Goodbye, Art," I say for the final time.

I can hear his voice breaking as he says, "I love you and I always will."

They're all gathered in the living room when I get home. I sit next to Uncle Stephen, who asks how it went.

"Can we not talk about it?" I ask. I suddenly feel exhausted.

I can tell my mom is disappointed, that she very much wants to talk about it, but Uncle Stephen quickly says, "Of course. We can never talk about it if that's what you want."

My mother gives me a look that at once tells me she supports and loves me. Then she says, "Sweetie, we were talking . . ."

Uh-oh, a sweetie sentence.

"Let's let Stephen share the news," my dad says.

News? I've been gone for like thirty minutes, and already there's news that needs to be shared. I brace myself.

Stephen turns to face me. "Christmas is coming up," he says. "You know how José loved the holiday season. He was such a goofball when it came to stockings and Christmas carols and all that stuff, and I loved it of course, and your mother doesn't want me to be alone for the holidays, and this could be my last Christmas . . ."

"Oh God," I say, and it's like all the sadness that was hiding under the anger comes out in a rush. Tears, so many of them, flowing down my face.

"No, no, this is good news!" my mom says, hugging me. "It's happy news."

"The nice thing about dying is that you can spend whatever you have," Stephen says. "And of course I was always planning on leaving the little I have left to you and to ACT UP, but before I go, I thought I could take us all on a holiday, a proper vacation. I think, maybe, that's the best possible way to spend the money."

"And we decided," my mom says with a big smile, "that you should pick the destination, Judy. It's your last holiday as a child, and we want you to choose."

"Anywhere in the world," Stephen says.

I don't know what to say. I'm processing all this. This isn't who we are. We are not the Grants, who jet off to foreign lands like they're just another borough of New York. And Stephen is sick. "Is it safe, I mean, for you to be away from your doctors?"

"I don't care anymore," Stephen says. "I want to do something special with the people I love most. The only thing you need to concern yourself with is where we go. Be creative. Japan. Hawaii. London. Italy. We could do a cruise!"

Where do we go? I'm not there yet. They're asking me to accept that Stephen is dying. I know he's not. I know something is going to change. A new medicine. A cure. And then I have a thought that I hate, a feeling of guilt, because I know that if I say yes, I'll be taking Stephen away from Art when he needs him most.

"I can't . . . ," I say.

"You can and you will," Stephen says. "And if not, I'll choose for you."

My mom gets up and sits on the other side of me. She holds my hand. "You've always wanted to go to Paris, haven't you?" she asks. "You used to talk about it as a little girl. Remember how I used to read you *Eloise in Paris*. That was your favorite."

An image comes to me, of myself as a young girl, my mother reading that book to me. God, I want to be small again. I want things to be uncomplicated. "Of course," I say. "I mean, the fashion . . ."

"I know a few queens who work in fashion," Stephen says. "Maybe we could get tours of the couture houses."

"But is this what you guys want?" I ask. "Maybe we should just go to a beach, and you guys can relax and read or something."

"Sweetie," my mom says, "this is about what you want. The only thing we care about is being together and making you happy. We are the people who love you most." God, that hurts, because before today, Art would be among those people, and now he's not. He's so not.

I think of Paris. Black-and-white pictures of stylish people on the banks of the Seine. The sound of Edith Piaf's voice coming from Stephen's stereo. Runway shows. Gaultier. Coco Chanel. Givenchy. "Okay, *oui*," I say, finally smiling. "Let's go to Paris."

REZA

The last words Art said to me were "just be yourself," as if that were something I knew how to do. I was telling him the truth when I said today was the closest I felt to being myself, but as I take the elevator up to a home that still doesn't feel like mine, I'm overtaken by panic.

I don't know who I am, and I can't pretend to. I like men, but that doesn't mean I'm like all other men who like men, does it? I watch as the elevator floors light up, one after another, until I reach our floor. I'm sweating now, between my nerves and the heat pumping through the building's vents—I'm turning into a fountain. I pause outside the door. I consider turning back. Fleeing. Maybe Art and I should escape like he suggested. San Francisco. It's not somewhere I've ever thought about going, but maybe it's where I belong.

I take a breath, put my key in the lock, and slowly open the door. I tiptoe into the foyer. I can hear them in the living room. All of them. My mom. Abbas. Tara. Saadi. They're arguing loudly. I steel myself for what they must be saying about me. But as I creep closer, I realize they're not talking about me at all.

"Well, I'm sorry, I think it's messed up that no one knows she's Armenian," Tara says.

"Why does it matter where she's from?" my mother asks.

"It just does," Tara says.

"She doesn't hide it," Abbas says. "In fact, I met her at a charity event once, and we discussed how some Iranians have names that end with -ian just like Armenians."

"I'm not saying she hides it," Tara says. "I'm just saying most people don't know. I mean, her name is Cher Sarkisian. Imagine if all the little Armenian girls knew that, if all the little Iranian girls knew that. She's brown."

"We're not brown," Saadi speaks up. "We're Caucasian."

"Right—keep believing that," Tara snorts.

"Officially, it's true," Saadi says. "Check the census."

"Yeah, well, we're not treated like white people," Tara says passionately. "Look around, guys, people hate us. We're enemy number one these days. The revolution. The hostage crisis. The whole Western world hates us so much that it let Saddam Hussein use chemical weapons on us and did nothing."

"That wasn't on us," Saadi says. "That was on the people who are still in Iran. We left."

"Wow," Tara says. "Wow."

"Tara, please," my mom says. I can't see her, but I can feel my mom begging Tara's silence with a pleading gaze.

"It's okay, Mina," Abbas says. "This is great. These are issues our kids should learn to debate intelligently."

"I just . . . I'm worried about Reza," my mom says, and her voice suddenly chokes up. "Where is he?"

Hearing her sound so fragile makes me want to go immediately to her. I walk into the living room, and they all turn to look at me. There is still so much I don't know. Have they seen the news? Do they know what I am? Has Tara told them she's moving in with Massimo? "Hi," I say cautiously.

The long silence before anyone says anything makes me sure they've seen the news. They must have.

"Tara. Saadi. Why don't you guys go pick up some food for us?" Abbas suggests.

"And miss this?" Saadi says.

Abbas immediately shuts Saadi down with a hard stare. Saadi gets up, glaring at me as he passes me by.

Then Tara gets up and follows Saadi out. But before she leaves, she hugs me and whispers, "I'm proud of you, Zabber."

"I . . . ," I whisper. I want to whisper that I'm thankful for her. That I'm proud of her too. But I say nothing.

And then they're gone. And I'm alone in the room with my mother and Abbas, who holds her hand tight. She won't look at me. I wish she would. I want her to hug me and say she's proud of me like Tara just did.

"Reza, do you want to sit down?" Abbas asks calmly.

"Not really," I say, nervous.

"Do you want to take your coat off at least?" Abbas suggests. "You look warm."

I put a hand on my forehead, wiping the sweat away. I pull my coat off and place it on an armchair. Then I take my hat and scarf off. I still don't sit. I want to make running away from here as easy as possible.

"Reza *jan*, is there something you'd like to tell us?" Abbas asks, his tone so mild you would think he was asking me what kind of tea I would like.

"Mommy," I say. "I . . ."

I have every intention of finishing the sentence. But then my mom finally looks up at me, and her misty eyes make me break down in tears. And I can't speak. Words won't come to me. All I can do is cry.

My mom wipes away her own tears, takes a breath, and speaks. "Reza, I know you," she says, pleadingly.

How can she know me when I don't know myself?

"I know who you are deep down," she continues. "You're not like these other men. Maybe you think you are. Maybe it's a phase."

"But I've felt this way for so long," I say, words suddenly tumbling out of me. "I've always liked boys. Even before I knew what it meant."

"No," she says. "You're confused. You didn't have a consistent father. Now you do. You'll see. You'll change."

"I don't know if I can," I say. What I don't say is that I don't know if I want to. Because changing would mean never touching Art again.

"Of course you can," she says supportively. She believes I can do anything, even change this part of myself. "There were men in Iran who went through phases. We all knew they did. But they were married. They had children. It was just something they did on the side."

"We're not in Iran," I say. I don't want Art to be something I do on the side. And I don't want to marry someone like Judy and lie to her, or have children who don't know who I am and how I love.

"Could we . . . could we not tell anyone else?" she asks.

"I think everyone else knows," I say, trying not to snap at her. "I think it's obvious to everyone but you because you don't want to believe it."

She lets out a loud sob when I say that, and Abbas puts an arm around her. He doesn't say anything, though. He just holds her.

"How could I not see it?" she asks quietly, like she's talking to herself. "How could I not know my own son is like this?"

Like this. I'm *like this.* It suddenly hits me that there is no word for gay in our language. No word for coming out. In the language my mother speaks, I literally don't exist.

"I'm sorry," I say. "I'm so sorry. I hate hurting you." I sit next to her, and she instinctively grabs ahold of me and clutches me tight. "I'm sorry," I keep whispering as I rest a head on her shoulder.

I hate that I'm the one apologizing. I'm the child, she's

the parent. Her responsibility is to me, not the other way around.

We hug for what seems like an eternity. Then she pulls away and composes herself. "What happens now?" she asks.

"I don't know," I say honestly.

She looks to Abbas, like he's going to have all the answers.

"We'll take it a day at a time," he says, nodding slowly. "The most important thing is that you stay safe. Reza, do you understand what I'm saying?"

"I do," I say, embarrassed to be discussing this in front of my mother. If only they knew how safe I was.

"You and Bartholomew Grant's boy . . . are you . . ." Abbas trails off, concerned about my mother's ability to hear any more.

I nod.

My mom lets out a breath and shakes her head. "How could I not see it?" she whispers. Then, through tears, "My God, have you . . . are you . . ."

She doesn't say any more. She breaks down crying, and Abbas holds her in his arms, guides her head to his shoulder. He whispers to her that it's okay and strokes her hair.

I feel like a ghost. Like I'm not in the room anymore. They don't look at me or talk to me. I don't get it. I'm the one who just came out to them. I'm the one who is broken up inside. Why am I not the one being comforted? Why is no one telling me it's okay? Suddenly, I feel sick to my stomach, like I'm going to vomit. I rush away.

"Reza," my mother barely croaks out as I'm almost out of her view.

I turn around, the whole room spinning from my nausea.

"Reza, give me time," she says. "Please don't tell anyone else."

"I . . ." I want to tell her that the whole point of my coming out to her is that I can't hide anymore. The hiding is what was destroying me. And she's asking me to hide again. I do not say a word of that, though, because I need a toilet. I run to my bathroom and kneel in front of the toilet. I try to vomit, but nothing comes out. The room spins. I want my insides to be emptied of everything. No more family, no more shame, no more past.

I lay my head down on the toilet seat and close my eyes, thinking maybe my mother will have a change of heart and come to comfort me. But the next thing I feel is a hand on my shoulder, and my sister's voice is gently whispering, "Zabber. Are you okay?" I open my eyes. "I doubt you're hungry right now, but I saved some sesame chicken for you."

"I can't eat," I say, my voice sad and distant. "I feel sick."

"I'll just leave it here then," she says, placing the container near the sink. Then she sits next to me and rests her head on the other side of the toilet seat, an act of solidarity that almost makes me cry again.

"Did you talk to Mommy?" I ask, afraid of the response.

"No," she says, like this answer should have been obvious. "I came right to you. Anyway, you know she'll pretend nothing happened unless you push her again. That's what she does. Deny, deny, deny. It's the Persian way, little brother."

I manage to laugh. I didn't think that was possible anymore.

"Why do you think I'm always acting out?" she asks. Then, answering her own question, "Because I just want her to see me. To acknowledge me. You know?"

I raise my head up now. "I see you," I say. "And since I don't think I've ever said it, you're . . . amazing."

"Thank you, little brother," she says, a sad smile on her face. "But it's not about me right now. I mean, it's always a little about me, but we don't have to focus on that right this moment."

"Did you always know?" I ask, truly curious. "That I was, you know . . ."

"Gay?" she says defiantly. "It's okay to use the word, you know." She takes a deep breath, then adds, "Yeah, I always knew."

And yet she never made fun of me. Never threw it in my face. Never forced my hand before I was ready to come out on my own. All this time, I've resented my sister and protected my mother, taking my mom's side. How could I not see that my true ally was Tara?

I feel sick again, and this time I vomit. The smell of it

fills the room. Tara immediately springs into action. She flushes the toilet, wipes my mouth, pours me a glass of water from the sink, and gently places it to my lips.

"Tara," I whisper, my lips trembling, "do you think I'm sick?"

She flips her hair, gives me a wry smile. "You just barfed, so yeah, I think maybe you're a little sick."

"You know what I meant," I say, taking her hand in mine.

"Yeah, I know." She sighs. "Of course I don't think you're sick. I think you're smart. Anyone on this earth who doesn't love hot men is an idiot, as far as I'm concerned."

She manages to make me laugh again. "But if everyone loved hot men," I say, "then no one would love you."

"A valid point," she says, laughing too now.

"So, um, did you tell them about, you know, Massimo and school and . . ." I trail off.

She shakes her head. "I was going to," she says. "And then we saw you on the news, and I knew it wasn't the right time. I'll get there, but thanks for making it a little harder for me."

"Sorry," I say, shrugging my shoulders. I seem to be making life harder for everyone I love these days.

"Guess I know what it feels like now," she says. "Thinking you need to keep the peace 'cause your sibling is rocking the boat so hard."

I look at her and nod.

Then she stands up and gives me her hand. "Come

on," she says. "Let's get out of here."

"Where are we going?" I ask.

"You tell me where Art lives," she says with a radiant smile, "and I'll tell you where we're going."

I let her guide me up and then out of the bathroom. As we make our way to the front door, we see my mom, Abbas, and Saadi eating Chinese food in the dining room. "Are you joining us?" Abbas says.

"We're going out for a walk," Tara tells them. She's holding the container of sesame chicken and places it on the table in front of them.

"We'll keep some food for you both," my mom says with a sad smile.

"Thanks," I say.

There it is. Denial. We're all denying everything that just happened. Only Saadi's hateful glare reminds me of what I just did.

My sister leads me out into the cold, and I lead her toward Art's building. She asks the doorman to tell Art we're here to see him, and the doorman tells us Art left recently. So we sit on the stoop and wait. And then I see him. I would recognize that walk from miles away. The swinging hands. The frenetic legs, like they're always in a rush to get to the next destination.

"Oh my God, Reza," he says, when he sees me. "How did it go? Did you . . . Did they . . ."

"Can we not talk about it?" I ask desperately.

Tara stands up. She gives Art a quick hug, then says, "Okay, I think I'm gonna go see my own secret man now."

"Have fun," Art says. His voice is shaky. I can tell he hasn't had an easy time of it either. I wonder if he was with Judy. I am almost sure he was.

Before leaving, Tara takes my hands, pulls me up, and hugs me tight. "Don't let them stop you from enjoying this fine-ass guy," she whispers.

And then she leaves. And Art and I are alone.

"Where were you?" I ask.

"Can we not talk about it?" he responds.

We stand in front of each other. I won't talk about what happened with my mom. He won't talk about what happened with Judy. I glance to my side, aware of the doorman watching us. "Can we go somewhere?" I ask. "Somewhere happy."

"Where do you want to go?" he asks. "I'll take you anywhere."

"San Francisco," I say, joking. "The gayest place on earth."

He laughs. "A slightly impractical choice," he says. "Though it can be arranged after graduation." Then his eyes light up. "Wait, I know exactly where we're going," he says.

He takes my gloved hand in his, which feels awkward. Almost instinctively, we both take our gloves off and hold each other's hands. Who needs gloves when you've got the heat of passion anyway? The doorman's eyebrows rise when he sees our hands clutch each other, but at the moment, I don't care. Let him stare. Let Art's parents reject him. Let my mom deny me. Right now, all that matters is my skin against his.

He leads me south, then west, until I hear the hum of crowds and the twinkling sound of Christmas music. And then we turn a corner, and I see it. The Rockefeller Center Christmas tree. It's so tall, so bright. "A happy place," he says. "Obviously, ignore Christianity's intense homophobia and focus on the real spirit of Christmas."

"Come on," I say, smiling. "Let's go ice-skating."

We rush toward the line and wait our turn to get skates. We lace each other's skates up. Second to second, the mood changes. Becomes lighter. Our parents and Judy and the world feel farther away, until we're on the ice and it's like we're part of a mass of happy people floating on a frozen cloud. We skate side by side, laughing, racing, twirling. And then her voice booms over the loudspeakers. Madonna. She's singing "Santa Baby." Just for us.

I must be excited by hearing Madonna's voice, because I make a false step and fall. But he catches me. I'm in his arms now. He guides me up, toward him, my face hovering so close to his.

I want to believe we're the only two people in the world, and on the ice, but my eyes can't help but dart around. I see families, children, straight couples, people who could hurt us. "Art," I say, shaky. "There are so many people here."

"They don't matter," he says, so sure of himself.

"But they could . . ." I trail off. Hurt us. Judge us.

"Reza, we live in New York City," Art says with

sudden delight. "If we can't kiss each other in this city, then where can we kiss each other?"

Are we going to kiss each other? The thought of it makes me soar.

"San Francisco," I joke.

"Shut up," he says, as he swats me playfully.

"I just wish we were somewhere private," I say, an ache in my voice. I want to be somewhere that is just ours. I want to pretend we're the last two people on the planet.

"Privacy is overrated," he says. "I want to scream from rooftops right now. I want the world to see how beautiful you are, how right we are together."

He moves his head closer to me. I close my eyes, and I'm in darkness. Private. I can feel him inching closer to me. His warmth, his breath, his scent, all slowly making their way to me. Until our lips are almost touching.

"Is this really happening?" I whisper quietly.

Then he kisses me. Our lips meet and our tongues start to explore each other. I feel like there is electricity inside me and I'm all lit up. *This is what it's supposed to feel like.*

And yes, this is really happening.

MAY AND JUNE 1990

"A lot of people are afraid to say what they want. That's why they don't get what they want."

—*Madonna*

REZA

I think about sex almost all the time now. It's like some-thing inside my brain that was locked has been unlocked by Art, by his closeness. I used to think about sex some-times, but now it's an unstoppable force. I think about Art's hands on my body, my cheeks against his, his lips pressed against mine, his body on top of me, crushing me with its weight, at once making me feel weighted down under its mass and freely soaring above the world, like a cloud with wings. I can't even sleep anymore, because my thoughts about Art are racing around my brain.

Maybe the reason I think about sex in a continuous loop is that, despite being with Art for months, we have still not had sex. Yes, my hands have touched his body. His lips have touched my lips. But that's all. I haven't let anything else happen. The moment I come close to doing more—I feel the fear and instantly think about disease, death, blindness, and lesions. It paralyzes me.

So I just *think* about it, and then I make him stop when he wants to put his mouth where I know it should not go, and his fingers where I want them to go.

"Clinical trials are like motherfuckin' golf clubs," Jimmy says. "Only rich white men allowed."

We're at an ACT UP meeting. The community center is packed with people. Men in tight leather pants. Women in blazers. Men with suspenders and no shirts. Drag queens. Men who look like they will die soon. People who seem to come from a different planet than the one I have known all my life.

"Apologies to the rich white men in the room," Jimmy continues. "But y'all know it's true, and it's got to change."

"No apology needed," Stephen says.

Hearing Stephen use the word apology is hard. We had to apologize to him multiple times before he forgave us for what we did to Judy. But eventually he confessed that he saw our side of it, and he said his life was too short to punish himself by not seeing Art.

"Girl," Jimmy says, "I wasn't talking to you. You may be white, but you're not rich. You burned through whatever you had in *gay Paree*."

This is what we do on Monday nights. Art refuses to miss a meeting. He considers this romantic. I would rather be kissing under a Christmas tree.

"Focus," a woman with a shaved head says. "This protest must feel focused. The government wants nothing more than for us to be off-message. But we will be clear.

The NIH must include women and people of color in medical trials. How the hell are they supposed to *heal* our bodies when our bodies are not a part of their research?"

It's so hot in this room that our palms are sweating profusely. We clutch each other's hands here, in this room surrounded by other people like us. In the outside world, the straight world, I sometimes pull away from him when he touches me. At school, I fear the bullies. On the streets, I am terrified of being beat up. I wish for Art's courage as his sweat merges with mine. I look down at our hands, his fingernails painted in different colors of the rainbow, glittery and bright. Optimistic.

The facilitators of the meeting—Jimmy, the woman with the shaved head, two other men and one other woman—lead a discussion about the group's next action. They will storm the National Institutes of Health in Maryland. They will demand changes to medical trials. They will shine a light on the lack of inclusion, on the inherent corruption of AIDS research. I can feel Art's body fill with excitement as the protest is discussed. He loves this, and I love watching him love something. He's a force.

"Maryland isn't New York," Jimmy says. "There aren't as many angry queens and fierce feminists there. We need to encourage people to get on the bus and haul their asses down there. This action is vital."

I close my eyes and wish for just one hour without the fear of AIDS. I think about what I would do with this one hour, how I would get enough of Art to last the rest of my life. How I would fill myself with his fearlessness and passion.

My eyes open at a piercing, awful sound. I see whistles being distributed to everyone by the facilitators.

"Attacks against gay men are increasing," Jimmy says. "And we need to protect each other."

The whistles are meant to be worn around our necks, to be used in case of emergency. Is it not bad enough that our bodies are being attacked from the inside? Do they need to be attacked from the outside too?

Art places a whistle around my neck and whispers in my ear. "Do you, Reza, accept this whistle?"

"I do," I say, giggling.

He looks at me with expectation. I place a whistle around his neck and whisper, "Do you, Art, accept this whistle?"

"I do," he says. "I do and I do and I do and I do."

"You do?" I ask.

He laughs. Then, his face suddenly serious, he says, "And don't worry, if anyone tries to hurt you, I'll kick their ass so hard, they'll think they were hit by a tornado."

"Like the storm that takes Dorothy to Oz?" I ask.

"Exactly like that," he says.

Art is my tornado. He came into my life like a cyclone, and ever since, I have been in my own version of Oz. My life was once sepia toned, one color, bland. Now it is a rainbow world of excitement and anticipation.

He stares at me for a long time, and then, when it

seems we can't look at each other any longer, he leans in and licks my lips and smiles.

When the meeting ends, people don't leave. They cluster. They talk. They make plans. They trade numbers. They go to the fund-raising table to buy mugs and pins and T-shirts. Art wants to buy me something. He chooses a black T-shirt with a Keith Haring image on it, the words IGNORANCE = FEAR above the image and the words SILENCE = DEATH under it.

"Try it on," he says.

"Here?" I ask.

"No one cares. And I want to see you without a shirt on."

I take my T-shirt off and throw the Keith Haring shirt on. Art points his camera at me.

We saw Keith Haring at a meeting in January. Art worshipped him. After the meeting, Art told Keith how much he had inspired him, and Keith smiled shyly and thanked Art. A month later, he was dead.

Art snaps a photo of me in the Keith Haring T-shirt, and then he pays for two of them. One for himself, and one for me. "Why Keith Haring?" he asks, shaking his head. "Why isn't this disease killing assholes instead of artists? God doesn't deserve him."

He takes his T-shirt off before putting the new one on. Time stops when I see that jolt of skin. So much skin. I inhale it all, every beauty mark, every hair on his body, the contours of his torso and his shoulders and his nipples. And then time starts again when he puts the new T-shirt on and throws our old T-shirts into his book bag.

We have the same T-shirt on now, the same whistle around our necks. We are becoming one, or perhaps I am becoming him. I long to be him, to escape myself and crawl into the safety of his skin. The clink-clink of his camera against the whistle sounds like a metronome and reminds me how different we are. He is an artist. He has a voice. I am still finding mine. The whistles also remind me of those fish pins Judy and I wore, and how much it bothered Art. Judy has not spoken to me for months. She hates me, and with reason. I miss her. She was my friend. The only one I have ever had.

We walk with Stephen and Jimmy after the meeting. They have begun spending all their time together. They are not a couple in the romantic sense, but they have become companions to each other. They hold hands. Art tries to hold my hand, but I pull away. We could run into my mother. We could run into Darryl Lorde. We could be seen. I sometimes have moments when I look at my life from above and wonder how I arrived here. This is one of those moments. Who is this Iranian kid in a Keith Haring T-shirt holding the hand of a boy with rainbow nails and a ponytail walking next to two men on the verge of death? Is it me? When did I become this person? When did I become so . . . lucky?

"I need to run into the drugstore," Jimmy says.

"Our second home," Stephen jokes.

We follow Jimmy into Duane Reade, and he heads

toward the pharmacy counter to pick up a prescription.

We linger in one of the aisles with Stephen. Condoms line the shelves. Regular and jumbo. Ribbed. Yellow boxes. Black boxes. Latex and nonlatex. Flavors. *Flavors?*

"I think I'll wait outside," I say. "I hate air-conditioning."

"Reza," Stephen says, "if there's something you want to ask me about, you know, sex . . ."

"I am okay," I say.

"No, you're not," Art says. "You're scared and you won't let me . . ."

"Art," I look at him meaningfully. "Please."

I try to leave, but Art pulls me back in and hooks his arms around me, locking his hands at my rumbling belly. I squirm, but he doesn't let me go. "I tell Stephen everything, so he already knows what we've done, but more importantly what we haven't done. Let him give you the birds and the bees talk, Reza. He's good at it."

"Why is it called birds and bees?" I ask, hoping we can discuss language instead of intercourse.

"Because parents were too afraid to speak to their kids about human sex," Stephen explains. "So they relied on metaphors about bird and bee reproduction."

"Oh," I say. "I'm so fascinated by idioms. There are so many interesting Persian ones that make no sense in English. Like we don't say 'I miss you.' We say 'My heart has become tight for you.' And when we truly love someone, we say, 'I will eat your liver.'"

"Reza," Art says, exasperated, "you're working overtime to change the subject."

"I'm gonna give you the good news about sex first," Stephen says.

"This is how he started with me too," Art says.

"The good news is that when you're gay, you can't get pregnant. No babies. No unwanted pregnancies. No trips to the abortion clinic."

Am I supposed to be happy about this? I want children someday. I want to hold a baby in my arms, and feel needed, and know that whatever began with me doesn't end with me. I want to prove that I can be a better father than my father.

"And the bad news is that when you're gay, you can die from sex," I say, a hint of anger in my voice.

"Sex has always been dangerous," Stephen says. "Look up how many women die in childbirth every year. But yes, let's be real here. The bad news is there's a virus out there infecting gay men disproportionately. You want more good news though?"

I say nothing. The last time he gave me good news, it was that I would never become a father.

"Condoms!" he says with a lilt, waving his hand across the aisle like he's Vanna White. An old lady with white hair and a basket full of hair dyes gives us a glare. I am mortified, but Stephen shrugs her off. "Condoms work," he says. "They do their job well. All you need to do is use them right. If you want a tutorial, we can go home and practice with bananas."

"Or Persian cucumbers!" Art says. I blush and try

to push away from him, but his arms are still locked around me.

"Condom advice," Stephen says. "Always check the expiration date. They do expire."

"Unlike Persian cucumbers," Art says. "Those get better with age, like a fine wine."

"And never keep them anywhere hot. If you put one in your pocket for the night, use it that night or dump it. You don't want the condom to break."

This is something I will no doubt have nightmares about. Condoms breaking. Like a faulty dam.

"Make sure your lube is condom-compatible. Not all lube is."

"Lube is lubricant," Art explains. "Men need it, because we don't naturally get wet down there."

I feel my face burning from embarrassment.

"The jury is out on whether oral sex is safe or not," Stephen says. "But my advice is to use a condom for that too. Experiment with flavors if you want, though I think the flavored ones are gross. I don't want sex to taste like pineapple."

Does sex have a taste? Does it taste the same with different people? Am I supposed to be asking these questions out loud?

"And here's something important," Stephen says. "The straight world has defined losing your virginity as intercourse. That's *their* thing. But we get to define it for ourselves. And you never, ever have to do anything you don't want to do. As far as I'm concerned, sex is just intimacy between two people. You can define what that looks like for you, and what losing your virginity looks like for you. We're queer. We make our own rules."

"Oh, and don't feel like you have to buy into that tops and bottoms bullshit," Jimmy adds. He's just joined us, a prescription in his hand. "If you're a top, fine. If you're a bottom, fine. But you can be both, or you can be a top on Monday and a bottom on Tuesday."

"Who has sex on Monday and Tuesday?" Art asks.

Jimmy laughs. "Honey, before this disease, some of us had sex seven days a week."

That's what I want. To have sex seven days a week. With Art. Only with Art. Seven days of Art.

"I know there's a lot to be afraid of," Stephen says. "But I want . . . I just want to communicate to you that . . . that . . ." Stephen's voice shakes a little. Cracks.

"That sex is beautiful," Jimmy says. "That intimacy is beautiful. That feeling like one with another human being is why we were put on this planet. It connects us to everything good that exists inside us and outside us. And you can't be robbed of that. Stay safe, but don't lock yourself in a prison. Live."

Stephen nods and repeats the last word, "Live."

Live. A marching order given to me by two men with little life left in them, their future a ticking clock with the alarm set to go off at any moment. *Live.*

Stephen grabs two packs of condoms and goes to the counter to pay for them. He hands one to me and one to Art. "You don't need to tell me anything," he says.

"Promise you'll keep these just in case." After a pause, he says, "But don't keep them in your pockets! Store them somewhere cool."

Art walks me home, but he doesn't come up. I don't let him. "Art," I whisper, taking the condoms out. "Please take this with you. I don't think my mother could handle finding it."

He laughs. "You think your mother snoops through your stuff?"

"I think all mothers probably snoop through their children's stuff," I say. I don't know if I mean it. But I know that I took the first chance I had to look into Art's backpack. I know that I invade Abbas's pockets. I have to assume others are as duplicitous as I am.

He takes a condom from me and puts it playfully in his mouth, biting the edge of the wrapper. "I'll keep it somewhere safe," he says.

I shake my head, smiling. I'm not used to smiling this much. But I stop smiling when I go upstairs. My mom, Abbas, and Saadi are finishing dinner and ask me to join them. My mom asks me how my study group was. They think that's where I was. I don't have the energy to tell them the truth. My mom hasn't mentioned my coming out since it happened. She hasn't used the word *gay* or asked about Art. She just pretends it never happened, and the rest of the family seems to back up this fiction.

She's equally in denial about Tara, who moved out in early January, after finally telling her that she's now a bartender in love with a DJ. They argued for hours and my mom cried. But now it's like nothing happened. Tara and I have a new saying. Denial isn't just a river in Egypt, it runs through the whole Middle East.

At home, Saadi has become an expert at taking the cues and saying nothing about me. But at school, he and his friends are constantly taunting me. I've heard every possible word a homosexual could be called in the last few months, all spewed out of the hateful mouths of Darryl, Saadi, and their cronies. Faggot. Pansy. Mary. Butt pirate. Fruit. Turd burglar. Flamer. Nancy. Queen. Lately, they taunt us with lyrics from Madonna's new song, which they know we love, and which celebrates the underground ball scene.

This morning, as I walk into school, I hear them cracking each other up as they call, "Reza, are you ready to *strike a pose?*" I ignore them. Then, when Art approaches me, Darryl says to us, "Hey, ladies with an attitude, don't just stand there, let's get to it!"

Art looks up at them, with a defiance I wish I had in me. "Yeah, you fellas in the mood?" he asks lasciviously. "Because I've got some whips and chains in my backpack I'd love to try on you."

"I bet you'd like that," Darryl says in disgust.

Art approaches them slowly, methodically. "Don't motherfuckin' test me," he says. "And leave Reza alone, you hear me? Save the abuse for me. He's off-limits."

"He's got it easy here," Saadi says, smiling. "If he went back to Iran, they'd kill him."

That sends a jolt down my spine, because it's true. I escape the situation, searching for an empty classroom. As I do, I walk straight past Judy, who looks away from me as I cross her. She's standing with Annabel de la Roche and a group of popular girls I've never spoken to. They're laughing, pretending I don't exist.

I can't find an empty classroom, but I see the auditorium is open, so I rush in and take refuge in the costume room of the theater. No one will come in here this early in the morning. I can hear Art call my name. "Reza, stop!" he says as he catches up with me. He puts his arms around me. "They're dicks," he says. "You want me to beat them up for you?"

"No," I say quietly. "You tried that once, and it was horrible."

"But it felt so fucking good," he says gleefully, like he's already forgotten the pain of the blood and bruises on his face. "And it would feel even better doing it for you."

"I don't want hitting," I say, looking into his glimmering eyes. "I want . . . kissing."

"Well then, don't just stand there," he says, moving his lips closer. "Let's get to it." I shake my head, and smile, and kiss him. We've danced to "Vogue" so many times, always at Tara and Massimo's place. That's the only home we can be ourselves in. Massimo has all the remixes, and we all dance like lunatics. I'm a terrible dancer, but Art can move. He strikes poses like Linda Evangelista, his hand framing his head, his legs assuming frozen poses that look glamorous and athletic. We laugh. We sing along. We pretend we are Madonna, or her dancers, or Greta Garbo. I know everyone Madonna is singing about now. I know who Rita Hayworth is. I know how to give good face.

Art takes my hand. He holds it and kisses the tip of each finger. Then he takes my other hand, kisses each of its fingers. "Do you believe in reincarnation?" he says.

"I don't know," I say nervously. "We should go to class. We'll be late."

"I don't think I do," he says, ignoring me. "But I like the idea of it. Like what if we knew each other in a past life? What if we were Bonnie and Clyde? Or Cleopatra and Mark Antony? What if this isn't the beginning of us, but just a continuation of something that started a long time ago?"

"You're funny," I say. "What if we weren't extraordinarily famous people? What if we were just . . . normal?"

"Reza," he says. He says my name with awe, like I truly am extraordinary. "If past lives exist, then we were epic people."

"Okay, then I want to be Cleopatra," I say, excited. He's succeeded in getting me out of my head, into a fantasy.

He kisses the palm of my hand now. "And what would you wanna be in our *next* life?"

I don't know what I would want to be, so I say the first thing that comes into my mind. "A fish maybe. It seems peaceful underwater."

"As long as you're somewhere far from sharks and oil spills," he says. "But I like that idea. I'll be a fish with you." He sucks his cheeks in to make a fish face, and I follow suit. We mash our lips into each other, laughing. I briefly think of Judy, of those fish pins we wore.

"You want to practice putting condoms on each other tonight?" he asks with a mischievous smile.

"Where?" I whisper, as if there is anyone in here who can hear us.

"We could ask Stephen to use his place," he says, like he's trying to convince himself that's a rational idea. "Or your sister."

"I am not asking my sister if she'll let me have sex in her apartment!" I say, way too loud. "And let's backtrack. I'm not ready to have sex at all."

He makes a fish face again. "There's no AIDS underwater, you know," he says. "And even if there were, fish are immune."

My heart beats fast. Everything seemed so right just a moment ago.

"I have a crazy idea," Art says. "Let's go get tested. Me and you, together."

I look at him, confused. "Tested? For what?"

"What do you mean, for what? For HIV." He says it so matter-of-factly, like he wants to sign us up for piano lessons.

"Why would we need to be tested?" I ask, incredulous. "We've never done anything! Have you ever done anything? I have never done anything!"

"No, I already told you," Art says. "I've never had oral or anal . . ."

"And me neither," I say. I hate those words. Oral. Anal. I hate how graphic they are, how hostile they feel. I sometimes wish sex could be like it is in old movies, a passionate black-and-white kiss and separate beds.

"Then we have nothing to worry about, Reza. We take the tests. They come back negative. And then we can do whatever we want. We could, you know, explore . . ." He trails off.

"Is the test 100 percent?" I ask.

"Reza, stop, just stop."

"I don't believe anything is 100 percent," I say, my voice shaky. "The test may be wrong. Condoms could break. You heard Stephen. Even he said they can break. And even if neither of us has done anything with another man, maybe we got it some other way. Ryan White got it, and he was . . ."

"He was a hemophiliac," Art says. "He had *gallons* of other people's blood injected into his body. Have you had gallons of blood injected inside you?"

"No, of course not," I say. "But the test is a blood test. What if the test itself gives you AIDS? What if they use an infected needle?"

"Reza, I'm trying to find a solution here," he says, frustrated.

"A solution?" I ask, defensive. "Why, am I that big a problem?"

A wave of anger passes through him. His nostrils flare.

His brow sweats. Then he takes a few deep breaths. "Just work with me. Please. You are not going to be positive, and trust me, if you are, the CDC will want to study you. You've never done anything that could put you at risk." He takes my hand again, squeezes it a little too hard. "If we're really boyfriends, then I want to, you know, do all the things that boyfriends are supposed to do."

"I'm sorry," I say finally. "I'm scared."

"I would never hurt you, Reza," he says softly. "I promise."

"Of course you wouldn't *want* to hurt me," I say. "But you might. Someday. I don't want to hurt you, and I feel like I'm hurting you right now. I don't want to hurt my mother, but I know I'm hurting her."

"Reza, it's okay," he says.

"Nothing is okay," I say. "I want to skip to our next life sometimes, Art. Maybe in our next life there will be no AIDS and no homophobia." I take a deep breath. "I'm sorry, Art. I am so happy with you, but . . ."

"But?" he says, aggravated. Then I watch as he brushes off his annoyance and smiles. He puts his arms on my back, moving them slowly lower until they reach my ass. "This is the only butt that matters in our relationship. No other buts, okay?"

I laugh. I grab his ass stiffly, trying to be as coolly seductive as he is, feeling awkward and foolish instead. "Except for this butt," I say.

I melt into his arms. I want him so bad. I want him to ravish me. I let him put a hand down my pants, feeling the smoothness of my skin in his palms. He laughs.

"What's so funny?" I ask, blushing. "Is it me? I sound silly trying to be sexy, don't I?"

"You don't need to try to be sexy," he says with sweet sincerity. "You *are* sexy." He takes a breath, then laughs again. "It's just . . . Is there anything gayer than the two of us holding each other in the costume room?" he asks.

I laugh too, but there's sorrow behind the laughter.

"Hey, can I tell you a secret?" He holds my gaze with intensity.

"Of course," I say. "You can tell me all your secrets."

He turns his head toward my ear, then whispers, "I'm more patient than I seem. I'll wait for you. And in the meantime, I will eat your liver."

ART

I'm so in love with Reza, I feel like I'm bursting with it. But I haven't been able to say it to him yet. Maybe I'm afraid it'll scare him off. Or maybe I'm afraid that saying it out loud will break the spell. That's what it feels like. Like we're under a magic spell.

I live to make him laugh. If I could bottle those moments of laughter, I would turn them into a cologne and spritz myself with it every day, or I would turn them into bath suds and soak myself in his essence. But all this love only makes me want to fight harder, because if love is *this* beautiful, then anyone standing in the way of it is even more evil than I thought. All those homophobes in government, all those pharmaceutical companies profiting from our illness, all those parents kicking their children out of their homes, all those high school bullies tormenting the gay kid. My own parents, who won't say Reza's name, or allow him into their home, or even look me in the eye anymore—someone should make a horror movie about them, but it would probably be too scary. People want their villains to look like Freddy Krueger and Jason. They don't see killers in pearls and tailored suits.

My anger isn't reserved for them, though. I have stores of it saved up for others. For Mrs. Starr, who wouldn't let me create an ACT UP affinity group. For Darryl Lorde and all the assholes at school, who sneeze and cough words like "faggot" and "pansy" into their hands when Reza and I walk by.

And for Judy, who hasn't spoken to me since December, who avoids my gaze just like my parents, and who has quickly replaced me with a group of boring girlfriends. Annabel de la Roche is her best friend now. They do everything together. Judy always hated girls like Annabel, with her blow-dried hair and her sleek gray-or-beige clothes and her simple makeup. Classic. Effortless. Boring. Not to mention Annabel dated none other than Darryl Lorde freshman year. Now Judy and this beige lover of homophobes are best friends? I know I wronged Judy, but months have passed. I called and left messages. I dropped notes in her locker. I admitted what I did was wrong. I told her I loved her. I even gave her a first-edition copy of Shel Silverstein's *The Missing Piece* and inscribed a note telling her that she was my missing piece.

And nothing from her. Not a word. Not even an acknowledgment. Silence. So yeah, I'm angry with her too. I'm pissed off that she won't forgive me. Aren't friends supposed to forgive each other? I'm pissed off that because of her, I'm not invited to Sunday movie nights anymore. That I don't get to share my first love with my best friend, because, well, because he was her first love too. But still . . .

Sometimes, I even get pissed off at Reza. Probably too often. I didn't know before this how frustrating love is, how crazy it can make you. Like now, we just got out of the movies. We went to see *Longtime Companion*, me and Reza and Stephen and Jimmy, and we cried and cried through the movie. It's about a group of gay men and their one straight female friend, and it's about the first years of AIDS, and about death and friendship. I can't believe this movie about fags dying was made. I cried because the movie was so beautiful, and because the story was so poignant, and because the character Mary-Louise Parker played reminded me of Judy and I miss her. But also I cried just because this movie *exists* now, and if this one was made, then maybe more will be made. Maybe gay stories will be told.

Then Reza asks, "Do you think the people who need to see this movie will see it? I hope it is not just a gay movie."

"What does that even mean?" I burst out. "JUST a gay movie?"

Reza stumbles over his words. "I meant, I don't know, that . . ."

"This *is* a gay film," I say. "And I want things labeled as gay. Books and movies and all that. Don't we deserve our own stories?"

I can feel Reza tense a little. He can't handle this side of me. Stephen puts a palm on my shoulder.

"You could argue," Jimmy says, intervening to restore peace, "that it is a story about friendship, about life and death. That those themes are universal."

"Yeah," I say. "About GAY friendship. About GAY life. And GAY death. Don't you want black films to be called black films, Jimmy?"

"I do," Jimmy says. "But what's a black film, anyway? Is *The Color Purple* a black film when it was directed by a straight white man? I loved that shit and Oprah was robbed, but the whole film is viewed through the lens of a white person. Perspective matters."

I think back to photographing Jimmy for my project, of posing him like Diana Ross as Billie Holiday, per his request. Of setting up the lighting to frame his face in an otherworldly glow and finding the perfect angle. Did I capture the true him? Could I? Then I remember what Stephen told me once. That photographs say more about the photographer than they do about the subject. And if that's true, I hate that. Because I don't just want to photograph myself.

"I'm sorry," I say to Reza. "I'm just angry that the straightness is implicit in everything, that there are so few queer stories. I'm not angry at you."

Reza nods. "It's okay," he whispers. "I see what you're saying."

Stephen smiles. "Isn't the world more interesting when

not everyone thinks like us?" he asks, clearly directing his question to me.

"Said the ACT UP activist who storms the offices of people who disagree with him," I snap back. What's wrong with me? I just apologized to Reza, and now I'm picking a fight with Stephen.

"Art, there's a difference between denying sick people access to life-saving drugs and expressing an opinion about how to define queer film," Stephen says tiredly. "Pick your battles."

Jimmy asks Reza a question about Iranian cinema, and the two of them walk ahead of us, leaving me alone with Stephen. I feel like an idiot. "What are you and Judy watching tonight?" I ask, changing the subject.

It's Sunday afternoon, and I know Judy will go to her uncle's tonight, that they will continue a tradition I was once a part of.

"I don't know," Stephen says, uncomfortable. He doesn't talk about Judy to me.

"Okay," I say. "Well, tell her that I still miss her."

"I have," Stephen says. "She will come around, you know. I just don't know when. And I hope it's before . . ." He takes a breath. "Let's talk about something else. How are you and Reza doing? Did my sex tutorial help?"

I shake my head. "He's too scared to do anything but kiss. And even that scares him sometimes. He bit his lip and he wouldn't kiss me until it healed. Which was, like, three days. I couldn't kiss him for three days. It was like torture."

"His paranoia is normal," Stephen says. "A lot of guys are scared. And remember that he just came out. He hasn't had all the time you've had to accept all this."

"But isn't he supposed to wanna rip my clothes off? Isn't he supposed to, you know, find me irresistible?"

"Oh, Art," Stephen says, smiling. "I'm sure he does find you irresistible."

"If his fear lets him resist me, then obviously I'm resistible," I grumble.

I look ahead at Reza walking with Jimmy, arm in arm. He's supposed to be mine, and yet he won't give himself to me. Not fully.

"Sometimes I wonder whether I would choose to be from your generation or mine," Stephen says thoughtfully. "I'd be alive if I were your age."

"Stephen, you're alive," I say forcefully. "You're here walking with me."

"You know what I mean," he says. "But if I were your age, I would never have had all those years of freedom without fear. I can't imagine falling in love with José and not being able to be intimate with him, to make our bodies one. I wouldn't trade those moments for anything, not even for more years."

"Thanks for rubbing it in," I say ruefully.

"Sorry," Stephen says with a shrug.

"You think Reza will ever be ready?" I ask.

"I do," Stephen says. "But I don't know when."

To recap: He thinks Judy will forgive me, but he doesn't know when. He thinks Reza will sleep with me, but he doesn't know when. And despite telling Reza I'm more patient than I seem, I'm as impatient as a human being gets. I look at Stephen and say, "I'm sorry I got all pissy earlier. I'm not a good person like you, but . . ."

"Art," he says, "you're a great person."

Reza and Jimmy have stopped and are waiting for us to catch up. When we do, Jimmy says he's tired and needs a nap before Judy arrives. We say our goodbyes, and then it's just me and Reza. We walk for a bit. Sunday nights are hard. The absence of Judy cuts deeper on Sunday nights. I want to put all this energy I have somewhere.

"Hey," I say to Reza. "How would you feel about coming to the darkroom with me?"

"Really?" he asks.

"Yeah, why not?"

"I just, I always thought, that it was . . . private, or you know, a sacred space for you." God, he's cute, stammering away like that about sacred spaces when *he's* my sacred space.

"Follow me," I say. "There's no place I wouldn't let you into." I hope he caught the not-so-subtle hint there.

I lead him to the darkroom I use, which is on the ground floor of an Upper West Side office building. I pay a fee per month, the best money I've every stolen from my criminal of a father. For that fee, I get access to trays and tongs and chemicals, but that makes it sound so technical. It's magic. You walk in with nothing, and you leave with an image.

Reza seems fascinated by it all, by the red lights, by the strong scent of the chemicals, and by the black-and-white photos I have hanging from clothespins above my workstation: Old Hollywood–style shots of Stephen and other activists. Jimmy with a gardenia in his hair. Those homophobe bankers at the New York Stock Exchange. And then I see Reza's eye catch an image that's almost covered up by another. It's the photo I took of him at that first protest, the one he pretended not to be at. He's part of a crowd, but it's unmistakably him. He stares at the photo and smiles.

"It seems sad now," he says.

"What?" I ask.

"That I lied to you about being at that protest," he says.

"You've come a long way, baby," I say.

"I also lied to you about your book bag," he says, cringing a little. "When you left it at my house. I opened it. I read those notecards. I smelled your underwear."

"You did NOT," I say, giddy.

"I did. I'm awful." The blush on his cheeks is accentuated by the darkroom lights.

"You're all kinds of awful," I say, impishly. "Now can we please be awful together?"

He turns his attention back to that image of himself as if there's an answer to a riddle buried inside it. Then he turns to me and says, "You are so talented."

"You think so?"

"I know so," he says.

"I see things," I say. "I mean, I know that sounds crazy. But it's like, I don't snap a photo unless I see its energy. I know they're all black-and-white, but they have colors to me. Auras. And if they don't, I don't take them. And if the aura doesn't survive when I print the picture, then I throw it out. And I want . . . I want them to mean something. I want to contribute something. To capture all this, so that a hundred years from now, or a thousand years from now, people will remember it all and know that we existed. That we lived."

"How did you start?" he asks.

"I always liked taking pictures," I say. "My mom had a camera, and she said when I was a kid and she was always taking photos of me, I would take the camera from her and take photos of her. She has an album somewhere at home of Polaroids I took when I was, like, five years old." My heart aches a little bit thinking about those Polaroids of my mother with her Farrah Fawcett hair and her chic palazzo pants and fringe dresses, of my father with a fuller head of hair and a thick mustache. My parents, through the lens of five-year-old me, were always shot from below, making them imposing and fabulous. When did that all change? When did I realize the divide between them and me was too big to cross? When did they go from being my favorite subjects to the villains in my story?

"Then Stephen gave me my camera the year I started high school, as a birthday gift, and it all took off from there. I became obsessed." I remember those early days with my camera, learning everything about lenses and apertures and focus. Practicing on Judy and Stephen. Making them pose for me. Their exasperation when they had to sit too long as I figured out how to get the focus just right, not too sharp, not too hazy. God, I miss Judy. "I guess that's it. Sometimes, I worry that I prefer life through a lens to *life*, you know. In a lens, I can . . . structure things. Frame them the way I want them to be framed. It's safe."

His eyes pierce through me. "I don't think there's anything safe about it," he says. "Your pictures are not safe. Everything about you, Art, is so . . ."

"Risky?"

"Bold," he says. "Brazen."

I think of my mom saying my photographs were "nice." She doesn't get me. But Reza does. He sees me.

"Brazen," I repeat. "I want to be brazen with you."

He laughs, then looks down at the floor, like he wants to escape this moment.

"Hey, you want me to teach you how to print a photo?" I ask.

He nods, and the lesson begins. As we print a portrait of a female activist in a cowboy hat, staring the camera down like John Wayne, I lead Reza's hands toward the tongs and show him how to gently place the paper in the different baths.

"Careful not to touch the chemicals," I say.

"Okay," he says.

"Safety is crucial in a darkroom. You should always wear closed shoes."

"Okay," he says.

"If you do touch anything, always wash your hands right away. And be very careful not to get any in your mouth or eyes," I say.

"What happens if you do?" he asks.

Our photo is in the final bath. I leave it in there and turn him around to face me. "Nothing will happen," I say. "I'll keep you safe. I promise."

I lick his lips. He always smiles when I do this, and I'll keep doing it until it stops making him smile. I pull him into me, crushing his body into mine. I kiss him, run my hands up his shirt, feel his smooth skin.

"Reza." I look into his eyes. I soak in the sound of his name. "Reza," I say again.

"Art," he says, tenderly.

"Say it again," I request.

"Art," he says. The sound of my name in his accent makes me feel like a new person, like he's invented a better version of me. It almost brings tears to my eyes.

Having him in my arms, and in my darkroom, feels more intimate than anything I've ever experienced. It's like he's inside my beating heart, and our hearts are becoming one.

And then I say it. I don't even think about it. I blurt out because I have to.

"I love you."

There. It feels like a relief. The words linger in the air.

His eyes dart away from my gaze, but I can see him blushing. I love seeing him blush. He sighs and then he kisses me. When he pulls away, he whispers, "I love you too. I've wanted to say it so many times."

"Me too, so many times," I whisper. I can't believe this is happening, that he actually feels the same way I do.

I love him. He loves me. We said it, and the magic spell didn't wear off. I still want to kiss him, hold him, protect him. I need to feel his skin against mine. I try to pull his shirt off, but he resists. I make a decision. I can't control what he takes off, but I can choose what I take off. I remove my T-shirt. Then I pull my jeans off over my sneakers.

"Art," he whispers.

I ignore him. There's one thing left to take off. My boxer briefs. I remove them. I stand in front of him, exposed.

"Art," he says again, a little louder.

"Shh . . . ," I say. "Just look at me."

"I thought the chemicals could . . ."

"I kept my shoes on," I say. "There are no rules posted about anything else."

I approach him again, press my nakedness against his clothes. We kiss, but he's holding back.

"Please," I say, with desperation. "I need you."

"I need you too. . . ." He trails off.

"Just touch me," I say, as gently as I can in the heat of this moment. "Let's start there. You won't get anything from touching. I promise." I push my knuckles into the knots in his back, trying to release his tension.

"I'm afraid that if I touch you . . . that it will make me want more. That if I touch you, I will want to taste you. And if I taste you, then . . . if I open the door, then I won't know how to close it again. . . . Because I want you more than anything."

"We don't have to close the door," I say. "Never. Don't you see how lucky we are? We were born at exactly the right time to protect ourselves."

"But what if that's not true?" he asks. "What if there is another virus waiting in the wings? What if condoms turn out not to work? What if this is only the beginning of something even worse?"

"Please," I say. "Please just kiss me."

He does, but it's tentative. I want it to feel free, unhinged, passionate. I want to be an animal, to roar.

"Art," he says tentatively, "I'm serious. What if AIDS is our warning that something even worse is around the bend?"

"What if AIDS is our warning that life is short?" I ask. "What if it's telling us that we should love when we have the chance?"

"I do love you," he says. "So much. Now that we've said it, I want to keep repeating it. I love you."

"Then don't let fear run your life," I say. "Look at me. I'm standing naked in front of you. I'm yours. I'm all yours."

Something shifts in him. He softens. He runs his hands down my chest, his touch so warm. "What if we just hold each other?" he asks. He looks so beautiful illu-minated by the red glow of the lights.

I melt into him, my head on his shoulder. The smell of him merging with the chemicals makes me dizzy. And then I cry. I can't help it. The tears just flow. I want to tell him that this isn't what love is supposed to feel like. I want to tell him that love is supposed to soar, to be weightless. Our love is so heavy, full of fear.

"I'm sorry," I say, with a sudden laugh. "These are tears of joy. Seriously. I'm just so happy that I want more happiness."

"We'll have more happiness," he says. "So much more happiness."

He cradles my face in his hands and kisses my tears. Then he wraps my head in his arms and holds me tight.

JUDY

How did I get here? I'm not the girl who goes to high school parties with her girlfriends. I'm not the girl who even has girlfriends. But I'm standing next to my new friend Annabel de la Roche in her gorgeous two-story apartment, currently vacated by her parents, who had to go to Geneva for some kind of gala. Annabel's dad makes watches, like really expensive ones that cost more than my apartment. They have a safe deposit box full of them, and not even Annabel knows the code to it. When it was just Art and me, it was so easy to judge everyone else at school because we didn't need anybody else. I judged Annabel for always dressing in beiges and grays and always wearing dewy makeup, and obviously, I judged her for dating that asshole Darryl Lorde fresh- man year. It's easy to judge people when you don't talk to them, and I never said much to Annabel. But then, just before Christmas, she saw me sitting alone in the cafeteria, since I had no friends left, reading a guidebook to Paris. She told me Paris is her favorite place in the whole world, and that she has family there. She sat next to me and told me all about these restaurants I had to eat at. Like, a steakhouse so popular that you have to wait in line for an hour to eat there, but that's totally worth it 'cause of some magical green sauce they drape onto the steak. And a hole-in-the-wall patisserie where I would find the very best almond croissants and *pain au chocolat.* And a Moroccan restaurant where you sit on the floor in patterned banquettes and where you must order the pigeon pie. And meanwhile, I was sitting there listening to her and thinking that I didn't even know Annabel ate food. I thought she was one of those skinny girls who subsisted on raisins and V8. And she's going on and on about steak and pigeon, and I'm thinking that Art doesn't even eat meat, and that maybe I have more in common with Annabel de la Roche than I do with Bartholomew Emerson Grant VI. She asked me to bring her some stuff back from Paris. Little macaron cookies from her favorite place, and some copies of French fashion magazines she loves.

That's how it started with Annabel. I brought her the stuff back, and she thanked me by getting me an Anna Sui choker as a gift. And I was like, how does this girl who wears the most boring clothes I've ever seen even know who the fiercest new underground designer is? And how did she pick such a badass choker for me? I think that's when Annabel told me that she always loved my style, and that she wished she had the confidence to dress like me. I was so confused. I mean, I wished I had her body, and her perfect features, and her ease with the world, her ability to glide instead of stomp. But she was jealous of me? So we became friends. We shop together. We talk boys together. We've somehow gotten on the same cycle. We flip through the pages of French, American, Italian, and Japanese fashion magazines together. Sometimes we hang out with Annabel's other girlfriends—Cindy, Verena, Briana (I know, they sound like supermodels, and they look like 'em too)—but I've realized that Annabel's friendship with these girls is pretty surface. That the person she feels the closest to is me.

Annabel's having a party, and about twenty seniors are here. The whole penthouse apartment is full of hormonal teenagers, most of them drunk on the fruit punch that Annabel made, then spiked with her parents' vodka. "It's top-shelf," she told me. "So it won't give you a hang-over." She convinced me to take a sip before the party started, "to loosen up." The party is fun. That sip of fruit punch did loosen me up. Annabel made a super-fun play-list, and there's a small dance floor in the kitchen. When Wilson Phillips's "Hold On" comes on, Annabel and I belt it out together and dance. Our voices sound awful, but it's so much fun. Then Cindy, Verena, and Briana join us and we're like a girl group. Everyone watches us and claps when we're done. Seriously, I don't know how I got here. I always thought I hated girls, and now I'm group-hugging a bunch of them like they're my long-lost sisters.

The next song that comes on is Billy Joel's "We Didn't Start the Fire," and a group of the guys, including Saadi, decide they're going to challenge our performance. They line up in a row and sing the lyrics to the song, screaming out all the references to Doris Day and Marilyn Monroe and Roy Cohn and Brigitte Bardot. I have a pang of missing Art. If Art were here, he'd whisper in my ear, "Do you think any of these meatheads even knows who Doris Day is? They probably think that's just D-Day's full name or something." Art's voice disappears from my head when Annabel whispers in my ear, "These guys are worse than the New Kids on the Block."

"They certainly do not have the right stuff," I say, and she laughs. That's another thing I like about her. She's generous with her laughter.

"Do you feel the punch?" she asks.

"I mean, a little bit, I think," I say.

"Come on," she says. "One more cup."

"One more sip," I counter.

"My sister told me that the best thing you can do before college starts is build up a tolerance to booze. Otherwise, you'll get there and be way behind everyone else." She scoops some punch into a clear plastic cup and hands it to me. Then she refills her own.

"I guess I was never planning on majoring in alcohol in college," I say.

"Well, you can minor in it," she says with a mischievous smile.

I smile as I sip the punch. I don't know what being

drunk feels like, but I'm just a little more vibrant, a little more alive, like I have a light on inside me illuminating me from within. I feel creative, inspired. I wonder whether vodka punch can replace ice cream as my inspiration food of choice, and which one has more calories. "I wish you'd let me make you over," I tell Annabel. "You would look so fierce in, like, a body-hugging black dress with hot-pink slashes across it."

She laughs. "I would need, like, five more cups of punch before I'd wear anything like that."

"It's not about that," I say. "You know I heard that Madonna doesn't even drink or do drugs or anything. And look at what she wears!"

"Judy," she says, "I hate to break it to you, but I am so not Madonna."

Almost on cue, "Vogue" comes through the speakers, and everyone just has to dance. I bet Art and Reza love this song. I think back to that drag ball Uncle Stephen took me and Art to ages ago. It all feels so far away. I practically scream all the lyrics out as I dance, and each time Madonna mentions the name of an old movie star, I have a flash of a Sunday movie night with Stephen and Art. I think of all the movies we've watched. Uncle Stephen and I still have movie nights, and Jimmy joins us sometimes. But it's not the same without Art.

When the song ends, Cindy grabs the now-empty bottle of vodka and yells, "HEY, SUCKERS, LET'S PLAY SPIN THE BOTTLE!"

God, no. Please no. This will not end well.

Everyone else seems to love the idea and, in a flash, a bunch of dudes move furniture off the living room rug. A circle forms. Everyone agrees that as the hostess, Annabel should spin the bottle first and then we'll go clockwise. Of course I sit next to Annabel, counter-clockwise, so I'll be the last to spin that stupid bottle. The game begins. Annabel spins first and it lands on Verena. And to my surprise, they giggle, go to the center of the circle, and kiss each other. What I discover as the game goes on is that girls can kiss boys, and boys can kiss girls, and girls can kiss girls. But boys can't kiss boys. If a boy spins and it lands on another boy, they laugh, go, "Ewwwwww, gross" for a while, and then spin again. I'm so happy Art isn't here right now. He'd definitely go into some diatribe about the homophobia of high school party games.

Luckily, the tip of the bottle seems to avoid me for the first few spins. I pray I will keep being spared. I also pray that the game will end before my turn arrives, that some amazing song will get everyone back on the dance floor. But then Darryl spins, with a lot of force, and the bottle turns and turns for an eternity, and Darryl goes, "Come on, no whammies," and then the bottle slows down and lands on . . . me.

"Judy!!!!!!!" Verena squeals.

I must grimace, because Darryl says, "Hey, I don't have cooties."

It's hard not to think that when he says he doesn't have cooties, he's really saying he doesn't have AIDS.

I turn to Annabel and whisper, "I don't think I should. I mean, he's your ex . . ."

"It's just a game," she says, cutting me off. "And you'd be surprised. He's a decent kisser."

My name is still being chanted. Reluctantly, I head to the center of the circle until I'm facing Darryl Lorde. We're both on our knees, our faces close to each other. I can smell his breath. It smells like alcohol, Cool Ranch Doritos, and hate. Thoughts stream through my head, but one resonates more loudly than the others: that this will be my first kiss with a heterosexual guy. How absurd is that, and how awful would it be to have to always know my first kiss with a straight person was with this high school Roy Cohn?

As Darryl moves his lips close to mine, I turn away. "I'm sorry, I can't," I say.

"Seriously?" he says. "Do you only kiss fags?"

A few people laugh uncomfortably. I hear a few *ohs*, and *oh, shits*.

I stare Darryl straight in the eyes, like I have lasers in my pupils. "I'm just a little worried that bigotry is contagious," I say.

What have you done, Judy? It was just a game. This is what normal kids do.

I make a beeline to the fruit punch and I scoop a huge cup for myself. I chug it. It burns the back of my throat a little bit, but I don't care.

"Hey," Annabel, who followed me, says. "Are you okay?"

"I'm sorry," I say. "I know that was awkward."

"Why are you sorry? I wish I could tell him off like that. Nobody keeps him in check."

"Thanks," I say.

"He wasn't as bad when we dated," she says. "I mean, he was still kind of awful, but not like a full-blown asshole yet. He got so much worse after his parents' divorce. Not that there's any excuse for the shit he says and does."

The spin the bottle game has ended, but a few people loaf on the living room rug together. Some are on the couches, making out. A few people dance. There seem to be two Annabels in front of me. "I think, um, I need to lie down," I say.

"Come on," she says. She grabs a huge bottle of Evian from the pantry and leads me upstairs. "I think bottled water is the stupidest thing in the world, but my mom insists on buying it by the case."

"Uh-huh," I say. Her words echo like we're in a cave.

"Do you know Evian spells *naive* backward?" she asks. "What more evidence do you need?"

"Do you know that words that spell other words backward are called heteropalindromes?" I ask as she leads me up the stairs.

"Seriously?" she asks.

"Seriously," I say. "I have no idea why. Like, what's a homopalindrome, then?"

We reach her bedroom. It has huge windows with views of the Manhattan skyline. "You can lie down here," she says.

"I told my parents I'd be home by ten," I say.

"You still have half an hour," she says. "Trust me, drink that whole bottle of naive water and lie down. You don't want your parents to see you like this."

I stare out at the skyline. "Do you think gay people are just naturally cooler than straight people?" I ask.

"What? You're so weird," she says.

"I'm serious," I say. "Think about it."

She gives me a kiss on the forehead and says, "Water. Rest. I'll check in on you soon."

I lie down on her bed when she leaves, with its crisp white sheets. Her room looks like a hotel room. I close my eyes. I have no idea how long I'm out for when I hear the door open and then a deep voice say, "Sorry, I was just looking for another bathroom." I look to the side and see it's Saadi. He's stumbling and slurring a little bit. "I think Bobby and Rachel are hooking up in the downstairs bathroom, which is really rude to people who need to, you know, piss."

"Yeah," I say. "I guess."

"My mom refuses to go to a party in an apartment with less than three bathrooms," Saadi says.

"That's smart," I say. I don't know if I mean it. I'm just making conversation. And hearing about his mom reminds me that his stepmom is Reza's mom. Weird.

"You mind if I piss here?" he asks.

"If by *here* you mean in Annabel's toilet, then sure," I say.

He goes into her bathroom but doesn't close the door.

I can hear him pee. When he's done, he comes back into the bedroom and sits on the edge of the bed. "Hey," he says. "You doing okay?"

"You didn't wash your hands," I say.

"So?" he asks. "It's not like I pissed on my hands."

"It really is an epidemic," I say.

"What is?" he asks.

I think back to Art telling me that straight guys never wash their hands after they pee. But I just say, "Nothing."

Then he puts his unwashed hand on my arm, and says. "So, you like Persian dudes?"

"What?" I ask.

"You liked the little prince," he says. "And he's like a scrawnier, less attractive version of me."

"Oh," I say. "Are you . . ."

Is he hitting on you, Judy? Is this how straight guys hit on girls?

"I always thought you were hot," he says. "I don't get why girls are so skinny these days. Dudes want something to hold on to."

"Um, thanks?"

"You're welcome."

"I guess I'm a little confused," I say. "Since you like to make cracks about my weight."

"Yeah, sorry about that," he says. "I can be a dick."

"A major one," I say.

"What are you thinking?" he asks.

I don't even know what I'm thinking. Too many things. That despite my better judgment, I'm a little turned on. That hooking up with Saadi would be the ultimate revenge on Reza, and that maybe that's the best reason to go through with it. That any other girl at this party would definitely take this opportunity. "Nothing," I say.

"Everyone's always thinking something," he says.

"What are *you* thinking?" I ask.

"Honestly," he says, "I'm thinking that my stepbrother is an idiot for letting you go."

And that is exactly what I needed to hear. I grab Saadi by the collar of his blue Lacoste polo and I pull him close to me, and I make out with him. It's furious. Our tongues explore each other. Then his hands are all over me, up the shiny fabric of the purple dress I designed for the party, on my thighs. His breath is heavy, and his hips are thrusting urgently. I feel what I never felt when Reza and I kissed, an erection. Saadi is so hard. He sits up and takes his polo off. His body is thick and his chest has black hair on it. I put my hands on his chest. My fingernails are painted purple too, and they look kind of great against his skin. He puts his hands on my face with a tenderness that surprises me, and that's when I say, "Wait."

"What's wrong?" he asks.

"It's just . . . will you . . . could you, um, go wash your hands? You just peed."

He laughs. "Seriously?" he asks.

"Seriously," I say.

He jumps up and goes into the bathroom. I can hear the water running. When he comes back, he sits back down next to me. He puts his hand next to my nose, and I sniff them. "Now I smell like lavender," he says.

"Better than smelling like piss," I say.

He laughs again. "You're pretty funny," he says.

"And you're pretty," I say.

"Um, thanks?" he says, imitating me.

"Why are you friends with Darryl Lorde?" I ask. "Why do you stand around while he says such awful things?"

Saadi shrugs. "Who else am I supposed to be friends with?"

"There are other choices," I say. "You could be friends with me."

"As long as I wash my hands obsessively," he says.

"Not obsessively, just regularly," I say. "Also, as long as you stop being homophobic."

"You know, we can't all change the world, right?" he says. "Some of us just go along with things the way they are."

"I get it," I say. "I'm sure a lot of old Germans say the exact same thing."

He laughs. "Did you just compare me to a Nazi?"

"If *Das Boot* fits," I say.

To my surprise, he laughs again. "Is it weird that the more you dislike me, the more I want to kiss you?" he asks.

"Um, I don't know," I say. "Do you go to therapy?"

He pulls me into a kiss. I explore his mouth with my

tongue, feel every crevice of his body with my hands. The coarseness of his skin, the fuzz of his hair.

"Take my dress off," I say, shocked by the commanding tone of my voice.

He yanks at the back of my dress.

"Carefully," I warn.

"It's beautiful," he says as he carefully peels it off me. "So are you."

He looks at me, taking my body in. I guide him on top of me, feel his hardness. He wants to have sex, but I tell him I'm not ready.

"Maybe next time."

"Next time?" I ask.

He thrusts against me until he's done, and then he collapses, his head on my breast.

I catch a glimpse of Annabel's kitty-cat alarm clock. It's ten thirty. It'll be close to eleven if I run home now. My parents will kill me. Shit. "I'm so sorry, but I have to go," I say. I see the bottle of water next to me. I've only had half of it. I grab it and chug the rest, begging for it to sober me up.

"We'll do this again, right?" he asks.

"Uh, maybe," I say as I put my dress back on.

I run home, ready to beg my parents' forgiveness. They *love* Annabel, so it should be easy to come up with some excuse of what we were doing. My mom's just so happy I have a girlfriend. When I walk in, my parents are awake, just as I expected. And they look *livid*.

"Where have you been?" my mother asks. Tears well in her eyes.

"It's almost eleven," my dad says. He's wearing a watch that Annabel's dad gave him for his birthday last month. Seriously, all my best friends' parents give my parents absurdly extravagant gifts.

"Annabel and I were just watching a movie," I say. "We lost track of time." My mom shakes her head, still crying. I move closer to her. "Mom, it's okay. I'm sorry I worried you."

"We were about to leave," she says.

"Leave?" I ask. "To go look for me? You guys, I'm not a child anymore. I can—"

"To go to the hospital," my dad says, and my heart sinks. If the bottle of water didn't sober me up, this did.

We rush out to the hospital together, and we're greeted by Jimmy, who is in the waiting room, sweating anxiously.

"Jimmy, is he okay?" my mom asks.

"I don't know," Jimmy says. "They won't let me go back and see him. I told them I'm his health care proxy, and they say I'm not family. It's BULLSHIT." The front desk nurse cringes a little as Jimmy glares at her.

"Jesus Christ," my mom says, and my mom never takes the Lord's name in vain.

"He was asleep next to me," Jimmy says. "Then I heard him gasping for breath. Like he was fighting just to get enough air. And he was drenched. The whole bed was wet. I got him here as fast as I could, but . . . I just . . . I'm so worried." Jimmy sobs. It's like he's been holding all the anxiety in until someone else showed up to help. My mom lets him cry into her cardigan.

"It's okay," my mom says. "You did the right thing. Let's go see him."

My mom heads to the front desk nurse, explains that she is Stephen's sister, and tells the nurse that Jimmy is family to us, and that he will be coming to see Stephen as well. She doesn't even give the nurse a moment to respond or defend herself.

"Hey," Stephen says when we enter his room. He has so many tubes and wires and beeping machines around him, but he smiles like he's lounging in a palace or something.

"Uncle Stephen," I say. I try hard to hold it together. I want to transmit strength to him, but seeing him like this is tearing me up inside.

My mom immediately goes to him and holds him, tears in her eyes. I know she doesn't like crying in front of him, but she can't help it. She's not as strong as her brother.

"Don't worry so much," Stephen says. "It's just a touch of toxoplasmosis."

"I was so scared," my mom says.

"The very attractive doctor says they caught it early enough to treat it," Stephen says. "I think he may have been flirting with me a little."

This is my uncle, a man who can make me smile even when he just almost died. Tears start to form in my eyes too, and I can see Uncle Stephen notices.

"Hey, Judy," he says. "You know I'd never go anywhere without saying goodbye to you, right?"

"I know," I say. "I know." I sit by his side. My mom holds one of his hands and I hold the other. My dad stands close enough for us to feel his support, but far enough to let us have this moment with Stephen.

"My girls," Stephen says as he clutches us tight. "I'm a lucky man."

"And Jimmy," my mom says. "If Jimmy wasn't with you . . ."

"You saved my life, girl," Stephen says.

"You've saved mine, girl," Jimmy says. "I'd have followed Walt out of this hellhole by now if it weren't for you."

"We're all grateful to you, Jimmy," my dad says with wrenching sincerity.

The doctor comes by to check on Stephen. He *is* hot, and he *does* seem to be flirting with Stephen. I wonder if that's his way of giving his patients a little extra reason to fight for their lives. As the doctor explains that Stephen's vital signs are looking promising, it hits me that he looks a lot like José before he was sick. It's uncanny—the messy black hair, the olive skin, the thick eyebrows, crooked nose, and soccer build. He even has José's way of biting his lower lip in between sentences. Somehow, the fact that this doctor looks like José gives me hope. It feels like a sign that Stephen will make it, that he'll be one of the ones to survive this thing and tell the story when all the rest of his friends are gone.

When the hot doctor leaves, Stephen turns to me. "Judy," he says in a whisper, "there's something I need to say to you before I go."

"But you're not going," I say. "The doctor just said you were doing great."

"I know," he says. "But it's time I said it. I want you to forgive Reza and Art." I look away from him. "But especially Art. He loves you."

"I know," I say. "But I just can't . . ."

"You want me to tell you a story? Stephen says. "In high school, I was teased mercilessly for being different, and I was so desperate to prove I was straight that I dated a girl. I convinced her that I loved her. And I let her fall in love with me."

I look at my mom, who nods her head. "Sara Massey," she says. "She was a friend of mine, too."

"Sara Massey," Stephen says wistfully. "I lied to her for almost a year. What I did to her wasn't kind, but I did it because I was scared. I did it because I thought the alternative was being called a fag, being beaten up. And on some level, I was trying to convince myself that I might be straight. I wanted to want her."

"Fine," I say. "I get it. But you weren't living in New

York City. And it was a totally different era. Things have changed."

"Not much," he says.

I shrug. "What you said explains what Reza did," I say. "But not what Art did. Art didn't date me because he wanted to be straight. He lied to me when I was his best friend."

"I know he did," Uncle Stephen says. "I think he felt ashamed of his feelings for Reza, and he didn't know how to tell you. What he did wasn't right, but it doesn't make him a bad person. It just makes him a human being."

All I can think of to say is "But Reagan and Jesse Helms are human beings, and that doesn't mean they need to be our best friends."

"Are they human beings?" Jimmy asks. "I always thought they were some sort of subspecies."

We all laugh, even my dad, mostly because we just need to laugh. I don't think my dad even hates Reagan all that much. He gives him a lot of credit for the fall of the Berlin Wall.

"There's something that would mean a lot to me," Uncle Stephen says. "Come to Maryland with us. Me, Jimmy, Art, Reza. We'll all be at the NIH protest."

"Oh Stephen," my mom says, "that can't be a good idea. You'll be so far from your doctors."

"The protests are what keep me going," Stephen says.

"Let us take care of you," my mom says.

"You know I'm not good at that," Uncle Stephen says.

"Besides, I'll be protesting outside the National Institutes of Health. If something happens, who better to treat me than them?"

My mom rolls her eyes. "You're impossible," she says.

"Agreed," Jimmy says. "Impossible, and impossibly hard to resist, so please say yes, Judy. We want you there. It would be very meaningful for your uncle."

I know I'll go. I would walk barefoot across the equator for him. But I don't want to be the only woman in our group. I'm done with that. I know now that it's nice to have another woman by my side, someone who sees things from my perspective and can support me in different ways than Art and even Uncle Stephen can. And so I say something that surprises even me. "I'll go on one condition," I say. "That you come with me, Mom."

My mom looks at me in surprise. "Me? I'm not really much of a protester."

"I think that's a great idea," Uncle Stephen says. "Come on, Bonnie."

"When is it?"

"May twenty-first," Stephen says. "It's on a Monday, but we're going for the weekend, because I have a surprise planned."

"What surprise?" my mom asks. "I hate surprises."

"Let me take care of you," Uncle Stephen says. "Stop worrying."

"Judy has school on Mondays. And I have book club that Sunday. I can't skip . . ."

"Mom, those ladies in pastel will forgive you for missing one book club. And what's the point of reading all these self-help books about being your best self if you don't live what they're saying? This is important."

My mom looks to my dad, who nods. "I'm good with my girls going on this field trip," he says. I see my dad and Stephen make eye contact, probably because they both referred to me and my mom as their girls. They have that in common. They've shared us all these years.

"Okay, fine," my mom says. "As if going to Paris wasn't living on the edge enough, now we're going to Maryland. Who am I?"

"You're Bonnie Bowman," Uncle Stephen says. "Mom and sister of the century, and the very latest member of ACT UP."

My mom the activist. I never thought I'd see this day. For the next half hour, we reminisce about Paris, about everything we ate and saw and all the clothes we tried on but couldn't afford to buy. Then the hot doctor comes back and says that Stephen should rest, and Stephen loudly says that the doctor is just trying to get rid of us so that the two of them can be alone. We all leave, and as we do, my mom turns to me and says, "Don't think I've forgotten how late you were tonight. I expect you to tell me everything." Everything. The punch. The spin the bottle game. Saadi's hairy, thick body on top of me. I feel myself blush.

"*Risky Business*," I say.

"What?" she asks.

"That's the movie Annabel and I were watching. It's so good. Annabel has a total Tom Cruise thing. She's seen that movie, like, twenty times, and she knows *Cocktail* by heart."

My mom gives me a side-eye. I know she doesn't believe me, and I know I'm lying to someone I love. But it doesn't make me a bad person, I tell myself. It just makes me a human being.

#76 Madonna

She is not ashamed, and therein lies her massive power. Because shame is their weapon. People who feel shame remain hidden, and that's exactly how they want us. And then along comes Madonna. She was quickly written off as a flash in the pan, a one-hit wonder, but not by the people who recognized immediately that she was not just a singer, not just a dancer, not just a performer. She was, and is, a revolution. Just look at the way she responded when *Playboy* and *Penthouse* ran nude photos that were taken of her when she was young and broke. She said three words: "I'M NOT ASHAMED." Those words are why her presence in the world gives me hope for the future, that more queer kids will come out sooner, that more women will feel the freedom to own their sexualities, that maybe someday shame will be something kids don't feel anymore. Before I became sick, I was out with José one night, on a dance floor. Madonna came out and sang one song, "Holiday." No one had heard of her yet, but within seconds, we were communing with each other, with her, and with a new way of thinking. "You can turn this world around," she sang, and she meant it. To turn the world around is to create a revolution, isn't it? She is a revolution in every sense, a radical change and a celestial body in orbit. She's turning this world around and showing us how to follow in her footsteps. I don't know if shame has a true opposite—perhaps pride, but that doesn't feel quite right. So, as far as I'm concerned, the opposite of shame is Madonna. Long may she reign.

REZA

We all plan to arrive in Maryland separately. Stephen and Jimmy got there earlier than us, to prepare for the protest. Judy's mom rented a car and is going to drive the two of them. And Art and I are on the train. I love trains. I think they're my favorite means of transportation. The rhythmic rumbling of wheels on tracks, the windows that give you rapidly changing views of foliage and industrial buildings and car lots. And the mystery of them. Like we are in an Agatha Christie novel. I try to explain this to Art, and his face lights up. "Let's play Count the Fags," he says. "Decode the mystery of these passengers."

"I hate that word," I say, frowning.

"Get over it," he says. "I've reclaimed it, and so should you. We'll start at the top of the train, and we'll get to the bottom. Which Stephen once told me is pretty much his journey."

"What is?" I ask.

"He started as a top and ended a bottom."

"Oh," I say. I do know what a top and a bottom are. There was a notecard about that. But I don't know which one I am. I cannot let my mind even think about all that. I think that being a top would be like invading someone, and being a bottom would be like getting invaded. And both sound scary and unsettling. When countries are invaded, it's usually not good for either side in the end.

We make our way to the front car. Art is giddy with excitement, and it makes him even more beautiful than usual. "Look at me," he says. "I'm away from my parents, on my way to a protest, with the man I love."

Now that we've both said we love each other, we can't stop saying it. We declare it often. Proudly.

"Am I a man?" I ask, amused.

"You will be when I'm through with you," he says with a smirk.

Through with me? Will he be through with me? I don't want that to ever happen. I want to be with him forever, preferably in a relationship that involves lots of kissing and cuddling, and no exchange of bodily fluids other than saliva, which I have come to see as the only bodily fluid that is my friend. And sweat. I like his sweat. I can see some now, just under his armpits. I love the smell of him. I breathe him in whenever he's near me. He's wearing a tank top, ripped black jeans, and leather motorcycle boots. He has changed his hair again—this time the sides are buzzed but the top is long, and a wave of dyed aqua hair falls over the left half of his face, like an ocean wave. He's my queer Veronica Lake. I didn't come up with that, he did.

Art begins the game by slowly walking down the aisle of the first car. Upon seeing a man sitting next to his wife and two children, he whispers to me, "Fag number one."

"He's married," I whisper.

"So were Rock Hudson and Cary Grant," Art says. "That guy was cruising us hard."

We pass a group of men who Art says are probably going to the protest. One reads *The Advocate* magazine. John Waters is on the cover, gazing out at the reader as if he wants to tell them a secret. Another wears a SILENCE = DEATH T-shirt with a pink triangle on it. Art gives them a nod and keeps moving. As we make our way from one car to the next, he points out one man after another: a young college dude on the train with his buddies, a businessman using his briefcase as a pillow, an old man reading a tattered copy of Walt Whitman. He seems to know by instinct who is gay and who is not, and each time I question him, he tells me that his gaydar is impeccable.

"Gaydar?" I ask.

"Yeah," he says. "It's how I knew about you."

What can I say to that? He did know about me, even when I did not want him to. When we get to the end of the last car, we make our way back to our seats.

"I counted sixteen fags," he says. "Which puts this train right in line with the world at large, if it's actually true that ten percent of the world of gay."

"Eighteen," I say.

"Eighteen what?" he says.

"You forgot to count us," I say. "That makes eighteen. . . ."

He smiles. "Oh, wow. You can't say the word, but you're counting yourself as a fag, huh?"

He leans in close to me, licks my lips, then kisses me. I want to close my eyes, but I don't. I'm too paranoid about all the eyes on us. I'm sure I see a woman with a bad perm shake her head at us in disgust, and two teenage girls giggling as they whisper in each other's ears. But Art's eyes are closed. He doesn't care what these people think, and that's what I love most about him. I wish I cared less about other people, and more about myself.

When he pulls away from me, he holds my hand tight, and I don't pull away. No one knows us here, and in any case, they all just saw us kiss. We stare into each other's eyes. The train makes a stop.

"Are you nervous?" I ask.

"Not at all," he says. "Let them arrest me if they want to. I'm ready."

"Not for the protest," I say. "To see Judy."

His eyes flutter. He looks down, then out the window, so many trees outside, so many shades of green whizzing past us. "Judy . . . ," he says. "Yeah . . ."

"She wouldn't have agreed to be there if she didn't want to forgive you," I say.

"But she didn't want to come with us," he says. "I

mean, she's driving with her mom? Over taking a train with us? Her mom is probably going to play some self-help book-on-tape in the car and make Judy talk about self-improvement and the power of positive thinking."

"I love her mom," I say. "When we were together . . ."

Art quickly cuts me off. "You and Judy were never together. It wasn't a real relationship."

"I know," I say. I don't fight him. I would never stand a chance. But I know in my heart that, despite my lies, Judy and I did have a real relationship. There was true affection there, and laughter, and understanding, and fish pins. I was going to say that when Judy and I were together, her mother was always so welcoming and kind to me, and that those qualities seemed to rub off on Judy. In this moment, I realize that Art's parents are combative and reactionary, and that some of those qualities have rubbed off on Art.

"Of course I'm scared," Art says. "I don't even know what to say to her anymore. I don't want to see myself through her eyes. When I think about that, about how she must see me, I hate me too."

"I feel the same," I say. "I hope she forgives me."

"Yeah," he says. "She probably will. But you didn't know her very long. My betrayal is so much worse."

"Maybe you're right," I say, though I can't help feeling like he doesn't understand that what I did to Judy, and what I felt for her, matters too.

"You realize that we're going be sharing a hotel room," Art says. "Do you know what that means?"

"Room service?" I ask, joking nervously.

"Yeah," he says. "Definitely room service. And sex. Hotel rooms are basically made for sex."

"Why?" I ask.

"I don't know," he says. "I read that in a story in some porno magazine once." After thinking about it some more, he says, "Maybe it's 'cause the maids change the sheets every day."

"Where did you . . ." I stop myself from asking the question on my mind.

"What?" he says.

"Where did you get a porno magazine?" I ask.

Art laughs. He squeezes my thigh. "Oh, Reza. My innocent Reza. The first time I read a porn, I was twelve. I found my dad's stash of *Penthouse* and *Playboy* magazines in the back of his closet. *Playboy* was pretty much useless to me. But *Penthouse* has these sex stories in them, and they were very hot because there were men in them." I find myself getting hard, and he moves his hand to my crotch. "Just covering up the evidence," he says with a smile.

"Maybe you could . . . read those stories to me someday. You can't get AIDS from story time."

He laughs. "Any day you want." He squeezes my erection, and I find myself looking around, wondering who can tell what's going on. "You've never bought a porno mag?" he asks.

I shake my head.

"The gay ones are always hidden at the newsstands.

They're amazing. There's porn for all kinds of guys. *Honcho. Inches. Black Inches. Latin Inches.*"

"What about Iranian guys?" I ask.

"I think that might be a void in the gay porn market," he says. "You could fill it by becoming a porn star."

"That would make all my mother's dreams come true, wouldn't it?" I smile sadly.

"I can see it now," he says. "The debut issue of *Iranian Inches*, with cover star Reza, photographed by me."

"Okay," I say, smiling. As the train rumbles toward Union Station in Washington, I think about our hotel bed. I see me and Art in that bed, taking turns invading each other, helping each other figure out if we are tops or bottoms or both. But then I think . . . what if the maids are lazy and don't change the sheets? What if the sheets we will be sleeping in have other men's semen on them, possibly infected? This thought stays with me as we take a cab to the hotel we are staying in, and as we check in, and as we enter the room.

Art dives onto the bed like it's a pool, and I have a moment of panic. I want to put those sheets under a microscope and make sure they are clean. But there's no time for my paranoia to build, because Art leaps back up, takes my hand, and then pulls me onto the bed with him. He kisses me, his tongue exploring every inch of my mouth, his body grinding against mine, sweaty and hot. He's hard, and I am too. He turns me over onto my back, positioning himself on top of me so that his hardness rubs up against mine. He whispers my name into my ear, and I whisper his name in his, until our names cease to have a meaning, sounding more like moans than anything else. He thrusts faster and faster, until my name becomes more scream than moan, and then he rolls over to the side of me.

"Wow," he says. "Guess I won't be wearing these pants tonight."

I notice the gooey stain on his black jeans, and the wetness on my own blue jeans. "Oh," I say. "I didn't know that you . . ." I leap off the bed and go to the bathroom. I squeeze some shampoo from a tiny bottle onto a washcloth, get it all wet, and then rub the wetness off my pants. I wash my hands, perhaps too aggressively. I look at myself in the mirror. I tell myself I am okay, that nothing risky happened.

"You okay in there?" Art asks. "You do realize having two pairs of jeans and two pairs of underwear between us is, like, as safe as abstinence, right?"

"I know," I say. And then, closing the door, I add, "I'm going to shower before we meet everyone downstairs."

I turn on the shower, take off my clothes, and get inside. As I touch myself, I imagine Art thrusting on top of me, screaming my name. I close my eyes and let the hot water wash all evidence of my passion away.

The lobby of the hotel we are staying at looks like it has not been redecorated in a few decades, which gives it an eclectic charm. Art touches everything in the lobby nervously, commenting on the ugly paintings and dirty lampshades. Anything to distract him from how scared he is to see Judy. And then . . . her voice.

"Art," she says hesitantly. "Hi, Reza."

We both turn at the same time. She wears tight tie-dye leggings with a flowy pink dress over it. A thin black belt, black leather boots, and a black choker complete the look, which is fantastic. She looks incredible. Her mother stands by her side and says hello to us.

"Thank you for coming," Art says after we have said our hellos. There's a humility in his voice I've never heard before.

"I came for Uncle Stephen," Judy says curtly. "Not for you."

Mrs. Bowman flinches when Judy says this. She holds her daughter's hand for support.

"I know that," Art says, masking his hurt. "But we're still here together."

"We're not together," Judy says. "I'm here with my mom, and you're here with Reza."

"I know," Art says. "I just mean, well . . ." If he expected immediate forgiveness, he's not getting it.

"You look great, Judy," I say, and already I want to wipe the stupid smile off my face. I'm trying too hard.

"Thanks," Judy says, but she doesn't sound thankful. She sounds like she hates me. "Though the last time you told me that, you weren't exactly being honest."

"Boys," Mrs. Bowman says, looking slightly uncomfortable. "Do you know anything about this surprise

Stephen told us about? I hate surprises."

"He didn't mention a surprise to us," Art says, relieved for the change in subject. "What kind of surprise is it?"

"That's what I'd like to know," Mrs. Bowman says. "Because if it's something like throwing grenades or lying down in front of traffic . . ."

"It has nothing to do with the protest," a voice says. It's Jimmy. We all turn to see him behind us, in a maroon velvet jacket over a T-shirt and jeans. Jimmy gives each of us a big hug, and then he addresses the surprise again. "Stephen worked hard to arrange something for us to do tonight that he thought would be meaningful and, perhaps, would bring back happier days."

"For us?" Mrs. Bowman asks. "Isn't he joining us?"

"Stephen couldn't make it," Jimmy says sadly. "And trust me, I was going to stay behind with him, but he insisted I be here. He said if I don't storm the NIH for him, he would never forgive me, and you all know that he is a very hard man to say no to."

"I don't understand," Mrs. Bowman says. "Why couldn't he make it? The doctor said he could go back home."

"Is he okay?" Judy asks, her voice trembling.

Jimmy can't answer that question without his eyes welling up with tears. He turns away from us for a moment, and then he says, "Look, he's been better, but he'll bounce back. He has before. And he wants photos of tonight. I promised him that, Art, so you better snap the hell out of all the glamour, girl."

"What glamour?" Art asks. "We're in Bethesda."

Jimmy reaches into the inside pocket of his velvet jacket and pulls out an envelope. He hands it to me, of all people. "He thought you should open it, Reza."

My hand shakes as I hold the envelope. "Me?" I ask. Why did he want me to open it? I'm the least important person here, the one with the weakest connection to Stephen. Why me?

"Well, go ahead, Reza," Mrs. Bowman says. "You'd think my brother would know that surprises just give me knots in my stomach."

I tear open the envelope and tickets fall out onto the floor. Six of them. I pick them up and stare at them, and my eyes zero in on a single word: Madonna. And then: Blond Ambition Tour. Capital Centre. Landover, Maryland. My heart races.

"Oh. My. God," I say in disbelief.

"And by God, you mean Madonna," Art says, wrapping his arms around me with excitement. "Holy shit, holy shit!" he adds for emphasis.

"Bartholomew, language," Mrs. Bowman scolds him.

"I can't believe it," Judy says, beaming. I can see her fighting against her excitement, not wanting to seem too happy in front of us. "We're going to see Madonna. Live. In person. Like, she'll be in front of us."

"Breathing the same air," Art adds.

For a moment, we're united in our joy. Then Mrs. Bowman looks over to Jimmy. "Is the show appropriate for children? Wasn't she just arrested in Canada for . . ."

"Mom," Judy says, annoyed. "She masturbates on-stage, big deal."

Mrs. Bowman flinches. And then, with a shrug, she says, "Well, at least masturbation is safe sex." I could not agree more.

"Guess that means we're all going to see Madonna!" Judy squeals.

Art hugs me, jumping up and down with excitement. "We're. Going. To. See. Madonna." He says each word like it deserves its very own punctuation mark.

Art, Judy, and I start singing, *We're going to see Madonna, we're going to see Madonna . . .*

Jimmy, amused, takes the tickets back and hands one to each of us. We realize that the sixth ticket won't be used. It's Stephen's ticket, and Jimmy suggests that we find a nice queen to give the ticket to outside the show.

The venue is mobbed when we get there. So many people, mostly women and gay men. Madonna T-shirts everywhere. Jelly bracelets. Girls with their bras on over their T-shirts. Boys in blond wigs with a long ponytail reaching down their spines. Desperate fans asking anyone if they have an extra ticket. As we try to decide who to give the ticket to, Art says, "Imagine playing Count the Fags here. The game would never end."

"What did you say, Bartholomew?" Mrs. Bowman asks.

"Oh, nothing, it's just a game that we . . ."

"There's nothing funny about using a word like that," she snaps back before Art can finish. The edge in her voice reminds me that Mrs. Bowman is as angry at me and Art as Judy is. She is Judy's mother, her protector.

"I'm reclaiming the . . ."

Again, she doesn't let him finish. "You know what, Art? I heard that word hissed at my brother like a dagger throughout his childhood, and I don't want to hear it ever again. So if you're going to reclaim it, wait until I'm not around."

I await Art's know-it-all response, but to my surprise, he simply says, "Deal."

"That's the one," Jimmy says. "Look at him." Jimmy points to a teenage boy, probably my age, wearing a white mohair sweater that swims on him like a dress. The sweater has a pink and yellow geometric design on it, and he pairs it with tight white pants and white platform boots. His black hair is pulled back in a long ponytail, and a crucifix dangles from his headband. I wish I had the confidence to dress like him. He clomps around, asking anyone if they have a ticket.

"I approve of his fashion sense," Judy says. "That sweater is like Saint Laurent meets a suburban Christmas party. It's fabulous."

"Then you do the honors," Jimmy says, handing Judy the extra ticket.

We approach the boy together, and Judy puts a hand on his shoulder. "Hey, I'm Judy," she says. "First of all, I'm obsessed with your style. But more importantly, would you like a ticket to the show?"

"Yeah, but I only have fifty bucks," he says.

"It's free," Judy says.

The boy's eyes open wide in disbelief. He hugs Judy and practically yells out, "I think I'm in love with you."

"Just what she needs," Jimmy says drolly. "Another queen in love with her."

We head in with our new sixth, whose name is Mario, and who was born in Mexico, and who has not spoken to his parents since they found him in his mother's heels. He left home and moved to Washington, DC, where he lives with a cousin of his who works at a newspaper there. Before he left home, he packed all his mom's best clothes to take with him.

We awkwardly circle around each other as we decide who will sit where. Jimmy goes in first, and then Mrs. Bowman enters, and then Mario enters. Judy goes in next, and then me, and then Art. I'm in between the two of them, feeling the tension.

"Hey," I say to Mario, leaning over. "What's your favorite Madonna song?"

"'Gambler,'" he says. "It's so underrated."

"Mine is the one that's named after me," Jimmy says.

"Yeah, but 'Jimmy, Jimmy' is, like, her worst song," Art says, with love.

"Which still makes it better than everyone else's best song," Mario says.

"Fair point," Art concedes.

Madonna is a safe topic of discussion, and so we talk

about our favorite looks, hairdos, videos. Everyone seems engaged in the conversation except Mrs. Bowman, who confesses that despite liking that she's a strong woman, she doesn't "get Madonna."

And then the lights dim, and in an instant, the crowd goes wild, no one more than me. We scream in unison, like a tsunami of sound that we are sending over to the stage, which practically vibrates with energy like a mating call. We are calling our goddess to us. Lights flash. An electronic beat begins. An industrial stage is revealed. Male dancers with sculpted bodies appear onstage, chains around them. And then, SHE is in front of us. Singing "Express Yourself." No, she's in front of *me*, because there's no one else in this room but me and Madonna. I cannot take my eyes off her for the first half of the song. But midway through, Judy bumps into me. She dances, feels the energy. And we look at each other, both singing along. A moment passes between us. Maybe she, like me, remembers wearing that "Express Yourself" lingerie, and how horribly that turned out for us. By the time the next song, "Open Your Heart," begins, I can feel something in Judy thawing, like the song is literally opening her heart. Judy smiles at me, a smile of forgiveness and empathy, a smile full of history. Here in this stadium, we are dancing, we are singing, we are forgiven, we are glowing, we are understood.

I glance at Mrs. Bowman a few times during the show. She watches with fascination, but with no sense of connection. When Madonna masturbates during "Like a Virgin," she covers her eyes with her hands and yells, "Oh, no. This is too much."

"It certainly is too much," Jimmy says with glee. "And that's why I love it."

But the show takes a turn when Madonna sings "Like a Prayer." She begins the song by simply looking up at the heavens and calling out, "God?" She speaks God as a question, like she's wondering where he has gone, how he's letting this world burn. The show goes from something fun to something challenging. After "Like a Prayer," she sings "Live to Tell," and at that point, the audience is in a hush. I hear a sob, and I turn to see it's Mrs. Bowman, tears flowing down her usually composed face.

One by one, we all turn to Mrs. Bowman, shocked to see her crying. Judy holds out her hand, and her mother takes it. Squeezes it hard.

Judy cries too now, and soon I do too, and Art.

"Oh, God," Mrs. Bowman says, still clutching Judy's hand. She rests her head on Jimmy's shoulder, her tears moistening the velvet of his jacket. He comforts her. It's hard to hear her words over the music, but I think she says, "He won't live, will he? He won't live to tell anything."

"Shh, baby, it's okay," Jimmy says. "Cry it out."

And she does. I do too. Because I am so filled with emotion. So much love. For Madonna, for the dreams she allows me to dream through her magnificence. For Art, whose hand I'm clutching so tight, who I cannot get enough of. For Judy, my first friend. For Jimmy, who I once feared touching. For Mrs. Bowman, who is so kind. And yet, there is still fear. Fear that Stephen and Jimmy will be gone soon. Fear that all these beautiful dancers on-stage with Madonna will be gone soon. Fear that this celebratory holiday we are experiencing will end. Fear that just as my life is beginning, it will come to a violent stop.

Will it grow cold, the secret that I hide?

I feel it all in the two hours that Madonna graces us with her presence. Joy and pride and love and fear and anger and passion. And one emotion I never thought I would feel: faith. Yes, faith. Because if the world could bring together this woman with these songs and these dancers in this place with me in it, then creation must be more powerful than destruction.

The last song she sings is her ode to family, "Keep It Together." Before the song ends, she hugs every member of her crew, starting with the grips and electricians. Her dancers keep dancing, and that's when it hits me that almost every one of her flamboyant, gorgeous dancers is a black man or a brown man. One of them even looks distinctly Middle Eastern. And they all seem gay.

Madonna dances until she is the only person left on-stage, the audience's clapping the only instrument she has left to accompany her. And to the sound of our beat, she repeats a mantra over and over, like her life depends on it. Like *our* lives depend on it.

Keep it together. Keep people together. Forever and ever.

We sing along. We cry tears, but now they are filled with joy. And we hold hands. By we, I mean Art, Judy, and me.

We are together again, just like Stephen planned. Whatever was unresolved between us seems to have been healed by this music, by this movement of our bodies and by the union of our voices. We find each other's gazes, and we sing along together. Singing these words is what we needed, more useful and powerful than all the apologies and accusations. We have been reminded that our unity is important.

ART

I knock on Judy's hotel room door an hour before we are set to go to the NIH. Mrs. Bowman opens the door. In the background, I can see Judy painting a sign that reads DEAD FROM HOMO.

"Good morning, Art," Mrs. Bowman says.

"Hey," I say. Judy looks up at me with a sad smile and a small wave. "I was thinking maybe Judy would want to grab breakfast before we go."

"Can you finish the sign, Mom?" Judy asks.

Mrs. Bowman looks over at the sign. "Of course," she says. "Dead from Homo . . . sexuality?"

Judy and I freeze.

"It was a joke!" Mrs. Bowman says. "Am I not allowed to engage in some dark humor to get through all this?"

Judy gives her mom a hug. "You're full of surprises, Bonnie Bowman," she says.

"You haven't seen the half of it," Mrs. Bowman says.

"Wait until you leave the house and I have a midlife crisis. I plan on wearing cone bras to work and—"

"Bye, Mom," Judy says with a kiss on Mrs. Bowman's cheek.

"See you in the lobby." Mrs. Bowman sits down and gets to work completing the sign.

Judy and I head out toward the elevator. We enter the lobby in silence. "Wanna grab a croissant and walk for a bit?" she asks.

"Yeah," I say. "Speaking of croissants, I can't believe you went to Paris and I wasn't there."

"I know," she says.

"And I don't even know where you went, what you ate, what you wore . . ." I look over at Judy, and she's smiling.

"I went everywhere. I ate everything. I wore nothing but Givenchy, darling." She laughs. "Seriously, Art, it was magical. It was more than a trip—it was like, I don't know . . ." She searches for the words. "It was like knowing that everything would be okay. That there are other cities, other communities, that there's just so much beauty in the world. Does that make sense?"

"Yeah," I say, sighing. "It makes total sense."

"We went to the Moulin Rouge," she says. "And we saw this crazy, bawdy show, and it made me think of you."

"Of course it did," he says. "I love me a courtesan."

"Their costumes were beyond. As was the top of the Eiffel Tower. And I love eating snails now. And I might like macarons even more than ice cream."

"Maybe you'll live there someday."

"Maybe," she says. "I don't know." She pauses, thinking. "Oh my God, wait, I have to tell you. There's ACT UP Paris. It's amazing. We went to a meeting."

"Wow," I say. "That's incredible."

"It's so cool," she says. "It's just like the meetings here, but in French. They asked Uncle Stephen to speak, and they treated him like the star that we know he is. I made a photo album of everything. I'll show it to you when we're back home if you promise not to mock my photography skills."

"*Moi*? Mock *toi*? Never!"

She laughs, and that sound heals something in me.

We get almond croissants at the hotel coffee shop, and then we head outside. Maryland isn't Manhattan. No crowds fight for space here; there's no crush of people, no skyscrapers hide the clouds above. It feels open, and foreign. Judy chooses a direction and starts to walk. "How are you and Reza doing?" she asks.

I don't answer immediately. I'm playing different answers in my head, wondering how they might be received, afraid of upsetting her.

"You can be honest," she says. "I'm a big girl."

"We love each other," I say finally.

"That's great, Art." Judy puts an arm around me, maybe to let me know she really means it. "I know this is awkward and I definitely wish I didn't date him before you, but you deserve to be loved."

"Thanks, Frances," I say, feeling unworthy of her. I know how major this is for her. I love her so much I want to hug and squeeze her, so I do.

She pushes me away with a laugh and says, "Okay, let's not be sticky about it."

I laugh, because she's quoting a line from *Mildred Pierce*, and no other teenager but us would probably get the reference. "You deserve to be loved, too," I say. "And unless you already fell in love with a Frenchman who you're hiding from us, I know you will."

"No Frenchman for me," she says. "The trip wasn't really about that. It was more about experiencing the city with Stephen, and weirdly enough, bonding with my parents. I don't know why I didn't realize this sooner, but I have really rad parents."

"Yes, you do," I say, trying hard to hide any trace of envy in my voice. "You're lucky."

"I know that now," she says. "I think, I don't know, that it's easy to take things for granted when you're young."

"Wait, are we old now?" I ask, and she laughs again.

"You know what I mean," she says, swatting my shoulder. "Anyway, we're older." She's right, we are definitely older. "So . . . ," she says, her voice dropping an octave. "Have you lost your virginity? Whatever that means to you. I know gay virginity is different."

I stop for a moment, not sure I'm ready to discuss all this with her. I don't want to alienate her. I don't want to betray Reza. But then I remember she's my best friend.

She's the person I'm supposed to talk through this stuff with. "He's still afraid," I say sadly. "So we mostly kiss. He won't even let me take his pants off."

She looks over at me with real empathy. "I hate AIDS," she says.

"I hate it too," I say.

We look at each other in silence for a long beat, saying nothing, letting all our hatred and fear bring us closer to each other.

"It'll be over someday," Judy says. "I know it will." I can tell what she's thinking. That it may not be over in time to save Stephen. But she doesn't linger in sadness. She shifts her tone and jokes, "And then you'll take his pants off."

I laugh and add, "Oh, I won't take his pants off. I'll *tear* them off. With my teeth. Like a tiger that's just been unleashed from zoo captivity."

She laughs again. God, I love her laugh. I love the way she makes me feel, like I matter. She has always made me feel that way. "And imagine all those years of anticipation built up inside him," she says. "It'll be the most insane sex of all time."

"Hopefully it won't be years," I say. "Maybe it'll just be a few more months."

"You think?" she asks. "You think the CDC or the NIH has the cure and is just sitting on it?"

"I have to believe that," I say. "I just have to."

"I know you do," she says. "I do, too. I just . . ." She looks deep inside me, like she can see my soul. "Sometimes I lose hope, Art."

Stephen is in the air now. His presence and his absence. We both know Stephen must be in really bad shape if he didn't come to Maryland. He orchestrated our reunion perfectly. I just hope it's not one of his final acts of goodness. I need him to keep fighting, keep adding more goodness to the world.

"I know," I say. I hold her hand, squeeze it tight, trying hard to transmit hope to her.

"Change the subject," she says, her voice quivering. "Please."

"What about you?" I ask quickly. "No new men at all now that you're a popular girl?"

"Oh, come on, I am *not* a popular girl," she says, a little embarrassed by the description. "And I don't want to be. I'll always be a proud freak." After a pause, her face reddens and she adds, "But, um, I might have hooked up with Reza's stepbrother."

"What?" I squeal, clapping my hands together. "No seriously, WHAT?!"

"And he may have called me since because he wants to do it again," she says.

"I'm sorry, but I need ALL the details. How did this even happen?"

"Well, I was a little drunk, so . . ." She's blushing even harder now.

"You gorgeous hussy," I say, and she laughs. "Do you like him?"

"No!" she says quickly. "But it was fun. That's okay, right?"

"Fun is definitely okay," I say. "You deserve fun."

"And he's one hundred percent straight," she says. "Which was a refreshing change for me."

"You deserve straight, too." I look at her with new eyes. She's still Judy, but she does seem different. More confident. More grown-up.

We both finish our croissants. "You're the first person I told that Saadi story to."

"What about your new best friend Annabel?" I ask, instantly regretting the snide tone.

"She's cooler than you think," she says, defensive. "Still, I haven't known her as long as you. It's not the same, you know."

"Yeah, I know," I say.

"Anyway, please tell no one. Especially not Reza. I don't want it to be awkward for him."

"Okay," I say, nodding.

"I think I've earned the right to have a few secrets of my own," she says, pointedly.

I put up my hands. "You have absolutely earned that right."

I realize this is it. We're friends again. We tell each other secrets once more. We trust each other. It'll never be me and her against the world the way it used to be. Too much has happened. I have a boyfriend now. And she has her girlfriends. But me and her, we're good again. We're us again.

"It's not always gonna be easy, is it?" she asks.

"What?" I ask.

"Us," she says. "Friendship."

"It's like what Stephen said about Joan Crawford in his notecard," I say. "That she was like Sisyphus pushing that boulder up a hill, except what she was pushing was the idea of 'Joan Crawford.'"

"I'm not sure I follow," she says.

"She survived—that's the whole point of her. Nothing came easy to her. You could always see her working for everything she had. And every time they tried to kill her, she came back. I guess what I'm saying is that . . . easy is overrated. We'll put the work in, and we'll survive."

Judy laughs. She can't stop.

"What's so funny?" I ask.

"It's just . . ." But she still can't stop the laughter. Finally, she catches her breath. "You've literally turned into Stephen," she says. "You used Joan Crawford's career as a metaphor for the survival of our friendship."

"If the shoe fits," I say. "We had our flapper phase and our MGM glory years. We just survived our box office poison days, and we're about to get signed to Warner Brothers. Watch out, 'cause there's an Oscar and a troglodyte in our future."

"I'm ready for it all," she says. "Bring on the trogs."

Now I laugh too. We laugh together. We laugh for the rest of the hour, and when our time together is up, we meet the others in the lobby as planned. Jimmy has been working with an affinity group that's planning on setting off multicolored military smoke grenades outside the NIH. As we all walk together, Jimmy explains this element of the action to us. "The whole idea is to get on the cover of the newspapers. See, a lot of papers are printing their front pages in color now. The rest is still black and white, but the front pages, those are bright and colorful. This affinity group had an ingenious idea. Basically, give the papers a color image that they cannot say no to. Rainbow smoke bombs outside the NIH."

"But is it safe?" Mrs. Bowman asks. "Because this movement is about saving lives, not hurting people, right?"

"No one will get hurt," Jimmy says. "It's totally safe. It'll just be beautiful and cinematic."

"Leave it to fags to turn protest into installation art," I say. Mrs. Bowman shoots me a look of death, and I correct myself. "Sorry. Leave it to *homosexuals* to turn protest into installation art."

"Where does one buy multicolored grenades?" Judy asks.

"*Soldier of Fortune* magazine," Jimmy says. "You can find anything in the back of a magazine these days."

"Wow," Reza says. "I guess you really can buy everything in America."

"Except life-saving medication," Jimmy says. "That's either too expensive or not approved yet."

No one says much after that. A somber silence hovers around us, like Stephen is walking by our side. I can almost feel him, smell him, hear him. And then I imagine José walking next to him, and Walt walking next to Jimmy. And James Baldwin leading us, and Michelangelo, and Oscar Wilde, and Judy Garland. They're all walking with us. When we arrive at the protest, one of Jimmy's friends tells us that over one thousand people showed up. "It's incredible," the activist says. "This turnout will show them how much we care." I want to tell him that even more people are here than he thinks, because there are spirits protesting alongside us.

Jimmy and the members of the affinity group run toward the entrance of the NIH, holding long poles, and then they ignite the grenades. I'm so mesmerized for a moment that I forget to raise my camera up and take pictures. That's how beautiful it is, how powerful. We have taken grenades, symbols of destruction, and turned them into symbols of love, of color, of hope.

And then, CHAOS.

People are chanting, demanding changes to the underrepresentation of women and people of color in clinical trials, demanding more and better treatment for all the opportunistic infections that come with AIDS.

The police are standing on guard, ready to make arrests, ready to pin people to the ground, handcuff them, silence them.

Activists lie down on the lawn, another die-in, their limp bodies a stark contrast to the lush green grass, glimmering in the springtime sun.

Other activists choose a more physical approach, using each other's hands to springboard onto the concrete of the building, literally becoming one with the structure as they chant.

Health Care Is a Right.

We're Fired Up.

Act Up, Fight AIDS.

NIH workers exit the building. They attempt to engage with protesters. Words are exchanged, loudly, passionately. Activists plead with them. So many people are screaming that I can only hear pieces of what each is saying.

". . . killing us. It's toxic . . ."

". . . BETTER DRUGS NOW . . ."

". . . opportunistic infections . . ."

". . . BLOOD ON YOUR HANDS . . ."

Jimmy gets in the face of an NIH suit. "And people of color? We're getting infected and dying at disproportionate rates, but where are we in your trials? Do our bodies not matter to you? DOES MY LIFE NOT MATTER TO YOU?"

A group of activists blows horns in unison. They blow a horn every twelve minutes, because that's how often someone dies of AIDS in this country.

Jimmy is still screaming at the NIH suit when a police officer approaches. The moment the policeman gets close to him, Jimmy goes limp, allowing himself to be cuffed and pulled away.

"Jimmy!" Mrs. Bowman screams.

"Art, take my picture," Jimmy yells. "Stephen wants to see everything."

I take his picture as he's pulled away, and it's horrible and beautiful all at the same time. I photograph it all, each frame so full of action. I snap Reza, his beautiful face surrounded by red, yellow, and green smoke bombs. I snap Judy, holding her sign that now reads DEAD FROM HOMOPHOBIA, the PHOBIA written in her mom's handwriting. Judy holds the sign high up in the air, and Mrs. Bowman's arm is draped proudly and protectively around her daughter. I snap it all, until I have no film left, until the protest is over.

We are not arrested, and Jimmy isn't held long. Mrs. Bowman says there's room for us in the car she rented, and so we all cram in. Mrs. Bowman says the car has a CD player and asks if any of us have some CDs with us. Reza pulls *Like a Prayer* from his Discman and hands it to her. On the way back to New York, we all sing along together, reliving the concert. When *Like a Prayer* ends, Reza pulls out *True Blue*, and we listen to that, singing extra loud during "Jimmy, Jimmy," and staring ahead in silence during "Live to Tell." By the time we reach the rental car place, Mrs. Bowman knows all the lyrics.

It's not time to say goodbye yet, though. First, we must go visit Stephen. "Should we take a cab downtown?" Mrs. Bowman asks.

"He's in the hospital," Jimmy says.

"I thought you said he was back home," Mrs. Bowman says.

"He made me say it, Bonnie. He knew you wouldn't go if you realized he was still in there." Jimmy's eyes are full of remorse. He hated lying. "It was important to him that we all took this trip. I promised him we would. And he wanted you there, Bonnie. He wanted you to experience it all."

Mrs. Bowman nods. "Let's go," she says urgently.

We head to the hospital together, and when I see Stephen, it's like my body splits into a million pieces. He looks like he has aged a decade in the last few days. He's thinner, paler, the life almost drained from his eyes. The machines and tubes around him and inside him seem to be working overtime to keep him breathing, and those breaths, every single one of them sounds like it's moving a mountain. He croaks out a "Hey" when he sees us. No one says anything. He looks over at Judy, me, and Reza and smiles. "You're friends . . . again," he says, his voice so weak that I wish one of those medical machines had a volume dial to bring his voice back up to its normal tone.

"Stephen," Mrs. Bowman says, taking his hand in hers, "how could you tell Jimmy to lie to us?"

"Look at me," Stephen says. "Are you really going to . . . pick this moment to give me . . . one of your lectures?" He struggles to finish the sentence.

Mrs. Bowman shakes her head. "No, of course not. I just want to be with you."

"I want you . . . with me, too," he says. "You and

Judy . . . stay with me . . . until I go."

"Oh, Uncle Stephen," Judy says, rushing to his side. "I'll sleep right here on the floor. I won't leave the hospital if you want me here."

"Not here," Stephen says. "I want to go . . . home." Everyone looks at each other, worried. "I don't want to go . . . here."

Mrs. Bowman looks at him and you can see her making a decision. "Okay," she says. "Okay. I'll go speak to the doctor. Jimmy, you're his health care proxy. Will you come with me?"

"Are you sure?" Jimmy asks, and Stephen nods. There's so much understanding between Stephen and Jimmy. I guess that's why Jimmy's the health care proxy, not Mrs. Bowman. Jimmy understands. He doesn't need a dictionary or a translator when he hears words like cytomegalovirus or cryptococcal meningitis or mycobacterium avium-intracellulare or toxoplasmosis.

Mrs. Bowman and Jimmy walk into the hallway to find the doctor. Stephen looks from Judy to me to Reza and back again. "How was the . . . concert?" he asks.

"It was amazing," Judy says. "She's God, basically."

"I am so grateful," Reza says. "It was the most thoughtful gift I have ever received. I think it, I don't know, changed my life. Is that silly?"

"It's not," Stephen says. And then, looking right at me, he says, "It's the power of . . . art."

"You were there," I say. I inch closer to Stephen. "You

were at the concert with us. And at the protest. I felt you. You were right by our sides."

"I know," Stephen says. "And you were . . . here with me, all three of you."

Reza's lips quiver in sadness. He doesn't know Stephen the way we do, once even feared him, and yet he has been welcomed into his family.

"I took pictures of everything for you," I say. "I even used color film for the first time to make sure you would see the color of those grenades."

"Were they . . . beautiful?" Stephen asks.

"They were," Judy says. "Like something out of a Technicolor musical. Vincente Minnelli couldn't have dreamed up something more gorgeous."

"No, but you will," Stephen says. "All of you. Keep . . . creating . . . beauty."

We all nod and catch each other's gazes. I feel these words etching themselves into my body, like a soul tattoo. *Keep creating beauty.*

Mrs. Bowman and Jimmy return. "You're going home, girl," Jimmy says.

"And I've spoken to Ryan," Mrs. Bowman says. "He's shopping for microwave dinners as we speak. Judy and I are staying with you."

Stephen just smiles, but then whispers, "Thank you."

"I'll go stock the fridge at his place," Jimmy says. "Any requests?"

"Diarrhea diet," Stephen says. "Rice . . . bananas . . . Gatorade."

"I know it well." Jimmy takes a deep breath. "This trip, it was special," he says. "I feel so close to each of you. We did something, didn't we?" Jimmy hugs us all and leaves.

"Why don't we go pack our bags, Judy?" Mrs. Bowman suggests.

"Okay," Judy says. "We'll see you soon, Uncle Stephen."

They give us hugs, and then they too are gone.

It's just me and Reza and Stephen now. We sit on either side of him. His gaze goes from me to him, him to me. Finally, he speaks. "I'm so happy . . . I lived long enough . . . to see Art . . . in love."

I can't help it. Tears roll down my cheeks. "I'm sorry. I hate crying in front of you. I just want to bring you joy."

"You, Art . . . have always brought me . . . . much more than joy." Stephen's eyes pierce mine.

I bury my face in his chest. "I love you. I love you. I love you." I keep repeating those words, thinking they might heal him.

Isn't love supposed to conquer all?

Then let it conquer AIDS.

Reza massages the knots in my shoulders as Stephen strokes my hair. And I keep saying the words.

I want love to be enough. I'll keep saying it until it is.

When Reza and I leave the hospital, he clutches my hand, which means so much. Usually, it's me clutching his hand, especially in public. "When Stephen dies . . ."

"Art, don't talk like that," he says. "He might be okay."

"It would be a miracle," I say, forcing myself to accept it.

"Miracles happen all the time," he says, looking to the sky, as if someone up there might be listening.

"When he dies," I say again, saying each word deliberately, "I don't think I can stay in this city. It's just going to feel like a ghost town to me."

"He's not dead, Art," Reza says. "He's not a ghost."

"If I go, will you come with me?" I ask desperately. "To San Francisco like we talked about? We could start a whole new life. Our life. No ghosts."

"Art, we weren't talking about leaving *now*." Reza looks away from me, like he's trying to escape this conversation.

"Not right now," I say, annoyed. "After he dies."

"You can't just escape your past, Art," he says.

"You did," I say, pushing him. "You escaped your dad. Wouldn't it be harder if you were in Iran, in the place where all your memories of him reside?"

"It probably would," he says. "But I didn't *choose* to escape. My mom moved our family."

"All the more reason to choose your own fate," I say. "Don't you want to create your own life?"

And then he says something that stops me cold. "Would I be creating my own life by following *you* somewhere *you* want to go? I didn't even apply to any schools on the West Coast."

Shit. He's so right. Here I am asking him if he'd follow

me, without even considering what he wants, or what he's planned.

"I'm sorry," I say, my voice laced with regret. "I guess all I want to know is that whatever happens, we'll be together."

He looks at me with certainty and says, "I'm not going anywhere if you're not."

JUDY

We move in with him. We are "his" girls. He uses the possessive to claim ownership of us, and for a few days, he truly does possess us. He possesses our time, our energy, our tears, and our thoughts. We do everything we can to make him eat. We sit on either side of him and watch old movies until he falls asleep. Morbidly, he chooses movies about illness. He says it makes him feel less alone to see glamorous women dying onscreen. We watch *Dark Victory* three times. Suffering is so beautiful in that film, each moment of disease romantic, deserving of a sweeping score and those epic Bette Davis close-ups, her eyes misty and searching. But nothing about Stephen's suffering is beautiful. He smells. He sweats. The diarrhea is so bad that he can't control it anymore. My mom cleans everything: the clothes, the soiled sheets, the toilet. She tends to him like he's her child, and not her big brother. And I get the strange experience of seeing how doting my mom must have been when I was a baby, to see how great of a mother she is. Sometimes he doesn't make sense. He calls me José, or Art, or Bonnie. And sometimes he makes so much sense. He looks me in the eyes, his eyes being the only part of his body that still has any remnant of glow, and he says something so simple and so true. "Judy, when I'm gone, I want you to love yourself as much as I love you."

Often, he's angry. This is a side of him I have rarely seen. He screams at my mom, at me, but mostly at himself. He hates what's happening to him. He's not ready. He wants to die. He doesn't want to die. He hates Ronald Reagan. He hates the FDA. He hates that Marilyn died before she could prove herself. He's furious that his mother won't come see him. He wants to hurt every bully from his high school. He wants to forgive the bullies, too. He works on a playlist of songs that he wants played at his memorial. "After You've Gone," by Judy Garland. "Don't Leave Me This Way," by the Communards. "Friends," by Bette Midler. "Once upon a Time," by Donna Summer. Songs that are at once sad and celebratory. He explains to us that the best dance songs are full of longing. They're about the desire to celebrate desire, because a dance floor is a place to morph your sorrow into grace. We listen to his song choices. Sometimes, for a few seconds, he has the strength to dance, so we dance. We belt out "The Way We Were," by Barbra Streisand, like we're auditioning for a girl group. The three of us. I barely sleep. My mom lets me skip school, and she doesn't go to work. We will be there when he goes. We've promised that to him, to each other, to ourselves. But being there requires vigilance, little sleep. Existence is hazy. Jimmy, Art, and Reza are with us often. Activists come and go. A lawyer from the immigration firm stops in to check Stephen's will. Drag queens sit by his bedside and sing. Only one person is missing. His own mother. My grandmother. My mom calls her twice a day, begs her to come, tells her she will forever regret not making peace with her son before he goes. But she never comes. I only talk to her once. I think maybe there will be a different result if the message comes from her granddaughter. So I take the receiver, and I say the word "Grandma," and then I break down in tears and can't say another word. I don't even know if it's exhaustion or anger or disinterest, but I realize I can't speak to her. I don't have the energy for her, for anyone but Stephen. I thank the heavens that he has my mom, and me, and that he created a family for himself, his queer family.

"Hey, where's that bottle of wine?" he asks, his voice clearer and stronger than it's been in days. In the hospital, with those tubes pulled in and out of his throat, he could barely speak. Now, his body is weak, but he can get a sentence out without gasping or clearing his throat.

My mom is roasting a chicken, hoping she can get him to eat some simple food. And I'm her sous chef, learning so much from her. How to give, how to care, how to be patient.

"Stephen," she says, "I'll pour you some more Gatorade."

"Give me the wine," he demands. "I'm done with fluorescent liquids."

My mom stops cold. She turns to me, her eyes welling, and asks, "Judy, can you get the wine?"

I don't understand her reaction, but I go ahead and search the kitchen for that special bottle of wine that Art's parents gave my parents, a bottle that my mom once said probably cost more than all the wine she's had in her life. It's a red bottle from France, and it's older than Stephen. I stare at the date on the bottle and I resent it. Why does this wine get to stick around longer than he does? I find a wine opener, and I realize I have no idea how to use it. I fumble with it for a few moments, frustrated. My mom approaches with a tender hand on my shoulder. She doesn't take the bottle from me, though. Instead, she guides me. And then she pours three glasses, though mine is more like a quarter glass.

We sit by his side and raise our glasses. "To my girls," Stephen says, and we all take a sip. The wine tastes rich and deep, almost like you can feel how old it is.

"To you, Stephen," my mom says, with so much love in her voice, "who always lived with so much courage."

"I had no choice," Stephen says.

"Of course you did." My mom runs a hand through

his hair, matted and clumpy from the sweating. "You could have hidden in the shadows."

"Maybe I'd still be alive if I hid," he says.

I feel split open. I don't even want to think that he could have been rewarded for living a lie. That's not how the world is supposed to work. He's the most honest, kind, and courageous man I know, and soon he'll be dead because of those very qualities. Dead because he dreamed himself into existence. Because he lived in truth.

"Uncle Stephen," I say, "don't say that. You're still alive. You're still here."

"I know," he says. "I know, Judy, my love. But I can't hold on any longer. And I don't want to put you through any more of my deterioration."

I put the wine down and hold on to his hand. "You're not putting me through anything. I want to be here. Just hold on. Tomorrow is another day."

"Are you quoting *Gone with the Wind*?" he asks, smiling weakly.

"Just trying to speak your language," I say. I'll quote old movies for the rest of my life if it will keep him alive.

"I always thought that movie was a little overrated," he says. "Though I do have a soft spot for Vivien Leigh. Poor thing would've been so much happier with Prozac. Medicine failed us both." Then, turning to my mom, he says, "Bonnie, can you pass me the pot of jelly beans?"

Suddenly it dawns on me. "No, Mom, don't give those to him!" She looks over at me, confused. "They're, like, some representation of everyone who's gone, and when he eats them, it's over."

"I don't understand," my mom says. "These jelly beans are . . ."

Stephen pushes himself up and grabs the pot of jelly beans. "I have found my own ways to cope," he explains to my mom. "A jelly bean for each soul I lost to AIDS. Maybe it's crazy, but sanity is boring." He puts a pink jelly bean in his mouth and chews. Then washes it down with another sip of wine. Then another jelly bean. And another. "Judy, will you call Jimmy, and Art and Reza? Tell them to come if they can."

"No!" I scream. "I won't do it. I can't do it, Uncle Stephen. You don't know what you're talking about. It's not time!" I'm sobbing now.

Stephen reaches over to the drawer of the end table by the couch. Inside are all his bottles of pills. Medication for the disease, and all the opportunistic infections, and then medication for all the side effects from the different medications. And morphine for the pain.

"You know I love you," Stephen says forcefully. "You know that, right?"

"Of course we do," my mom says.

"Bonnie, it's time," he says quietly. "Let me go."

My mom looks inside the drawer, and she sucks in a breath. I rush to her side, and then I see. The morphine bottle is empty.

"Uncle Stephen! No!" I'm sobbing now.

He doesn't say anything.

"Mom, we have to take him to the hospital!"

But my mom doesn't move. It's like she's frozen. She just looks at him with, I don't know, resolve. "Judy," she says quietly, "call Art and Reza. And Jimmy. And your dad."

"Please no," I choke out. "Please!"

"Sweetie, do what he says," my mom tells me gently. "The doctor said it's a matter of days."

"Judy," Stephen says. "Darling, I want to go surrounded by the people I love. Let me choose this. It's all I have left."

How can this happen? I'm not prepared to make these calls. I don't know how to tell a person that another person they love is dying. But I do it. Because he asks me to, and because if this is it, I want him to have as much love around him as possible. I get them each on the phone. And through tears, I somehow get the words out.

When I return to his side, he says, "Judy, you will have everything you dream of, and more. And I'll be watching."

I don't know what to say. I wish I could see into the future, see if I'll make him proud. Because that's all I want right now. To guarantee that I will. To live a life that's worthy of him.

"If you ever meet Madonna, if you ever make clothes for her, will you ask her a question?" This is how his mind works these days, going from one thought to another without explanation.

"Um, of course," I say.

"Can you ask her why Joe DiMaggio is in her 'Vogue' rap?"

I shake my head. Laugh a little. "Seriously, Uncle Stephen?"

"He doesn't fit. Greta Garbo. Marilyn. Dietrich. Brando. Jimmy Dean. Jean Harlow. And then, DiMaggio? He's an athlete. He struck balls, not poses. It makes no sense. I know it rhymes, but couldn't she have worked a little harder to find a rhyme for, I don't know, Joan Crawford or Barbara Stanwyck or Ava Gardner or poor, sweet Judy?"

"Uncle Stephen," I say, with all the conviction I can muster, "I promise you that if I ever meet her, I'll ask her that question. I promise."

"Good," he says, nodding. "I'm glad I stuck around long enough to hear that song. It makes me happy that kids today will know who Rita Hayworth is."

"They weren't all lucky enough to have Sunday movie nights with their amazing uncle," I say.

"I'm the lucky one," he says, smiling at me with love. "I got to watch you grow into the beautiful woman you are."

I feel a sharp ache. I'm not done growing up, and I don't know how to keep growing up without him.

My mom turns her wet eyes to me. "My beautiful daughter," she says, wiping her eyes like she's trying to see me more clearly. Then, turning to Stephen, she adds, "And my beautiful big brother."

Jimmy arrives first. He sits on the floor next to me and clutches Stephen's hand. Stephen smiles when he sees him. They nod in solidarity. "Is there anything you want me to tell Walt?" Stephen asks.

Jimmy shakes his head. He can't get a word out, but eventually he croaks, "Just tell the fool I miss him."

"Jimmy," Stephen says, "thank you."

"Shut up," Jimmy says. "I didn't do anything except keep you company, and you kept me company. And now . . ."

"Don't let go," Stephen says. "Fight it harder than I did. Finish that novel before you go."

Jimmy nods. "I'll try."

My dad arrives next. He doesn't say much, my father of few words. But he's here, with us, and that's all that matters.

Art and Reza arrive together. Art doesn't have his camera around his neck. Maybe he forgot it in the rush. Or maybe this is a moment he doesn't want to document, a moment he wants to experience without the remove of a lens. Reza looks apprehensive, unprepared to be here. And yet, I think, he's the one with the most direct experience with loss and with death. But maybe that doesn't matter. Maybe experiencing death once doesn't prepare you for experiencing it again. Death isn't something you can practice.

Art and Reza sit next to me and Jimmy, the four of us on the floor, my mom on the couch. Stephen is enveloped in tenderness. He looks around at all of us. "Judy, Art, Reza." Stephen says our names slowly, methodically, and then, even more slowly, he says, "Don't forget me."

"Are you kidding? No one who ever met you could forget you," Art says, tears running down his face.

"Not just me," Stephen says, looking to Jimmy. "Us. All of us. What we did. What we fought for. Our history. Who we are. They won't teach it in schools. They don't want us to have a history. They don't see us. They don't know we are another country, with invisible borders, that we are a people. You have to make them see." Stephen takes a strained breath. "You have to remember it. And to share it. Please. Time passes, and people forget. Don't let them."

"We won't," Art says, and I can feel just how much he means it.

Stephen closes his eyes. "We took care of each other, didn't we?" he asks. "This community. Gay people will make the best parents. Someday. Just look how we took care of each other. When no one else would."

"We're family," Jimmy says.

Stephen pulls out the final two jelly beans from the pot. He turns to Jimmy. "This one is Walt," he says. "And this one is José. Our great loves."

"Reduced to jelly beans," Jimmy says with a sad smile.

Stephen looks at each of us now, his gaze moving from

Jimmy to Art to Reza to me, and finally resting on my mom, his sister, who has never known a world without him. Neither have I.

He closes his eyes.

And then he's gone.

I can hear the sobs of my friends around me, or are they my own? My mom places a hand on his forehead and speaks before anyone else. "He was loved," she says.

She's right, but to me, nothing about this man will ever be past tense.

I whisper, "He is love."

REZA

I need supplies. I walk to a pharmacy as soon as it opens, when it's still empty and free of other staring customers. I purchase condoms and lube. Everything I need to lose my virginity. As I place the items on the pharmacy counter, I feel my face heat up. I can only imagine how red I am, how fiercely my embarrassment shows. But I go through with the transaction. I pay for the items. I look the cashier in the eyes and say thank you with as much confidence as I can muster.

Then I need a place, somewhere private. I knock on my sister's door, pharmacy bag in hand. I called her and told her there was something important I needed to talk to her about. She answers the door in a silk nightie, her messy hair tied above her head with a scrunchie. She waves me in with a yawn and a tired "Hey."

"Long night?" I ask.

"I'm a bartender," she says, annoyed. "Every night is a long night."

"I'm sorry," I say sincerely. "I, um, how is work these days?"

"I love nothing more than getting ogled by gross guys," she says, her voice laced with sarcasm. "And pouring them liquor that makes them act even grosser as the night goes on. On the bright side, I'm drinking less. Being around nasty drunks has made me realize how unattractive being wasted is. And I'm all about being hot."

I smile. "I'm sorry, that sounds tough," I say nervously, because I know what I'm about to ask her might be a little awkward.

She leads me to the kitchen. There's a small wooden table by the window, three mismatched chairs around it. "Well, maybe Mom will get her wish and I'll go back to college," she says with a shrug. I choose a chair and sit. "Tea? Coffee? Leftover ramen?" she asks. "I cooked it myself, and by cooked, I mean that I poured boiling water over it."

I shake my head. "I, uh, needed to talk to you," I say.

She pours herself some coffee and sits next to me. After a sip, she puts her hand over mine. "How are you doing?" she asks. "I know you were close to Judy's uncle. I'm so sorry, Zabber. This disease sucks."

I nod. "I knew him, I guess, but . . . not like Judy and Art did."

"Grief isn't a competition," she says. She looks at me

piercingly, and I realize we never spoke about our dad's death. Maybe I was too young. Maybe I resented her too much back then. Maybe she resented me.

"I know," I say, nodding. "I'm sad, but I'm sad for Judy and Art and Judy's mom more than anything else, if that makes sense."

"Sure it does," she says. She looks at me for a long time, sipping her coffee, waiting for me to say something. Finally, she asks, "Okay, what's up? Why'd you get me out of bed?"

"I, um . . . ," I stammer. "I was wondering if you would be okay with . . . It's just . . . See, the thing is that I can't go to Art's because his parents wouldn't let us . . . and I don't dare bring him over anymore because it would hurt Mom—"

"It's okay to hurt Mom, you know," she says. "I've made a career of it. I live with Massimo, I'm a bartender, and life goes on. You're gay now, and life goes on."

"But it wouldn't be fun for us," I say, blushing. "We need privacy."

"What wouldn't be fun?" she asks. And then her eyes open wide, and she laughs. She takes the scrunchie out of her hair and tousles it so it falls wildly around her shoulders. "Oh my God, are you asking me if you can use our apartment to have sex with Art?"

I can't see myself, but I can only imagine how fiercely my embarrassment shows.

"Is this the first time?" she asks, giddy.

I nod.

"Do you promise to use condoms?" she asks, with no hint of fear or judgment.

I pull a box of condoms out of the pharmacy bag, and she looks impressed. Then she stands up and screams with excitement.

"I'm so proud of you," she says, taking my hands and lifting me up to hug me. "My little brother is becoming a man."

"I don't know about that," I say.

I hear Massimo enter the kitchen, his voice raspy and exhausted. "What's going on?" he asks, going straight for the coffee. He's wearing nothing but white boxers that are practically see-through. "Why are you screaming?"

"I'm taking you out to dinner tonight," Tara says to Massimo gleefully.

"Okay," he says, unexcited. "Is it a special dinner?"

"It is," she says. "Because while we're at dinner, Reza and Art will be here. In our apartment. Getting. It. On." Tara cracks herself up, but Massimo barely reacts.

"Okay, I think I should go," I say, embarrassed. "I'll come back tonight. Thanks."

When I'm back home, I call Art's home. I can't wait to tell him to meet me at Tara's this evening. His mother answers the phone.

"Hello?" Her voice makes me wonder if she's been crying.

"Mrs. Grant, it's Reza," I say tentatively. "I'm calling for Art."

"How are you, Reza?" she asks, with more empathy

than I've ever heard from her.

"Okay," I say.

"I'm so sorry for your loss," she says.

"Thank you," I say. I don't know which loss she's speaking of. Is it the loss of Stephen, who she seemed to hate? Or is it the loss of Art, who is threatening to go to Berkeley instead of Yale, leaving us for another ocean?

"Here's Art," she says.

"Hey," Art says when he gets on.

"Will you meet me at my sister's place tonight?" I ask boldly.

"Sure. Is she hosting us or something?"

"No, she won't be there," I say. "It'll just be . . . us."

He takes a few breaths as he puts it together. Then he whispers, "Wow. Reza, of course I will meet you at your sister's empty apartment. You know I will."

Now that I've made the decision, I can't wait for it to be tonight. I don't know what to do with myself in the intervening hours, so I start by running a bath and I soak. I close my eyes. That is when I hear a ghost, but it's not Stephen this time. It's my dad. He's outside the bathroom door, screaming at me. In Iran, I used to take baths to escape his rage, but his voice would pierce the calm, even when I submerged myself under water. *Go away*, I scream at him in my head. But he doesn't. He's telling me all the things I know he would've said if he were alive. That I am disgusting. That I am an embarrassment, and a disappointment, and dead to him now. *You're dead*, I think.

You're dead. And I'm finally starting to live.

When I leave, I don't tell my mom where I'm going, and she doesn't ask. That's the thing about her denial. It stops her from asking me anything she's too scared to hear the answer to. She pretends to believe me when I say I'm going to a study group at night, or that I'm going to Maryland for a school trip. She doesn't ask anything, and I don't offer anything. It makes me so sad, but it's better than anger or rejection. At least that's what I tell myself.

I make my way to Tara's apartment. She opens the door and hugs me hard before she goes. Massimo awkwardly pats my shoulder before saying goodbye. I can tell he's probably not all that comfortable with this scenario, but also too in love with my sister to say much. I pace the apartment until the buzzer rings.

Art.

The time it takes for him to walk up the stairs is interminable, but the moment I see him, all my anxieties turn into excitement. I've wanted him for so long. Why have I been so scared of letting myself have him?

"Hi," he says, as he kicks the door closed behind him.

"Hi," I say, blushing.

"So, um, this is a surprise," he says. "I mean, I didn't think you would—"

I cut him off with a kiss, holding the back of his head, pulling him into me.

"Wow," he says when I let him go. "Who's brazen now?"

"I'm sorry," I say. "Was that too much?" I realize I've

become accustomed to him being the aggressor, and to me resisting. Maybe I'm no good at making moves.

"No, no," he says, smiling. "That was perfect."

"Okay," I say. "I don't know what I'm doing. I just know I want to do it."

I guide him to Tara and Massimo's bedroom and close the curtains. We fall into bed together, and I keep kissing him. There's no aggressor anymore. We're both initiating everything, like our bodies are synced up to the same rhythm. When I pull away from him, he's lying down and I notice his combat boots on the white sheets.

"We should take those boots off," I say.

"Go ahead," he says, smiling slyly.

I move toward his feet and try to pull the boots off unsuccessfully. I pull harder and harder, to no avail. We laugh, and I'm grateful for the laughter.

"Let me help you," he says, sitting up and yanking the boots off. He throws them onto the floor with a thud. We sit in front of each other for a moment. "Guess we should take the rest off, right?" he says.

"Okay," I say. A wave of excitement passes through me at the thought of us naked together.

He starts first. He peels his tight ripped jeans off in the blink of an eye, and then his tank top. And finally, with a smile, his underwear. He waves his underwear around in the air and tosses it at me. I duck and laugh.

"Your turn," he says.

"Yeah," I say, every part of me thrumming with anticipation.

I can feel my arms shaking as I slowly take off my black jeans and my T-shirt. I pause before taking my underwear off. I search his eyes for the reassurance I need. "Art," I whisper. I want to tell him I'm scared, but I know he knows that. So I just whisper his name again. I like feeling it on my tongue. "Art." And then again, more decisively, "Art."

We lie naked next to each other, and we kiss for what feels like either a split second or an eternity. It's a kiss that stops time. There is no past or future, just this moment, just this kiss.

Time starts again when he removes his lips from mine and kisses the back of my ears, my neck, my shoulders, my chest. He works his way down. "I want to kiss every part of you," he says. And he does. When he takes me inside his mouth, it's almost over.

"Wait, slow down," I beg him. And then, when he does, I just repeat, "Wow. Wow. Wow." I must sound like an idiot, but I don't care. I don't feel like an idiot. I feel like me.

I pull him back up when I can't take any more, and I do the same to him. I kiss and lick every inch of skin on his body, tasting the expanse of him, drawing him into me. The moment my lips leave his neck, I miss it already. Then when they leave his chest, I miss that. I want all of him, all at once, all the time.

"I love you," I whisper, my breath heavy.

"Me too," he says, laying me on my back and finding his way on top of me.

I turn to the bedside table and grab a condom. I give it to him with a smile and a nod. "Wow," he says. "Wow, I didn't think . . ."

"What?" I ask, mischievous. "You thought I'd remain like a virgin forever?"

He beams. A hand on my cheek, he says softly, "*Quien es este niño?* Who's that boy?"

I realize I'm a new person now, the person I've been waiting to be. I feel it's only right to quote Madonna back to him, so I kiss him once more, then whisper, "I'm a young boy with eyes like the desert that dream of you, my true blue."

His smile radiates love. "True blue," he repeats.

He tries to open the condom wrapper but fumbles with it. He tries his teeth. I grab it from him and tear it open. I try to put it on him, doing my best to block out why the condom is necessary, trying to forget all those images of death and disease. My hands shake as I place the condom on him. "I think you're putting it on upside down," he says, laughing.

"Really?" I turn it over and try it the other way. It finally slides on.

He smiles. I smile. We have a layer of protection between us now. He squeezes some lube onto him, then onto me. I wrap my legs around him, pulling him closer to me, or deeper into me, because he's in me now. We thrust and grunt and sweat until we almost fall off the bed.

"I need to catch my breath," he says. Then, with a

smile, he adds, "I think this is the first team sport I like."

I laugh. "I'm sure your dad would be very proud if you tried out for the varsity sex team."

This makes him laugh. "Like an athlete," he jokes. Then he whispers tenderly, "Reza, are you doing this because you want to, or because you think it'll make me stay?"

I kiss his neck, tasting his salty sweat. I lick the skin behind his earlobe, a hidden piece of him that feels all mine. "Maybe I thought about that," I say. "But that's not why I changed my mind. Whether you stay here or go west, I needed to do this. You had to be my first."

He nods, then shakes his head. "Hey, why are we talking so much? Aren't we supposed to be having mad, hot, passionate sexual intercourse right now?"

"You started talking!" I laugh.

"Me?" he asks, a roguish grin across his face. "You're the one inventing new school sports."

"Shut up," I say, blushing. "Or I'll never let you onto the junior varsity blow job team."

He laughs and kisses me. The heat quickly returns. He enters me again, and it's like we are flying together, soaring above the world and its problems, and there is no more death or grief or distance.

We collapse into each other when we're done. After a while, Art gets up and opens the curtains. He's speaking to me, but I'm still in a haze, floating.

"That was incredible." And then, sadly, "I wish I could tell Stephen about this."

I crawl out of bed. It hurts a little to walk, but in a good way, like my body wants to remember him inside me. I walk over to him. I wrap my arms around him, and we gaze out at the city together. We don't say anything for a very long time. We just stare at the city that brought us together.

The next morning, I put on the most celebratory item of clothing in my closet, the beautiful shirt Judy designed for me. Stephen requested we all wear something fabulous to his memorial. He wanted it to be a celebration of life, not of death. I stare at myself in the mirror. When she first designed this for me, I did not feel worthy of it. Now it feels right. This shirt was designed for someone who loves himself.

There is a knock on the door, which means it's Abbas. Nobody else in my family knocks. "Come in," I say.

Abbas enters. He wears a black suit, a white shirt, and a pink tie. "Your mother and sister are both running five minutes late," he says.

"Because they are getting dressed or because they are arguing?" I ask.

He smiles as he sits on my bed. "A little bit of both."

He stares ahead at my Madonna posters, records, magazines, all funded by money I stole from him, and suddenly I feel a desire, no, a need, to confess. "Abbas, I . . . there's something I need to tell you." He turns his head to me curiously. I take a deep breath. "I stole money from you. More than once. From your pockets when you were in the shower, and . . ."

"I know," he says, with no trace of anger.

"You do?" My throat feels suddenly dry.

"When you grow up and make your own money, you will always know how much you have in your pockets too," he says.

"But you didn't say anything?" I ask, shocked. "Why?"

"At first, I thought it could be Saadi." He crosses each of his legs over the other so that he's sitting on my bed like a pretzel. He leans closer to me, speaks in an intimate whisper. "But then I noticed the things you were buying and I knew it was you."

I can't believe this. He knew all along. "Did you tell my mom?" I ask.

He shakes his head. "I knew you wouldn't do it forever. And I knew that you needed these things. These records and posters. If you were spending the money on something unhealthy, I would have stopped you."

"Wow," I say, with surprise and gratitude. I sit on the bed next to him. "I learned how to do it from Art. He steals from his father. But his dad deserves it. You don't."

"Thank you," he says, a hand on my knee. "I appreciate that." Then he pulls me into a hug and says with sincerity, "I'm proud of you."

I almost push him away. It's too foreign to hear a man claiming to be my father say words like that. "Why?" I ask.

"Because it took courage to tell me what you did," he says. "And courage to be who you are."

"Do you think my mom is proud of me?" I ask, my

voice shaking. I'm so afraid of the answer.

"I know she is," he says with certainty. "Even if she doesn't know how to say it yet." He looks me deep in the eyes. "She loves you so much. But you must understand we come from a culture with no history of this. She hasn't been exposed to people like you, or to gay rights. I've been in New York for a decade. I've met people, seen things. She needs time."

"How much time?" I ask.

"I don't know, Reza," he says, shaking his head. "She's scared. She's scared life will be difficult for you, scared you could get sick. Being a parent is terrifying. All we want is to protect our children, and there is so much out there to fear. So much to blame ourselves for."

"I'm scared too," I say, on the verge of tears now.

"I know," he says, pulling me into a hug. "It's okay to be scared."

I appreciate him. So much about him. His gentleness, his patience, his understanding. The second chance at life he has given my mother. The way he has accepted me and my sister. "I love you, Baba," I say.

Abbas smiles, moved. He may not be the father who created me, but he is the father who loves me. I always thought my own father hated me, but Stephen said to me that nobody truly hates anyone. Hate is just fear in drag, he said. So maybe my father was just afraid of me. But Abbas isn't.

"Your mother will come around," he says. "Just the fact that she's attending this memorial is a big step. We didn't know him. We're doing this to be with you."

"I know," I say, allowing myself a little bit of hope that perhaps things will change soon with my mother.

Abbas stands up. He gives me his hand. "Shall we?" he asks. "I think it's time."

I let him help me up, and together, we find my mom and Tara. My mom looks beautiful in a black dress. Tara is wearing a tight, colorful, low-cut dress. I would never know this if not for Judy, but I think it's Pucci. Tara looks a little bit like a drag queen, which is fitting for the occasion. And her hair is newly permed by one of the girls she bartends with.

"You like it?" Tara says, as she twirls for me. "New dress. Vintage, obviously."

"You mean someone else wore that before you?" my mom asks, making a face. "Did you wash it?"

"And new perm," Tara says, ignoring my mom.

"I don't know why they call it a permanent," my mom says. "Nothing is permanent."

"Some things are permanent," I say.

She looks at me with curiosity. I know she understands what I was saying, that I'm not going through a phase. That this is who I will always be.

Massimo and Saadi, who were in the living room together, emerge. Saadi wears khakis, a button-down, and his white hat. Massimo somehow seems to match Tara in a bright shirt with tight white pants. "How long do I have to stay?" Saadi asks.

"As long as I do," Abbas says.

We go to the memorial together, but there are too many of us to fit into one taxi. It's Abbas who suggests my mom and I take one cab, while he rides with Tara, Saadi, and Massimo.

So I join her in the back of the first taxi that pulls to the curb. At first, we each stare awkwardly out of our windows, but then she turns to me and says, "I don't want life to be hard for you, Reza."

It's just one sentence, but it means so much. "It's not hard," I say, quickly realizing what a lie that is. "What I mean is that, yes, it is hard, but I can't change it." I close my eyes for a second, wishing for eloquence. "I think what I'm trying to say is that I wouldn't change it if I could."

"Really?" she asks, surprised.

"Because it's been hard," I say, a revelation coming to me. "But as hard as it's been, it's also been the best thing that's happened to me. The things I've felt this year, the love, the community, I wouldn't trade them in for an easier life. I don't want to be like Saadi, playing sports and being boring."

"Go easy on Saadi," she says gently. "He had a hard time with his mother."

"What do you mean?" I ask.

"I'm not—" She stops herself, then says. "Please don't repeat this, but she fell in love with someone else and left abruptly," my mom explains. "She didn't want custody. Why do you think he barely ever sees her? Just imagine how hard it is for a kid to have a parent who doesn't want them."

"Um, I don't have to imagine that hard," I say bitterly.

She gives me a sad look. "Oh, my boy."

"Why didn't you tell me this before?" I ask.

"Abbas doesn't like to talk about it. Neither does Saadi. It's hard for them." She shrugs. "Maybe our culture is different. We have the same problems as everyone else; we just pretend we don't."

"We definitely have the same problems," I say. "And by the way, if you're going to ask me to go easy on Saadi, I'd say the same goes for you and Tara."

She nods, taking this in. She almost says something but stops herself. Then she looks up at me and says, "All I wanted for so long was an easier life. It was always so hard. I wanted an easier life for myself, but also for you and Tara. And now I have one. But Tara doesn't. And you don't."

"But you love Abbas, don't you?" I ask.

"Of course," she says. She leans into me. "I would never have married him if I didn't love him. Never."

"And I can't be with someone I don't love either," I say. "And neither can Tara."

Her eyes well as she hears this, like she's understanding in a new way. She holds my hand and kisses it. "Okay," she says.

We don't say anything else. It's enough for now.

The memorial is being held in one of Stephen's favorite nightclubs. The owner was a friend of his, and a member of ACT UP. He has allowed the space to be transformed for this celebration. When we walk in, the stereo is blasting the Communards' "Don't Leave Me This Way," and a few people are dancing. Jimmy is one of them, but he looks more like Diana Ross in a red dress, high heels, and a sky-high wig. He looks like a star. Art's photographs line the walls. Photos of protests and actions. Photos of Stephen and José. Photos of Judy. Photos of Jimmy and other activists posed like glamorous movie stars. And photos of me. I freeze in front of the photo of me outside that stock exchange protest. I almost don't recognize myself. I was so much younger then, and yet I almost feel younger now. So much freer. Art's arms wrap around me. "I love you," he whispers in my ear.

I turn around to face him. I want to kiss him so badly, but I know my mother's eyes are probably on me, and she couldn't handle seeing that. "Did your parents come?" I ask.

He shakes his head. "I didn't think they would," he says. "Or maybe I did. I don't know. I guess I hoped that maybe death would make them see things differently. Death is supposed to bring people together, right?"

"I'm sorry," I say. I know how it feels to have a parent who can't love you. I also know how it feels to have a parent who can.

"It's okay," he says. "Look at all these people Stephen brought together. Who needs two more?"

Judy catches my eye. She's at the buffet table, next

to her parents and Annabel de la Roche, serving herself a plate of arroz con pollo. She whispers something to Annabel and then walks over to us. We hug her. "Uncle Stephen didn't cook the food," she says. "So it's really good."

"It's kind of weird to have food in a nightclub," Art says.

"He left very specific instructions," Judy says wistfully. "The menu. The art. The soundtrack." As she says this, the song changes to Sylvester's "Be with You," and even more people join the dance floor. I recognize so many of them from the protests and meetings. Men on the verge of death finding a moment of joy through music. Women with conviction singing the words to the song with all the force of their love and commitment. *I want to be with you forever. I want to share this love in heaven.*

When the dancing stops, and when people have eaten and hugged and said hello, the memorial itself begins. The owner of the club gives the first speech. He says that Stephen used to be a regular at this club, even before he met José. And then Stephen and José were regulars together. And then it was just Stephen again. And now it's us. He describes Stephen as someone "who knew how to live, even when he was dying," and I love that. A Judy Garland impersonator sings "Over the Rainbow." A man with a guitar sings a slow, mournful version of Marilyn's "I Wanna Be Loved by You." My sister clutches Massimo, tears in their eyes. My mother's and Abbas's eyes are misty. Even Saadi seems moved, his baseball hat pulled a little lower, perhaps to hide the emotion in his eyes. And am I imagining it, or does Saadi keep glancing over at Judy? Jimmy gets up onstage and explains that Stephen's favorite cinematic funeral scene was from *Imitation of Life*, "the Lana Turner and Juanita Moore version, obviously." He then lip-synchs the song from that scene, Mahalia Jackson's "Trouble of the World," imbuing every movement of his lips with so much passion that it sometimes feels like it really is his voice we are hearing.

Stephen has asked Judy and Art to speak together. I'm sure this was intentional, that he wanted to make sure they had to work together, remember together, grieve together. Their friendship mattered to him, and it probably matters even more now that he's gone. "Hey, everyone," Judy says. "I'm Judy, Stephen's niece. You know, the girl he named after Judy Garland. No pressure there." There are loud cheers from the crowd. She and Art speak of Stephen's love, his mentorship, his guidance. At the end of the speech, they read Stephen's notecard about love. "The most important four-letter word in our history will always be love," Judy says, before Art finishes with "That's what we are fighting for. That's who we are. Love is our legacy."

After the speeches, there is more music. More dancing. All his favorites are on the mix. Bette and Barbra and Grace Jones and George Michael and Diana. Then Madonna's "Keep It Together" comes on, and it feels like he's playing it just for us. Judy pulls me and Art and Annabel to the dance floor. Mr. and Mrs. Bowman join us. Jimmy shimmies to the middle of our circle, spinning with abandon. I wave Tara and Massimo over, and Tara puts her arms around me, swaying with me. My sister, the first person who accepted me. I realize how much I love her. Even my mom and Abbas and Saadi reluctantly join the circle. We all dance. Family, new friends, old friends, keeping people together forever and ever.

The night ends. We give hugs, we say our goodbyes.

I tell my family I'm going to stay behind with Judy and Art. Before my mom leaves, she gives me a long hug and whispers in my ear, "I'm sorry for your loss." Then she lets me go but keeps searching my eyes for something. She places a hand on my cheek. "I love you," she says.

"I love you, too," I whisper. I hug her once more, because I need to. And because she deserves my love and acceptance and patience, just like I deserve hers.

And then there is me, and Art, and Judy. The three of us. We decide to go get ice cream. We sit on the stoop of a downtown tarot card reader, tasting the sweetness, saying nothing for a long time. Through the window of the building, the tarot card reader waves to us. I wish she would tell me my future, flip over a card that will ease all the fear inside me. But I don't step inside. This is not a time for crystal balls, or a time to think about the future. It's a moment to honor the past.

Judy puts her head on my shoulder. Art is on the other side of her. When he finishes his ice cream, he puts his head on her lap, and she runs her hands through his hair tenderly. We're so connected, and yet something inside us has shifted, just as something in this universe has shifted. When someone leaves this planet, they take so much with them. So much energy. So much connective tissue.

"Let's walk," Art says, and we do. I hold his left hand. Judy holds his right. It's not until I see the river again that I realize he has led us directly west, to the very edge of this island. Art looks out, not at the water, but out past it. I watch him gaze at the horizon, like he's trying to see what is beyond it.

JUDY

It's been almost two weeks since Stephen died. Life has felt like a blur ever since. My mother's tears, endless. Art's decision to leave, unbelievable. I sometimes think I dreamed it all, but I didn't. It's real, too real.

"I want you both to come with me," Art said as he stared out at the Hudson River. "We belong together, the three of us. Let's start over in San Francisco." I brushed him off. I thought he was just looking for an easy way to escape the pain of grief. I told him it isn't that easy. "Maybe it is that easy," Art said. "How do we know until we try? We'd be like the three heroines of *How to Marry a Millionaire*, living in a pad together. Except instead of marrying millionaires, we'd be changing the world."

I went along with the joke. I said that if we were going to be like the heroines of that movie, I'd be Lauren Bacall. Art said he'd obviously be Marilyn, which meant Reza would be Betty Grable. And Reza asked who Betty

Grable is. And we managed to laugh through our tears.

But there were more tears in store for us. And more anger. With every day that passed, Art became more resolved. At first, he decided he would go to Berkeley in the fall. Then he announced he wouldn't go to Berkeley at all. He wouldn't go to college, because that would mean taking more money from his dad, and he was done with him.

I guess I always knew he had to escape his parents' world to forge his own path. I just didn't realize his parents' world encompassed the entire East Coast, and I didn't think that once he made this decision, he would choose to leave so soon. "I need to go before I change my mind," he told me.

Now the day of his departure has arrived. Reza and I wait for Art in the lobby of his parents' apartment building. "How'd it go?" I ask when he emerges holding a small carry-on suitcase.

"As good as it could have," he says. "My dad wished me luck and told me never to ask for money." He shakes his head as he says this, but then his face softens and his eyes well up. "And my mom cried. A lot."

"I'm so sorry," I say, my heart breaking a little. "Your parents love you. I know they do."

"It's just, their love comes with a lot of conditions," he says. "Anyway, it's not them I'll miss most. It's you guys."

He looks into Reza's misty eyes. Reza says nothing. His lips just quiver, words hovering under them that won't come out.

"Before we go," Art says, "can we stop by a photo-copy place?"

We walk to the nearest Kinko's, the wheels of Art's suitcase loudly banging against the uneven sidewalks. When we get there, Art pulls out Stephen's notecards. There are one hundred and thirty-one of them, and we each take a third and head to separate copy machines. Art's stack begins with #1 Adonis and ends with #41 Divine. Mine begins with #42 DSM and ends with #83 Mineo, Sal. And Reza's begins with #84 Minogue, Kylie, and ends with #131 Woolf, Virginia. We copy each card one by one, making two copies of each. The machines light up each time a new copy is made, little sparks thrown into the world. We have three stacks when we're done. Two copies, and the original note-cards.

"I think the originals should go with you," I say. "It's what Stephen would have wanted. He wrote them for you."

"Thank you," Art says, with genuine surprise. Then he takes my hand, and says, "Thank you for sharing him with me. He was your uncle."

"Art, stop," I say. "He didn't belong to me. No one belongs to anyone."

I see Reza glance at Art when I say this. Maybe Reza wanted Art to belong to him, or vice versa. I know Reza considered leaving with Art. He even asked me to talk through the decision with him. We made a pros and cons list. There was only one pro to leaving: Art. There were a lot of cons. Ultimately, Reza chose college and his family.

"Hey, I have an idea," Art says, his face lighting up. "I think we have time."

"What is it?" I ask.

Art tells us. We make one more copy of the cards, and then we go around scattering them around the city like ashes. We leave #69 King, Billie Jean, in a restaurant booth. #130 Woodlawn, Holly, we place in a mailbox. We put #24 Cockettes on a car windshield, and countless cards on storefronts.

We hand a businessman #68 Jorgensen, Christine.

We stop two fabulous models and give them #74 Lorde, Audre.

To our taxi driver on our way to the airport, we bequeath #95 Provincetown.

In the airport, we leave them in the bathroom, on the magazine stands, inside suitcase carts, until they are almost gone.

All but one. We go to an airport store selling magazines, medicine, trinkets, and souvenirs. We consider placing the final card in front of the latest issue of *Vanity Fair*. Anjelica Huston is on the cover, looking fierce in a red dress I kind of wish I'd designed myself. Stephen would've approved, but it doesn't feel right. We browse the rest of the shop. Yankees hats, and I Heart NY T-shirts, stuffed bears with a map of the state on them, key chains. Finally, we see a display with hundreds of plastic Statue of Liberty figurines standing next to each other. That's where we choose to place the card. #75 Love.

We stare at it together, read it as if it's Lady Liberty's new epitaph.

"Was it love?" Reza whispers to Art. "Or was it like love?"

I realize I'm a third wheel here. I grab a copy of *Harper's Bazaar*, and I excuse myself to the corner of the store. Madonna is on the cover, obviously, her hair more platinum than ever. In red block letters, the cover reads "SEX IS ALIVE and well." I flip the pages and read. But it's a small store, and I can hear them.

"It was love," Art says. "True blue."

"Then why would you leave?" Reza asks. "Who leaves their true blue love?"

Art says nothing.

"Am I not enough?" Reza says.

"You're perfect," Art says. "I'm the one who's fucked up. And I hate myself sometimes, Reza. For always wanting more. For never being satisfied. For hurting people."

"Then don't hurt people," Reza begs. "Stay."

I want to jump into the conversation and echo everything Reza is saying. Don't hurt me, Art. Don't go. Don't leave me in this city without my best friend. Don't break my heart.

"You will always be my first," Art says.

Reza sobs now. It's so loud and so horrible that I want to rush over and hold him. Everyone in the store looks over at them, concern on their faces, but like me, no one dares interrupt.

"I have no regrets, Reza," Art says, holding him now. "Do you?"

"No," Reza says. "No."

Art's eyes well up. "I get how crazy and impulsive this is. But I'm impulsive, and maybe that's one of the things you loved about me . . ."

"Love," Reza says. "I still love you."

Then Art whispers the final words of the card still resting near them. "Love is our legacy," he says.

"Love is our legacy," Reza repeats.

I feel a wave of gratitude that these two found each other. The idea that Reza and I were once a couple seems absurd. I'll find my true first love someday. And when I find him, I'll never let him go like Art is letting Reza go. Never.

"I didn't deserve you," Art says to Reza.

"Shut up," Reza says. "You did, and you do. And if you change your mind . . ." Reza doesn't finish the sentence. If Art changes his mind, Reza will be waiting. I will, too.

I look at the time and approach them. "You're going to miss your flight," I say.

We leave the store and walk toward the security line. Art has his camera around his neck, and he points it at me and Reza. He snaps a photo.

"Really?" I ask, shaking my head lovingly.

"I want to remember this moment," he says, smiling.

"You better come visit," I say sadly.

"I'll be here for my MoMA show next year," he says jokingly.

I smile. Art dreams big, and he's always let me dream big. "And I'll be in San Francisco next year. They're closing down the Golden Gate Bridge and turning it into a catwalk for my debut show."

We both turn to Reza, wanting him to play the game, to make some grand proclamation of where he'll be next year. "Stop looking at me," he says. "I don't even know what I want to do yet."

"Just tell us what you dream about," Art says. "In your wildest dreams, what would you be?"

"I don't know," he says. "Happy?"

"Everyone wants that!" Art says. "It's a cop-out of an answer. Say you want to be an astronaut, or you want to cure AIDS, or you want to be a movie star, or Madonna's manager."

"I think," Reza says longingly, "I'd like to be a father someday. To have my own family. Does that count?"

Art looks genuinely surprised, like it's the last answer he was expecting. "Yeah," he says finally. "It counts."

We stare at each other for a few moments, and then I say, "You really are gonna miss your flight, Art."

"Okay," he says. "Well, I guess this is adieu then."

I smile. One of Stephen's favorite songs is "Comment Te Dire Adieu," and it's like he's here with us when Art uses that word.

"Okay," I say.

"Good luck," Reza says, and he gives Art a hug.

They clutch each other, their hands on each other's necks, like they're bottling this moment so they can drink it in when they're apart.

When they let go, Art pulls me into a hug. I feel like I could stay here forever, in his arms, like we're one being, sharing a heartbeat, finishing each other's sentences. Who else knows who I had a crush on when I was ten, and how terribly my first attempt at shaving my legs went? Who else will understand when I want to quote old movies?

"Hey, don't let anyone else call you Frances," he says with deadpan seriousness. "You'll always be *my* Frances."

I don't know what to say to him, so I say nothing. I just pull away from him and look deep into his eyes. They're moist. Mine are too. I nod. I'll always be his Frances. And he'll always be my best friend.

He walks away from us backward, waving his hand, until he bumps into a lady, who doesn't seem amused. Then he turns around, facing away from us, and disappears into the crowds going through the security lines, headed to different cities, other countries, fresh starts.

Reza and I stand there for a moment, frozen. Above us is the list of all the destinations planes are headed to. Some flights are boarding, some delayed. The departure times changing on the screen mesmerize us, and Reza says, "If you could pick one city from that list and go right now, which would it be?"

"Do I get to take anyone I want?" I say. "Because it's not really the city that matters; it's the people I'm with."

He nods. I don't answer the question, and neither does he.

"It's Sunday," I say.

"Movie night?" Reza asks, as if he can read my thoughts.

"Movie night," I repeat. "Annabel might come over, but she loves old movies. Is that cool?"

"Of course," he says. "She seems nice. And three is a nice number, as it turns out."

We head out of the airport, toward the chaos of the taxi line. The air outside is thick with cigarette smoke and the scent of perfume. We get in the back of the taxi line, behind a woman traveling alone with three children. She holds a baby, and her two toddlers pull at her. She speaks a language I don't know, making everything she says to her children sound musical. The taxi line inches forward, and we all inch with it. One of the woman's children stares at me, and I stare back, playing peekaboo with her. I wonder who all these new arrivals to the city are. Where did they come from, and where are they going?

The woman turns around, and that's when I notice her baby is holding a piece of paper, chewing on its edges. No, it's a notecard. Stephen's notecard. *Love.*

I asked a question, and Stephen answered. We all come from love. And that's where we're going too. Where we are now, that's the complicated part.

JUNE 2016

"It's always wrong to hate, but it's never wrong to love."

—*Lady Gaga*

ART

Some traditions must end, but sometimes, in their place, a new tradition is born. Sunday movie nights couldn't last forever. Not without Stephen, not after I left Reza, Judy, and New York for San Francisco. But we started something new after I left. Every June, on the anniversary of Stephen's death, me, Judy, and Reza meet in New York City. Sometimes Jimmy joins us too, having survived just long enough for protease inhibitors to extend his life, though not without severe side effects. I was luckier, the drugs more sophisticated by the time I tested positive. But Jimmy fights on, lives on, and writes on—five novels and counting—in Paris, where he has chosen to live among the spirits of James Baldwin and Josephine Baker, two of his favorite ghosts. He told me once that if someone had predicted back then that he'd live longer than Michael Jackson and Whitney Houston, he'd have told them they were crazier than the whole Psychic Friends

Network put together. And yet there he was, in June of 2016, on the twenty-sixth anniversary of Stephen's death, dancing the night away with us at, where else, an eighties night in the East Village. "Into the Groove" was playing and the sound of Madonna's beckoning call made us feel young again. Judy's children were sleeping soundly, her husband watching them for the night. Reza's kids were with his husband in Connecticut, where Reza teaches classes about the sociology of pop culture. We were all dressed in outrageous and glamorous clothes designed by Judy, she being the preferred designer of rock stars, drag queens, and plus-size girls. It was Jimmy who got an alert on his phone first. A gunman had opened fire at the Pulse nightclub in Orlando, a place named to remember the owner's brother who died of AIDS, in honor of his pulse to keep living, keep fighting. By morning, we would know more details. Forty-nine killed. Fifty-three wounded. We were all supposed to go home, but we couldn't. We needed to be held by people who understood that every queer life taken is tragedy on top of tragedy, a loss of family, and so much trauma relived. We needed to be with people who knew our history. Stephen's notecards will belong to my child one day, and now I'm adding some more. So much has happened since Stephen left us. Prop 8 and RuPaul and DOMA and *Ellen* and Don't Ask, Don't Tell and Tori Amos and Chechnya and Laverne Cox and *Will & Grace* and PrEP and Gaga and Queen Bey and Pulse.

Here's what I learned from Stephen: You are not alone

and never will be, because you have a beautiful, constantly evolving history full of ghosts who are watching over you, who are proud of you. If you ever feel lonely, just look up at the sky. José and Walt and Judy Garland and Marsha P. Johnson are always with you, and so many more. Just ask them to listen, and they will. Tell your story until it becomes woven into the fabric of *our* story. Write about the joys and the pain and every event and every artist who inspires you to dream. Tell your story, because if you don't, it could be wiped out. No one tells our stories for us. And one more thing. If you see an elderly person walking down the street, or across from you at a coffee shop, don't look away from them, don't dismiss them, and don't just ask them *how* they're doing. Ask them where they have been instead. And then listen. Because there's no future without a past.

AUTHOR'S NOTE

I realized I was gay before I had a word for it, before I knew there were thriving gay communities. Like Reza, I was born in Iran, and I moved to New York from Canada when I was young. But unlike Reza, I wasn't exposed to its gay community. All I knew of the feeling inside me was fear and shame. All I saw of gay life was death. I thought I had a choice between being myself and staying alive, which isn't a choice at all. Either way, I wouldn't truly be living. The generation I come from wasn't old enough to be on the front lines at the beginning of the AIDS crisis, nor were we young enough to come of age when treatment was available. We were coming into our sexuality with fear drilled into us, and it worked. That fear protected me from making risky decisions, but it also made it difficult to accept myself, since for most of my youth I viewed my sexuality as a death sentence. Writing this book was a way for me to reconnect with the scared teenager who still lives somewhere inside me, and to thank the friends, family, artists, and activists who helped me on my journey from shame to acceptance.

My first exposure to a celebratory depiction of gay life came through, who else? Madonna. I fell in love with Madonna when her very first video was released. I made my parents take me to the Virgin Tour when I was *way* too young for it. I created a Madonna Room in our home as a place of worship, a place where I could be with the person who let me dream big and seemed to understand and accept me before even I did. Yes, a Madonna Room, and it would be over a decade before I would come out to my parents! She was so much a part of my life that she practically became a member of our family. So when she started to explicitly and courageously include queer life in her work, there was no way to shield me from it. She was also a portal into other queer art. Thanks to Madonna, I discovered filmmakers like Pedro Almodóvar and artists like Keith Haring, and I learned about the underground ball scene. Thanks to Madonna, I saw queerness not as a death sentence, but as a community and an identity to be celebrated. My gratitude to her is boundless.

In high school and college, I was exposed to more queer culture. One high school teacher introduced me to gay films like *Paris Is Burning*, *The Times of Harvey Milk*, and *Maurice*. I started to read queer authors. The impact of these works, and of the mentors who shared them with me, cannot be understated. This book could never exist without the spiritual mentorship of all the storytellers who gave voice to queer life and to the AIDS era. Those men and women helped shape who I am long before the idea for this novel came to me, and they guided me as I researched this novel. I hope anyone who reads and likes this book uses it as a portal into further exploration, and is inspired to read the words of James Baldwin, Audre Lorde, Armistead Maupin, Randy Shilts, Paul Monette, Edmund White, Andrew Holleran, Sean Strub, Tony Kushner, Amy Hoffman, Tim Murphy, Patricia Powell, and Cleve Jones, to name a few, and then watches films like *How to Survive a Plague*, *Longtime Companion*, *Parting Glances*, *Tongues Untied*, *BPM*, *Angels in America*, and *Torch Song Trilogy*, to name a few.

This book is an ode to the heroes and heroines of the AIDS movement, activists who saved lives, without whom I and many others would likely have met different fates. While the protests depicted here are all real, I chose to fictionalize the activists themselves. I didn't want to put words into the mouths of people I admire as much as Larry Kramer, Marsha P. Johnson, Sarah Schulman, Keith Haring, Peter Staley, and others. To them, and to anyone else who was a member of ACT UP or other activist groups, thank you from the bottom of my heart. I recognize that my health and my freedom would not exist without your heroism. ACT UP was a diverse coalition of men and women of all races. Its leaderless structure, its affinity groups, and its joint actions with feminist groups spoke to an inclusive, diverse, and democratic movement that has served as a model to other activist groups. I am not a historian, and this isn't a work of nonfiction. Though the important facts here are well researched, I did make some small changes for storytelling purposes (for example, I may have shifted Madonna's Maryland Blond Ambition tour date up by two weeks). If you would like to learn more about the true history as it happened, I hope you'll research these heroes and their work. It is thanks to them that so many of us have the abundant lives we have.

There is another person who was integral to my coming out and self-acceptance: my first boyfriend, Damon. He forced me to come out to my parents, threatening to break up with me if I didn't. He pushed me past many of my fears and boundaries. He had in him the flamboyant spirit of an activist. He also had a tremendous amount of darkness, which he shielded me from during our relationship. Years after we broke up, he died of an overdose. He isn't the only one. I know too many members of our queer community who have taken their own lives or overdosed. There is still shame to work through, still residual fear.

In college, a friend conducted a survey for a class, asking his classmates where they saw each other with each passing decade. None of the gay men he spoke to, myself included, saw a life for themselves past forty. I am past forty now, with the family I always wanted but never imagined for myself. A loving partner who accepts me as I am, and who knows as many *Mommie Dearest* quotes as I do. Two incredible kids who light up my life, and have a lot of favorite Madonna songs. I am blessed to live in a time that allows me to live and love freely, but there is still work to be done. When people say that history repeats itself, they tend to mean it in a negative way. But there is so much that can be good about history repeating itself. Activist movements can learn from past activism. Storytellers can be inspired by artists who speak to them. Families and communities can honor their ancestors. We owe so much to those who came before us, and perhaps by honoring the best of the past, we can repeat the best of history instead of the worst of it.

ACKNOWLEDGMENTS

I've wanted to write this story since I was a teenager but was too afraid to. I began my career as a screenwriter in Hollywood, often being told to stop writing about Iranian and queer people. My editor, Alessandra Balzer, pulled this story out of me after I pitched numerous ideas I thought were more "commercial." I am deeply grateful to her for encouraging storytelling that is personal and daring, and to the whole team at Balzer + Bray/Harper-Collins for supporting that mission.

Writing a book is a solitary and insecure experience, but much less so with an agent who gets you. Mitchell Waters is always there for me when I need someone to send pages to and discuss them with. There would be no books without him, and I am deeply grateful to him and the Curtis Brown team, including Steven Salpeter, Anna Abreu, and one of the people who has had the greatest impact on my life and career, Holly Frederick.

I hope you judge books by their covers, because Michelle Taormina and Alison Donalty have created such beautiful covers for my books. Thank you to them, and to Dave Homer, who created the stunning cover art.

Brandy Colbert, Mackenzi Lee, and Robin Benway, you inspire me and so many others with your words. Thank you for being early advocates of this story.

Writing about teenage life in an era close to when I was a teenager brought back so many memories of the friends and mentors who lit up my life as a teen. A few friendships in particular felt very alive in me as I wrote these pages. Lauren Ambrose, my fish friend forever, made my teenage self feel alive and creative and still does. Tom Collins made me feel seen and accepted, and still does.

There is no greater gift to a writer than reading rough drafts and giving honest feedback. Thank you to Richard Kramer, Mandy Kaplan, and Ronit Kirchman for taking the time to help me find my way.

It was so important to have input from people who were involved in ACT UP, and Jim Hubbard and Philip Pierce provided input and more. Thank you, Jim and Philip, for your guidance.

As I was writing this, James Teel gave me an original ACT UP sweater, which was one of the most thoughtful and inspiring gifts I've ever received.

Friendship and community keep me going in so many ways, and a few people I wouldn't be here without are: Jamie Babbit, Susanna Fogel, Nancy Himmel,

Ted Huffman, Erica Kraus, Erin Lanahan, Joel Michaely, Busy Philipps, Mark Russ, Melanie Samarasinghe, Micah Schraft, Sarah Shetter, John Shields, Lynn Shields, Mike Shields, Jeremy Tamanini, Amanda Tejeda, Serena Torrey Roosevelt, and Lila Azam Zanganeh.

Big thanks to the authors in the young adult community who have accepted me with open arms. There are too many names, but if we've lip-synched, paneled, or shared a meal together, I appreciate you.

One of this book's most pivotal scenes is set against the backdrop of my favorite Madonna song, "Keep It Together." I've always loved the song's message about family being gold, probably because I have a huge family that loves and inspires me. Huge thanks to *la famille*: Maryam, Luis, Dara, Nina, Mehrdad, Vida, John, Lila, Moh, Brooke, Youssef, Mandy, Shahla, Hushang, Azar, Djahanshah, Parinaz, Parker, Delilah, Rafa, Santi, Tomio, and Kaveh. And big love to the Aubry and Kamal clans: Jude, Susan, Kathy, Zu, Paul, Jamie, and company.

So much gratitude for my parents, Lili and Jahangir. They took me to the Virgin Tour when I was eight, and to the Blond Ambition Tour when I was thirteen, and that says all you need to know about the kind of open-minded, amazing people they are. And big thanks to my brother, Al, who shares my love for celluloid and has always supported my self-expression.

Tom Dolby, our friendship, collaboration and creative kinship has helped me grow in so many ways. Thank you.

Jennifer and Jazz Elia, you are family to me. I love you with the ferocity of Nadal's new backhand.

Jonathon Aubry, I could never have written this book without my place by your side. You inspire me, cheer me on, and allow me to disappear into hotel rooms when I need quiet time to write. Nothing about us is *like* a love story. It is a love story, and I still smile every day knowing I found my Pally. Your heart fits me like a glove, and this book is for you.

Evie and Rumi, as I write this, your most requested Madonna songs are "Open Your Heart" and "Crazy for You," which is perfect because you have both opened my heart in so many ways, and I couldn't be crazier for you. You teach me every day to be more patient, loving, and creative. I can't wait for you to read this book, so I can tell you all about a time when there were no cell phones or internet, and when I was a starry-eyed kid who dreamed big, but could never have dreamed of one day having the privilege of raising the two greatest children in the world. Never forget that if I hold the lock, you hold the key.